Cindi Myers is the author of more than fifty novels. When she's not plotting new romance story lines, she enjoys skiing, gardening, cooking, crafting and daydreaming. A lover of small-town life, she lives with her husband and two spoiled dogs in the Colorado mountains.

Nicole Helm grew up with her nose in a book and the dream of one day becoming a writer. Luckily, after a few failed career choices, she gets to follow that dream – writing down-to-earth contemporary romance and romantic suspense. From farmers to cowboys, Midwest to the West, Nicole writes stories about people finding themselves and finding love in the process. She lives in Missouri with her husband and two sons, and dreams of someday owning a barn.

EAGLE MOUNTAIN CLIFFHANGER

CINDI MYERS

SMALL TOWN VANISHING

NICOLE HELM

MILLS & BOON

First Published in Great Britain 2022
by Mills & Boon, an imprint of HarperCollins*Publishers* Ltd
1 London Bridge Street, London, SE1 9GF

www.harpercollins.co.uk

HarperCollins*Publishers*
1st Floor, Watermarque Building,
Ringsend Road, Dublin 4, Ireland

Eagle Mountain Cliffhanger © 2022 Cynthia Myers
Small Town Vanishing © 2022 Nicole Helm

ISBN: 978-0-263-30362-9

1022

This book is produced from independently certified FSC™ paper to ensure responsible forest management.

For more information visit: www.harpercollins.co.uk/green

Printed and Bound in Spain using 100% Renewable electricity at CPI Black Print, Barcelona

EAGLE MOUNTAIN CLIFFHANGER

CINDI MYERS

For the Ouray Mountain Rescue Team

Chapter One

Hannah Richards accelerated up the mountain road in her battered Subaru, torn between wanting to hurry and the need for caution on the narrow, winding lanes. A callout for Search and Rescue always fired her adrenaline, and a swift response could mean the difference between life and death. But experience working in these mountains made her hyperaware of the hazards that lurked in the picturesque setting. Snow softened the sharp edges of the landscape around her, like a puffy white comforter draped over the ridges of the surrounding mountains. The road was a thin black ribbon wound around the peaks, with no guardrails separating the narrow shoulder and the deep ravine to her right.

She took her foot off the gas as she neared a pullout that offered a view of the frozen waterfall and the canyon below, a popular photo spot. The motorist who had called to report the accident said the van had gone off the road just past this pull off. Yes, there was a set of tire tracks gouged deep in the snow, veering off the road and into the ravine below.

Hannah stopped the Subaru and checked her rearview mirror. No one coming. Carefully, she backed to the pullout and parked, then hurried to get out and collect her gear bag from the back. As a paramedic, she always traveled prepared for an emergency. She had been out shopping when the call from the 911 dispatcher came in, which had allowed her to be first on the scene. But if the van was very far down in the ravine, she'd have to wait for a climbing crew to determine the safest route down to her patients. Every member of Eagle Mountain Search and Rescue was trained in emergency first aid, but for serious cases—and driving off the side of a mountain definitely qualified as a serious case—it was up to the two paramedics, one nurse and one doctor on the SAR roster to deliver the kind of high-level care any survivor of this accident was likely to require.

She slung a pack with most of the supplies she might need over one shoulder and walked back to the spot where the tire tracks disappeared over the edge. As she walked, she checked her watch. The call from the motorist who had seen what he described as a "boxy white van" go over the side had come in approximately twenty minutes before. The outside temperature up here was twenty-one degrees. It would probably be colder in the ravine. Every minute counted if someone had managed to survive the plummet over the edge.

She walked alongside the tire tracks, post-holing through deep snow. A recent training exercise, conducted by the Rayford County Sheriff's Department, had stressed the importance of preserving evidence at the scene, in order to aid law enforcement in determining the cause of the accident. About a foot from where the ground fell away, Hannah stopped and peered over the edge.

The white van lay on its side about a hundred yards down the steep slope, resting against a large boulder. It looked as if a giant had hit it with a hammer—the top and sides dented in, steam pouring from beneath the crumpled hood. Hannah cupped her hands to either side of her mouth and shouted. "Hello! Can you hear me? I'm with Search and Rescue! Help is on the way!"

A scuffling noise to her left startled her, and she jumped back, heart pounding, and was amazed to see a man clambering up the slope toward her. Blood streamed down his face and drenched his clothing, mingling with the mud smeared on his hands and his pants from the knees down. At the sight of her, the man drew back and let out a groan.

He was probably in shock, or disoriented from what appeared to be a head wound. "It's okay." Hannah held out both hands. "I'm a paramedic. I'm here to help you. Can you tell me your name?"

The man stared at her, and she shrank from the menace in that look. People reacted strangely when they were in shock, she reminded herself. "My name's Hannah," she said. "You look like you're injured. I'd like to help."

A car door slammed and Hannah whirled to see a sheriff's deputy striding toward her. "What's the situation?" he called as he hurried toward her.

"The van is down there." She pointed down the slope. "And we've got at least one survivor. Sir, how many people—" But when she turned back toward the bleeding man, he had vanished.

"Sir!" She rushed toward where the man had been. "Sir!"

The sheriff's deputy moved in beside her. "A man was right here," she said. "He was climbing up the slope, and he was bleeding."

"Do you think he fell back down? It's pretty steep."

"Maybe." She could see the path the injured man had made through the snow coming up the slope, footprints and flecks of red on the snow marking his route. Had he descended the same way?

A siren announced the approach of a rescue vehicle. Relief surged through her when she recognized SAR Captain Tony Meissner and the vehicle they had termed the Beast, a specially modified Jeep that had seen better days, but held most of the team's gear—everything from oxygen tanks to a litter outfitted with oversize wheels for moving patients across rough ground, to equipment for extracting people from cars or hauling them out of mine tunnels, canyons or rivers.

Tony, a tall, bearded man in his late thirties who worked as a surveyor in his life outside SAR, was in his second year as leader of the search and rescue team. Calm and organized, he was good at quickly assessing a situation, and knew how to utilize each volunteer's strengths and compensate for their weaknesses.

With Tony was nurse Danny Irwin. Tall and lanky, with a mop of sandy hair, Danny had the weathered complexion of someone who spent all his spare time out of doors. Another medical person could come in handy if they had more than one victim with major trauma, though Hannah still felt a little awkward around him since their recent breakup after a brief affair. The split had been amicable, both of them agreeing they were better friends than lovers. But she was still learning to differentiate between what could sound like flirting and Danny's general charm.

"I'm Deputy Jake Gwynn." The sheriff's deputy stepped forward to introduce himself to Tony and Danny. He looked to be about Hannah's age—mid-twenties, with thick dark hair, dark brown eyes and high cheekbones. He had a handsome face that would make most people look twice.

"The new guy." Tony threw open the doors of the Beast and began hauling out ropes and other climbing equipment. "I remember you from the training a couple weeks ago." He looked past Gwynn to Hannah. "How far down is the vehicle?" he called.

"About a hundred yards," she said. "The slope is sixty to seventy degrees. The van is wedged against a big boulder, pretty smashed up. But there was at least one survivor. He was climbing up toward me, then he was gone."

"Could have lost consciousness and fallen." Danny came around to join Tony in pulling gear from the Beast. "We may have to climb down past the vehicle to find him."

"What can I do to help?" Gwynn asked.

"Traffic control," Tony said. "This road is too narrow and dangerous to have people slowing down or even stopping to rubber-neck. We need you to move them along."

Two more vehicles pulled into the parking area behind Hannah's Subaru: volunteers Sheri Stevens and Ryan Welch piled out of Ryan's red Jeep, with Ted Carruthers tight behind them in a big black truck. Another sheriff's department vehicle soon joined them.

Danny and Ryan, whose curly auburn hair had earned him the nickname Red, began laying out the climbing gear. "I'll go down first," Sheri said. No one argued; the tall blonde was one of the team's best climbers.

"I'll go down alongside and run a line we can use as a handhold to bring up the Stokes basket," Tony said. "Ted, you monitor things up top. Hannah, you and Ryan come down after Sheri and I have had a chance to assess things."

"We need to find the man I saw," Hannah reminded him. "He had a head wound and probably other injuries. He might be disoriented."

"I'll go down and start a search for him," Danny said. He looked at Hannah. "Show me where you saw him coming up the slope."

While she walked over to show Danny, Deputy Gwynn and a fellow deputy put out cones to close off one lane of traffic. This forced any passing vehicles to move by at a crawl, but gave the team more room to work.

Gwynn rejoined them shortly after Danny and Sheri had started their climbs down. "If somebody will make note of the plate number of the vehicle, we can start searching for the name of the owner, who may be the driver," he said.

"I'll get it," Ted said, clipping into his harness. The oldest volunteer at sixty, Ted was a fit, wiry man with thick gray hair and a neat goatee.

Gwynn stood beside Hannah and watched the team members descend. Sheri moved rapidly, propelling herself with agility and speed, as if she was skipping down a well-worn trail instead of an icy sixty-degree slope. "I'm Jake," Gwynn said.

She nodded, her gaze still fixed on Sheri. "I'm Hannah."

"Have you been with Search and Rescue long?"

"Four years." She glanced at him. He looked fit. She'd heard through the grapevine that he was single—that kind of news traveled fast in a small town, where the dating pool was limited. Not that Hannah was actively looking, but she was single and didn't necessarily want to stay that way forever. Still, now was not the time to be flirting with the new guy.

If, indeed, he was flirting. Maybe, as a cop, he was used to asking questions. "It's a volunteer position, right?" he asked. "What do you do the rest of the time?"

"I'm a paramedic, for the county." That was her paid position, but there was considerable overlap with SAR. If a SAR call went out when she was on duty as a paramedic, she was free to respond—on the clock, as it were—as long as she wasn't already involved with transporting or otherwise tending to a patient.

The hand-held radios they used to communicate over short distances— fancy walkie-talkies, really—crackled, and she keyed the mic of hers. "What have you got?" She'd bet it was Sheri, first on the scene. She had been the fastest on the descent.

"The driver is DOA," Sheri said. "Still strapped into the seat. There's a passenger, and I'm pretty sure he's dead, too. There's a lot of blood, like maybe he got sliced by windshield glass or a piece of metal. We're going to have to move the driver out of the way to get to him. Somebody send down the Jaws."

The hydraulic extractor and cutter, commonly known as the Jaws of Life, could spread open crushed metal, giving a team member more room to work on an injured person, or to extract a body or other items from the wreckage. "I'll bring it," Hannah said, and went to collect the tool from the van.

The Jaws in its carrying case weighed about fifty-five pounds. Instead of trying to carry it and her medical pack, Hannah fastened a line to the handle of the carrying case, and tied it securely. She handed the free end of the line to Jake. "Feed this down to me," she instructed. Not waiting for his answer, she started climbing down.

Unlike Sheri, Hannah didn't particularly enjoy climbing. She did it because it was one of the requirements of the job, and she'd had plenty of training and opportunities for practice. She took her time, carefully placing her hands and feet, the cold of the snow seeping through her gloves and boots, though her waterproof pants and gloves did a good job of keeping out the wet. Every couple of steps down, she paused and tugged on the Jaws to drag it down alongside her. She didn't look down, counting on Sheri to alert her when she was almost to the wreck. As long as she kept her gaze focused directly in front of her, or up the way she had come, she didn't have to think about what could happen if she slipped on the steep, icy rock. Yes, she was in a safety harness tied off to a piton hammered in the rock above, which, she knew from her training, would catch and hold her if she fell. But the sensation of swinging free into space, while it exhilarated some climbers, like Sheri, filled Hannah with a terror she did not care to repeat anytime soon.

"Almost down." Sheri's voice, firm and confident, sounded close, and a few moments later Hannah felt her teammate's hands on her hips, steadying her to a stop. When she was sure Hannah was secure, Sheri moved over to unfasten the Jaws. Tony moved to help her and together the two of them worked the contraption into the crushed driver's side door.

Hannah inched her way around the vehicle, trying to see past the damage to the figure slumped in the passenger seat. A big Black man, so not the man she had seen up top. He looked like someone had dumped a bucket of red-brown paint down his front—the metallic stench of blood made her throat convulse. She was sure he was dead, but she called out to him anyway. "Hey, mister!" she shouted. "Can you hear me? I've come to help you." No response, but then she hadn't expected any.

Danny moved in beside her. "I found some tracks in the snow, but no sign of your wounded man," he said. "We'll have to search for him after we've got a better handle on things here." He moved away to begin stabilizing the vehicle, placing blocks and even anchors to, she hoped, keep it in place until they had removed everyone inside. He tossed her a chock and she wedged it firmly under the tire, then did the same for the other two tires she could reach, while he fastened one end of a heavy chain to the front axle and the other to a tree upslope.

It took another agonizing half hour to expand and cut away the metal around the door until it was wide enough for Tony to lean in and examine the driver. He backed out, shaking his head. "He's already cold," he said. "We'd better get him out now." Once rigor set in, it would be that much more difficult to move the body.

As soon as they had dragged the driver—white, overweight, with thinning blond hair and a lot of head trauma—onto the ground, Hannah scrambled into the van, ignoring the blood and gore, the broken glass and bits of metal. Up close, the man in the passenger seat looked even worse. He was young, maybe late twenties, and he was wearing a uniform. She wiped blood from the gold star on his chest. Law enforcement, though she couldn't make out what branch. She forced herself to reach in past the blood to feel for the pulse at his neck. She had heard all kinds of stories about people surviving horrific injuries, so you always had to check.

What she found this time made her draw back in horror, with a yelp of protest. "What is it?" Sheri asked. "Are you hurt?"

Hannah scrambled backward out of the van, then stumbled over to the side and was promptly sick. Sheri patted her back. "It's okay," she murmured. "All of us have seen something at one time or another that made us lose it. Just give yourself a minute to pull yourself together."

With shaking hands, Hannah accepted the bottle of water Sheri passed her. She rinsed her mouth, then pressed cold hands to her cheek. "It was just shock," she said.

"You okay?" Tony joined them.

Hannah nodded. "The passenger is some kind of law enforcement officer," she said. "And I don't think he died in the crash."

Tony's eyes narrowed. "What do you mean?"

Hannah closed her eyes, verifying that her memory of what she had seen in there was correct. She forced the words out past the tightness in her throat. "I'm pretty sure his throat was cut," she said. "He was murdered."

Chapter Two

"We need a law enforcement presence on scene."

Jake was coiling up the rope he had used to help convey the Jaws of Life to the accident site when an older man, one of the SAR volunteers, approached. "Captain says we have a situation down below," the man said.

"What's happened?" Jake shoved the coil of rope into the back of the SAR Jeep and turned to face the older man.

The man—gray haired and craggy, with skin like leather, shook his head. "Tony thinks we might have a crime scene on our hands. He'd like you down there ASAP."

"Of course." He looked toward the drop-off. "I'll need help getting down there."

"Done much climbing before?"

Jake made a face. "Does the climbing wall at the gym count?"

The man shrugged. "It's something. I got a harness for you over here." He gestured toward a black truck. "My name's Ted," he said as Jake followed him to the truck.

"I'm Deputy Jake Gwynn."

"Okay, Deputy Gwynn. We got you the harness. A helmet. Gloves." Ted shoved each of these items at Jake as he spoke. "Hold on tight, watch your step, don't look down. If you slip, the harness will catch you. Ryan is going to climb down alongside you and coach you through everything. You shouldn't have any problem."

Not if you'd done it before, Jake thought, as he buckled the helmet under his chin, then stepped into the harness and pulled it up around his hips. He was from Eastern Colorado—the flat part, with not a mountain in sight.

But he said nothing of this to his guide. "Over here." Ted led him to the edge of the drop-off and handed him a rope. "I'll be belaying up top here, and Ryan will be alongside, so you'll be fine."

Ryan wore a bright red helmet plastered with stickers for various outdoor equipment manufacturers. He clipped into a rope that ran parallel to Jake's. "Take it slow and listen to my instructions," he said. "If you get stuck, stop and wait for my help."

Though Jake's heart hammered with trepidation at the climb, he was also excited about what he might find at the wreck. He didn't want bad things to happen to people, but he liked the challenge of solving crimes and stopping bad guys.

Focusing thoughts on what he might find at the wreck helped him make it down the slope. That, and Ryan's firm coaching. The soles of his winter boots kept slipping in the mixture of mud and snow on the slope, but he held tight to the rope and managed to keep from falling. When he reached the place where the van had come to rest, the pretty redhead he'd met earlier, Hannah, helped him unhook and climb out of the harness. "What's going on?" he asked.

She shook her head. "You'd better see for yourself and decide," she said. "But I warn you—it's pretty grisly."

"You need to take a look at the guy in the passenger seat," Tony said.

It was grisly, all right, and Jake had to clench his jaw tight to maintain control as he looked at the man in the passenger seat of the van, his head almost severed from the neck. Jake forced himself to take his time and make as thorough an examination as possible, being careful not to disturb the scene, though the SAR personnel had probably already inadvertently destroyed evidence. Then again, the plummet off the road could have done that, too.

"I don't see anything that would cause a wound like that accidentally," Tony said after Jake emerged from the van.

"No, I'd say that was done deliberately," Jake said. The wound had looked deep, made with a very sharp blade.

"Any idea who he is?" Ted asked. "We saw the uniform."

"Bernalillo County, New Mexico," Jake said. "His badge says Deputy Green. I'll have to contact them. The van isn't marked, but it has government plates."

"Huh," Tony said. "I didn't notice that."

"Have you looked in the back yet?" Jake nodded toward the rear of the vehicle.

"No. We thought we'd better wait for you."

The side door of the van was blocked, so Tony held back the driver's seat while Jake crawled inside. Then Tony played the beam of a powerful light over the back seat. "Looks like that seat belt's been cut," he said, spotlighting the cleanly cut edges of the safety belt.

Jake's foot nudged something and he looked down at a metal eye fixed into the floor of the vehicle. A short piece of chain was threaded through the eye, and beside the chain lay a pair of leg irons. A chill that had nothing to do with the ambient temperature ran up his spine as the meaning of that chain registered. He took the flashlight from his utility belt and began searching beneath the front seats. Something glinted, and he bent awkwardly and used a pen from his pocket to drag the item forward. "Are those handcuffs?" Tony asked.

"They're handcuffs." Jake backed out of the vehicle to find the rest of the SAR team around the opening, looking at him expectantly. "Looks like they were transporting a prisoner," he said.

"So the prisoner took advantage of the crash to get away," Tony said.

"Or the prisoner caused the crash when he made a break for it." Jake turned to Hannah. "Tell me everything you remember about the man you saw when you first got here. What did he look like?"

"He looked hurt," she said. "He had blood all over his head and his clothes."

"What was he wearing?"

She frowned. "I wasn't paying attention."

"Think. You saw something, even if you didn't consciously register the fact. It could be important."

She nodded, and closed her eyes. After a moment, she opened them again. "He was wearing a white jumpsuit. Or it had been white, before there was blood and mud all over it. But he didn't have a coat or hat. He's liable to freeze to death out here."

"Where's the closest place he could go for shelter?" Jake asked.

She looked around them, as if getting her bearings. "I don't know. We're twelve miles from town, over some pretty rugged terrain."

"There aren't any houses nearby," Tony said.

"What about the huts?" a tall, thin man asked.

"The huts?" Jake asked.

"There's a series of backcountry huts," the thin man said. "They're designed so backcountry skiers can spend the night. The huts are roughly a few hours on skis apart. They're not fancy, but there's a woodstove and firewood and bunks, some basic supplies in each one."

"How far is the nearest hut?" Jake asked.

The man scratched his chin. Unlike the other male SAR volunteers Jake had met, this man was clean-shaven. "A couple of hours? But that's with winter gear. It would be a lot tougher going in street clothes, without a coat or snowshoes or anything."

"So you're saying our guy would probably freeze to death before he got there?" Jake asked.

"Not necessarily," Tony said. "He's got to climb and all that strenuous activity would warm him up a lot. And it just depends on what kind of shape he's in and how determined he is. You'd be amazed what people can survive if they're stubborn enough. Sometimes that really is the only difference between making it out of an ordeal alive—some people just refuse to give up."

"I need to go after him," Jake said.

"That's our job," Tony said. "The search part of search and rescue."

"He's already killed one man," Jake said. "And I think he's probably armed. Deputy Green's weapon holster is empty. I can't let you go after him alone."

"Then you'll come with us." Tony looked around, then pointed to the thin man. "Danny, you've spent the most time on these trails. You come with us."

"I need to talk to the sheriff, see what he thinks," Jake said. "But Hannah should come, too." At her look of surprise, he added, "You're the only one of us who's seen this guy. That might prove useful."

She nodded. "We'll need the right equipment," she said. "Boots with crampons."

"Snowshoes, too," Danny said. "Skis would be good in places, but too hard to maneuver on the rough stuff unless you're really good. Like expert good."

"I can hold my own on skis, but I'm no mountaineering expert," Jake said.

Ted clapped him on the back. "You talk to the sheriff. Meanwhile, Hannah and Danny, go back to town and get the equipment you need. The rest of us will finish up here."

"We'll need to get forensics in here to photograph the scene and look for evidence, and you'll need the coroner," Jake said.

Ted nodded. "There's nothing we can do for either of the victims in this case, except stand by to help retrieve the bodies when the coroner is done." He looked up, squinting at the sky. "You'd better get a move on. We've only got a few hours before we start losing light."

DANNY MADE THE climb back up to the road first, then Hannah followed. "You okay going after this guy?" Danny asked as they waited for Jake to climb up.

She bristled. "Why wouldn't I be?" She didn't exactly relish the rough journey, but this was the kind of thing she had signed on for and trained for. And this man, even if he was a criminal and possibly a killer, was hurt and would need medical care.

Danny shrugged. "Just seems kind of dangerous."

She stared at him. "A lot of the stuff we do is dangerous." She waved her hand at the chasm below them. "This right here is dangerous."

"Nah, this is just a challenge. It's not dangerous if you know what you're doing."

She was saved having to argue with him by Jake's arrival. "Can you ride into town with me?" he asked. "We can stop by the sheriff's department, then you can help me round up the equipment I'll need."

"Sure." She appreciated that Jake didn't mind looking to her for help. She followed him to a sheriff's department SUV and waited while he shifted a pile of papers and gear from the passenger seat. She was scarcely buckled in when he swung the vehicle around and hit the siren for the drive back to town. As soon as they hit the city limits for Eagle Mountain, he ordered his phone to call the sheriff.

"What's up, Jake?" Sheriff Travis Walker sounded calm and easygoing, but Hannah knew he had a reputation as being no-nonsense. Her father had said that Travis was a man who worked more than he talked, and that had earned the young lawman the support of a lot of people in town.

Jake ran through the particulars of the crash, summing up with, "We've got a fugitive, probably armed, loose in the high country. He isn't dressed for the weather, so he'll probably head for the closest shelter, which is one of the backcountry ski huts. I want to take a couple of the search and rescue team members up there to look for him."

"Who are you taking?" the sheriff asked.

"There's a guy, Danny, who's a local ski patroller. He knows the way to the closest hut. And the paramedic, Hannah. The man we're looking for was likely hurt in the accident, so he'll need medical attention. And she got a good look at him before he ran off, so she'll recognize him."

"I'm going to send Gage with you. He knows the area as well and you need another officer backing you up."

"Yes, sir."

"I'll track down Deputy Green's supervisor and get the particulars on our fugitive," Travis said. "I'll keep you posted."

Jake ended the call, and slowed the cruiser as they neared the center of town. He switched off the siren and glanced at Hannah. "Who can lend me the gear I'll need?"

"What size boots do you wear?" she asked.

"Thirteen."

"Then you can borrow my dad's stuff." She pointed ahead of them. "Turn left on Seventh Avenue and go all the way down to the Alpiner Inn."

The Alpiner was a two-story affair built to resemble a European chalet, with bright blue doors and shutters. In the spring, Hannah's mom filled the window boxes with red geraniums, but this time of year the boxes were mounded with snow. Jake pulled the SUV under the portico over the entrance and he and Hannah piled out.

The lobby was empty, so Hannah hit the bell on the front desk. Her mother, a petite woman with her riot of faded red curls tamed beneath a pink bandanna, bustled out of the back room. "Hannah?" She turned to Jake and took in his uniform. "Is something wrong?"

"Is Dad around? Deputy Gwynn needs to borrow some gear."

Her mom looked over her shoulder as Hannah's dad, Thad, came through the door. Despite his slightly bent frame and tonsure of white hair, his clear blue eyes and practically unlined face made him look younger than his sixty-two years. "Hello there." He smiled at Jake, a question in his eyes.

"Deputy Jake Gwynn." Jake stepped forward and offered his hand. "Your daughter said you had some winter gear I could borrow."

Thad shook Jake's hand. "Sure thing. Where are you headed?" he asked.

"There was a wreck on the highway up on Dixon Pass," Hannah said. "An injured man wandered off and we have to look for him. Jake needs some good climbing boots and warmer outerwear."

"But why is the deputy going along?" Thad asked.

Hannah looked to Jake. She had hoped to avoid alarming her parents, by making it seem that this was an ordinary rescue call. "We don't know this man's history and we have reason to believe he's armed," Jake said. "I'm going along as a precaution, but I'm new to the area, so I need to borrow some gear."

Thad nodded. "Come on back then."

They followed her dad through to the back of the building, where the family lived. "I heard the sheriff's department had a new hire," Thad said as he rummaged through his closet. "How do you like Eagle Mountain so far?"

"I'm very happy to be here," Jake said. "It's a beautiful place." He turned to study a display of medals and trophies next to the closet, many of them featuring images of climbers. "Are these all yours?"

Thad leaned out of the closet to see what had caught Jake's attention. "Yeah. I used to be a professional climber. I haven't competed in years, though I still keep my hand in, helping out with local clubs. Climbing is how I ended up in Eagle Mountain."

"I'm impressed," Jake said. There must have been two dozen awards in this case, in addition to several framed commendations.

Thad ducked back into the closet. "Have you spent much time in the backcountry?" he asked.

"Some," Jake said.

"You'll need these." Thad handed him a pair of stout leather boots, fitted with crampons.

"We need snowshoes, too," Hannah said.

Thad nodded, then looked Jake up and down. He dived back into the closet and came out again with a pair of insulated coveralls, patched at one knee with silver duct tape. "They're not pretty, but they're warm," he said. "What about a helmet?"

"I have one of those," Jake said. "We work enough rock slides and avalanches it's standard issue."

"What else then?"

"This should do it, Dad. Thanks." Hannah tugged at Jake's arm. "We're in a hurry." If they stayed, her father, who loved to talk, would start asking for more details, either about the accident, the man they were looking for or Jake himself.

Back in the lobby, Hannah said. "I'm going to get my gear. I'll meet you back outside."

She tried to slip past her parents, but her dad was watching for her. "This doesn't sound like an ordinary search and rescue mission," he said. "Who is this man you're looking for?"

"All I know is that he was in a car accident and he's hurt," she said. "He may be in shock and lost. I have to go help." She patted his shoulder. "Don't worry, Dad."

"Worrying is my job," Thad said. "It gets added to the job description the day your first child is born—you'll see."

She kissed his cheek. "I'll be fine," she said, then hurried up to her room before he could say more. She loved her parents, and loved that they were still close, but living at home at twenty-four did mean sacrificing a bit of privacy and independence. The pluses outweighed the minuses, but she sometimes envied those of her friends who had the luxury of keeping a few secrets from their folks.

When she returned to the SUV, Jake was hanging up the phone. "We know the fugitive's name is Charles Cutler—he goes by Charlie. He's thirty-seven, and he's a convicted murderer. He was serving time in New Mexico and was being transported to Junction for a trial for a murder in Colorado." he said. "The sheriff is trying to find out more. The deputy who was killed is Armando Green, twenty-eight, from Albuquerque, on the force for two years. The driver was a civilian, Geoffrey Calloway."

She piled her gear into the back on top of his, then slid into the passenger seat. "Those poor families," she said.

"Gage is going to meet us in the pullout near the crash site," Jake said. He shifted the SUV into gear. "Cutler isn't some kid who made a rash mistake. He's a hardened killer. I don't think it's a good idea to involve civilians in this hunt."

"I'm not an ordinary civilian," she said. "Search and Rescue members are trained to work with law enforcement." Not that she had ever been in this kind of situation before, but she did have training. "I know how to stay out of the way and how to follow orders," she added.

He frowned but didn't say anything. He didn't use the siren on the way out of town this time. Hannah looked for some way to break the tension between them, but Jake spoke first. "Have you lived in Eagle Mountain long?" he asked after a moment.

"I grew up here. There at the inn. Where are you from?"

"Eastern Colorado. A little town called Haxtun."

"Sorry. I've never heard of it."

"Most people haven't. My parents have a ranch out there. They raise cattle and wheat."

"At least you're not a city boy."

"No, I'm not." His mouth twitched, as if he was amused.

She squirmed. "I just mean that if you grew up in a rural area, you probably know a little bit about dealing with the elements. They have big blizzards out there on the plains, don't they?"

"Oh yeah."

"And you really did handle the climbing well today. I've seen people freak out when they had to do something like that. It still scares me, even, and I've had hours and hours of training."

"I would have thought since your dad was a pro you would have been climbing since you were a kid," Jake said. "I saw all his trophies. He must be pretty good."

"I never had Dad's talent," she said. "I do it because it's part of my job. You looked like a natural, though."

"I was in good hands," he said. "I'm thinking it will be a little different up on the mountain."

"We'll be on trails part of the time," she said. "Trails with snow and ice, but that will make the going a little easier."

"First we need to see if we can pick up Cutler's trail. If he's still bleeding, that will help."

"If he's still bleeding, he may not get far," she said.

"Then that will be to our advantage."

She winced inwardly. Even though she knew the man they were searching for was a killer, the image of him, bleeding and terrified, was burned into her brain. All her training was devoted to helping people without judgment. She couldn't change her thinking now.

They neared the pullout and Jake slowed the SUV. Her Subaru was still there, along with another sheriff's department SUV. Sergeant Gage Walker, the sheriff's brother, got out of his vehicle as they pulled in behind him. A little taller and a little blonder than his brother, Gage was a friendly guy who often stopped by the inn to check on things or talk fishing with her dad.

"Hello, Hannah," Gage said. He came around to the back of Jake's SUV, where they were unloading their gear. "Danny's waiting for us at the trailhead on the other side of the waterfall. Did Travis tell you about this guy we're going after?"

"He said he killed three people."

"Uh-huh. Two women and a man." He glanced at Hannah, then away. "Pretty violent."

"He slit that deputy's throat and took his weapon," Jake said.

"Yeah, well, there's something else, something Travis just found out."

Jake and Hannah both stopped what they were doing and faced him. "What is it?" Hannah asked.

"Before Charlie Cutler was a killer, he was in the army. He went through the army's mountain-warfare school in upstate New York. That's summer and winter mountaineer training, rough terrain evacuation and mountain sniper training."

Jake swore under his breath.

"Right." Gage clapped him on the back. "We're about to go after a guy who's been trained to thrive in conditions most people couldn't even survive."

Chapter Three

They met up with Danny at the trailhead. Already the sun cast long shadows across the snow. In another hour they would be in full shadow, and an hour after that, twilight. Jake's heart raced with a sense of urgency. Hannah and Danny assured him they had trained for nighttime rescues, but darkness and colder temperatures made everything more difficult.

And this time they were going after a killer. Someone who could take advantage of the darkness to hide.

They started hiking up the trail, Danny leading the way, followed by Jake and Hannah, with Gage bringing up the rear. "It's going to take a couple of hours to reach the hut," Danny said. "We'll have a little more light after we cross the ridge into the valley where the hut sits, but we'll be coming back in the dark."

"Don't turn on your headlamps until we have to," Gage said. "If Cutler is up here, he'll be able to spot any lights approaching from a long way off and we don't want that."

"Right," Danny agreed. "Then we'd better hurry."

He set a swift pace up the steep path. No one said much, saving their breath for the climb. The narrow path wound up the mountain along a thin ridge, fields of pristine snow on either side, a canopy of blue overhead. If they hadn't been in search of a dangerous killer, Jake might have enjoyed the trek.

"It looks like this trail gets a lot of use," Jake said, as they neared the top of the first long switchback. The snow on the trail was packed down, with many boot prints, and slick ice in the sunny spots.

"This is the shortest route up to the huts and some really good skiing," Danny said. "And the avalanche danger is pretty low on this side, because the highway department regularly sets charges to release the snow to keep the road clear."

"Makes it harder to track our fugitive, though," Gage said.

"We don't even know Cutler came this way," Hannah said.

"It's the easiest route up the mountain, so he's an idiot if he didn't head this way," Danny said.

"Except he has to know someone would come after him," Hannah said.

"I don't see any tracks off the trail," Gage said.

"Would he have known about the huts?" Hannah asked.

"There's a sign at the trailhead," Danny said. "If he saw that, he'd have known this was his best bet for shelter. He'd want to get there before nightfall."

"What if someone else is already at the hut?" she asked.

"I hope they aren't," Gage said. "For their sake."

Hannah's stricken expression told Jake she understood that Cutler was likely to kill anyone who got in his way. That included all of them.

About five hundred yards up the first steep incline,

Danny stopped and pointed to the ground at their feet. "I think that's blood," he said.

Jake knelt and examined the drops, bright red where they had frozen on the snow. "This looks pretty fresh," he said.

"It could be an injured animal," Gage said.

"Maybe." Jake straightened and stared up the slope. "But I don't think so."

"Yeah, I don't think so, either," Gage said. They started out hiking again. Danny quickened the pace, moving just below a trot. The altimeter on Jake's watch showed just over ten thousand feet and he could definitely feel it, breathing hard, his heart pounding. He told himself that Cutler, who had been in a prison in Albuquerque, would be at a greater disadvantage, living at a lower altitude.

At the top of the next switchback, they met two men hiking down, skis strapped to their big packs. "Have you passed anyone on your way down?" Jake asked.

"Nobody," the older of the two, with a full red beard, said.

"You're starting up kind of late," his friend said.

"Were you at the hut?" Jake asked.

"We passed by there," the bearded man said. "It didn't look like there was anyone there, so you should have the place to yourselves."

"Thanks," Jake said, and they moved on. At the top of the next switchback, Jake motioned for Hannah to move past him, and he dropped back to speak to Gage. "What do you think?" he asked.

"I think if we get there before him, we can hide and take him easier," Gage said.

"Right. But if he was ahead of us, and those two didn't

see him, where did he go? We're above tree line and there aren't a lot of places to hide around here. We spotted those two long before we met up with them."

"I don't know," Gage admitted. "I haven't seen any place where anyone has gone off trail, but maybe they teach things in that army course that we don't know about. They must have stuff in their training about evading the enemy."

"They probably taught him how to sneak up and ambush someone from behind, too," Jake said, keeping his voice low so Hannah and Danny wouldn't hear.

Gage grimaced. "And we're pretty exposed up here on this ridge."

"I'd feel better if we didn't have civilians with us," Jake said.

"I've worked with Search and Rescue before," Gage said. "They've got solid training and they know how to follow orders. Don't worry about them."

What some people called worry was Jake's idea of being prepared for the worst. But he merely nodded and moved up alongside Hannah again. "How are you doing?" he asked.

"I'd be enjoying myself if we were doing this for some other reason." She flashed him a smile. "It's beautiful up here."

"It is." Except those clear skies and open snow fields made him feel like a target. Still, he reminded himself, as far as they knew, Cutler only had a pistol. He'd have to get pretty close in order to fire on them. "Thanks for agreeing to come with us," he said.

"If you find Mr. Cutler, you'll need me," she said.

He hoped that was the only reason they needed her. A man who would cut the throat of a sheriff's deputy the way Cutler had wouldn't hesitate to kill anyone else he thought was in his way.

HANNAH KEPT HER eyes on the ground, searching for more spots of blood alongside the trail. Those first spots had been so vivid, a scattering of bright red against the stark white. But they hadn't seen any more. Was it because Cutler had staunched the flow, or because he had left the trail at some point and struck out in some other direction?

They only had another hour or so before the sun set behind the mountains, which meant that no matter what they found, they'd be descending in the dark. She had hiked with a headlamp before, but coming down would be a lot colder. It was cold enough now, the tips of her fingers, even in insulated mittens, going numb periodically, until she shoved them deep into the pockets of her parka to thaw, and her cheeks stinging. She told herself as long as she could feel them she didn't need to worry about frostbite. Coming down, they would be a lot more fatigued, too. It was the kind of conditions that were ripe for mistakes.

When she lifted her gaze from the trail, her view was of Jake Gwynn's back. For a flatlander, he was handling the climbing well. Unlike her, he wasn't focused on the trail. Instead, he constantly scanned the area around them, his attitude alert. While she knew, objectively, that Charlie Cutler was dangerous, Jake accepted it as fact. He was probably used to expecting the worst from people, while her training was to seek out the best in everyone. That dissonance between what the facts told her and what she wanted to believe added to the unreal quality of this whole afternoon.

Up ahead, Danny stopped and waited for the rest of

them to catch up. "The hut is just over this next ridge," he said. "About another half mile."

"Can you see this trail from the hut?" Jake asked.

"No. The hut sits in a little depression, in a sheltered area. If you're inside, you really can't see anyone until they're up on you. There aren't many windows, in any case, which makes it easier to heat."

"If Cutler is in there and has built a fire, we'll be able to see the smoke," Hannah said. "We'll probably smell it before we see it."

"He'll know we're likely to come after him," Gage said. "So he might not light a fire. If I remember, there are supplies in the huts, right?"

"Yeah," Danny said. "Water and firewood, but also some blankets, first aid and emergency supplies, and some canned food."

"All right," Gage said. "When we get within sight of the hut, you and Hannah need to fall back. We'll stop and observe for a while, then Jake and I will move forward."

Hannah and Danny nodded.

They started out again, a new silence enveloping them, as without discussion they tried to make as little noise as possible. Twenty-five minutes later they reached the top of the ridge, and stopped to look down on the hut, a simple A-frame painted a soft gray that blended with the shadows of the ridge above. Firewood filled a separate woodshed a few feet from the door, and an outhouse painted to match the hut itself sat twenty yards from the back door.

Danny sniffed the air. "No smoke."

Jake pulled a pair of binoculars from his pack and focused on the hut. "There are footprints leading to the doors, front and back," he said, his voice very low.

"Could be from other visitors," Gage said. "A lot of people use these huts."

Jake stowed the binoculars. "I'll go down first," he said.

"Better strap on snowshoes," Danny said. He swept his hand toward the expanse of snow between the trail and the cabin. "That snow is feet deep. Follow the ski trail in—it will be more packed."

Jake nodded and slipped the pack from his back to unstrap the snowshoes. He removed his crampons and stepped into the snowshoes, then bent to tighten them, his gaze focused on the cabin, which was still and silent.

"I'll cover you." Gage unholstered his weapon. "You two get down," he said to Danny and Hannah.

The sight of his drawn pistol made the danger seem so much more real, and she fought back a sickening wave of fear. She sat in the snow, pulling her knees to her chest, as Jake started down toward the hut. She wished she could see what he was doing. Then again, she didn't really want to see if Cutler shot him. She closed her eyes. The saying in SAR was you never knew what you'd find when you went out on a call, but she couldn't at her most imaginative have anticipated a day like today.

"Hey, it'll be all right." Danny moved closer and put his arm around her.

She shoved him away and glared.

He drew back. "You don't have to be so touchy."

And he didn't have to try to take advantage of the situation. She didn't need him to "comfort" her, thank you very much.

"What's going on down there?" Danny asked Gage.

"Jake is almost to the hut."

That was a good sign, wasn't it? Unless Cutler wanted Jake closer before he killed him.

Another long wait. Hannah focused on taking deep breaths, counting with each one. One...two....three... four...

"He's motioned for us to come on down." Gage stood and holstered his weapon.

Hannah rose, staggering a little on frozen feet, and joined the other two in fumbling into snowshoes. They started down to the hut, sinking five or six inches before finding a good footing. Anyone who came along would spot their trail from a mile away.

The whole area was in full shadow now, blue in the dwindling light. Jake came partway up the trail to meet them. "If he was here, he's gone now," he said. "The place is empty. We should stop and get warm, maybe eat something before we head back down."

"It's getting too dark to track him now," Gage said. "But if we can determine which way he headed, it will give us a head start tomorrow. We can probably get a helicopter up here to help out."

They walked spread out across the snow, headed toward the hut. The idea of a hot drink and a chance to sit down for a while sent a burst of energy through her. Another few hours and this would all be over and—

Before she could finish the thought, something whistled past her. Then a body slammed into hers. She sank into the snow, the breath knocked out of her, then realized the sounds around her were shots. Jake lay sprawled on top of her. "Are you okay?" she asked, trying to throw off his weight enough to sit up.

"Stay down," he ordered, and rolled over enough to draw his weapon, just as another bullet struck near them, snow flying up where it struck like feathers from a burst pillow. The sound it made was soft, almost gentle, in sharp contrast with the fear that gripped her. Were they going to die here, slaughtered like animals in the midst of so much beauty?

Chapter Four

Jake fired in the direction the shots had come, the report of his weapon loud and echoing, overlapping a similar report from Gage's gun. Their fire wasn't returned, so he lowered his gun and listened. His own ragged breathing filled his ears, then Hannah whimpered and squirmed beneath him. "I can't breathe," she whispered. "Could you get off of me?"

He hadn't even realized he was still sprawled on top of her. When the first shot had rang out, he had acted on instinct, pushing her down and shielding her. Now he knelt beside her, knees sinking in the snow, snowshoes kicked up awkwardly behind him. "Are you okay?"

"I'm okay." She raised herself to all fours and looked toward the hut. "Is he in there?"

"I don't think so. Not anymore."

Gage crawled over to them. "I think he was firing from behind the outhouse," he said. "But he's gone now. I can just about make out his tracks headed away from there."

Jake pulled the binoculars from his pack and focused on the outhouse, then shook his head. "The light's too bad to make out anything." He lowered the glasses and stared down the slope. "Do we go after him, or head back?"

"If we could get inside for a bit, drink some water and have something to eat, we'll do better on the trip down," Hannah said. "And we might be able to tell if he took any supplies from the hut when he left."

"She's got a good point," Gage said. He stood and offered a hand to Hannah. "Let's go down."

Jake's pulse hammered in his ears all the way down to the hut, and by the time they reached the door he ached from holding himself so rigid. But no further shots rang out. Gage led them in a wide arc around the steps in front of the hut. The door stood partly open, as if Cutler had exited in a hurry.

The inside of the hut was as cold as it had been outside. Danny switched on his headlamp, and Jake took a flashlight from his belt and played the beam across the interior, revealing a single room with a woodstove against the back wall, a table and chairs in front of the stove and triple bunks on either side wall. A single cabinet on the back wall to the left of the stovepipe stood open, the contents tumbling out. "Looks like he rifled through here," Gage said.

"He used the first aid kit." Hannah moved to the table, her headlamp spotlighting a tangle of bloody gauze, unwound bandage and an open tube of antibiotic cream. She frowned at the disarray. "I can't really tell much about the nature of the wounds from this. He was bleeding—maybe from broken glass from the wreckage?"

She reached out toward the roll of bandaging but Jake caught and held her hand. "Don't touch anything more than necessary," he said.

She nodded and he released her and stepped back.

Danny moved to a wooden locker at the end of one set of bunks. Gingerly, using only one finger, he raised the lid. "He's been in here," he said. "There was a pack in here with more first aid and emergency supplies missing."

"You're sure?" Jake moved in beside him.

"We stocked all the huts at the beginning of the season," Danny said. "The packs are designed so that in an emergency, someone could carry what they need to someone who was hurt on the ski trails."

"What did the pack contain?" Gage asked.

"Basic first aid supplies—bandages, a splint and instant ice packs." Danny tilted his head, considering. "There were a couple of emergency blankets—those foil-looking things that utilize the body's own heat for warmth. Some chemical heat packs and emergency food—energy gels and bars. Extra socks and gloves and a hat." He peered into the locker again. "I think last time I was up here someone had left one of those big wool Nordic sweaters in here, too. That's gone."

"So he has a pack, warmer clothing, food and first aid supplies," Gage said. "He's in a lot better shape that he was when he left the van a few hours ago."

"He must have taken the deputy's rifle with him when he left the van too," Jake said. "I didn't think about that at the time, but that wasn't a pistol he was firing at us."

"We'll have to contact the Bernalillo County Sheriff's Department and find out what kind of weapon Green would have had, and how much ammunition," Gage said.

"My guess is Cutler has plenty left," Jake said. "He didn't fire that many shots."

"He just wanted to buy time to get away," Gage said. "We'll need to close this area to the public until we find him."

"Good luck with that," Danny said.

"What do you mean?" Jake asked.

"I mean there are probably ten trails that access this basin," Danny said. "You don't have the personnel to station someone at every trailhead. You can post signs, but people will ignore them. It happens every fire season. The forest rangers spend a lot of time running people out of closed areas. It's always the same story. 'I didn't see the sign' or even 'I didn't think one or two people would be a problem.' There are always people who think the rules don't apply to them."

"Maybe if the signs say a killer is on the loose, people will take them seriously," Jake said.

"You can try," Danny said. "But I wouldn't count on it."

"We need to eat and get warm before we head back down," Hannah said. "I know we're not supposed to touch anything, but we're not going to make it down safely if we don't get some fuel in us."

"Go ahead," Gage said. "We're not going to find anything here that tells us where Cutler is headed or what his plans are."

Hannah moved to the gas cooktop and picked up the kettle. "I'm going to get some snow to melt for water for coffee," she said. "Danny, can you fix something for us to eat?"

"I'll go out with you," Jake said. He moved with her toward the cabin's back door. "Let me go out first. Just in case Cutler is still out there."

Her eyes widened, but she said nothing, only nodded and stepped back, cradling the empty kettle under one arm, her snowshoes under the other.

He slipped outside, snowshoes in hand, and waited in the shadow of the hut, ears straining to hear anything but his own breathing. After a long moment, he looked back toward Hannah and nodded. "Switch off your light," he said, keeping his voice low.

She did as he asked and he moved closer so she'd be sure to hear him. "Can you see well enough to move around without a light?"

"Yes." She bent and began strapping on her snow-shoes.

He put on his own snowshoes and took a few steps away from the hut, braced for the impact of a bullet. Yes, he had on a ballistics vest underneath the insulated coveralls, but he didn't have faith the vest would make much difference to a slug from a high-powered rifle.

Nothing happened. Quiet wrapped itself around him, and he wondered if this was what sudden deafness was like. He looked up at the first stars shining out from the canopy of blackness, like pinholes punctured in a blackout curtain.

Hannah moved up alongside him. "We need to get a ways from the hut," she said. "To be sure the snow is clean."

"All right."

Moving in the dark was awkward, but they made it about a hundred yards before she stopped and scooped the kettle into the snow. Then she turned and hurried back to the hut, so that he had to jog to keep up with her, snowshoes making muffled slapping sounds against the powdery snow.

Back inside, someone had started a fire in the wood-stove. Danny had placed a cutting board on one of the bottom bunks and was slicing summer sausage and cheese. Gage had pulled one of the chairs from the table over to the stove and sat in it, reloading his pistol.

"Your perp took all the chocolate," Danny said. "This

is all from my pack. There's crackers and dried mango, too." He indicated a couple of plastic bags beside the cutting board.

"There's still coffee in here." Hannah took a plastic container of grounds from the single cabinet.

They ate quickly, then Hannah and Danny cleared up the remains of their meal. "Before we go, I want to see if we can figure out which way Cutler headed," Jake said. "It will give us a head start when we pick up the search again in the morning."

"Good idea," Gage said. He stood and began pulling on his parka. "You two wait and we'll head back down together," he told Danny.

Jake pulled on his borrowed parka and a balaclava, then strapped the helmet on over that. At the back door, he and Gage put on their snowshoes, and set off toward the outhouse. Ten steps from the doorway, darkness closed around them. He had a moment of vertigo, suspended between the soft snow and the stinging cold of the night air. "You think Cutler is still out here?" Gage asked.

"Why would he still be here?" Jake asked.

"Maybe waiting for us to leave? He could spend the night in the hut."

"He's bound to know we'll keep looking for him. And we'll start the last place we saw him—here." Jake shook his head. "I think he's on his way to the next hut."

"Then we'll start one search team there at first light," Gage said. His footsteps crunched softly on the snow. "Come on. Let's see if we can find any sign of him."

As Gage and Jake exited out the back door, Hannah dropped into the chair by the fire that Gage had vacated and sipped the last of the coffee. Danny pulled a second chair alongside her. "Wild day, huh?" he said.

"All I want to do is get home," she said. Even the thought of having to hike in the darkness back down to her car exhausted her.

"Finding that deputy this morning was rough," Danny said. "Don't let it get to you."

"I won't." She hadn't even been thinking about Deputy Green, as terrible as that was. He wasn't, unfortunately, the first dead person she had seen working Search and Rescue.

"What do you think of the new cop?" Danny asked.

"He's okay." She stared into the fire, aware of Danny watching her. "He's not a whiner."

"Maybe he'll last longer than some of the others. Seems like we've gone through a lot of deputies in the past few years."

"You know what it's like in small towns," she said. "People come here to get experience, then move on to some place that pays better or is less expensive to live— or both. It happens everywhere, not just the sheriff's department." One of the reasons she continued to live at the Alpiner with her parents was that it was so hard to find dependable employees who would stay on the job. She worked three twelve-hour shifts a week as a paramedic and had the other four days off to help at the inn.

"He seems pretty into you," Danny said.

She frowned. "You're imagining things."

"I didn't imagine the way he threw himself on you when the bullets started flying. I was standing just as close and he didn't try to save me."

"Are you jealous?" she asked.

He said something obscene.

Fortunately, he didn't have time to pick up the discussion. The back door opened and Jake and Gage stepped in, stamping their snowshoes on the rubber door mat. "Did you find anything?" Danny asked.

Gage pushed back the hood of his parka and shook his head. "It's too dark to tell much of anything. There are tracks over behind the outhouse, but no way to tell much. We'll be back up at first light tomorrow with a search team."

"If you need help, I'm up for it," Danny said.

"Thanks," Gage said. "But this will be all law enforcement personnel."

"Yeah, I guess with a cop dead, it will be an all-out manhunt," Danny said.

"We want to make sure he doesn't kill anyone else," Jake said. "How far is it from here to the next hut in line?"

"Five miles," Danny said.

"Is that the closest shelter?" Jake asked.

"Pretty much," Danny said.

"There are some mine ruins not far from that hut," Hannah said. "Some of the buildings aren't in bad shape. He might try to hide there. Less chance of running into other people, at least this time of year."

"What about transportation out of here?" Jake asked.

"Other than going back down to the highway or into town—he could hijack a vehicle at a trailhead," Gage said.

"He could hike over the ridge into the town of Paradise," Danny said. "It's not the easiest route, but it's not impossible. From there he could go just about anywhere."

"Is there a path or a road he'd follow to do that?" Jake asked.

"There's an old Jeep road," Danny said. "It's closed this time of year, but if he's motivated enough…" He shrugged.

"I think he's motivated," Gage said. He looked around the cabin. "Let's get out of here."

They headed out, changing out of their snowshoes when they reached the trail. Hannah's headlamp cast a trembling blue circle of light in front of her and cold seeped through the layers of her clothing, until she could no longer feel her fingers and her teeth chattered. She forced herself to move faster, trying to generate warmth. But as they moved around a ridge and into the open, the wind buffeted them, sending her staggering sideways.

Jake caught and steadied her. "Careful," he said. "It's really icy here."

She leaned into him an extra moment, grateful for his steadiness—and for the way he blocked her from the wind. Ha! Danny thought Jake was attracted to her. Maybe he merely appreciated her usefulness as a windbreak, too.

She set out walking again and Jake stayed close behind her. "What do you remember about Cutler's injuries?" he asked.

So this was what they were going to talk about. So much for having any chance to relax and forget why they were up here. "He was bleeding from the head," she said, forcing herself to recall the image of the man standing at the edge of the ravine. "His clothes were covered in blood. A lot of it. And there was blood running down his face. But even minor head wounds can bleed a great deal, so it's possible this was just minor lacerations. Still, I got the impression he was in pain. And…and frightened." That moment when their eyes met, it had been like looking into the eyes of an injured animal. Or a child.

The look was one she had seen in other victims—sometimes it was the last thing she saw before the light faded and life ebbed away.

She shrugged her shoulders, shaking off the thought. Cutler might have been frightened, but he was upright and moving and far from death. The fact that he had made it to the hut despite his lack of winter clothing spoke to his stamina and fortitude—or, as Gage had said, desperation. "Was he.. was he facing the death penalty?" she asked.

"New Mexico and Colorado don't have the death penalty anymore," Jake said. "But I imagine he was looking at spending the rest of his life behind bars."

She shoved both hands in the pockets of her parka and hunched against the wind. The prospect of permanently losing his freedom might make a person take all kinds of crazy risks.

"He's in bigger trouble now," Jake said. "He killed Deputy Green, and the driver probably died because of Cutler's actions. Don't feel sorry for him."

"I don't," she said. Not when she thought about Deputy Green and the driver. Her head ached from fatigue and cold and altitude, and maybe from trying to make sense of a fragmented picture she was only able to see in bits and pieces. Charlie Cutler was an injured man and she was supposed to help injured people. He was also a multiple murderer who wasn't likely to show her any mercy if they met up again.

She lifted her head and tried to see into the blackness beyond the circle of her headlamp. Was Cutler out there in that cold darkness? Was he watching them, even now? If so, what was he thinking? Would the answer to that question make her even more afraid?

Chapter Five

Hannah had agreed to work the front desk of the inn the next morning, so she reluctantly hauled herself out of bed and made it downstairs in time to handle checkout for two couples who were departing that day. She was finishing up their paperwork when her mom, Brit, emerged from the back room, coffee mug in hand. She slid the coffee toward Hannah. "I thought you could use this."

"Thanks." Hannah wrapped both hands around the mug and drank deeply of the coffee laced with sugar and heavy cream. Her mother wasn't a believer in skim anything.

"Did you find the man you were looking for?" Brit asked.

Hannah shook her head. "No. The sheriff's department is going out to look more this morning."

"I heard a helicopter fly over a few minutes ago and wondered," Brit said. She settled onto a stool behind the counter. A trim woman dressed in leggings and a lace-trimmed tunic, Brit Richards still had the smooth, creamy complexion of a much younger woman. Only the fine lines fanning out from her blue eyes and the streaks of white in her fading red hair betrayed her as slightly north of fifty. "I'm glad you're not going this time. I don't like to think of you anywhere near a murderer."

Hannah set down her coffee and faced her mom. "How did you know the man is a murderer?"

"Ashley stopped by last night after you left to tell us about the Bernalillo County sheriff's deputy who was killed. She said the killer was loose somewhere near Dixon Pass." Ashley Gray was one of her mom's best friends and worked for the city—right next door to the sheriff's department. "She didn't know you were searching with them, or I'm sure she wouldn't have told me," Brit added.

Hannah sighed. News like this wouldn't have remained a secret for long. Any number of people regularly monitored the emergency channels online and passed along the latest news about police and fire calls. "The man they're looking for was injured in the car accident," Hannah said. "Danny and I went along to take care of him if he was found."

"I don't see why they had to take both of you," Brit said.

"Danny was guiding them to the ski hut, and I... I was actually the only person who saw this man," Hannah said. "The sheriff's deputies thought it would be a good idea to have me identify him."

"But they don't need you to identify him today?"

"I guess not." Hannah had a feeling the shots Charlie Cutler had fired on them had persuaded the sheriff's department not to involve Search and Rescue any further. "I'm sure the paramedics on call today are standing by in case they're needed." Part of her wished she was on the schedule today, though she had decidedly mixed feelings about facing Charlie Cutler again.

"Deputy Gwynn seemed very nice," Brit said.

"Yes," Hannah said, bracing herself for what she suspected was coming.

"Good-looking, too. About your age. Is he single?"

"Mom." Hannah tried to put a warning in the single syllable, which Brit ignored.

"I know it's not easy to meet eligible men in a small community," Brit said. "It's always interesting when someone new moves in. I imagine he'll get a lot of interest."

"I'm sure he'll have his pick of people to date," Hannah said.

"You never know, dear. I wasn't interested in getting married at all when I met your father."

"I know, Mom." She knew all about her parents' meet-cute when he collapsed a tower of canned goods in the grocery store where her mother was working a summer job between semesters of college. As they picked up cans together, her dad asked her out. Her mom said no. He came by every day after that, waited in her checkout line to buy a pack of gum and eventually persuaded her to go out with him. Two months later, they were married. It was a crazy, romantic story, and one Hannah thought was very unlikely to happen to her. For one thing, meeting at the scene of an accident involving a violent killer definitely didn't qualify as a meet-cute.

She was saved from having to explain this by the ringing phone. "Alpiner Inn," she answered. "This is Hannah. How may I help you?"

"Hannah, it's Jake. Deputy Gwynn."

"Good morning, Deputy," she said, aware of her mother watching her. "Is the search over already?"

"Not yet. No sign of him at the second hut."

Her stomach tightened. So Charlie Cutler was still at large. Was he even alive? He wouldn't be the first person to freeze to death in the mountains in winter. If he was still alive, what would happen when the searchers cornered him?

"The helicopter is searching the area now," Jake continued. "And some of us are getting ready to head out again. I called because I need to get your statement about yesterday."

"My statement?"

"We need a formal statement of everything you saw at the crash site. For the case file."

"Oh, of course. Do you want to do that now? Over the phone?"

"No. Could you meet me at the sheriff's department this afternoon? Would two o'clock work for you?"

Hannah turned to her mom. "I need to go to the sheriff's department at two to give a statement about what happened yesterday," she said.

"That will be fine," Brit said. "Tell Deputy Gwynn I said hello."

"I can be there," Hannah said.

"Great. If anything changes, I'll let you know."

She hung up the phone and turned to find her mother smiling. "Wear that new blue sweater this afternoon," Brit said. "It's a great color on you."

"Mom. This is serious police business. I'm not trying to impress anyone."

"Well, you don't want to show up in a stained sweatshirt, do you?"

Hannah looked down at the sweatshirt, which advertised a local outdoor guide service. She hadn't noticed the yellowish blotch across her stomach when she had grabbed it this morning. "I'll go change," she said.

"The blue sweater," her mother said.

Hannah stomped up the stairs to her room. The inn had an elevator, but she seldom used it, preferring the workout from the stairs. She unlocked her door and walked to her closet, determined to find anything to wear but the blue sweater, but after discarding half a dozen choices, ended up with the sweater anyway. It was a personal favorite—soft and well fitting, and comforting. Wearing it made her feel good, and she needed all the confidence she could get if she was going to be giving an official statement to law enforcement. Even though she hadn't done anything wrong, it still felt intimidating.

Her mother nodded in approval when Hannah returned to the front desk, then left to talk to their housekeeper, Jade. Hannah spent the rest of the morning answering the phone, steering guests toward good places for lunch and trying not to brood over Charlie Cutler, Jake Gwynn and the aftermath of what had seemed yesterday like a routine call for a traffic accident.

At two o'clock she walked into the lobby of the Rayford County Sheriff's Department. Though she had walked past the building hundreds of times, on her way to one of the shops in downtown Eagle Mountain, she had never been inside. The lobby was small and utilitarian, the walls painted gray and lined with photographs of officers past and present, in and out of uniform. A portrait of the sheriff, Travis Walker, was centered on the right-hand wall, one she recognized from his campaign posters. Tall, dark and handsome pretty much summed up the thirty-something sheriff, who had a good reputation in the community.

"You must be Hannah Richards." The woman who had emerged from a door to Hannah's left was old enough to have a complete head of white hair and a network of fine lines around her mouth and eyes. She wore blue-framed glasses and large blue hoop earrings. "I'll let Deputy Gwynn know you're here."

The woman moved to the desk at the back of the room and Hannah continued to study the pictures. She hadn't located one of Jake—maybe he was too new to the department. "Thanks for coming, Hannah."

She turned to find the man himself, his face slightly windburned and hair ruffled, but looking more alert and rested than she felt. "Come back here and we'll get this over with," Jake said, and held a door open for her.

She followed him down a hallway to a small, gray room outfitted with a single table and three chairs. "I need to record your statement and that will be easier in here," Jake said as he ushered her into the room. "Can I get you anything? Some water?"

"No, I'm fine." She pulled out one of the chairs and sat, while he settled opposite her and pulled forward a file folder. "Did you find any sign of Cutler yet?" she asked.

"No. He's not in any of the obvious places we thought he might seek shelter, but there's a lot of territory to cover out there. A lot of places to hide."

She nodded. "I guess so."

"We'll continue to hunt for him, and we're posting signs at all the trailheads warning people to be on the lookout for him, and not to confront him if they do see him. Maybe someone will spot him and contact us."

"I hope so."

He opened the folder. "Thanks for coming this afternoon. I'm going to start the recording." He hit a remote, then recited his name, her name and the date and time. Then he began laying out some photos in front of her. "Can you tell me if any of these pictures are of the man you saw at the accident scene yesterday?"

She leaned forward and studied the photographs. They were all of very similar men—white, mid to late thirties, with close-cropped hair. The thought flashed through her mind that she might not be able to identify the man she had seen. After all, they had only stared at each other for a few seconds, and he had been bleeding…then she came to the last photograph in the row and recognition jolted her. "That's him," she said, pointing to the photo.

"You're sure?" Jake asked.

She nodded. "The eyes, and that gap in his eyebrow." She indicated the space on the photo. "I hadn't really thought about it before, but as soon as I saw this picture, I knew it was him." In the black-and-white photo, Charlie Cutler faced the camera, unsmiling. He was better looking than she remembered, handsome even, in an un-polished way, clean-shaven and clear-eyed, with broad shoulders and erect posture. "He looks like a soldier, doesn't he?" she asked, recalling what Gage had said about Cutler's military background.

"Not just any soldier," Jake said. "I did a little reading this morning about the army's mountain-warfare school. The school has its origins in the Tenth Mountain Division that trained on the Continental Divide here in Colorado during World War II. The training includes winter survival and maneuvering in really rugged conditions. The people who complete that training are in a pretty elite group."

She shuddered, not wanting to think about the advantages that kind of training would give a killer.

Jake picked up the photo of Cutler and stacked it on top of the others and returned them to the file folder. "Tell me everything you remember about yesterday at the accident scene," he said.

She began with the callout. "The dispatcher said a motorist had reported seeing a boxy white van go off the road near the pullout for the falls," she said. "I was shopping at that end of town, so I drove up there. I must have been the closest, because I arrived first. I got out and looked things over. I could see the van below, and I called down and listened for an answer. If someone was alive, I wanted them to know help was on the way."

"When did you see Cutler?" Jake asked.

"I heard him first. Feet slipping on loose rock—like someone climbing up. Which in itself was pretty incredible. It's very steep there. We had to use ropes to get down. Yet he climbed up that snowy, muddy slope under his own power. And injured."

"So you heard him. Then what?"

"I turned toward the sound. He was standing there, just…looking at me. He had blood on his shirt and running down his face, and his clothes were very muddy. I said something to him—I think I introduced myself and asked his name. I'm sure I said I wanted to help. Then you arrived and I turned toward you—when I looked back, he was gone." She frowned. "You didn't see him?"

Jake shook his head. "I had just gotten out of my car and was focused on you. I couldn't see the edge of the ravine from where I was standing."

She nodded. "That's really everything. I probably looked at him for ten seconds or less."

"And you think he came from the wrecked van?"

"Yes. I'm sure he climbed up from there. The mud all

over him and the blood—I couldn't see any major injury, so I think maybe it was from broken glass." She frowned. "He would have been in the back seat of the van, in leg irons and handcuffs, though maybe he managed to get free of those and kill the deputy... Is that what caused the accident, do you think?"

"We're still trying to put the pieces together. Is there anything else you can tell us about your encounter with Charlie Cutler?"

"As a paramedic, my first assessment was that he was in shock. He looked dazed, and with the cold and all that blood, it would be a natural reaction. But then, he'd made the climb up the slope, and that would take a lot of physical strength. And he looked...frightened." She bit her lip. "You'd think I would be the one to feel threatened by him, but really, he looked harmless. A little lost."

"He probably was frightened," Jake said. "He could have been killed in the wreck, and he'd just murdered a sheriff's deputy. He had to know if he was caught he'd be severely punished. He probably saw me and my uniform and that's why he ran." His eyes met hers, dark with concern. "I know to you he was a hurt, scared victim whom you were there to help. But Charlie Cutler is definitely not harmless. Don't make the mistake of thinking that."

She nodded. His words sent an icy shard of fear through her. "Can you tell me about the murders he was convicted of? Gage said two women and one man?"

"The woman was a bank teller. He attacked her outside her apartment building one night. The man and the woman were a couple he attacked in a park one evening a month later." Jake's jaw tightened, lips compressed and pale.

"Is there something else?" she asked. "Something

you aren't telling me?" She leaned toward him across the table. "I want to know. I'm not going to freak out, I promise."

He exhaled a long breath, then reached over and switched off the recording. "This doesn't go any further than this room," he said.

She nodded. "I promise I won't tell a soul."

"Cutler was convicted of killing the three people I mentioned, but he's a suspect for five other murders, at least. He was being transported to Junction to be tried in one of those cases. All women." He swallowed, Adam's apple bobbing, then met and held her gaze. "The Bernalillo County Sheriff's Department sent over a file, with photographs of his suspected victims. All women in their twenties and thirties, athletic builds, with blue eyes and reddish hair."

She drew a sharp breath. The women he had described... "They all look like me," she whispered.

Chapter Six

"The search for escaped murderer Charles 'Charlie' Cutler continues in the rugged San Juan Mountains outside Eagle Mountain, Colorado. Cutler escaped custody four days ago after killing a Bernalillo County, New Mexico, sheriff's deputy while being transported for a new trial in Junction, Colorado. After stealing survival gear and supplies from a remote cabin, Cutler, who is reported to be suffering unspecified injuries, has vanished in a rugged, mostly roadless area where temperatures have hovered near zero every night. When asked whether he believed Cutler was still alive, Rayford County Sheriff Travis Walker stated authorities are approaching the search as if Cutler is still at large. The sheriff emphasized that anyone who thinks they have seen Cutler should contact local law enforcement and not attempt to approach, as he is known to be armed and is considered very dangerous."

Tony reached up and switched off the radio that sat on a high shelf in the Search and Rescue headquarters, sandwiched between a stack of report binders and a CPR practice dummy dressed in a pink-and-green floral aloha shirt. Most of the other two dozen members of the teams occupied various seating in the converted garage space that served as meeting room and training center, from folding chairs that creaked every time someone shifted their weight to a sagging plaid sofa Danny had found on the side of the road and hauled into the building. He sat at one end of the decrepit piece of furniture now, the other cushions occupied by Sheri and Ted.

The monthly training meetings were mandatory for SAR volunteers and included a regular mixture of bad coffee, griping, gossip and actual education. "Cutler's dead," Danny said as soon as the radio fell silent. "Some hiker will stumble on his body this spring."

"Some people don't turn up for years," Ted said. "Remember that body retrieval we did in Galloway Basin two summers ago? That woman had been missing for eight years."

"I heard Cutler was like, ex–Special Forces or something." The speaker was the newest member of the group, trainee Austen Morrissey, a baby-faced thirty-year-old with thinning brown hair and wire-rimmed glasses. "Someone like that could survive a long time in the wilderness."

"Sure, in the summer, if he could forage food and steal from tourists," Danny said. "Those granola bars he stole from the ski hut aren't going to get him very far."

"There are a lot of summer cabins off those Jeep roads up there," Ted said. "He could break into one of them and help himself and no one would know until the owners come back in June."

"What do you think, Hannah?" Danny asked.

Hannah had been trying to ignore the conversation about Charlie Cutler. She didn't want to think about him at all, though the memory of him staring at her, blood streaming down his face, would pop into her head at the oddest moments—when she was almost asleep, or when she was driving and let her mind wander. "I don't have an opinion," she said. "We don't know anything about Cutler and what he's capable of."

"We know he's capable of murdering four people," Danny said. "Five if you count the van driver."

Hannah looked away. The truth was, she had wondered about Cutler, and though she felt terrible about wishing someone dead, she had to admit she would feel safer if he was permanently gone. Knowing she resembled Cutler's previous victims made her uneasy. She told herself she was being irrational. Cutler had seen her for less than a minute and then he had been focused on eluding capture. Finding her and hurting her would be the last thing on his mind.

But weren't serial killers psychopaths? They didn't operate according to normal rules of human behavior. Still, with everyone in three counties searching for him, it would be almost impossible for him to get anywhere near her, wouldn't it?

"Cut the chatter and let's call this meeting to order." Tony banged his coffee mug on the wooden bench at the front of the room. "Today, we're reviewing ground-search techniques and tactics."

Chairs creaked and papers rustled as everyone settled in to review the types of searches, the makeup of search teams, use of compass points and landmarks, gathering clues and other important details to remember. Before Hannah had joined Search and Rescue, she hadn't realized how science based some of their activities would be. Searchers had to be familiar not only with the topography of the area they were searching, but with how people tended to behave when lost, injured or trying to run away. Search and Rescue members had to be more than fit, willing volunteers. They had to devote hours to training and learning specialized skills and knowledge.

Halfway through a segment on planning a search, the headquarters phone rang at the same time Tony's cell phone vibrated. Immediately, tension radiated through the room. "Hello?" Tony answered the headquarters phone. He listened to the caller, making notes on the whiteboard mounted beside the phone. "We'll have a team right out," he said, and hung up.

"Car accident?" Danny was already on his feet.

"SUV rollover on Dixon Pass," Tony said. He scanned the room. "Hannah, I want you, Chris, Ryan and Ted. I'll coordinate from here in case we need life flight."

Hannah knew Danny wanted to protest. He was the type who wanted to go on every callout. But one look from Tony silenced him. Hannah pulled on her parka and followed the others to the next bay to retrieve the Beast.

The night was dark and clear, the cold cutting against her bare face as Hannah climbed into the back seat next to Ryan. Christine Mercer, a local artist with purple streaks in her short black hair, sat in the passenger seat next to Ted, who had insisted on driving. The oldest member of SAR, he fought hard to maintain the appearance of seniority. He was in terrific condition for a man who was sixty, but no one his age would have the stamina and strength of a twenty-something like Ryan, and Hannah sensed Ted was acutely aware of that.

SAR headquarters had been purposely located on the side of town nearest Dixon Pass and the ice climbing cliffs, two areas that accounted for at least half their emergency calls—maybe more than that in winter. The pass was the gateway to much of the backcountry terrain popular with skiers and climbers, and the road itself turned treacherous in inclement weather. Ten minutes after loading in, the Beast slowed as they approached flashing lights just this side of the top of Dixon Pass. The red-and-blue revolving lights cast kaleidoscope patterns across the black pavement and the snowy cliffs alongside.

"I bet the vehicle slid on ice," Ted said as he pulled the Beast in behind a highway patrol black-and-white. "It looks slick out here."

As Hannah exited the vehicle, she had a disorienting flash of déjà vu. The place she was standing was directly across the road from the spot where she had first seen Charlie Cutler.

"Come on," Chris said. She handed Hannah her gear bag and together they joined the group of law enforcement personnel and civilians by the side of the road. The four men and one woman were standing uphill from a black SUV that lay on its back like an upturned bug, one side resting against the rock cut that had been made when the road was built. The windshield was smashed and various bits of trim dangled from the vehicle, but it was in better shape than Hannah would have expected from a rollover.

"What's the situation?" Chris asked the highway patrolman closest to her.

"Looks like the driver got too close to the side, one or two wheels dropped off the edge of the pavement, he overcorrected and the vehicle rolled, then skidded to a stop against the wall here." The officer gestured.

"He's lucky he didn't roll the other way and the wall stopped him." At the sound of the familiar voice, Hannah looked past the highway patrolman to Deputy Jake Gwynn. He nodded in greeting, then gestured to the man and woman who sat on the ground by his patrol SUV. "We thought there was someone trapped in the vehicle but turns out we were wrong. The driver and passenger were able to get out of the vehicle on their own just before you arrived , but you might check them out."

"Nobody else in the car?" Ted asked.

"No one," the highway patrolman said. "Sorry about the false alarm."

Hannah introduced herself to the couple by the sheriff's department vehicle. Both of them bore traces of white dust from their SUV's airbags. "How are you feeling?" she asked. "Any injuries? Cuts? Bruises? Any swelling? Anything hurt to move?"

"Maybe a few bruises," the man said.

"Mostly we're just shook up," the woman said. She looked across the road, where the pavement dropped off into the canyon. "When I think what could have happened if we'd been on the other side I feel sick."

"Let me check your vitals, make sure everything is okay," Hannah said.

They didn't protest as she looked them over. As they had said, the only consequences of their accident were a few bumps and bruises and a fright that would probably stay with them for a while. "Do you have someone you can call to come get you?" she asked when she was through.

"My brother is on his way from Junction," the man said. He looked at the upside-down SUV. "Do you think the insurance company will total it? I've only had it a few months."

"I'm sure it will work out," Hannah said as she repacked her gear. She wasn't even sure the man had been speaking to her, but it seemed the polite thing to say.

She left the couple and returned to the group by the road. The other three members of the SAR team were ranged around the upside-down SUV, discussing the damage or the accident itself or maybe even what might have happened if the vehicle had been less sturdy or the driver and his passenger less lucky.

Jake was deep in conversation with the highway patrolman. As Hannah approached them, she overheard part of their conversation. "You should definitely get another year or so of local experience under your belt before you apply," the other officer was saying. "By then there should be a few more positions opening up."

"I figure the variety of investigations and situations I'll get with the sheriff's department will look good on my CV," Jake said. He glanced up and saw Hannah and smiled. "Everything okay with the driver and passenger?"

"They're going to be sore tomorrow, and they're still pretty shook up, but they should be okay." She set down the heavy gear bag. "He said his brother is on the way."

"Right. And a wrecker." Jake looked back at the vehicle. "At least we don't have to haul this one out of the valley."

"Were you in on that van that went over the side a few days ago?" the highway patrolman asked. "The one with Charlie Cutler?"

"Hannah was first on the scene," Jake said. "I came along just after her."

The patrolman turned to her. "I'm Phil Landers," he said. "It sounds like that whole situation was pretty hairy."

Hannah shrugged. The very nature of the work they did was "hairy," but she didn't feel like pointing that out. Today was an exception—they had showed up prepared to do everything from pulling someone out of the icy river below after climbing down to them across ice, rock and snow, to using the Jaws of Life to extract victims with multiple traumatic injuries, then establishing a place for the medical transport helicopter to land. Instead, everyone got to go home unharmed. It didn't happen like that very often.

"Here's the wrecker." Officer Landers nodded at the approaching vehicle. "I'd better get him lined out."

Jake moved closer to Hannah. "It's good to see you again," he said. "How are you?"

"I'm okay." She could pretend she hadn't heard his conversation with Landers, and spend the rest of her spare time wondering what it meant. Or she could risk offending him and ask. She didn't like uncertainty, so she opted to ask. "I caught some of what you were saying just now. Are you looking for a new job?"

"I like my job here," he said. "But eventually I'll probably want to move on, to somewhere with more opportunity for growth. A state job could provide that."

"I guess so." Logically, it made sense, though the idea that he could already be thinking of leaving when he had just got here didn't set well with her.

"No news on Cutler," he said—because he thought she wanted to know, or because he wanted to change the subject...or both?

"I heard a report on the radio this evening," she said. "Some of the rest of the crew were saying they think he's dead."

"It's a possibility," Jake agreed. "Not many people would survive for long in the wilderness in the middle of winter."

She met his eyes, and saw her own conviction reflected back at her. "You don't think he's dead, do you?" she asked.

"I don't." He moved closer still, his voice low. She could see the five-o'clock shadow along his jaw, and caught the scent of woodsmoke on his clothes. Did he have dinner at the barbecue place in town? "I've been reading the file Bernalillo County sent over," he said. "One thing I got from it is that Cutler is a planner. Cutler knew he was going to be transported. I don't think he merely seized the opportunity of the crash to get away. I think he caused the crash and had a plan. He knew where he wanted to go and what he wanted to do."

"Was he familiar with this area?" she asked.

"He wasn't from here, but it's possible he visited at one time. And you can learn a lot from internet research."

She wrapped her arms around herself, warding off a sudden chill. "You're not making me feel any better," she said.

"I promise if we hear anything about him, you'll be one of the first to know."

Why? she wanted to ask, but this time she didn't. There was a small bit of comfort in thinking that Cutler might be dead, or at least very far away from here.

Chapter Seven

After he admitted his ambition wasn't to stay with the Rayford County Sheriff's Department forever, Jake didn't miss the chill in Hannah's attitude that had nothing to do with the weather. He wanted to protest that he wasn't doing anything different from what a lot of other people did. Small departments like this were the perfect place for an officer to gain experience and learn on the job, but Rayford County would never have specialized divisions like vice or violent crime, or even its own SWAT team. With Rayford County, Jake could get a taste for investigation and forensics, but if he wanted to focus on those areas, he would need to look further afield. There wasn't anything wrong with that.

He was about to tell her as much when the rest of the Search and Rescue crew decided it was time to leave. Hannah said goodbye and turned away. Maybe he'd find the opportunity to talk to her later. He hoped so. He really liked her and wanted to get to know her better. After all, he planned to stay in Eagle Mountain a couple more years, at least, and after that he might very well land a job with highway patrol or even the Colorado Bureau of Investigations that would keep him in the area.

He was still brooding over this the next morning at the

sheriff's department. Travis stopped by his desk. "How are you with dogs?" the sheriff asked.

"Dogs?" Jake sat up straighter. "Sir?"

"Yeah. Do you get along with them?"

"Yes, sir. I like dogs." There had always been multiple dogs on the ranch when he was growing up, mostly heelers and the occasional Australian shepherd. Their job was to help manage the livestock, but they all became family pets. One heeler, Lacy, had slept at the foot of Jake's bed for years.

"There's a stray who's been hanging around downtown," Travis said. "Nobody claims him. A couple of people have tried to catch him but they haven't had any luck. I need you to round him up and take him to the shelter in Junction."

"Wouldn't that be a job for, well, a dog catcher?" Jake asked.

"Today, that's you." Travis tapped the corner of the desk. "Last report, he was spotted in the alley behind the brewery. The kitchen help have probably been leaving scraps for him."

"Do you have a description?" Jake asked.

"Medium sized, brown, long legs, long ears, some kind of hound."

This was small-town law enforcement in a nutshell, Jake thought as he headed out on foot toward the brewery. One day you're tracking a dangerous killer; the next you're on the hunt for a stray hound.

At least it wasn't a bull that had jumped the fence. At his initial interview with the sheriff, Travis had told him his background in ranching was a mark in his favor. "We do a fair amount of putting back cattle that have gotten out of their pastures," Travis said. "They're valuable property for the ranchers, plus they're a traffic hazard if they wander around loose."

On his way out the door the office manager, Adelaide, waylaid him. "You'll need this," she said, and held out a purple leash.

"Thanks," he said, and tucked the leash in his pocket.

"Good luck," she said. "From what I hear, this pup is pretty skittish."

He walked a couple of blocks, then turned into the alley behind the brewery and slowed his steps, scanning the area for any sign of a brown hound. Snuffling noises led him to the dumpster, a long tail poking out from behind it. Leash in hand, he moved closer. "Come here, pup," he said softly.

The dog looked up, then charged past him. Jake stumbled back and almost fell. "Oh no, you don't!" he shouted, and the chase was on. He raced down the alley after the canine, and emerged onto the sidewalk, almost colliding with a large woman laden with packages.

"I'm sorry, ma'am," Jake said, stopping to retrieve a fallen parcel and return it to her.

"Was that your dog?" the woman asked, eyeing the leash in his hand.

"No, ma'am. Just a stray that I'm trying to catch."

"Well, watch where you're going."

"Yes, ma'am." Jake looked past her, searching for the dog. He caught a flash of brown fur across the street, in the vacant lot between an art gallery and a T-shirt shop, and crossed the street at a fast walk, leash in hand.

For the next hour, Jake pursued the dog over four blocks of downtown Eagle Mountain. Several times he got close enough to touch the tips of the dog's fur, but every time the dog darted away. He had obviously been on his own a while—he had the dirty, hungry look of ne-glect. He was definitely more frightened than fierce, and Jake was more determined than ever to get him to safety.

In the alley behind Mo's Tavern, Jake managed to grab hold of the dog's ruff. "It's okay, boy, I'm not going to hurt you," he murmured, and reached for the leash, now looped in his belt.

The dog lunged forward suddenly, sending Jake sprawling in the dirt of the alley.

"You're never going to catch him that way."

He looked up to see a young woman standing just out-side the door to the tavern, a cigarette in one hand. Jake stood and brushed off his uniform. "I'm open to sugges-tions," he said.

"He's hungry. Try bribing him. Wait a minute." She stubbed out the cigarette in the bucket of sand by the door and disappeared into Mo's. A few seconds later she emerged with a paper to-go bag and handed it to Jake. "Boneless chicken wings. No sauce. It's his favorite."

"If you've been feeding him, why haven't you caught him?"

She smirked. "He's not hurting anyone."

"He looks in pretty rough shape to me," Jake said.

"He's better off running free than locked up in some shelter." She shrugged. "Give him the chicken. At least he'll have a meal."

Bag of chicken in hand, Jake continued to the end of the alley onto the street. "Hello, Deputy!"

Jake looked up to see Thad Richards striding toward him. "Good to see you again," Hannah's father said. "How are you doing?"

"Good." Jake looked past him. "Have you seen a brown dog around here?"

"A dog? What kind of dog?"

"Just…brown. Long ears. Kind of a hound?"

Thad joined Jake in scanning the street. "Can't say that I have. Has he done something wrong?"

"No, he's just a stray. I'm trying to catch him to take him to a shelter in Junction."

"Maybe you should just keep him. Dogs are really good company."

"That's not very practical," Jake said. "I live in an apartment."

"You have Becky Pratt's old place, above 1890 Antiques?"

Jake nodded. By now, he wasn't surprised that Thad knew this. There were very few secrets in a town this small.

"I know Becky," Thad said. "She loves animals. She won't mind you having a dog."

"I work pretty long hours. It wouldn't be fair to an animal to leave him alone so much."

"Take him to work with you. I mean, police dogs do it. Maybe you could train him as a police dog."

Jake suppressed a laugh at the idea of that dog ever being police dog material. "Do you have a dog, Mr. Richards?" he asked. Maybe the hotel owner would like this one.

"We have three. Dachshunds. We love 'em. Hannah's crazy about dogs."

"I'm sure the shelter will find this dog a good home," Jake said. "But first, I have to catch him."

"Try liverwurst."

"Liverwurst?"

"My dogs go crazy for it. Smells to high heaven."

"I got some chicken from Mo's." He held up the grease-spotted paper bag.

Thad nodded. "That might work. But with the liverwurst, he'll be able to smell it from across town."

"Thanks for the tip. I'd better get back to work."

"Sure thing. Feel free to stop in at the Inn anytime. I think Hannah would like that."

This statement drew him up short. "Thanks. I'll do that."

"It's great having Hannah living with us, but I worry sometimes that she should be out on her own, not stuck here in this little town."

"Eagle Mountain is a good place to live," Jake said. "Hannah seems happy here, working as a paramedic and volunteering with Search and Rescue."

"Yes, but is she going to be happy doing that for the rest of her life? Maybe she should go to college, see more of the world." Thad shook his head. "You think about these things when you're a parent—wanting your kids to have opportunities you never had."

Why was Thad telling him all of this? And what was he supposed to say? "I'm sure Hannah will figure it out," he said. "Now I'd better see if I can find that dog."

"I'll tell Hannah you said hello."

Jake wasn't sure how Hannah would feel about that, but he didn't have much time to ponder the situation when the dog darted across the street right in front of him, a tall woman in pursuit. She drew up in front of Jake, panting. "That's the third time this week that dog has stolen food off the patio tables at the café," she said. "You've got to do something about him."

"I'm trying to catch him to take him to the shelter in Junction," Jake said.

The woman frowned. "You need to find his owners."

"I don't think he has an owner," Jake said.

The frown cut deeper lines into her face. "People who would dump a dog deserve to be strung up by their thumbs," she said. She looked in the direction the dog had vanished. "I hope you catch him. I don't like the idea of him going hungry, but he can't steal food from my customers."

"Yes, ma'am. I'm on it."

Several times in the next hour, Jake thought of giving up, but if he went back to the station now he'd have to admit that a dog had outwitted him, and that stung his pride. Instead, he kept up a, well, dogged pursuit of the canine until, in late afternoon, he cornered him by yet another dumpster in yet another alley. But this alley had no outlet at the other end.

Jake stopped a few feet from the dog and squatted on the ground. "Hey there, pooch," he said in a gentle voice. "Are you as tired of running all over town as I am?"

The dog stood facing him, tongue out, panting. He had the typical hound dog's sad, brown eyes. Jake thought he was full grown, but not very old, and the outline of his ribs showed beneath his rough red-brown coat. Jake took out the chicken and unwrapped it. The dog's ears pricked up and he ran a big pink tongue across his lips.

There were three chicken wings. Three chances to earn the dog's trust and get close enough to slip the leash over his head and around his neck. Jack tossed one wing to him. It landed a few inches from his nose and the dog quickly gobbled it up.

"You've had a rough time of it, haven't you?" Jake asked. "You could probably use a friend." He tossed the second wing, and it landed halfway between him and the dog.

The dog hesitated, then took a few steps forward, grabbed up the wing, then retreated.

Jake held out the third wing. It was the largest of the three, gleaming with fat. The scent of it made Jake's mouth water—he could imagine what it must be doing to the dog.

The dog's nose twitched, and he licked his lips again. Then he gathered himself and lunged for the wing.

Jake was ready. He slipped the noose of the leash over the dog's head and pulled it tight. He didn't want to choke the animal, but he needed to be able to control him.

The dog's response surprised him. Instead of lunging and trying to get away, the dog looked up at him with a resigned expression, let out a sigh, and lay at his feet.

Jake tugged at the leash. "Come on," he said. "Come with me."

The dog rolled onto his side and lay there, panting.

Jake stared down at the animal. He tugged on the leash, but the dog's only response was a low moan.

"Come on," Jake pleaded. "I can't drag you."

Another moan from the dog, and a *thwap* of his tail against the packed dirt of the alley.

And that was how Jake ended up carrying forty pounds of hound dog through the streets of Eagle Mountain to the sheriff's department, to the amusement of many passersby, several of whom took out their cell phones to capture the scene. Jake ignored them, just as he tried to ignore the ripe odor of the dog in his arms, a smell that called to mind dirty floors, old shoes and something that had died some time ago.

The sheriff and Adelaide had both gone home for the

day when Jake entered the sheriff's department. Deputy Shane Ellis looked up as Jake staggered in with the canine, then rose in alarm. "Is he hurt?" Shane asked. "Do we need to call the vet?"

"He's not hurt." Jake set the dog on the floor. The animal shook himself, then looked up, wagging his tail.

"What are you going to do with him?" Shane asked.

"I'm going to take him to the shelter in Junction."

Shane checked his watch. "I'm pretty sure they're closed now. You'll have to wait until morning."

"Great." Jake stared down at the dog, who looked back up at him with hopeful eyes. "What am I supposed to do with him until then?"

"There's nobody in the cells," Shane said. "He should be safe in there."

The two of them, followed by the dog, walked downstairs to the basement holding cells. The dog followed them inside and Jake got a bowl of water for him and shut the door.

"He should be happy in there," Shane said.

They left the dog lapping up water, and headed back upstairs. As soon as they were out of sight, the howling began, a mournful, melodious bugling that could probably be heard on the next street over.

The two men exchanged looks. "That's going to draw some complaints," Shane said.

"I've got to stay around and finish up some paperwork," Jake said. "I'm sure he'll quiet down in a little bit."

Shane nodded. "I'm on patrol tonight," he said. "I'll head out."

He left, but the howling continued. For the next half hour, as Jake tried to focus on paperwork, the noise didn't cease or decrease in volume.

Finally, Jake returned to the cells. As soon as the dog spotted him, he stopped howling and walked to the door of the cell, tail wagging.

"People are going to think I'm torturing you," Jake said. He knelt in front of the cell and scratched the dog's ears. The dog sank onto his haunches and moaned, eyes closed.

Jake checked the time. It was after six thirty. He was hungry and needed a shower. He couldn't stay here all night babysitting this dog. But he couldn't leave the dog here to disturb the peace, either. Finally he sighed and stood, and retrieved the leash. "Come on," he told the dog. "I guess you're coming home with me. But just for tonight."

ANOTHER WEEK SLIPPED by with no further sightings of Charlie Cutler. Hannah decided the people who said he had died out there in the wilderness were right. She put the whole episode out of her mind and focused on her work with the paramedics and at the hotel, and her volunteer job with Search and Rescue. All three activities kept her so busy she scarcely had time to sleep. A rash of house fires, home mishaps, heart attacks and traffic accidents kept the ambulance on the road most days, and mishaps among ice climbers and backcountry skiers led to a record number of Search and Rescue callouts for February.

The call to search for a missing skier late in the month found Hannah, Ted, Danny, SAR Lieutenant Carrie Andrews, Austen and Tony in a snowy basin high in the mountains, with a trio of friends who had become separated from a fourth companion during a cross-country trek between the ski huts.

"Mitch Anderson," a man in a yellow ski jacket and black helmet introduced himself. "I'm the one who called."

"Tell us what happened, Mr. Anderson," Tony said.

"Al—Al Grantham—was behind the rest of us, but not too far," Mitch said. "We lost sight of him and stopped at the top of a hill to wait for him. When he didn't show up after ten minutes, Del and I went back to look for him."

"We skied to the last place we'd all been together and tried to follow his tracks from there," a petite woman in a purple ski helmet said. "We thought we were following his tracks, but there are so many, going in all directions."

"We decided we'd better call for help before one of the rest of us got lost, or we got too far off the main trail and triggered an avalanche," Mitch said.

"You were smart to do that," Tony said. "Take us to the last place you saw him."

They skied single file along the ridgetop trail. The day was clear and calm, the single-digit temperatures moderated by the intense sun and lack of wind. A beautiful day for a backcountry outing. Hannah hoped the group's memory of their beautiful day wasn't about to be ruined.

She estimated they had skied perhaps a quarter mile when they stopped. "We were all together here," Mitch said. "We stopped to take a picture. When the rest of us went on, Al said he'd be along in a minute."

"Why was he hanging back?" Tony asked.

"I thought he just, you know, needed to relieve himself or something. We'd been skiing a couple of hours since we left the last hut. But Al is a good, fast skier. I figured he'd catch up soon."

Tony studied the crisscrossing ski tracks across the top of the ridge. No tracks veered into the soft snow on either side. "Could he have turned around?" he asked. "Gone back for something?"

"I can't imagine why he'd do that," Mitch said.

"What is your friend wearing?" Tony asked.

"Orange ski pants, a blue jacket and a black helmet," the woman, Del, said. "He's a big guy, so he should be easy to spot."

"He had a red bandanna, too," Mitch said. "From a Killington resort. He grew up in that area."

Tony nodded. "Hannah, you and Austen go back down the trail toward the second hut," he said. "Radio if you spot anything." He scanned the area. "I haven't had any reports of new avalanches in this area, but let's check our transceivers."

Hannah dutifully pulled out her avalanche transceiver, which had been on since they left the parking lot. Tony ran through the tests to make sure the devices were working in both transmit and search mode. If someone was buried in an avalanche—or even hurt and separated from the group—others could search for the signal and locate them.

"When you get to the hut, stay put and radio in for further instructions," Tony said. "The rest of us are going to check out some of these side paths." He indicated some faint trails that looked too old to have been made by the man they were looking for. But sun and wind could obscure fresh tracks or make old ones look newer, so they had learned to follow every avenue in a search.

Hannah led the way down the trail toward the hut, with Austen following. She hadn't worked with him much, though they had partnered once in a climbing exercise and he had proved himself competent and dependable. He was the newest member of the team and she didn't know him well. He had moved to Eagle Mountain from Denver and seemed eager to involve himself in his new community. "Have you done searches like this before?" he asked.

"A few. More in summer than winter, looking for missing hikers." She had been involved in some avalanche rescues, too, or rather, body searches, since they had never managed to find anyone alive. She shook off the grim memories.

"It's kind of eerie, isn't it?" He looked around them, at the expanse of snow. "It's so big, it makes me feel insignificant. And exposed."

Another shiver went through her. Now that Austen had mentioned it, she did feel exposed—vulnerable. In their bright ski clothes they were very visible against the white snow. Anyone with a pair of binoculars or even good vision would be able to track their progress along the ridge from a long way off.

She had had the same feeling the night she and Danny accompanied Jake and Gage to search for Charlie Cutler—the uneasiness of realizing what a target you presented for a killer with a gun. She tried to shrug off the sensation. "No one cares that we're here," she said.

"You're right." He gave a nervous laugh. "I need to remember that."

They continued along the trail. "What do you think happened?" Austen asked after a moment. "I mean to the guy we're looking for."

"Al." It always helped to think of the person by name. They weren't a vague statistic or a job to do, but a real person who needed help. Remembering that kept you going when you were cold or tired or wishing you were anywhere but out looking for them.

"Yeah. Why didn't Al catch up with his friends?" Austen said.

"Maybe Tony is right and he decided to ski back this way," she said. "Maybe he remembered that he left something at the ski hut."

"He should have let his friends know."

"He probably thought he could get there and back before they missed him. Or before they missed him enough to call for help. Maybe he thought he was closer to the hut than he was. Or he could have gotten disoriented and skied down one of the side trails." It was easy to get lost up here with few landmarks to guide you.

"That wasn't very smart," Austen said.

"Our whole job is necessary because people make not-so-smart decisions all the time," she said. "It's part of being human."

"Some of the people we help aren't doing anything dumb," he said. "They're just in the wrong place at the wrong time. The road ices over and they can't see the ice, or another car forces them to swerve the wrong way, or the ice they're climbing has a flaw they can't see and it gives way."

"It's not a good idea to try to fix blame on anyone," Hannah said. "We're about helping, not judging."

"I guess so," he said, though he didn't sound convinced.

Hannah picked up the pace, partly to reach their destination more quickly, and partly to put some distance between Austen and his questions. She didn't want to talk any more. She'd rather focus on the search, scanning the area around her for any sign of a disturbance.

They were within sight of the second hut when a flash of color in the snow ahead made Hannah wobble in midstride. Not orange or blue like the clothes of the man they were looking for, but red. A splash of red, like blood on the snow.

Or blood on the body of a man, stripped of all his clothing and lying in the snow twenty yards off the trail.

Chapter Eight

"How are you on cross-country skis?" Deputy Dwight Prentice stopped by Jake's desk a little after three o'clock and posed the question.

"I do all right," Jake said. Eastern Colorado had plenty of snow, but no mountains, so he had grown up cross-country skiing. "Why?"

"We just got a call from Search and Rescue," Dwight said. "They were called out to search for a skier who went missing between the first and second huts, above Delaware Basin. They found his body. Looks like murder."

Jake shoved back his chair and stood. "Maybe Charlie Cutler didn't die out there after all."

"Maybe not. Anyway, the easiest way to get up there is to ski the trail. Search and Rescue is waiting for us."

"I'll need to borrow some skis. I didn't bring mine with me." That was an oversight he would have to correct the next time he visited his parents.

A scuffling noise beneath Jake's desk distracted them. A brown dog, cleaner than before and already beginning to fill out, emerged, wagging his tail. "Why do you have a dog under your desk?" Dwight asked.

"He's the stray who was running loose around town." The dog shoved his head beneath Jake's hand and Jake rubbed the velvety ears. "He howls like crazy if I try to leave him alone."

Dwight smirked. "I thought you were supposed to take him to the shelter in Junction."

Jake looked down at the dog, who regarded him with worshipful eyes. "Yeah, well, by the time I caught him the shelter was closed. I took him home for the night and I guess I never quite made it out to the shelter."

Dwight laughed. "You sucker." He leaned over and patted the dog. "What's his name?"

"I'm calling him Gus. It seems to suit him."

"Does the sheriff know he's here?"

"Not exactly." Jake pulled on his jacket.

"He can't come to a crime scene with us," Dwight said. "Especially not up in the high country."

Jake frowned at the dog. If he left Gus at his apartment, his howling would be sure to draw complaints. He couldn't leave him to run loose at the sheriff's department. "I guess I'll have to figure something out."

"You'll need to find some skis, too. I think Mountain Outfitters will rent you some."

"I'll take care of it," Jake said, an idea forming. He might be able to solve the problem of the skis and the dog at the same time. "I'll take care of Gus, too."

"Make it quick," Dwight said. "Can you meet me back here in half an hour?"

"You bet."

Gus took his now-usual position in the back seat of the sheriff's department SUV. He had wanted to ride in the passenger seat, but the image of himself with the dog as his partner had been a little too cutesy for Jake to bear, so he had insisted the dog ride in back, shielded from public view by the heavily tinted back windows.

Jake found a parking spot directly in front of the Alpiner Inn, snapped the leash on Gus's collar and led the dog inside.

"Well, hello there!" Thad Richards greeted them from behind the front counter when they entered. "I see you have a friend there, Deputy."

"This is Gus," Jake said. "I was wondering if you could watch him for a few hours while I'm on a call."

"Sure, we could do that." Thad came out from behind the counter and squatted down to greet the dog.

"I have another favor to ask, too," Jake said. "I need to borrow some cross-country gear—skis and boots, and those insulated coveralls you loaned me before. I promise I'll get my own gear soon."

"No problem." Thad stood. "I'll get them right now."

He disappeared into the back of the hotel and a few moments later, Brit Richards emerged. "Hello, Deputy," she said. "Thad told me we're going to be dog sitting." She smiled at Gus, who wiggled his entire rear end in greeting.

"I hope you don't mind," Jake said. He unclipped the leash and Gus hurtled forward and stood with his front paws on the counter. "Down!" Jake commanded.

"It's all right. He won't hurt anything." Brit rubbed his ears. "Aren't you a pretty boy?" She looked at Jake. "Where did you get him?"

"He was a stray," Jake said, not wanting to go into the whole story. "He doesn't like being alone."

Thad emerged from the back room, loaded down with skis, boots and coveralls. Jake hurried forward to relieve him of the burden. "Thanks so much," he said.

"Is something wrong?" Brit looked worried. "Does

this have anything to do with the call Hannah went on a little earlier?"

"Maybe." Jake balanced the borrowed skis and clothing. "As far as I know, all the Search and Rescue personnel are fine. Sorry I can't stay to talk—I need to get on the road. Thanks for looking after Gus."

He hurried out the door and into his SUV. He'd have to buy the Richardses a gift card for the nicest place in town to thank them for being such a big help.

Twenty minutes later, he and Dwight were strapping on skis. They headed up the trail toward Hut #2, and within thirty minutes he spotted the peaked roof of the hut, and just beyond that, the cluster of people gathered at the side of the trail.

He searched for Hannah and found her, standing to one side, her arms hugged across her chest as she spoke with the SAR commander, Tony. "Someone's covered the body," Dwight said. "They shouldn't have done that."

Sure enough, the body was hidden beneath a silver emergency blanket. Tony looked up and spotted them and joined them as they kicked off their skis. "Before you say anything, I promise we didn't touch the body or disturb it in any way," he said. "But we had to cover it. His friends were freaking out about the state of him."

"What is the state of him?" Dwight asked.

"Naked. And it looks like his throat has been cut. There's a lot of blood."

Dwight nodded. "I can see how that would be upsetting."

Hannah and another man moved in behind Tony. "We found him," Hannah said.

The man with her nodded. "He was just lying out there

in the open, blood everywhere." He swallowed hard. "It was pretty shocking."

"What's your name?" Jake asked.

"Austen. Austen Morrissey."

"We'll get your statement in a minute, Mr. Morrissey," Jake said. He moved over beside Hannah. "You okay?" he asked, keeping his voice low.

She nodded. "It was a shock."

"How long had he been missing when you found him?" Jake asked.

"Close to two hours. His friends waited an hour before they called us out."

He nodded. "Stick around. I'll probably have more questions after we've looked at him."

Dwight was already kneeling beside the covered body when Jake joined him. "The snow around here is really disturbed," Dwight said. "Some of it is probably from the SAR team but those tracks might be the killer's." He indicated a set of ski tracks setting out from the body. "Better radio for backup."

While Jake put in the call, Dwight carefully lifted the emergency blanket from the body. The man beneath it was tall—Jake guessed over six feet—and fit, with sandy hair and beard, a tattoo of snakes and flowers down his left arm, the ink standing out against his pale, pale skin. Blood stained his chest and bloomed on the snow around him from the gash in his neck. "Deputy Green's throat was cut, too," Jake said. "It's how Cutler killed all his victims."

"His murderer took his skis, helmet, gloves, goggles and every stitch of clothing," Dwight said. "That points to Cutler, too. He would have wanted all those things."

"How did he get close enough to cut his throat?" Jake

looked around them. "You can't sneak up on anyone out here."

"Maybe he pretended to need help," Dwight said. "Most people wouldn't ignore someone stranded or hurt up here, so far from other aid." He straightened. "Let's talk to his friends, then to the SAR volunteers."

The victim's three friends huddled together out of sight of the man's body, arms around each other. The woman had been crying, while the two men looked grim. Dwight and Jake introduced themselves, then listened to their story of an outing among friends gone wrong. "I don't know why he would have turned back," the woman, Del, said.

"You say you had lunch at the ski hut," Dwight said. "Could he have left something behind there and gone to retrieve it?"

"I can't imagine what," she said.

"We weren't even there that long," one of the men said. "And if he did go back, why didn't he tell us?"

"Did you see anyone else while you were out here this morning?" Jake asked. "Someone in the distance, or anyone near the hut?"

All three shook their heads. "There's never many people up here during the week," Del said.

Jake nodded. He and Dwight had seen no one else on the way up here.

"Was he the type of person to go out of his way to help someone else?" Jake asked.

"Yes." Del didn't hesitate to answer. "He would stop on the side of the road to change a stranger's tire, and he always gave money to street people." She sniffed. "I can't believe someone would do this to him."

One of the men put his arm around her and looked at

the two deputies. "Do you think this has anything to do with that man who went missing up here a while back? I read he was a convicted murderer."

"We don't know," Dwight said.

"We saw the posters about him at the trailhead," the other man said. "But we didn't pay much attention. Maybe we should have."

And maybe the sheriff's department should have insisted on closing the area to all recreation, though local officials had balked at the idea, Jake thought. And with no sign of Cutler for almost two weeks, closures would have been difficult to enforce. He and Dwight took the contact information of the three and told them they were free to go, then moved over to the SAR team.

Hannah and the rest of her team were gathered to the side of the trail, sipping coffee from thermoses. Dwight and Jake split them up to interview them. The group that had taken the side trail reported they had seen nothing unusual. "I don't think the trail had been used much since the last fresh snow," Carrie, a sturdy thirty-something blonde, said. "We turned around as soon as Hannah radioed that she and Austen had found the body."

"Did you see anyone at all while you were up here, other than the dead man's friends?" Dwight asked.

"No one," Tony said.

No one else had anything useful to add. By the time they had collected everyone's statements, Sergeant Gage Walker and Deputy Ronin Doyle had arrived to help process the scene. The SAR team headed back down the mountain and the sheriff's department personnel set to work. "I want to follow those tracks and see where they lead," Jake said, indicating the ski tracks leading away from Al Grantham's body.

"Good idea," Gage said. "But be careful. If this is Cutler, he's still armed and we know he won't hesitate to kill a cop."

"Right," Jake said. Nothing like setting out across a wide-open expanse of terrain, feeling as if you had a target on your back.

Dwight and Jake set out, skiing parallel on either side of the tracks, alternately scanning the area around them, and watching the ground for any evidence the skier might have dropped. "If this is Cutler, where has he been for the past two weeks?" Dwight asked.

"There must be summer cabins up here he could break into and stay for a while," Jake said. "He was injured in the car wreck when he escaped. Maybe he was healing before he set out again."

"You know some people are going to say we stopped looking for him too soon," Dwight said.

"We threw everything we had into searching for him for three days after he escaped," Jake said. "We didn't have the resources to keep it up." But it was hard to believe they couldn't have done more. A man was dead, and they might have been able to prevent it. The thought galled.

After about fifteen minutes, Jake stopped. "What is it?" Dwight asked.

"He's skiing parallel to the trail," he said. He indicated the ridge above them. "He's far enough away, and far enough down in elevation that someone on the trail would be unlikely to see him unless they were looking."

"Are you sure they couldn't see him?" Dwight looked up toward the trail. "I think I could see someone on the trail."

"You might be able to see the top of their head," Jake

said. "Or more likely, hear their voice. But look how the terrain undulates. The snow has drifted. I don't think someone up there would notice him unless they looked very carefully."

"Where's he going?" Dwight asked. "The trail leads to the first hut."

"Maybe he went there."

But well before they reached the first hut, the tracks turned upward, crossed the ridge and the main trail, and set off on a parallel course on the opposite side of the trail. The terrain was much rougher here, less open. "It would be easier for him to hide here," Jake said, as they picked their way around a trio of snow-covered boulders.

"You can't see the trail at all from here," Dwight said.

"No, but you'd be able to hear anyone talking. Sound carries. Listen." They stopped and the murmur of conversation from somewhere above drifted down. Jake couldn't make out any words, but he could track the movement of people on the trail by the sounds of their voices.

"What's he doing, going back the way he came?" Dwight asked. "Is he tracking the rest of Al's party? Planning to kill them also?"

"I don't know," Jake said. "He killed Al to steal his skis and clothing. I don't know if he'd risk attacking a group of three. Maybe he wanted to see what they would do—if they would go back and find the body."

"Or maybe he wanted to see who else showed up," Dwight said. "Like law enforcement."

"Or Search and Rescue," Jake said. He stopped again, the thought hitting him like a blow to the chest.

"What is it?" Dwight asked. "What's wrong?"

Jake shook his head. "It may be nothing."

"What? What did you think of?"

He met his fellow deputy's gaze. "Hannah is the only member of Search and Rescue who saw Cutler the day he escaped from custody. And he got a good look at her. She looks like the women he killed—and the other women he's suspected of killing."

"You think he was tracking her," Dwight said.

"I hope I'm wrong," Jake said. But the knot in his gut told him this hunch was too big to ignore. If Cutler had fixated on Hannah—if he had remained in the area because of her, even—then he was going to be a bigger problem than they had anticipated.

"CHARLIE CUTLER CAN'T be after me," Hannah protested when Jake told her about the ski tracks and his theory. The rest of the SAR team had already started back toward the parking area, but Jake had asked her to stay to talk with him. "He doesn't even know me. He saw me once, for all of fifteen seconds."

"If I'm right and he was trailing the SAR team, he saw you for longer than that." Jake shoved his hands into his pockets and began to pace, his skis still stuck in the snow beside the trail. "I read his psychological profile in the file Bernalillo County sent over," he said. "He has a pattern of choosing a victim—usually after a chance encounter—and stalking her. One of the women he killed was a barista in a coffee shop he visited once. Another was a passenger on a bus he rode. The profiler said he has a type and feels compelled to follow and kill them."

The idea that a known murderer could be stalking her was terrifying—and surreal. She looked around at the sunlit snowscape. What had been beautiful before now seemed menacing. "Where is he now?" she asked. "Where did the tracks lead?"

"They stopped at the edge of a ravine." He shrugged. "They just…stopped."

"Did he go down in the ravine? Did he fall?"

Jake shook his head. "We don't know. The tracks went right up to the edge, then there wasn't any sign of him. No footprints. No disturbed rocks—nothing."

"He didn't just vanish."

"We've called for a tracking dog and more searchers. Maybe he backtracked and we didn't see it. Or maybe he did something to hide his tracks. We'll figure it out."

She wished she shared his conviction. If Charlie Cutler had managed to survive up here on his own for the past two weeks, what was to keep him from eluding them indefinitely? "What am I supposed to do in the meantime?" she asked. "I can't quit my job and hide in my room."

"Maybe you could take a leave of absence or…"

"No. That isn't possible or practical. We don't even know if this man is a real threat to me."

"I'm not willing to take a chance that he is."

"Then find him."

He looked pained. "We're going to. But in the meantime, you could be in real danger."

She struggled to rein in her frustration. "I appreciate your concern, and I promise I'll be careful. But I can't stop my life—or let down the people who are depending on me—because of a threat that might not even be real."

He pressed his mouth into a thin line, and she was sure he was going to argue with her, but he only shook his head and moved toward his skis. "I'll go with you to your car."

"Thank you." She wasn't foolish enough to suggest

striking out on her own when Charlie Cutler might be nearby.

They set out skiing. He let her take the lead and she soon fell into a familiar rhythm, gliding along the trail, enjoying the exertion and the warm sun on her face. She wasn't going to think about the dead man, or the live one who might or might not be stalking her, or anything but this moment.

That was the theory, anyway. Getting her mind to stick to that plan was another. For now, she was grateful for the man with the gun who skied right behind her. Though why she had faith Jake could do anything against a man who seemed to appear and disappear at will, she couldn't say. Maybe she was merely comforted by the idea that she wasn't entirely alone in this.

Her Subaru sat apart from the half-dozen law enforcement vehicles that now filled the parking lot, including two new arrivals, one of which included a German shepherd with a coat that proclaimed Canine Officer. She noted the vehicle was from neighboring Delta County.

She turned to Jake. "Thank you for seeing me back to my car," she said. "I'll be okay now."

"I'll wait until you're inside the car," he said. "With the door locked."

She refrained from rolling her eyes, and carried her skis to the car. She loaded them into the rack atop the car, aware of him watching, then circled around to the driver's side and started to climb in. Halfway in, she froze.

"What's wrong?" Jake hurried to her side.

She pointed to the windshield. A scrap of red cloth fluttered from beneath the wiper blade. "That wasn't there when I left," she said.

Carefully, Jake lifted the wiper blade and caught the

edge of the cloth with a gloved thumb and forefinger. "It's part of a bandanna," he said. He held it up and she stared at the words Ski Killington in white script across one corner. "Al Grantham was wearing a Killington bandanna," she said, her voice pinched and strained sounding.

Charlie Cutler had taken that bandanna. He had left it here as a message. One that said, *I know you. I'm watching you.*

Chapter Nine

The enormity of finding one man in this vast area struck Jake as a law enforcement team gathered at the trailhead nearest the second hut to conduct a ground search. Not a single structure or even a tree broke the expanse of snow and sky that spread out in every direction. Even with sunglasses the glare of the sun off the snow made him squint, and once they began to move out across the landscape he lost all sense of direction.

They were searching for any clues Charlie Cutler might have left behind, but what those clues might be no one could say. A forensics team had combed the area around Al Grantham's body and both of the closest ski huts, but as far as Jake knew, they had come up with nothing. Gage had bagged the bandanna left on Hannah's car and dusted the car itself for fingerprints, but the windshield and every part of the car Cutler might even have brushed against had been wiped clean. They had questioned the few people who had been in the parking lot, but no one had seen anyone suspicious, or anyone near Hannah's car.

Then again, Cutler wouldn't have looked suspicious. He would have looked like anyone else in the area at that time—a man with skis, wearing a helmet, goggles and bulky ski clothes that would have made him unrecogniz-able to almost anyone, even those who might know him well, which no one here did.

Jake wanted to find Cutler, to see that he was pun-ished for his crimes, to prevent him from harming other people, but most of all to protect Hannah. He had felt her terror when she had spotted the bandanna on her car and realized who must have put it there.

But wanting something very badly wasn't enough. It was going to take more than will to find Cutler in these rugged mountains. Ski tracks crisscrossed the area near-est the parking lot. The tracks grew fewer as they moved farther from the road, but wind picked up the snow and sent it swirling across the ground to settle once more yards away, leaving the surface as smooth and even as if swept by a broom. He moved steadily forward, scanning the ground with little hope of finding anything. Ten feet on either side of him, other law enforcement officers did the same, but even that bit of order disintegrated quickly as deep gorges or icy cliffs forced them to deviate from straight lines.

Occasionally, he heard the throb of helicopter blades from the air search, but the vastness of the landscape swallowed up even that sound before the chopper was out of sight. The crunch of his skis on hard-packed snow and the whistle of the wind against his helmet was the primary soundtrack for the search.

By three o'clock the peaks to the west sent long shad-ows over the landscape. A deeper chill set in, and Jake found he was exhausted, even though he felt he hadn't done anything. His head throbbed dully—probably from not drinking enough water. He forced himself to drain the water reservoir in his pack as he joined the others in the parking lot. "The air search didn't spot anything, either," Gage reported.

"Will they try again tomorrow?" someone behind Jake asked.

"Not unless we have another sighting that helps us narrow our focus," Gage said.

Another sighting or another murder, Jake thought grimly. But what else could they do? There was too much territory to cover. Too many places for a man like Cutler, who had been trained in stealth, to disappear.

"YOUR BLOOD PRESSURE is one-twenty over eighty-three, Gail. Right where it was last time." Hannah slipped the stethoscope from her ears and unfastened the blood pressure cuff.

Gail Hunnicutt, a regular on the hike-and-bike trail that ran past the fire station, stood and pulled on her coat. "Thanks for checking for me, Hannah. I'll go home and write it down on the sheet I keep for my doctor."

"Anytime. Have a good rest of the day." She waved goodbye to the older woman and was surprised to see Danny slip in as Gail exited.

The sight of Danny was jarring. She had expected to see Jake, since he made it a point of stopping by every day to check on her. She couldn't decide if it was endearing or annoying—probably a little of both.

"Hey," Danny said.

"Hey, yourself." She stowed the blood pressure cuff in a drawer and replaced the stethoscope on its hook and faced him. "What are you doing here?" Danny hadn't shown up at the fire station since the two of them had split up.

"It's almost quitting time for you, isn't it?" He leaned

against the wall beside the door, arms crossed over his chest. "I thought I'd see if you wanted to grab a beer."

"Danny." She drew out his name. What was he playing at?

"Just friends." He smiled, and she tried to ignore the tug in her chest, left over from the early days when she had been so besotted with him—before she figured out that the two of them together were never going to work long-term.

"I thought maybe you'd want to relax a little," he said. "You've had kind of a rough week."

Understatement. Charlie Cutler—what he had done, where he might be, where he would strike next—was all anyone wanted to talk about. Most people didn't know about the "message" he had left under the wiper blade of her car, but everyone knew about the murder of Al Grantham, and they all speculated on how Cutler had survived in the snowy wilderness so long. Add in a week of callouts for her regular job and two SAR expeditions— one for a fallen ice climber, another for a person trapped in a car by a snowslide—and she was wrung out. Suddenly sitting in a cozy tavern and having a beer sounded like exactly what she needed. Especially since her only other alternative was going home to the inn and having her mom and dad fret over her.

"Sure," she said. "Are you buying?"

He grinned. "The first round, anyway."

Twenty minutes later, they had walked across the park to Mo's, and settled at a high table across from the bar. "Any more news on Charlie Cutler?" Danny asked as a server set two mugs of draft in front of them.

"No. And talking about him isn't my idea of relaxing."

"Sorry, I just figured you'd be the first to know, since you're so tight with that deputy."

"Do you mean Jake? We aren't tight." They weren't anything. Not really. He had decided she could be Cutler's next victim, so he kept checking on her. And yeah, he'd stopped by the inn a few times with his new dog, but that was mostly to talk fishing or skiing with her dad. He was just a friendly guy who was passing through on his way to some place bigger and better.

"I see you with him all the time," Danny said.

"What, are you spying on me?"

He laughed. "Hard to miss the cop car parked in front of the inn all the time, or over at the fire station."

"There's nothing between me and Deputy Gwynn." She took a sip of beer, then set down her glass and fixed him with a hard look. "But even if there were, it's none of your business."

"Hey, I'm still your friend. I care what happens to you. I'd hate to see you hurt."

"What make you think Jake would hurt me?"

"You told me the reason you and I couldn't be a couple was because you're looking for a long-term commitment and I'm not," he said. "And you're right about me. But Deputy Jake isn't your long-term man, either. He's got short-timer written all over him. He's here to get some experience for his résumé and move on. It's practically built into the job."

"Not everyone who hires on with the sheriff's department leaves," she said. "For every deputy who moved on, there were others who were making a career with the department.

"The people who stay are from here," Danny said. "Or they came here looking for something specific this place has to offer. Jake doesn't fall into either of those categories."

"You're probably right." She shrugged. "And it doesn't matter, because Jake and I aren't involved."

"So you're not dating anyone right now," he said.

"No." She drank more beer, mainly so she wouldn't be tempted to elaborate—to tell him she was "taking a break" or some other excuse. Only two months had passed since they'd agreed to call it quits and she didn't have to explain herself to him.

He leaned toward her across the table and spoke in a quieter voice. "In that case, what do you think about taking our friendship in a different direction?"

"What are you talking about?"

"We'd still be friends," he said. "But friends with benefits. And hey—" He held up a hand to silence her protest. "Before you work yourself up over the idea, think a minute—we were good together. You can't deny that. We had a lot of fun. And I really miss you. Maybe you miss me, too."

She stared at him, torn between telling him off and agreeing to what she knew would be a stupid idea. Because Danny was right—the two of them had been good together. Deciding to break if off with him hadn't been easy. But it had been the right decision. "I guess since you can't have me anymore, now I'm irresistible," she said, trying to inject the words with sarcasm.

"Hey, I never stopped wanting you, babe." He reached for her hand, but she pulled it away and pushed back her chair.

"No, thanks," she said. "I don't think I'd be good at an arrangement like that."

"You never know until you try." He grinned—the

same boyish, goofy grin that had won her over so many times before. But not tonight.

"Thanks for the beer," she said, and left.

The cold night air hit her like a slap, clearing her head a little. She stopped to zip up her parka and pull on gloves, then set off across the park, old snow crunching beneath her boots. She was halfway across the playground area when someone called her name.

She turned to see Jake being pulled toward her by a large brown hound. "Hello, Gus," she said, rubbing the dog's ears. "And hello, Jake."

"Hello." He looked down at the dog. "Gus, sit."

The dog stared up at him, wagging his tail.

Jake reached into his pocket and took out a treat. "Sit," he repeated.

Gus sat with a thump! He snatched the treat as soon as it was within range, then immediately popped back up. "He's a work in progress," Jake said.

"Is he still going to work with you?" she asked.

"Yes. When I'm in the office he hangs out under my desk, and he rides in the back seat of the cruiser. I keep waiting for someone to object, but so far, no one has."

"He's obviously bonded with you." She rubbed the dog's chin and he leaned toward her hand, in danger of falling over.

"What are you doing out here by yourself?" he asked.

"Just walking back to my car from Mo's. And before you say anything, I didn't even have half a beer."

"I wasn't going to say anything." He studied her more closely. "Are you okay? You look a little upset."

"It's nothing." She wasn't about to share her conversation with Danny. She'd like to pretend it had never happened.

"Are you sure? You haven't seen anything suspicious,

or that made you feel unsafe? It doesn't matter if you think it isn't important. You can tell me."

His genuine concern touched her. "Really, it's nothing like that," she said. "Just a stupid argument with someone I know. Nothing important."

"Good." But he didn't relax. "I'll walk you to your car," he said, and fell into step beside her. She noticed he wasn't in uniform, but wore gray knit joggers and tennis shoes, and a worn leather jacket with a black lamb's-wool collar.

"So what have you been up to?" she asked.

He shrugged. "Just the usual. I returned a lost wallet to a tourist and took a report from a store manager about a shoplifter who has since vanished."

"So...no news about Charlie Cutler?"

He didn't answer right away, and she began to feel uneasy. "*Is* there news about Cutler?" she asked.

"I wasn't going to say anything. I didn't want to upset you."

She wrapped her arms around herself. "Too late for that. What is it? Has something happened?"

"A man who owns a cabin in the high country snowmobiled up there to check on things and found someone had broken in. It was Cutler."

"How can you be so sure?"

"There were fingerprints. A perfect match for Cutler."

"That was a lucky break," she said.

"No luck involved," he said. "He went to a lot of trouble to leave very clear prints on a glass where we would see them. He wanted us to know he was there."

"Why would he do that?"

"I'm not qualified to answer that, but I don't like that he's still in the area. Why is he staying around here?"

Unless he's waiting to kill me, she thought, but she couldn't say the words out loud. Speaking them would make the threat too real. "I haven't seen or heard anything at all threatening or unusual," she said. "And I've been hypervigilant."

He nodded. "That's all we can do. We're combing the area up there, searching for him. And we're plastering every trailhead and cabin with posters warning people to stay away, and to report any sign of him to us."

They reached her car and she fished out her keys. "Thanks for letting me know," she said. "And thanks for walking me to my car."

"Where are you headed now?" he asked.

"Home, I guess."

"Want to get something to eat?"

Was he asking her out? "Where?"

He looked down at the dog. "My place? It's easier than leaving him in the car while we go in. I'm not a bad cook."

The idea appealed to her. Eating at his place was private, unlikely to attract the attention of gossips. And it wasn't the inn, where her parents tried to pretend they weren't worried and only magnified her own anxiety. "Thanks," she said. "I'd like that." If nothing else, she could use the evening to find out more about Jake's plans for the future. How long did he see himself staying in the area—and how did his answer make her feel?

JAKE HAD BEEN thinking about asking out Hannah since the day they had met, but she was a hard person for him to read. He hadn't missed her hesitation when he had suggested dinner. Maybe she thought he was rushing things, inviting her to his apartment instead of to a public place.

But she had said yes and was with him now, climbing the stairs to his apartment. "Are your parents expecting you?" he asked as he unlocked the door. "Will they worry?"

"I'll text them." She pulled out her phone. "It's not as if they deliberately keep tabs on my comings and goings, but they would probably worry." She typed for a few seconds, then pocketed the phone.

He pushed open the door and Gus barreled in ahead of them. The dog snatched up a stuffed duck and brought it to Hannah. "Is that your toy?" she cooed. "Do you want me to play?"

While she tussled with the dog, Jake made a quick pass through the living room, gathering coffee cups and random shoes and stashing them in the kitchen and his bedroom. When he returned to the living room, Hannah was standing in front of his bookcase, studying the titles.

"It's mostly law enforcement stuff," he said.

"So I see. I don't think I'll be asking to borrow *Practical Homicide Investigation* anytime soon."

"I read fiction," he said. "But it's mostly ebooks."

"Oh, me too," she said. "I'm always grateful for books on my phone when I'm stuck waiting somewhere." She turned to survey the rest of the room. "Nice place."

Though small, the one-bedroom apartment featured high ceilings, full-length windows and hardwood floors. "There's a plaque downstairs that says the building was constructed in 1910," he said. "I think originally the shop owners lived here."

"You were lucky to get it," she said. "Rentals are scarce around here."

"You mentioned that's one reason you live at the inn."

"I used to have my own place," she said. "I moved back home when my mom was diagnosed with cancer."

He opened his mouth to say he was sorry to hear that, but she cut him off. "She's fine now, but I needed to be close while she was undergoing treatment. Then they lost a couple of long-time employees and I started filling in." She shrugged. "It's just easier this way. We turned one of the guest suites into a little efficiency apartment for me. It's not as nice as this, but the price is right."

"Let's go in the kitchen and see what I can find to eat," he said.

The kitchen was small, but modern, with quartz counters and black stainless appliances. Hannah pulled out one of the black iron bar stools and sat at the small island. "I'm not picky," she said. "But I am hungry."

He opened the refrigerator and surveyed the contents. Eggs, tomatoes, onion— "How about shakshuka?" he asked.

"Will you think I'm a dope if I admit I don't know what that is?" she asked.

"Poached eggs in tomatoes and onions," he said.

"Sounds good," she said.

"It's fast, too," he said, pulling ingredients from the refrigerator. "We can talk while I cook."

"Where did you learn to cook?" she asked.

He switched on the oven and slid in a half loaf of French bread he pulled from the pantry. "My mom. She was big on teaching her kids to be self-sufficient. My two sisters and I were each responsible for dinner one night a week." He pulled several jars of spices from the cabinet.

"Smart woman," Hannah said.

"Both my parents are pretty sharp." He began chopping tomatoes.

"Can I do anything to help?"

"No. This won't take long. Tell me how you came to be a paramedic."

"First, you tell me how you ended up in law enforcement."

"My father never said, but he would have liked it if I stayed on to run the ranch," he said. "But I saw how hard they worked, how much debt they carried and how they were at the mercy of so many things that were out of their control—weather and commodity prices and competition from foreign markets. I wanted something more stable. I went to college to study economics and thought I'd work in a bank."

She tried, and failed, to stifle a bark of laughter. "Sorry," she said. "I'm just having a hard time picturing you as a banker."

"Yeah, well, I figured out pretty quickly that I would be bored silly working in a bank. So I was looking around for something else when I met a law enforcement recruiter at a campus career fair. I attended a citizen's police academy, did some ride-alongs. I was hooked and I ended up enrolling in the state's police academy after I graduated college."

"What was it that hooked you?" she asked.

"The job is never routine. You have to be independent and think on your feet. And it's a real rush, helping people. I like the problem solving. I even like the training." He started dicing the onion and garlic. "I want to learn more, to get better at my job and move up the ranks so that one day, things will be better for my family."

"And you think there's more opportunity with highway patrol," she said.

He moved to the stove and switched on a burner, and

drizzled olive oil in a pan. "I know there is. The starting salary there is more than deputies who have been here three years make. And I can branch out to criminal investigation or a drug task force—all kinds of things."

"I guess that makes sense," she said.

He added the onions and garlic to the pan. "Your turn. Why a paramedic?"

"I was going to be a veterinarian," she said. "Until I found out how many years of schooling that took and how much it cost. I was working in a T-shirt shop downtown when my mom got sick. She had a rough time of it with some of her early treatment and we had the paramedics at the inn several times. I got to know some of them and they let me know about a program the town has to pay for the training if you agree to a three-year contract."

"And you like the work." He added tomatoes to the pan and fragrant steam rose.

"I do. Like you said—it's a rush to help people. And I discovered I'm really calm in a crisis, which helps."

"So how did you end up with Search and Rescue?" he asked.

"At the time, I was the only paramedic who wasn't part of the group," she said. "They guilted me into joining, but I ended up loving it. I stayed even after the rest of them moved on. I liked testing myself physically and mentally. And with all the training, I'm in the best shape of my life."

He grinned. "I hadn't noticed."

She laughed and he joined her. "I know you're not doing it just for the exercise," he said. "It's a big commitment to help people who are mostly strangers."

"It is." She slid off the stool and came to stand beside him. "But now that I'm part of the team, they're like my family. We all depend on each other and we're all working for something bigger than ourselves."

He nodded and took an egg from the carton. "Law enforcement is like that, too."

She watched as he cracked four eggs into the pan, then set the lid on. "Those need to cook for a few minutes. I don't have any wine, but I probably have time to go down the street to the liquor store."

"Water is fine," she said.

He set plates, silverware and glasses in front of the two barstools, then checked the eggs. "Almost done," he said, and switched off the heat.

They made comfortable small talk while they ate. Gus lay on the floor between them, sad brown eyes fixed on them. "I'm really glad you kept him," Hannah said as she rubbed the dog with the toe of her shoe. "It's probably just as well I didn't go to vet school—I would have taken in every homeless pet I came across."

"I didn't realize how much I missed having a dog until Gus came along." He dropped a bite of egg and the dog snatched it up.

She fell silent and when he looked over he realized she wasn't looking at him or the dog anymore, but somewhere in the distance. "What is it?" he asked.

She shook her head. "It's not exactly polite dinner conversation."

He pushed his plate away. "We've eaten everything," he said. "So tell me."

She took a deep breath. "It's Charlie Cutler. Do you really think he's staying in the area because of me?"

"We don't know," he said. "Really, we don't. He may be staying here because he doesn't have anywhere to go.

Or maybe he enjoys toughing it out in the wilderness, getting the better of the small-town cops."

"You said you read his file. You said he picked out his victims ahead of time and stalked them?"

"He observed them long enough to learn their routines," he said. "But he can't do that with you. He can't risk coming into town where you live. Someone would notice him. Eagle Mountain is too small and we've made sure his picture is everywhere."

She nodded. The fire station had one of the sheriff's department posters, with Cutler's photo, on the front door, as did the library. Even her parents had tacked one to the bulletin board in the breakfast area of the inn.

"The thing is," she said, "he can keep tabs on me when I go on calls in the area. By now he knows I'm with Search and Rescue. Maybe he even knows I'm a volunteer. Maybe he killed Al Grantham so Search and Rescue could respond and he'd have a chance to watch me."

He covered her hand with his own—her fingers were ice-cold. "Cutler killed Alan Grantham in order to steal his winter clothing and skis," Jake said. "Having those things greatly increased his chances of survival."

She nodded. "Of course." She didn't move her hand away, and he became more aware of the softness of her skin, of the delicate structure of bones beneath his hand and the herbal scent of her hair cutting through the savory aromas of their dinner. He tried to think of something to say to ease her mind.

"The other women Cutler fixated on didn't know he was after them," he said. "They didn't have a chance to take precautions, to vary their routine or make sure they were always with other people. You have that advantage over them, and I think it's a big one."

She nodded, and turned up her hand to lace her fingers with his. "You're right. And when I am on a call, I've got the whole SAR team watching out for me."

"And you've got me," he said. His gaze shifted to her lips. He wanted to kiss her, but wasn't sure if now was the time.

She looked away, a faint blush warming her cheeks. "Thanks for dinner," she said, slipping her hand from beneath his and standing. "Let me help you with the dishes."

He fed Gus, then she washed while he dried, but the breeziness they had enjoyed when she had first arrived had given way to a different energy, an awareness that buzzed between them as they brushed against each other, then pulled away, or locked eyes, then quickly averted gazes. It was a tantalizing game of keep-away.

The last dish done, Hannah dried her hands and turned to him. "I'd better go," she said. "Thanks again for a lovely evening."

"I should be thanking you," he said. "This beat eating in front of the TV by a mile." He followed her to the coat hooks by the door. "Let me walk you to your car."

The dog whined and pawed at his leg. "Correction. Gus and I will walk you to your car."

The night was clear, a wash of stars glittering against the blackness overhead. The sharp cold burned their cheeks and Hannah shoved her gloved hands deep into the pockets of her parka. "Beautiful night," he said, though he was looking at her when he spoke.

She nodded. "You should see the high country at night.

There's zero light pollution and the number of stars is amazing. I sometimes look at them when I'm on a Search and Rescue call and I'm trying to take my mind off how cold and tired I am."

"Do you have to go on a lot of night calls?"

"More so in the summer," she said. "It can take a while to locate lost hikers, or even to get to a person who's been injured at high elevation. Sometimes we have to bring them down in the dark, or on a few rare occasions, wait for enough light for a helicopter to airlift them out. Looking at the stars and picking out constellations helps to pass the time."

"You really are amazing," he said.

They reached her car and she hit the button on the key fob to release the locks. "Not amazing," she said. "Just too stubborn to give up." He reached up and brushed his cheek with the tips of her fingers. "Thanks again," she said.

"Can I kiss you good night?" he asked.

"Oh yes."

He slid one arm around to pull her closer, and pressed his lips to hers. Soft and pliant, warm and sweet, the sensation spreading through him. She moved closer, shaping her body to his, and he deepened the kiss, the sweep of her tongue across his lips sending a fresh jolt of heat through him. He lost himself in that kiss, and would have gladly stood there with her for hours, but Gus grew impatient and tugged at the leash.

Reluctantly, Jake broke the contact and lifted his head to stare into her eyes, which looked back at him, dark and a little sleepy with desire. She stepped back, smiling, and opened the door of her car. "Good night," she said.

He waited until she drove away before he started walking back across the park. It had been a good night. The first of what he hoped would be many others.

Chapter Ten

Jake was leaving Kate's Café at lunch midweek when he almost collided with highway patrol Officer Phil Landers. "Hey, Jake, how's it going?" Landers said.

"Good, Phil. How are you?" Jake moved away from the door to the restaurant and unfastened Gus's leash from the bench on the sidewalk. The dog greeted him enthusiastically.

"I'm great," Phil said. "Good-looking dog. Is he yours?"

"This is Gus." Jake patted the dog, then straightened. "What have you been up to?"

"A lot. I'm glad I ran into you before I left town. You won't be seeing me around here anymore. I'm transferring to Denver."

"That's a good thing, I hope," Jake said.

"Oh yeah. A promotion, actually. Like I told you, there's lots of opportunity for advancement in state patrol. Have you put in your application yet?"

"I thought I'd wait until I'd been on the job here a little longer."

"I'd do it now, get your name in line. You never know when something is going to open up."

"I'll think about it," Jake said. "Good luck in Denver." Phil went into the restaurant and Jake continued down the sidewalk, back toward the office. Should he put in an application with state patrol? He had planned to stay in Eagle Mountain another year or two, at least, to gain more experience. Would the state even want an officer who was still so green?

It would be better to wait, he decided. Plus, he really liked Eagle Mountain. He was just settling in, getting to know the area and the people.

Getting to know Hannah Richards. She'd been a little standoffish at first, but he felt like they were really getting along now. Dinner with her the other night had been special, and the kiss they had shared after he walked her to her car had held the promise of more. He wanted to stick around and see what developed there.

Lost in thought, he didn't hear the man calling his name at first. Tony Meissner had to step in front of him to get his attention. "Just the person I wanted to see," Tony said when Jake stopped on the sidewalk outside the sheriff's department.

"What can I do for you, Tony?" Jake ordered Gus to sit and the dog obeyed. He was definitely getting better.

"Search and Rescue is conducting a training exercise up in Galloway Basin Sunday," Tony said. "I thought you might like to join us."

"Any particular reason you want me there?" Jake asked. Were they worried about Charlie Cutler?

"I'm hoping you'll like it enough you'll decide to sign on as a volunteer," Tony said. "We're always looking for new people, and having a deputy on the roster could come in handy sometimes."

"It sounds interesting," Jake said.

"It is. And you'll learn skills that could be useful in your regular job, too," Tony said. "You get to spend time out of doors with a bunch of great people, and help the community."

"Sure. I'll come to the training," Jake said. He would get to see Hannah, just one more reason to participate.

"Nine o'clock, at the parking area on the highway," Tony said. "You'll see all the cars. Dress for a day out of doors."

Tony left and Jake pushed open the door to the sheriff's department, Gus at his heels. While Jake turned down the hallway to head to his desk, Gus stopped by Adelaide's desk, where the dog knew the office manager kept a box of biscuits for him. Though she claimed not to approve of the dog, she kept her desk stocked with goodies for him, and had even presented him with a bandanna printed with the sheriff's department logo. "Now he looks like he belongs with the department," she had said as she tied the bandanna around his neck.

Biscuit eaten, Gus joined Jake at his desk, where a note in Adelaide's handwriting instructed him to "see the sheriff." Jake ordered Gus to stay and walked the few feet to Travis's office. Travis looked up when Jake tapped on the door. "Jake, come in."

Jake entered. He wondered if he would ever get over the feeling of being called into the principal's office when he was singled out by his boss like this. "I wanted to let you know you may be hearing from the FBI," Travis said. "They've taken an interest in Charlie Cutler."

"Yes, sir." Jake wasn't surprised the feds would be part of the search for a fugitive wanted in two states.

"I notified the regional office as soon as Cutler escaped in our territory," Travis said. "I was hoping they'd kick in on the search but I didn't hear anything until this morning." His expression was as stoic as ever, but Jake thought he detected a note of disdain in the sheriff's voice. "If an agent calls you, give him whatever information he needs. I've already let them know we haven't had much to go on. We're trying to check all the back-country properties Cutler might be using as shelter, but a lot of them are accessible only by snowmobile this time of year and we don't have the personnel to check them all. I suggested the FBI might send some people to help, but I didn't get the impression they thought that was necessary."

"Does Cutler have any contacts in this area?" Jake asked. "Friends or family who might help him out?"

"Not that I know of," Travis said. "According to his file, his family are all in Utah."

"Not that far away, as the crow flies," Jake said.

"The FBI hinted that they think that's where Cutler was headed when he escaped."

"But he didn't leave," Jake said. "I don't think it's because he couldn't. He's already demonstrated he has the skills to survive, even thrive, under harsh conditions."

"He stayed because he likes the way he's living now," Travis said. "Or he enjoys taunting local law enforcement. Or because he's fixated on his next victim."

"Hannah Richards." The words tasted bitter.

"Has Hannah reported anything unusual since that bandanna was left on her car?" Travis asked. "Do you think she would tell us if she had?"

"I think she would tell us. Cutler really frightened her. But she hasn't said anything. Maybe he's focused on someone or something else now."

"I don't like playing guessing games with him," Travis said. "We're not going to let our guard down. If you talk to the FBI, make sure they know that, too."

"Yes, sir." Jake returned to his desk, mind churning. He had read through Cutler's file again, searching for any clue about what the murderer might be up to. He was beginning to think that in order to catch criminals, he needed to learn to think like a criminal—an unsettling realization.

SUNDAY MORNING, the SAR team assembled in the parking area near Galloway Basin, a popular backcountry skiing area, for field training. A storm had moved in during the night and it was still snowing when they arrived, with occasional gusts of wind sending the snow swirling around them or blowing hard pellets of ice straight at them. "Did you order this weather just for us?" Ted asked Tony as they gathered in front of their parked vehicles.

"It's perfect weather for our training today," Tony said. "The topic is winter wilderness first aid. We're going to be practicing assessment and treatment, with an emphasis on some problems particular to winter, such as hypothermia and frostbite, as well as practice some techniques for transport over snow and ice. Ah, and we have a new volunteer with us today."

The others turned to see Jake striding toward them. "Hello." He nodded to the group in general, and smiled when his gaze locked with Hannah's.

"Deputy Gwynn asked to join our training today, as he thought it might be useful in his work as a deputy," Tony said.

"Please, call me Jake."

"All right, Jake," Tony said. "I assume you're certified in basic first aid and CPR."

"Yes, sir," Jake said.

"Then you can start us out with that section of the training. Austen, get our Resusci Anne out here."

Austen hauled the CPR dummy dressed in the bright Hawaiian shirt out of the back of Tony's SUV and arranged her on the packed snow in front of the parking area. "We'll start with solo CPR," Tony said.

Jake knelt in front of the dummy and went through the protocol of checking for a pulse, opening the airway and beginning chest compressions. Above him, Tony talked about the procedure. "Jake is doing the standard of thirty chest compressions and two rescue breaths. Ideally, he would continue to do this until help arrived. In the real world, we know that help could take an hour or more to get to him." He consulted the stopwatch in his hand. "You're at one minute, Jake."

Jake nodded and continued. He was breathing hard now, but kept going.

"If we're on a call as a team, we don't have to depend on one person to administer CPR," Tony said. "Someone starts, and someone else takes over when the first rescuer begins to fatigue. You'd probably have a pair trading off performing chest compressions and rescue breathing." He studied the stopwatch and after a long interval—during which the sound of Jake's efforts were loud in the snowy silence—Tony called, "Okay, you can stop now, Jake."

Jake sat back, panting. "What did you notice about this exercise?" Tony asked.

"I'm pretty winded," Jake said.

"We're at eleven thousand feet here," Tony said. "Less oxygen and even for someone in good physical condition, CPR is strenuous. Not only are you winded, but what you probably didn't notice was that your chest compressions were not going as deep as they need to in order to be most effective. A 2014 study in the *American Journal of Emergency Medicine* reported that the quality of chest compressions began to decline after only thirty seconds at altitude, and continued to decline, even if the rescuers did not report feeling fatigued. So what's the takeaway?"

"If you've got more than one person able to perform CPR, switch off more often," Danny said.

"Yes," Tony said. "Carrie, you and Danny get down here and switch off every other set of compressions."

As Danny and Carrie took his place, Jake moved over beside Hannah. She hadn't seen him since their dinner a week ago—and their kiss by her car. "You didn't tell me you were thinking of joining SAR," she whispered as Carrie and Danny demonstrated the awkward quick transition.

"All right, Austen, you come in here and let's work with three people in a relay setup," Tony said.

"I ran into Tony in town earlier in the week and he suggested I might want to participate in some of the training," Jake said. "He'd like to have a law enforcement person as part of the regular team."

"I can see how that would be useful sometimes," she said.

The CPR demonstration ended and they moved on to risk assessment for both patients and rescuers, diagnosing and treating frostbite and hypothermia. "Let's talk about warming techniques," Tony said. "Hannah, come be the victim."

Hannah joined Tony at the front of the group. He instructed her to lie down, then discussed the methods of assessing hypothermia in the field. All of this was information they had reviewed in the classroom previously, but standing in the mountains with snow swirling around them made the challenges of the assessment more real.

They discussed handling and treating various levels of hypothermia, with and without other injuries or conditions. All Hannah had to do was lie still while Tony, assisted at various times by Ted or Ryan, demonstrated various procedures.

"All right," Tony said, when the discussion of hypothermia was concluded. "Let's move out a little and we're going to practice patient transport in both stable and unstable snow conditions."

Hannah rejoined Jake. "It's a lot to remember," he said.

"And we get tested on this stuff, so get ready to study," she said.

The team members strapped on snowshoes and followed Tony about a half mile from the group, each carrying some piece of equipment, from ropes to a plastic litter, and various first aid equipment. They walked in single file, packing down a trail that could be used when coming back out with an injured person or persons.

They reached the area Tony had selected for the exercise and spread out. "What are those buildings up there?" Jake pointed up the slope to a cluster of ruins.

"That's the Jack of Hearts Mine," Danny said. "Or what's left of it."

For the next hour Tony laid out various possible rescue scenarios and they discussed the best approaches, then practiced those approaches, taking turns being the victims and the rescuers. It took real physical effort and strength to move the weight of an injured person, plus any supplies used in treating them, over rough terrain in wind and snow, plummeting temperatures and thin air.

By the time Tony signaled the break for lunch, everyone was winded and chilled. "Let's head up to the mine and get out of this wind," Danny said.

"I'd like to see it," Jake said. He turned to Hannah. "Do you want to come?"

She had been looking forward to sitting in her car with the heater running, but shrugged. "Sure. Why not?"

"We'll have to approach from the east to avoid that cornice on the west side," Danny said. "With all this snow dumping, it's liable to be unstable." Hannah and Jake followed him along a ridge that led away from the mine, then back through a wooded area to what he told them was an old Jeep road. The long hike in snowshoes warmed Hannah, so by the time they reached the mine site, she was feeling more enthusiastic about exploring the place.

The mine site consisted of a couple of small cabins and one larger building. The cabins were little more than piles of logs and tin, but the larger building, though gutted inside, still had four intact outer walls and a solid, though rusting, roof. Danny led the way to the door, kicking aside the snow until they could push open the heavy door and tramp inside.

All of the windows in the building were broken or missing, and at some point the openings had been boarded, but someone had ripped the plywood from one of the larger openings, letting in enough light for the three of them to see most of the interior. Large pieces of rusting metal—what must have been an old woodstove—lay scattered in the back corner of the building.

Danny kicked off his snowshoes and walked over to one of these. He nudged at a pile of charred wood and ash with the toe of his boot. "Someone's had a fire here," he said. "And not that long ago, from the looks of it."

Hannah could smell the smoke now. "I didn't notice any woodsmoke smell on the way here," she said.

"The wind was blowing it away from us," Danny said.

Jake moved over beside him, and crouched down to hold his hand over the remains of the campfire. "The coals are still warm," he said.

"That trash isn't antique, either." Danny pointed to an empty can that had once held chili, and a flattened cracker box.

A shiver raced up Hannah's spine. "Do you think it was Charlie Cutler?" she asked. Who else would be camping out here in February?

"Maybe." Jake straightened and began examining the rest of the cabin. Hannah looked up at the second floor of the building. So much of the flooring was missing that she could see all the way to the underside of the metal roof. But was there enough flooring left for Cutler to be hiding up there, looking down on them?

"If he was here, I think he's gone now." Jake stood in the opening of what would have been the back door. The door itself hung from one rusting hinge at an acute angle. Jake pointed out the opening and Hannah moved in behind him and looked at the ski tracks headed away from the cabin.

"Those couldn't have been made more than a few minutes ago," Danny said from behind her. "It's snowing hard enough, they would have been covered otherwise."

"He was just here," Hannah whispered.

"You don't know it was Cutler," Danny said. "The parking lot is full of cars. Maybe someone else was up here, having lunch and warming up."

"How many people come up here by themselves?" she asked. "If they do, they're not being very smart."

Danny shrugged. "That doesn't mean those tracks are Cutler's."

Jake had turned away from the door and was investigating the rest of the cabin. He paused at the front door. "It was Cutler," he said. "He left us a message."

Hannah and Danny hurried to join him. The door, hewn from fir logs and darkened with age, was crisscrossed with graffiti of all kinds, but at eye level a new message had been gouged deep into the wood, the letters bright against the dark boards: CC <3 HR.

CHARLIE CUTLER LOVES *HANNAH RICHARDS*.

"You don't know that's what those initials mean," Danny said when Jake voiced his suspicions. "They could stand for Chris Carson and Heidi Rogers."

"Who are Chris Carson and Heidi Rogers?" Hannah asked. Though pale, she remained calm.

"I don't know," Danny said. "I made the names up. I'm just saying that those initials could be anybody."

"They could," Jake agreed. "But I don't think they are."

"How would he even know Hannah's name?" Danny asked.

"I think I introduced myself, when I saw him right after the accident," she said.

Jake returned to the back door and stared out at the ski tracks—or where the ski tracks had been. The fast-falling snow had already mostly covered them.

"You can't go after him." Hannah spoke from just behind him. He had been so engrossed in staring in the direction the tracks had disappeared that he hadn't heard her approach.

He glanced back at her. "He could be very close," he said.

"And he has skis and at least one gun—maybe more. If he really has been watching me, then he knows who you are, too. He knows you're one of the deputies who's been hunting him. He's already killed one cop. Why would he even think twice about killing you?"

He nodded. "I won't try to go after him." Not alone, for all the reasons she had named, and for another— he wouldn't leave her alone, knowing Cutler could be nearby.

"We need to get back to the others," Danny said. "Tony is going to give us grief for being gone so long."

"I'll need to drive to where I can call this in," Jake said. His phone wasn't getting a signal here.

"We haven't eaten lunch yet," Hannah said. "Not that any of this has improved my appetite, but we've burned a lot of energy this morning and it's not smart to be out in the cold and hungry if you can help it."

"So we eat and move at the same time," Danny said. He looked around. "I'm man enough to admit I'm a little spooked and I'd just as soon get out of here."

"Yeah, me too," Hannah said.

"Then let's go," Danny said.

They donned their snowshoes again and set out. Hannah dug in her pack and pulled out her lunch. "Peanut butter?" Jake asked, catching the scent as she bit into the sandwich.

"Hey, it keeps well, it doesn't matter if it gets crushed or cold or hot, and I happen to like it." She took a bite. "What are you eating?"

"Summer sausage, cheese sticks, nuts and an apple."

"All good trail food," she said. "You get an A on the food portion of wilderness training."

"Extra credit for dessert," Danny said. He pulled a large Snickers bar from the pocket of his jacket. "Chocolate, nuts and sugar. Perfect energy food."

"I see your candy and raise you cookies." Jake brandished a large oatmeal cookie.

Both men looked to Hannah. "I could go with either," she said. She plunged a hand into her pocket and drew out a bright yellow package. "I'm a peanut M&M's woman, myself."

"Not your mother's brownies?" Danny asked, sounding disappointed.

"Not today."

Danny clapped Jake on the shoulder. "You haven't lived until you've tasted one of Brit's brownies," he said. "She bakes them for all the SAR fundraisers and they always sell out."

The sudden camaraderie surprised Jake. He had gotten the impression before that Danny resented him—whether it was because the other man didn't like law enforcement or perhaps was jealous of Jake's ill-concealed interest in Hannah, he hadn't been able to tell. But maybe it was just a veteran's natural resentment of a newcomer to a tight-knit group like Search and Rescue. Maybe at the training today Jake had managed to earn a little respect and acceptance.

They moved out of the wooded portion of the hike and began to make their way down the hill toward the parking area. The snow had let up somewhat and the sun even showed signs of peeking through. "It figures the weather would improve when we only have a couple more hours of training," Danny said.

"Be careful what you wish for," Hannah said. "If the weather turns too good, people will want to get out in the fresh snow and the chances of someone making a mistake and triggering a slide go up."

"If they do, at least we'll be close," Danny said. "Unless, of course, they're on the other side of the county."

"You know they will be," she said, and laughed.

The sound released a tension in Jake he hadn't even recognized he had been holding in. The sight of those initials carved on the cabin door had solidified his theory that Cutler had fixated on Hannah. He had worried that truth would terrify her. But maybe it only confirmed something she had learned to live with. It didn't mean she wasn't afraid, but she wasn't letting that reality defeat her.

Then again, he should have realized a woman who regularly risked her life to save others wouldn't frighten easily. "What are we going to cover this afternoon?" he asked. Depending on what the sheriff decided about pursuing Cutler, he might have time to take in at least part of the afternoon training before another law enforcement search team convened at the mine.

Danny turned to answer him, then his eyes widened and he swore—loudly. Jake whipped around to see what had caught his attention and added his own curse. With a sound like whitewater rapids, snow cascaded down the slope to the west of the mine site. Snow rose in clouds and re-formed into waves, ripping down the mountain, tearing up trees by the roots and tossing them up like twigs.

"Carrie!" Hannah's scream rose over the sound of the avalanche, and Jake's gaze shifted to take in two people in the path of the snowslide, both in the bright yellow parkas that were part of the search and rescue group's uniform, one short and one tall. As he watched in horror, they disappeared in a wave of snow.

Chapter Eleven

Hannah took off running, snowshoes slapping awkwardly, pack bouncing on her back. Danny caught up with her, then passed her, and they joined the others in running toward the slide path. Tony was barking orders, directing them where to search while he and Ted set their transceivers to receive signals from Carrie's and Ryan's units.

"Over here!" Austen shouted, and they converged, quickly, but carefully, on a section of the slide. Already the snow had set like concrete, and they attacked the snow with shovels, hacking at it with all the force they could muster. Hannah moved back to let the others dig, and did a mental inventory of the medical supplies in her SUV and what she knew Danny and Tony carried in their vehicles. They had plenty of stretchers and splints, supplemental oxygen, bandages...

"I'm okay! I'm okay! Find Ryan!" Carrie shouted as Austen and Ted hauled her from the snow. She protested as they moved in to examine her. "I'm fine. I've taken worse falls on my mountain bike. Just find Ryan."

"We've got Ryan!" Danny called.

Ryan was less ebullient than Carrie, and emerged cradling his left arm. Hannah moved in and she and Danny examined him. "If it's broken, I don't think it's a bad break," Hannah said. "But you'll need an X-ray to be sure."

"I'm betting it's just a bad sprain," Danny said.

"That better be all it is," Ryan said. "I'm supposed to compete in ice climbing in two weeks."

"Two weeks might be a little soon," Hannah said.

His answer was a growl of frustration. She and Danny walked with him to rejoin the others. Carrie had removed her knit cap and was brushing snow from her hair with her fingers. "Good thing we were at the very bottom of the slide when it let loose," she said, looking back up the slope. "I thought we were low enough we were safe, but I guess I was wrong."

"I thought I saw someone up there," Ted said. "I caught a flash of blue just before everything came down. I was about to yell to the guy that he was stupid to be up there."

"He wouldn't have heard you," Carrie said. "Not all the way up there."

"I'd like to find whoever it was and shake some sense into him." Ryan rubbed at his arm. "I think you're right," he said to Danny. "I don't think my arm is broken."

"Whoever was up there could have been caught in the slide," Tony said.

"I don't think so," Hannah said. "I saw everything from the first and there was no one else caught."

"I agree," Danny said. "If someone set this off, they were above the slide itself—out of danger, but a danger to others."

"The ski parka Charlie Cutler stole from Al Grantham was blue," Jake said.

The others turned to stare at him. He had stayed back while the others searched, letting them do the work they were trained for. But now he rejoined them. "You think this was Cutler?" Tony asked.

"When Hannah and Danny and I went up to the mine at lunch, we found signs that Cutler had been there," Jake said. "Very recently."

"He had just left when we got there," Danny said. "We could see his ski tracks out the back door, and you know how hard it was snowing then. He must have left just as we were approaching. He'd had a fire in there and it was still warm." He glanced at Jake. "If it was Cutler."

"Do you think he set off that slide deliberately?" Tony asked.

"Maybe," Jake said.

"But why?" Carrie asked. Then she shook her head. "What am I saying? He's killed several people. Maybe he just likes putting others in danger."

"Maybe," Jake said, but something in his voice made Hannah look at him more closely. He looked...guarded. As if he was trying to hide something—from all of them, or just from her?

"We all need to leave the area," Jake said. "I've got to drive to where I can call this in, and we'll probably pick up the search for Cutler here." He turned to Tony. "I'm sorry to disrupt your training."

"I think we've had enough for today." He turned to the others. "You heard what the man said. Let's pack it up and go home."

"Danny, will you go with Hannah and see that she gets safely home?" Jake asked. "All the way home?"

"You bet," Danny said.

Hannah wanted to protest but she saw the sense in what Jake was asking. If Cutler really was targeting her—

and it looked more and more as if he was—then she shouldn't be alone in any place where he might get to her.

She helped the others to gather equipment and load it in Tony's SUV. Danny, who had ridden to the training with Ryan, walked with Hannah to her Subaru. She hit the key fob to unlock the doors, then froze at the sight of something yellow caught beneath the rear wiper blade.

"What's that M&M's packet doing underneath your wiper blade?" Danny asked.

He reached for the packet, but she put out a hand to stop him. "Don't touch it," she said. "Not until Jake has seen it."

Danny stared at her. "Are you okay?"

She shook her head. "I think…" She swallowed, trying to manufacture enough saliva in her suddenly bone-dry mouth to speak. "I think Cutler left that," she said. "It's why he set off the avalanche, so he'd have time to leave this for me."

Was it a taunt? A threat? Or Cutler's idea of a love note? She clutched her stomach, willing herself not to be sick right here in the parking lot. She was ready for this to be over. Now.

JAKE FELT SICK to his stomach as he stared at the candy wrapper stuck beneath Hannah's wiper blade, a warning flag that Cutler had been this close. "How do you think he got hold of it?" he asked Hannah. He tried to keep his voice calm, not wanting to add to her fears, though he could see she was pale and shaky.

"I must have dropped it when the avalanche happened," she said. "The last thing I was thinking about then was litter."

He nodded and looked at the others who had gathered

around. "We all need to leave the area right away." He looked past them, to the few skiers who had gathered, probably drawn by the outcry. "I'm with the sheriff's department," he said, raising his voice. "I'm closing this area immediately. You all need to leave at once."

A few people started to protest, but Tony turned and addressed them. "You heard the man! Everyone needs to get out of here. It's not safe."

"Thanks," Jake said.

"I'll stay and help you make sure everyone clears out," Tony said.

"Carrie, will you and Danny stay with Hannah?" Jake asked. "Make sure she gets back to the Alpiner Inn. Don't leave until you're sure she's inside with her parents."

"We'll take care of her." Carrie put her arm around Hannah's shoulders.

"I'm sorry, but you'll need to leave your car here for now," Jake said to Hannah. "I'll make sure you get it back as soon as possible."

She nodded, her eyes glazed. Jake moved in closer and took her gloved hands in his. "You're safe," he said. "And I'm going to make sure it stays that way."

Her eyes met his, and the fear in them sent anger burning through him. He hated Cutler for making her feel this way—for transforming the strong, lively woman of this morning into this trembling, fearful one.

Gradually the area emptied out. Hannah left with Carrie and Danny. Tony stayed with Jake until the last of the skiers had driven away and the only vehicles left in the lot were Hannah's Subaru, Tony's SUV and Jake's personal Jeep. The two of them set up barricades to close off the lot. "What's this guy Cutler playing at?" Tony asked.

"I don't know," Jake said.

"I heard he'd killed a bunch of women. Is he after Hannah?"

"He could be," Jake said. "That's the second time he's left something on her car. Or at least, we think he's the one who left the items." He didn't mention the graffiti in the cabin. No one else needed to know about that.

"We'll all keep an eye on her," Tony said. "She's special. We don't want anything to happen to her."

Jake nodded. Hannah was special. Maybe that was what drew Cutler to her. He saw that quality in her and for some reason wanted to extinguish it.

He left the parking area right behind Tony, and hit the siren coming off the pass, racing toward the sheriff's department. He called the sheriff on the way in and gave him a summary of what had happened. "I'll call out the search teams," Travis said. "Maybe we'll get lucky and be able to track him in the fresh snow."

"Can we get eyes in the air?" Jake asked. A helicopter might be able to spot something searchers couldn't.

"I'll try," Travis said. "But we only have a couple of hours of daylight left. I doubt we have time to mobilize a chopper."

Travis didn't mention his budget, but Jake knew that was a consideration, too. Air support cost hundreds, if not thousands, of dollars an hour, and the department had already spent a small fortune on the hunt for Charlie Cutler.

An hour later, he was back on the mountain, in a line of officers spreading out in all directions from the parking lot and the Jack of Hearts Mine. There were plenty of ski tracks in the area, but they had no way of knowing which ones belonged to Cutler. They also had a high avalanche danger to contend with.

A forensics team searched the mine buildings and collected a few items, and examined the exterior of Hannah's car. "There's really nothing there," Gage reported when they gathered at the sheriff's department much later that night. By then the search had been called because of darkness and another snowstorm blowing in.

They reviewed everything that had happened that day, and everything they knew, but it all added up to a big nothing. Cutler had vanished into the wilderness again. They knew he was still in the area, and he was apparently focused on Hannah. "The next move is up to him," Travis said. "As hard as it is, all we can do is wait."

Jake was exhausted by the time he left the office, but too keyed up to sleep. It was after eleven. Too late to bother Hannah and her parents, but he drove to the Alpiner Inn anyway. The front door was locked and a sign said to ring the bell if you needed assistance. He hesitated, and peered in the window, trying to see if anyone was in the lobby.

Thad Richards opened the door. He looked ten years older, dark circles beneath his eyes, his tall frame hunched. "Jake! Is everything all right? Has Cutler—"

"We haven't found him," Jake said. "I just wanted to check on Hannah. How is she doing?"

"Her mother persuaded her to take a sleeping pill and go to bed. Then Brit did the same. Both of them were worn-out."

"You look beat yourself," Jake said.

"I am, but someone had to stay up. Come in. I just made some hot chocolate. There's plenty for two."

Jake waited while Thad locked the door behind them, then followed him into a little kitchen off the lobby. "We use this for the breakfasts we serve guests," Thad explained. He opened a cabinet and pulled out a box of hot chocolate packets, then took a couple of mugs from hooks on the wall. "Have you been up on the mountain all day?"

"We searched until it wasn't safe to do so anymore," Jake said. "I think part of the problem is there are so many of us hunting for him, Cutler can see and hear us from a long way off, and he has plenty of time to get away."

"Hannah told me he set off an avalanche while the SAR team was up there." He emptied the chocolate packet into the mugs, then added water from an electric kettle. "You're lucky he didn't do the same to the searchers."

"I think he was smart enough not to try to play cat and mouse with us this evening." He accepted the mug of chocolate and took a sip. The hot, sweet drink hit him in a soothing wave and he sighed.

"I appreciate all you're doing to help Hannah," Thad said.

"I'm not doing anything," Jake said. "Not enough, anyway."

"She's been through an awful lot these last few years," Thad said. "Did she tell you she moved back home to take care of her mother when Brit had cancer?"

"She mentioned it, yes."

"Then I had my accident. The worst part of the whole thing was seeing how torn up Hannah was about it."

"She didn't say anything about you being in an accident," Jake said.

"She doesn't like to talk about it." Thad set aside his empty mug. "I fell climbing ice in Caspar Canyon three years ago. Hannah had just signed on with Search and Rescue and was on the call. She didn't know it was me until she saw me lying there on the ground. It really shook her up."

"You look like you're doing okay now."

"I can predict the weather with my joints now." He rubbed at one knee. "I healed up okay, but it was a close call. I'm sure Search and Rescue saved my life. When I saw how upset Brit and Hannah were, I promised them I'd stop competing."

"Was it hard to give it up?" Jake asked.

"Not as tough as I thought it would be. I think I was at a place in my life where I had done a lot of exciting stuff, climbed all over the world, and had a display case full of medals. It's enough for me now to stay home and climb every once in a while just for fun. And my girls are a lot happier with my decision. That means a lot. It takes a load off my mind knowing you're watching out for Hannah. I feel like she's safe with you around."

Jake wished he could be so sure.

"This Cutler guy isn't going to last out there in the mountains much longer with everyone looking for him," Thad said. "I don't care how much training he has—he's going to run out of places to break into and things to steal."

Jake didn't share Thad's confidence. Cutler had already survived on his own for a month. And it didn't matter how many more days or weeks Cutler could survive in the wilderness. He only had to make it long enough to get what he wanted. And what he wanted, apparently, was Hannah.

WORD ABOUT THE candy wrapper left on Hannah's car and its significance had spread, until she began to feel like some rare species of wild animal, everyone around watching to see what she would do next. Her mother had suggested she might like to go visit her grandparents in Oklahoma for a few weeks, her boss had offered her a leave of absence and even Tony had offered to temporarily take her off the SAR roster "until things calm down."

"What do they think I'm going to do?" she complained to Danny as the two of them sorted through the search and rescue team's medical supplies, refilling depleted items and tossing out anything that had expired. "Sit in my room with the door locked until Cutler is captured?"

"No one wants anything to happen to you." He squinted at the expiration date on a package of alcohol wipes and tossed them to one side.

"I do appreciate everyone's concern," she said. "And it's reassuring, knowing so many people are watching out for me. But it's also a little stifling." She was a strong, independent woman who climbed mountains and rappelled into canyons. She hated feeling so helpless and dependent on other people for protection.

"At least Deputy Jake is sticking close," Danny said. "It's like you have an armed bodyguard."

Hannah tossed the rolled splint she had been examining into the supply bin and stared at him. "The other day you were giving me a hard time about getting too close to Jake."

"Yeah, well, that was before I figured out he's chiefly interested in you as a way to get to Cutler."

That certainly hadn't been her impression of Jake. When they had kissed after dinner the other night, she was pretty sure he hadn't been thinking about Cutler at all, although there hadn't been a repeat of that night. She had told herself that was because they were both so busy, but was she wrong? "What are you talking about?"

"I just put two and two together," Danny said. "He's here to beef up his résumé, wants to get on with the state cops or a bigger department. Capturing a fugitive would look great on his résumé. And that fugitive is fixated on you. So if Jake stays close to you, he ups his chances of nabbing Cutler. It's a good plan, really."

Hannah felt a little sick to her stomach. Danny had to be wrong. But he was a man. Maybe he was better at reading another man than she was. "So you don't think Jake has any romantic interest in me?"

Danny was bent over a plastic tote of supplies and his voice came out muffled. "I should have believed you when you said he didn't," he said. "But when I saw him at the training Sunday it made sense."

"What made sense?"

"That line he gave Tony about wanting to learn skills to be a better cop—it was really just an excuse to stick close to you in the area where Cutler was known to be roaming around. It may even be why he was so eager to go check out the Jack of Hearts Mine. He probably figured it would be a good spot for Cutler to lay low, and bringing you along might lure his quarry out of hiding."

"Wait—you think Jake deliberately used me as...as *bait*?"

Danny straightened and looked at her. "Don't get upset. He wasn't going to let you get hurt. It was a good idea, really."

"It was a horrible idea. And I don't believe Jake would do such a thing." But what if she was wrong? "Did he tell you that's what he was doing?"

"No. But it just makes sense."

"More sense than that he might be interested in me?"

"Sure, he was probably attracted to you. You're cute

and fun to be with. But guys figure out pretty quick when a woman isn't interested. You've made it real clear you don't want anything short-term and I'm sure he knows it."

"You seem to have spent a lot of time thinking about this."

He shrugged and went back to combing through the box of supplies. "I probably know you better than most people," he said. He fastened the lid on the box he had been sorting. "Are you done with that box?"

She looked down at the now-rearranged supplies. "Yes."

"Great. Then I'll just take this expired stuff to be boxed up at the office. Tony said we can send it to a charitable group that distributes it overseas."

Hannah stared after him as he carried the bag of expired items from the room. Obviously, Danny was wrong when he claimed to know her better than most people. If he knew anything about her at all, he would have realized she was furious with him right now.

She was gathering her things to leave when Jake walked into SAR headquarters. He had made a point to check in with her at least once a day since last Sunday, and until now she had enjoyed seeing him. She liked that he kept her informed about their search for Cutler, even though there was little real news to offer. But she felt a flash of irritation as he greeted her now.

"I need to talk to you," she said. She wasn't one to stew over suppositions when they could clear the air right now.

His smile faded. "Uh, okay."

He started to pull out a chair at the table in the center of the room but she shook her head. She could hear Danny and Tony talking in Tony's office, and other members of the team were liable to walk in at any time. "Outside," she said. "In my car."

Jake followed her to the parking lot. His sheriff's department SUV sat in the slot next to hers and as they approached, Gus stuck his nose out the partially open window and gave an excited yip. "Hey, Gus," she said, and reached in to pat the dog.

Jake waited beside her Subaru until she unlocked it. "Is something wrong?" he asked. "You look upset."

She took her time arranging her backpack and water bottle and digging out her sunglasses, trying to choose her words. Finally, she turned to him. "Danny thinks you're sticking so close to me because you see me as your ticket to capturing Charlie Cutler and making a name for yourself."

He stared at her, mouth in a tight line.

"Well?" she said.

"I told you I was ambitious. That isn't the same as ruthless. Is that what you think of me?"

"I told him he was wrong—but is he? He said you suggested going up to the Jack of Hearts Mine because you knew it was a likely place for Cutler to be and you wanted to draw him out. You figured if I was with you, Cutler would be more likely to surface."

He swore and looked away.

"Are you angry because Danny is wrong or because he figured you out?" she asked.

He looked back at her, face flushed, his gaze burning into her. "I'm angry that you think so little of me," he said. "That you would believe I'd use anyone that way—especially you!"

"I don't think it!" she protested. She clutched her head in her hands. "I just... This whole thing is so stressful and Danny was so sure…" Her voice trailed away. Now that she was saying all this out loud, she could hear how ridiculous it all sounded.

Jake inhaled deeply and slowly blew out the breath. "I don't know what Danny's problem is. Maybe he's jealous. I heard you two used to be a couple. Maybe he doesn't want you interested in me, so he's making sure you think I'm a bad guy."

"Danny and I agreed we weren't right for each other," she said. "He's just a friend."

"Maybe now that you're no longer together, he wants to be more than a friend."

She thought of their conversation at Mo's, when Danny had proposed they be "friends with benefits." "I don't feel that way about him," she said. "But I am pretty upset about everything that's happened. It's hard enough to figure out relationships without the pressure of a…a stalker, too."

Jake took her hand in his. "I'm sticking close because I care about you," he said. "Would I like to catch Cutler? Of course I would. Once he's caught, he won't be a threat to you any longer. As for Danny's theory that I dragged you up to that mine looking for Cutler—Danny was the one who suggested we go up there at lunch. If I had thought Cutler was up there, I would have gotten you as far away from there as I could."

She leaned toward him until their shoulders touched. "I'm sorry I accused you of putting ambition ahead of everything else," she said. "I knew even when I was hearing Danny say those things that he was wrong, but I've been so on edge and… I'm just sorry."

"It's okay." He rubbed the back of her neck, a soothing gesture, and a sensual one, too. "Will you have dinner with me tonight?" he asked.

"Yes. I'd like that." She turned her head and their lips met and she closed her eyes and relaxed into the kiss. This was what she needed right now. To forget everything but how good being in his arms felt. She needed to shut off her brain and stop debating whether Jake was right for her or wrong for her and just let herself feel something good.

And the kiss was very good. The kind of kiss she felt with her whole body, the warmth from his lips spreading through her chest to her stomach and lower, a physical reminder that while she might be threatened, she was here and alive, with a man she believed truly cared for her—a man she was growing to care for also.

A door banged in the distance, the sound startling them. They drew apart and she looked up to see Danny striding toward her. "Time to come back inside," he said, when she lowered the window. "We've got a call about a fallen climber."

Chapter Twelve

The ice climber had fallen on a steep, technical pitch in Caspar Canyon, where natural seeps and waterfalls had formed a wall of ice that attracted both professionals and amateurs from across the country. Plenty of people had been on hand when one end of the climber's rope came free, but all had been helpless to stop his plunge into the rocky gorge below.

Hannah told herself that this was just like any other call, helping someone who was injured, but as soon as she stepped out of the Beast at the entrance to the canyon, she was reminded of that day, three years ago, when her father had been the injured man. Seeing him lying there, broken and bleeding, had overwhelmed her. It was just as well that Ryan, the commander at the time, had relieved her of her duties as soon as he realized her father was the man they had been called to help.

Her dad was fine now, she reminded herself. Completely healed, largely because Search and Rescue had gotten to him quickly, administered medical care and seen that he was transported to a trauma center, where he was wheeled into surgery a mere two hours after his fall. She had the opportunity to provide the same level of care to someone else now. She would do it for her father. The idea made her feel stronger.

The first challenge rescuers faced was getting to the injured man, who was reported to be a forty-year-old, experienced climber from Montana. He had fallen into a deeper gorge at the far end of the canyon. Sheri and another volunteer, Eldon Ramsey, rappelled one hundred feet into the gorge to assess the man and radioed their findings to Tony and the others waiting above. "I've got Brock Franklin here," Sheri said. "Mr. Franklin is conscious, but in a lot of pain. Difficulty breathing. Looks like some broken ribs, maybe a broken pelvis, probably punctured lung."

Hannah winced—"a lot of pain" didn't begin to describe what Brock Franklin was probably experiencing.

"I'm sending Hannah down with oxygen, and we'll send a litter on a separate line," Tony said.

Hannah steeled herself for the trip down. Descending rock was anxiety inducing, but slick ice made the climb down even more harrowing, not to mention cold. She reminded herself that she was attached to safety lines and had a whole team of people looking out for her. That was the thing about being part of Search and Rescue—you never had to face the difficult tasks alone.

She managed the descent with only a few jarring slips, and Eldon, a cheerful Hawaiian native who had discovered a love of ice and snow and relocated from Oahu two years before, greeted her at the bottom and helped her out of her harness. She could hear her patient moaning and gasping for breath. The same way her father had moaned and gasped. Again, she stopped to steady herself.

"Everything okay?" Eldon asked. Maybe he had heard

about her father's accident, though he hadn't been with SAR then.

She nodded. "All good." She pushed the memory of her father aside and knelt beside the man. "Hello, Mr. Franklin," she said. "I'm Hannah. I'm a paramedic. I'm going to see if we can't get you breathing a little easier." She quickly assessed him, then turned to Sheri and Eldon. "I think if we reposition his head he'll be able to breathe easier."

"Let's get the neck brace on him," Eldon said.

With the man's head and neck stabilized, Hannah was able to reposition him to open his airway a little wider. That and the supplemental oxygen and some painkillers gave him a little relief. "Do you have him in the litter?" Tony radioed.

"Not yet," Sheri said. She looked to Hannah, who nodded. "We're going to move him now," Sheri radioed. "Give us a few minutes."

"Take your time," Tony said. "We've got a boom truck coming from the power company. We're going to drop a line from the boom and try to lift him straight up, but we need some time to set up everything."

Moving Franklin into the litter was a slow, excruciating process. There was no way to do so without causing the man pain, but no way to get him the help he needed without going through that pain. By the time he was secured in the aluminum litter, blankets and chemical hot packs tucked around him to make him as comfortable as possible, all three of the rescuers were sweating and chilled.

The truck from the power company had arrived and extended its boom out over the gorge, and a large crowd had gathered to watch the process. Two more volunteers descended to set anchors and guide lines, and to fasten the litter to the lines using techniques they had practiced many times but that Hannah, at least, had never used in the field. "Hannah, you need to ride the litter up with him," Tony radioed down. "Keep the lines from getting tangled and keep him calm."

"Okay." Her brain was screaming that it really wasn't okay, but there was no other answer. Tony thought she was up to the task, so she would be up to the task.

This involved donning a harness and sling and being pulled up along with the litter. Instead of thinking about being dashed to death on the rocks if the rope snapped or the pulley failed, Hannah focused on Franklin. She put her hand on top of his body and spoke to him. "Hang in there, Brock," she said. "You're doing great. We're going to go for a quick ride and before you know it you'll be in the ambulance and on your way to help. You're a strong guy and you're going to get through this."

"Stupid mistake," he muttered. "I should have checked the rope."

"You can come back next year and do the climb right," she said, hoping she wasn't lying. They wouldn't know the true extent of his injuries until he could be examined at the hospital, but she had seen people come back from worse. Her father, for instance, though he no longer traveled the world to climb treacherous slopes in remote areas as he had done so much in his younger years.

And she had seen people die from lesser injuries, but she wasn't going to think about that now.

By the time she looked around, they were almost to the top of the gorge. The lift was so smooth she had scarcely felt it, and might have enjoyed the sensation of floating in midair in other circumstances.

Fifteen minutes later they were out of the gorge and Brock Franklin was on his way to the hospital in Junction. Checking her watch, Hannah was surprised to find that the whole rescue had taken just over three hours.

"That went well," Tony said, coming up alongside her.

She nodded. "It did." Now that is was over, she could admit to feeling a little shaky, but good.

"How was the ride?" Tony asked.

"Actually, it was kind of a thrill."

He laughed. "I'll remember that, if we have to do it again." He fell into step beside her as she walked to her car. She didn't ask why he was accompanying her. Since the incident at the training Sunday, her SAR teammates had made it a point not to leave her alone at any time on a call. She appreciated their watchfulness, especially when she returned to her car. She lived in dread of finding another of Charlie Cutler's messages.

But no message awaited her this time. No notes beneath her wiper blades, nothing left on the hood or near the car. She unlocked the vehicle and climbed in, and relief flooded her as she realized that this time, at least, Cutler had left her alone.

THE WHOLE SHERIFF's department had lived and breathed the search for Charlie Cutler much of the last month. When Jake wasn't actively searching for the fugitive, he was reviewing Cutler's case file, searching for some clue as to his intentions and his next move, or he was checking in with Hannah to make sure she was all right. The normal duties of a sheriff's deputy in a small, rural county continued, but the usual round of barking dog complaints, traffic violations, one bar fight and a petty theft didn't demand copious amounts of time and attention, leaving Jake to fret over Cutler almost every waking hour.

When the sheriff convened a special meeting about the case, Jake hoped this meant there had been a new development—something that would lead them to finally track down and apprehend the fugitive. The first thing he noticed when he filed into the conference room with his fellow officers after leaving Hannah on Thursday was the slender man in a business suit who stood with the sheriff. "Looks like the feds finally showed up," Dwight muttered as he took his seat alongside Jake.

Jake checked out the man again. Short hair, upright posture, and no-nonsense expression. Eyes that took in everything in the room. He looked like a cop all right. "What's he doing here?" he asked Dwight.

"We're not getting anywhere on our own," Dwight said. "We need help, so maybe he's it."

The sheriff introduced the man as Special Agent Carter Sherrell with the FBI's Grand Junction office. "The FBI is assuming direction of the hunt for Charlie Cutler," Sherrell said. "We appreciate the work your department has done to this point, but we have reason to believe Cutler has left the area and is headed to Utah."

"What makes you think that?" Gage asked.

"We've interviewed Cutler's cell mate in Albuquerque and he says Cutler shared his plans to try to escape during his transport and make his way to Utah," Sherrell said. "Cutler has family and friends in the Salt Lake area he believed would hide him."

"But we have evidence that Cutler was in this area as recently as Sunday," Jake said.

Only a slight tightening of his jaw betrayed Sherrell's feelings about this question. "I've read the reports relating to the incident Sunday and the evidence for Cutler being at the scene is tentative at best. There were any number of skiers in the area who could have set off that avalanche, the graffiti on the door of the old mine building is cryptic and could stand for anything and the candy wrapper left on the female paramedic's car could have been merely an attempt by someone to chide her for littering. I find it highly unlikely that Cutler, who fled the scene of the accident the day of his escape wearing only jail coveralls and tennis shoes, could have survived the hostile conditions in that area for going on a month now."

"He stole supplies," Dwight said. "Winter clothing, food and a gun."

"Which he would need to get over the mountains to Utah," Sherrell said. "But there was no need for him to remain in such a hostile area."

"So you don't believe he remained in the area because he was focused on his next victim?" Jake asked.

The only word Jake could find to describe the FBI agent's smile was *condescending*. "We don't believe Ms. Richards was ever in any danger."

Jake wanted to believe the man, but his attitude of dismissing the on-the-ground expertise and experiences of him and his fellow officers made his conclusions suspect.

Jake apparently wasn't the only person in the room with doubts. "Our understanding is that Cutler had special training in wilderness survival, especially winter survival, from his time in the military," Gage said. "He would be more equipped to deal with harsh conditions in the backcountry than most people."

"And we believe he used that training to get him over the mountains and into Utah, where we hope to apprehend him shortly."

The deputies exchanged looks. Clearly, there was nothing else they could do. "Thank you for your time," Sherrell said. "Now you can get on with your regular duties."

"That's all for now," Travis said, and after a few seconds' hesitation, they shoved back their chairs and filed out of the room.

"I hope he's right and Cutler is in Utah," Deputy Jamie Douglas said.

"Or maybe he just wants everyone to think that's where he is," Deputy Ronin Doyle said.

"If he is still up there, he won't sit around and do nothing," Gage said. "He'll break into a cabin or vandalize some property and we'll hear about it."

"Or he'll kill someone else," Dwight said. "I'd just as soon not find out he's still here by responding to another murder."

Jake clenched his jaw so tightly it ached. He was thinking that he hoped the person Cutler went after wasn't Hannah, but he couldn't say it.

"We'll all be keeping our eyes and ears open," Gage said. "We can't devote manpower and resources to an all-out search anymore, but that doesn't mean we stop looking." He turned to Jake, as if reading his thoughts. "Don't go up in the high country alone. If a couple or three of us decide to go cross-country skiing or drive up to check out some mine ruins on our own time, there's nothing to prevent us from doing so. Solo outings up there are a bad idea anytime, but especially with the possibility of an armed fugitive who hates cops on the loose. Understand?"

Jake nodded. "Yes, sir." He'd be careful, but he wasn't going to let down his guard on the FBI's say-so. There was too much at stake.

AFTER HELPING CLEAN up at the rescue site, Hannah drove to SAR headquarters for the usual review of the rescue and to help put away gear. "Want to come with us to Mo's?" Sheri asked when the meeting broke up.

"Thanks, but I have something else to do," Hannah said.

"Something with a certain good-looking deputy?" Sheri teased.

"Maybe."

"I thought you two had been spending a lot of time together." Sheri nudged her with her elbow. "Good for you. He seems like a good guy."

"Yeah. I think so."

She had been tired when she left SAR headquarters, but the thought of seeing Jake again energized her. Back at the inn, she headed to her room to shower and change. Her dad stopped her on the stairs. "Everything go okay on your call?" he asked.

"It went great, Dad."

"I heard it was a climber."

"Brock Franklin. Do you know him?"

Thad shook his head. "There are so many new people these days. Is he going to be all right?"

"He's going to be fine." She thought so, at least.

"What happened?"

"I'm not sure. His line came loose. He said he made a mistake."

"It happens to the best of us," Thad said. "I'm glad he's okay."

"Me too, Dad."

"And you're okay?"

"I am." She patted his arm. Today had been stressful, but she'd gotten through it and that had felt so good.

She cleaned up and was downstairs in time to greet Jake when he entered the lobby. Dressed in jeans and a soft blue shirt, he definitely looked good. And smelled good, too. She sniffed his spicy aftershave, but resisted the urge to bury her nose against his neck.

Good thing, since her father spoke from behind her. "Hello, Jake. No Gus?"

"I'm crate-training Gus and he's doing pretty well," Jake said. "I thought it was safe to leave him alone at my place for a few hours."

"I don't suppose you have any news about Charlie Cutler?" Thad asked.

"The FBI thinks he's in Utah," Jake said. "He told his cell mate in Albuquerque that's where he intended to go. We know he has family and friends there."

"Do you think they're right?" Thad asked.

"I don't know," Jake said. "But I figure the feds have information they don't necessarily share with us."

"It would be a relief to know he isn't around here anymore," Thad said, stating the obvious.

"Good night, Dad," Hannah said, as she slipped into her jacket. "Don't wait up."

"Have a good time, sweetheart."

She slid into the front seat of Jake's Jeep and he leaned over and kissed her, a brief but fervent meeting of their lips.

"What happens now, with Cutler?" she asked, as he started the Jeep.

"The FBI is in charge. We won't let down our guard, but there's not much else we can do." He glanced at her. "Try not to think about it too much. Maybe the feds are right. That would be good news."

She nodded. She wanted to believe Charlie Cutler was

out of her life, but after so many days of fearing him around every corner, it was hard to turn off that vigilance with the blink of an eye.

"How was your day?" Jake asked.

"Just the usual," she said. "I helped save a guy's life, and rode a stretcher one hundred feet straight out of an icy gorge."

"This, I want to hear all about," he said.

He drove to the Thai restaurant and over pineapple fried rice and spicy prawns she told him about the call-out to Caspar Canyon. "Is he going to be all right?" Jake asked when she was done.

"I think so," she said. "We got to him quickly and though his injuries are severe, he should recover completely, unless something showed up at the hospital that we couldn't pick up on."

"Your dad told me he was injured climbing there a few years ago," Jake said. "He said you were on the call. That must have been hard."

"It was," she said. "I was still a trainee and though I'd seen some pretty bad things in training, it's different when it's your dad." She laid down her fork. "I really thought he was going to die and I couldn't handle the idea."

"Was the call today hard for you, remembering your dad?" he asked.

She nodded. "I was really nervous, at first. But once I focused on my patient, it was all about him, not me. Keeping that in mind, and knowing that I could do what I needed to do when it counted, that I didn't have to fall apart, made me feel a lot better. Like I've grown and matured."

"Your dad told me he quit competing because it upset you and your mom so much."

"He wouldn't have given it up if he wasn't ready to," Hannah said. "He seems happy now, sticking to local events. And I feel better knowing he's taking fewer risks."

"Ironic, considering the risks you take every day."

"Maybe, but I'm still young. Dad isn't. And don't tell him I said that."

Jake grinned. "I wouldn't dream of it."

They finished their meal and outside the restaurant, she stopped and looked up at the almost-full moon, such a brilliant, pure white against the black sky. "It's such a perfect night," she said.

Jake brushed his warm fingers across her cool cheek. "It's good to see you looking so happy."

"I am happy," she said. "It's beginning to set in that this whole ordeal with Charlie Cutler might be over." She laced her fingers with his and squeezed.

"What do you want to do now?" he asked.

"Let's go back to your place."

His answer was to pull her to his side in a warm hug. A few minutes later, they stood outside the door to his apartment. "Gus isn't carrying on, so that's good," he said as he unlocked the door.

Inside, the silence continued as he switched on more lights, then helped her out of her coat. Hannah looked toward the large crate beside the sofa. "From here, it looks like Gus is sound asleep."

Jake walked over and unlatched the door of the crate. "Hey, Gus." He leaned down to look inside. "We're home."

The dog lifted his head and blinked sleepily, then his tail began thumping hard. "I need to take him out," Jake said as the dog emerged from the crate. "You can come with us or wait here."

"I'll wait here." She sat on the sofa and patted the wiggling dog while Jake clipped on the leash.

"Lock the door behind me," he said, and kissed her, then came back and kissed her a second time, a deeper, more sensual kiss. "Just to give you something to think about," he said.

She was still tingling with the aftereffects of that kiss once Jake and the dog were gone. Restless, she strolled around the room. It was a simply furnished, clean space, without a lot of personalization. No house plants or photos on the wall. Was that because Jake hadn't had time to add these things, or because he didn't intend to be here long enough to bother?

But even that thought couldn't nudge out the happiness that filled her. Today had been such a good day, from the rescue to the news that Charlie Cutler was out of her life, and the dinner with Jake. She wanted to carry that euphoria into the night.

When she heard Jake's key in the lock she was waiting to wrap her arms around him and pull him close. He responded eagerly, pulling her tight against him and deepening the kiss, leaving no doubt of his desire for her.

"I could get used to that kind of greeting," he said when he finally released her. He unsnapped the leash from the dog's collar. "I need to feed Gus. You could wait for me in the bedroom?" He asked the last as a question, as if verifying her intentions.

"That sounds like a great idea," she said.

Jake's bedroom was like the rest of the apartment, furnished only with the basics of a queen-sized bed, a six-drawer dresser and a nightstand. A navy blue comforter draped the bed and the nightstand held only a single lamp and a phone charger. Hannah sat on the edge of the bed—the mattress was firm, but comfortable. But she didn't really care about the bed or the decor. These observations were only a distraction from what was to come.

She debated undressing and slipping under the covers, but that felt like rushing things. They ought to take their time tonight, and get to know each other bit by bit. Undressing could be awkward, or it could be a fun game. Better to make it the latter—a game she was eager to play with him.

He was grinning when he slipped into the room and shut the door behind him. "Gus never had his supper delivered so fast," he said.

He pulled her close and kissed her again—the man definitely knew how to kiss. He didn't simply mash his lips to hers; he made love to her mouth, alternately tender and insistent, awakening every sensitive nerve ending, which carried the message to the rest of her body that she definitely needed to take this further.

She broke the kiss and pulled back to look at him. "You taste like mint," she said. "Did you brush your teeth?"

"Yeah, well, all that garlic at dinner…"

She laughed. "No fair." She covered her mouth with her fingers, but he tugged her hand away.

"I love the way you taste," he said, and proved it by kissing her again.

By the time the kiss was over, he had backed them to the bed, and they fell onto the mattress, still entwined. She began to unbutton his shirt, letting her fingers brush his bare skin, and the crisp whorls of hair on his chest as she did so, then sliding across his firm abdomen, feeling the muscles contract beneath her fingers.

She slid her hands up once more, and pushed the shirt off his shoulders, and kissed the hollow of his shoulder. He was breathing harder now, his own fingers slipping beneath her fleece top, gliding over her skin.

They helped each other wrestle out of the tangle of their shirts, and he nudged her gently until she lay on her back. He began kissing his way along the top of her bra, his tongue teasing at the flesh beneath, until she was panting. He reached around and unsnapped the clasp, then pushed the garment out of the way and drew one sensitive nipple into his mouth. Sensation rocketed through her and she bit back a moan.

He moved to her other breast, and fumbled with the button of her pants. She caressed his back, delighting in the movement of his muscles beneath her touch. When he eased her pants down her hips, she wiggled out of them, then lowered the zipper on his jeans and slid her hand inside the fly to grasp his erection, the sharp intake of his breath, coupled with the feel of him, hot and hard, sending a stab of need through her.

Within seconds, he was naked and pulling her close again, their legs and arms twined as they sought as much contact as possible, warm flesh to warm flesh, mouth to mouth, hands caressing, stroking, grasping. Hannah broke one kiss with her laughter. "What's so funny?" Jake asked, his hand cupping her bottom.

"Not funny." She shook her head. "Just so…wonderful."

He grinned, and buried his face against her neck, nipping and making her laugh all the more with the joy that surged through her.

Then her smile vanished and he kissed his way down her body, every brush of his mouth making her more aware of her need for him. When his mouth reached her center she closed her eyes and gave herself up to the sensation, the heat and tension building. His fingers stroked the inside of her thighs, then moved up her body once more to caress her breasts as his mouth teased and coaxed. She tried to hold back, to make the moment last, but sensation swamped her, her climax overwhelming and wonderful.

He held her for a moment, and she thought she had never been so completely happy, and so utterly drained. And then his erection nudged at her hip and he leaned over to kiss her once more, and she wanted him all over again.

He pulled a condom from a box in the drawer of the bedside table and she watched as he rolled it on, aroused by the sight of him touching himself. She pulled him to her and guided him inside her in a moment that could have been awkward, but wasn't. After only a few moments they found a rhythm that felt good to them both. She gripped his back, then his waist, and watched as desire transformed his expression into a beautiful fierceness. She felt his climax all the way to her toes, and to the top of her head, touching every part of her. She had enjoyed good sex before, but she had never felt more connected to another person.

They lay together for a long time afterward, silent at first, then talking of little things—how much he was enjoying getting to know the people of Eagle Mountain, stories of her early days with Search and Rescue, when she had plenty of medical training but zero skills at rescue. "I guess it's like anything else," she said. "You feel so in over your head at first, and then everything becomes familiar and the next thing you know, you're the old-timer helping to train the rookies."

"I thought there would be more of that here," he said. "That it would take a while for me to find my feet and be accepted. But I guess since every deputy at the sheriff's department does everything, you're all on a pretty even footing from the start. I like that."

The conversation faded and she was drifting to sleep when the buzz of a phone startled her. She struggled to open her eyes and found Jake already sitting up on the side of the bed. "It's mine," he said, and reached down to fish his phone out of the pocket of his pants.

He answered and listened for a moment, making noncommittal noises, then ended the call, placed the phone on the nightstand and lay back down beside her.

"Is everything okay?" she asked.

"That was Sergeant Walker," he said. "He wanted to let me know the FBI has had a positive sighting of Cutler at his cousin's house in Draper, Utah."

"So Cutler really did leave?" She had already wanted to believe it, but this was the confirmation she hadn't even realized she was waiting for.

"Looks like it." Jake tightened his arm around her shoulder. "I guess we really can stand down."

She closed her eyes. Stand down. Relax. Her life could get back to normal, or as normal as life ever was when you worked Search and Rescue.

Chapter Thirteen

A large color photo of Hannah being lifted with the litter out of the gorge filled the front page of the next edition of the *Eagle Mountain Examiner*, the caption identifying her by name. Thad insisted on framing the photo to display at the front desk of the inn, and some joker tacked a clipping of the photo on the bulletin board at SAR headquarters, a superhero cape drawn in at Hannah's shoulders with red marker.

A much smaller article at the bottom of the page detailed information about Charlie Cutler's sudden appearance in Utah, where, it was stated, authorities expected to make an arrest soon.

A stretch of fair but cold weather led to an increase in calls for assistance from Search and Rescue, as people rushed to the backcountry to enjoy the snow and sunshine. Not everyone who decided to snowshoe into the mountains or skip the lift lines to ski untracked wilderness had the expertise or equipment to take care of themselves. The team was called to rescue a young couple who had taken a popular ski trail, but become disoriented and lost. They had no map or compass and hadn't familiarized themselves with the area before. When Hannah and three others reached them, they were only feet from the trail that would have taken them safely to the parking lot. It was a happy ending to what might have been a disaster, but it was also frustrating that the couple had not done more to look after themselves.

Another day they had to retrieve a man who admitted he had never backcountry skied before, who had gone too far on a trail that was rated difficult, fallen repeatedly and, since he wasn't dressed properly for the weather, had gotten wet and become hypothermic, as well as exhausted. He, too, survived the ordeal with no consequences thanks to Search and Rescue volunteers.

"I didn't sign on to take care of people who are too stupid to take care of themselves," Austen complained as he and Hannah finished up their reports on the hypothermic skier.

"It can be frustrating," Hannah agreed. "All we can do is try to educate people so they don't make the same mistakes next time. And that man could have died if we hadn't been here to help. He had a real emergency, and that's what we're here for."

He scowled, but said nothing more. Hannah predicted he wouldn't last long-term in Search and Rescue. People cycled in and out of the organization all the time. Some couldn't handle the time commitment, some didn't have the physical fitness necessary, some had life events that prevented them from continuing, and others, like Austen, signed on with expectations that differed too greatly from the reality of everyday wilderness rescue. The work required a passion and dedication that not everyone possessed. Hannah hadn't truly believed she would be a good fit for the work when her coworker had persuaded her to give it a try but to her surprise, she had found a place in the group. She could truly say if she gave it up, she would miss it, even the hard, grueling days, and the days when her best efforts couldn't save an injured person, or the days when by the time SAR was called, it was already too late. And yes, even the days when she ended up rescuing someone who should have had the sense to stay home.

And then there were the calls that took everything out of you—every bit of physical stamina and mental courage and technical skill. Those were the calls that challenged and exhausted you and in the end, made you feel that you had made such a difference that all the suffering had been worthwhile, and you would do it all over again.

"Nobody should kid themselves—this is going to be tough." That was how Tony greeted the volunteers who assembled at the base of Mount Baker shortly after 1:00 p.m. on a Saturday afternoon. Hannah had been getting ready to meet Jake to drive into Junction to take in a movie and dinner, and maybe hit up a club when the call came. Jake hadn't balked or complained when she called to cancel—she supposed one advantage of dating a cop was they accepted that emergencies happen.

"According to the 911 call, we've got a skier stuck on a ledge on the west side of Mount Baker, about two hundred feet below the summit," Tony continued. "He fell skiing down that couloir that runs down the right side of the front face of the mountain."

"He fell there and he's alive?" Ryan asked.

"His partner says so. He was able to communicate with his friend where he lay on the ledge, then he climbed back up to the summit, got a cell signal and called it in. The skier—" Tony consulted his notes. "His name is Jeremy Prather, forty, from Junction. The guy with him is Vick Balin, also from Junction. Vick says Jeremy was conscious, but in a lot of pain, but was able to convey that he thinks he fractured his femur, and may have done some damage to his knee and some ribs."

"I think I know that spot," Ryan said. "I've climbed that route in the summer. It's going to take us at least four hours to hike up there—probably more, depending on conditions."

"What about a chopper to take a couple of medical people up there to triage?" Danny asked.

Tony shook his head. "We don't know what kind of condition the snow is in up there. Even if we could get a chopper over before dark, if the snow is unstable, a helicopter could bring it all down right on top of the guy."

"So we hike in," Ryan said.

"Right," Tony said. "And we don't rush. No sense any of us getting hurt, too. We know setting out this is going to be a night operation, so we take our time and do it right. Ryan, you lead, since you know the trail. Hannah, you and Danny decide what medical equipment we need to haul up there." He called out the names of other personnel and assigned each of them to specific duties.

Hannah and Danny convened in front of the medical supplies. Danny was already pulling items from the bins. "We'll need splints. An air splint. Supplemental oxygen." He began checking off items as he piled them on the table in front of them.

"He'll need pain meds," Hannah said.

"Right. Do we have any medical history on this guy?"

"I don't think so," Hannah said. "But he was healthy enough to be up there skiing."

She retrieved the key for the locked cabinet where they stored their supply of drugs, and reviewed what was available. Taking too much or the wrong things was a waste, but keeping the patient as comfortable as possible was a priority. Tony hadn't mentioned a head injury, which would make treatment easier, but until someone was able to examine the man, they would have no idea of the true extent of his injuries.

Thirty minutes later, Hannah was seated next to Tony in the front seat of the Beast, barreling down a snow-packed county road toward the trailhead at the base of Mount Baker. Ryan and Eldon were fifteen minutes ahead of them, intending to set out to pack the trail and clear any obstacles. Sheri, Danny, Ted, Austen and Chris rode in the rear of the Beast, crowded in with an intimidating array of equipment, from an aluminum litter and oxygen canisters, to a large orange vacuum mattress that reminded Hannah of a swim float. Every bit of that equipment would have to be transported up the mountain on the backs of the rescue volunteers.

Tony parked at the trailhead with the headlights of the Beast illuminating the start of the trail, which from this vantage point appeared to be a narrow, muddy track heading straight up through thick forest. Hannah and the others climbed out and began unloading their gear. No one said much as they worked. This was when Hannah saw the real value in the hours of training. They had been through similar situations before and knew what they had to do. She stifled a groan as she eased into her pack, which must have weighed forty pounds—more than she was used to carrying.

She reminded herself that the others were carrying at least this much and more. Sheri even had the vacuum mattress strapped to the back of her pack, adding two feet to her height. They started up, and before they had traveled a hundred yards Hannah was sweating in her heavy parka, various muscles and joints complaining from the strain. *Think about the patient,* she told herself. *Think about Jeremy.* How was he handling the pain? Was he warm enough? Was he in shock? Was he terrified, lying there injured on the side of a mountain in the dark? She would be afraid in that situation, though she would have one advantage over most other people. She would know that down here at the bottom of the mountain a whole team was working to get to her, to do everything they could—including risking their own safety—to make sure that she was all right.

JAKE WAS DISAPPOINTED his date with Hannah had been canceled, but he wasn't surprised. It might as easily have been him calling her to say he had to report in to work to handle an emergency. They would get together again soon. In fact, they had scarcely been apart since the night she had stayed over at his apartment. They weren't actually living together, but close. The intensity of their relationship surprised him, but it felt right. More right than anything he had experienced with any other woman.

The big drawback to all those good feelings was that right now he was worried. She hadn't given him many details about the call she was on, though she had mentioned something about someone having fallen while skiing down a mountain. "It's going to take a while to get to him," she said. "So don't expect to hear from me before morning."

Too restless to sit at home, he leashed Gus and took him to the park. The dog was more than happy to accompany him, and spent the next half hour sniffing every inch of the path around the perimeter, with special attention to the area around the picnic tables, where he snagged what Jake thought was a chicken wing, though he'd only had a glance at the item before it disappeared down Gus's gullet.

Reluctant to return home just yet, Jake turned toward the sheriff's department. He would just check in with whoever was on duty to see what was going on. Maybe they'd even know something about Hannah's fallen skier.

Deputy Dwight Prentice was the only person in the squad room when Jake and Gus entered. He looked up from his computer at their approach. "Hey. Aren't you supposed to be at the movies or something?"

"Hannah had a callout," Jake said. "Some guy fell off a mountain." He walked to his desk and flipped through the papers in the in-box. "Anything interesting come in?"

"Nothing." Dwight yawned and stretched his arms over his head. "It's a quiet weekend for once."

"Any news from the feds on Charlie Cutler?" Jake asked. "Did they make an arrest?"

"No word," Dwight said. "But then, I'm not sure they'd bother to tell us if they did."

Jake sat at his desk and logged into the computer, then pulled up the files on Charlie Cutler. "What was the name of that special agent who came and talked to us?"

"Special Agent Sherrell," Dwight said.

"Yeah, here it is." Jake picked up the phone.

"What are you doing?" Dwight said.

"I'm going to call Agent Sherrell and ask him for an update."

"On a Saturday afternoon?"

"Why not?" Jake dialed the number and listened to it ring. Once…twice…by the fourth ring he was expecting a voice mailbox to answer, but instead Sherrell's clear, clipped voice said, "Hello. Who is this?"

"This is Deputy Jake Gwynn in Eagle Mountain,"

Jake said. "What can you tell me about Charlie Cutler? Did you make an arrest?"

Silence. Jake knew Sherrell was still on the line because he could hear him breathing. "Agent Sherrell?" he prompted.

"No, we did not arrest Charlie Cutler," Sherrell said. "The man we thought was Cutler was actually a cousin who looks very much like him. We brought him in for questioning, but he swears he hasn't heard from Cutler."

Jake felt cold all over. "Are you saying Cutler was never in Utah?" he asked.

"We don't know. We still feel that's where he was headed. All we can say for sure is that Charlie Cutler was not at that house in Draper."

"You don't know where he is," Jake said. "In fact, he's very likely still here in Colorado."

"We don't know that, either," Sherrell said. "Have you had any more sightings of him?"

"We haven't been looking for him," Jake said, his anger barely contained. "You told us not to bother."

"I'm not going to debate this with you, Deputy," Sherrell said, an edge to his voice.

"No, I'm not going to waste time doing that, either." Jake ended the call and sagged back in the chair.

"They didn't get Cutler?" Dwight asked.

Jake shook his head. "The man they thought was Charlie Cutler was a cousin. Cutler probably isn't even in Utah. I bet he's still up there in the mountains. Where Hannah just went on a rescue call." He clenched both hands into fists, wishing he could punch Sherrell— though that wouldn't do anyone any good, he knew. Except it might feel good, to let off some of his frustration.

The feds had been so sure they knew better than a bunch of small-town cops.

"Hannah isn't up there alone," Dwight said. "She's surrounded by a whole team of people. People who care about her. Cutler isn't going to get to her, even if he did find out where she was. And I don't see how he would."

Jake nodded. "You're right. She's not alone and she'll be fine." He stood and snapped his fingers. Gus, who had been napping beneath the desk, jumped up, tail wagging.

"Where are you going?" Dwight asked.

"I think I'll drive out to the trailhead at the base of Mount Baker," he said. "See how things are going, and if they need any help."

To Dwight's credit, he did not remind Jake that Search and Rescue did not need the help of someone who had been on exactly one training exercise, or that Jake would be unlikely to even see, much less speak to, Hannah, who would be busy doing her job. But he could at least pass on the information that Charlie Cutler might still be at large in the area and they should all be on guard.

And on the slim chance that Cutler might show up, Jake wanted to be there, armed and waiting for him.

Chapter Fourteen

If the climb up the mountain had been challenging in
the fading daylight, as darkness descended it became
the stuff of nightmares. Hannah switched on her headlamp, but no matter how she tilted the beam, it could
illuminate only a small area in front of her, spotlighting the orange mass of the vacuum mattress on Sheri's
back, or the gleam of the metal oxygen canister carried
by Danny, or the steep drop to one side of the trail, or a
tree root that tripped her as she passed, sending her forward hard on her knees, or the bare branch of a tree just
before it slapped her in the face.

A third of the way up the trail they encountered snow,
mixed with mud at first, then slick with ice, and finally
thick and fluffy, though Ryan and Eldon had done their
best to pack it down. Walking was treacherous, especially when she was unable to see her feet. One inch off
the narrow packed path and she would sink to her knees,
the heavy pack throwing her off balance and wrenching
her sideways. Soon her ankles and knees and hips and
back ached and she wanted to scream in frustration. At
this rate they wouldn't reach the top of the mountain
until daylight.

"Here, grab this. It will be easier." Sheri turned and

guided Hannah's hand to a stout rope at the side of the trail. "Ryan and Eldon fixed this up for us," she said.

The rope made the going much easier, and she appreciated having something to hold on to, an extra insurance against plummeting off the side of the mountain. Every hundred feet or so they would stop and wait while Ryan or Eldon pulled the rope up and reattached it, but the pauses allowed them all to catch their breath, and they made better time overall.

The trail flattened for a bit and Tony called for them to regroup. He had left Ted at the trailhead to coordinate from there. "Everybody take a minute to rest, hydrate, get something to eat," he said. "How's everyone doing?"

They all muttered variations of "okay" and "all right." No one wanted to be the first to complain. They were all tired and sore, but also aware that a man lay injured at the top of the mountain, whose life depended on them gutting it out and soldiering on. Hannah leaned against a rock outcropping, letting the rock take some of the weight of the pack. "You can take that pack off if you want," Danny said, coming to stand beside her. "I'll help you get it back on."

"No," she said. She was afraid if she removed the pack, she wouldn't have the strength to face putting it on again.

"Look at the moon," he said, and pointed toward a mountain peak across from them, and the silver edge of the moon just beginning to appear from around the side of the peak. "Another hour or so and it will be all the way up. It will make walking easier."

She realized it was already lighter, their figures casting shadows on the snow. She hugged her arms across her chest, cold. Now that they had stopped, the sweat she had worked up on the climb was chilling her.

"Unzip the vents on your jacket," Danny said. "You should have done it before we started out."

"Yes, Dad," she teased.

"Don't start that," he said. "Just because you don't want me as your lover, you don't have to pretend I'm that much older than you."

"We're much better off as friends and fellow team members," she said. "You know it, even if you won't admit it."

He let out an exaggerated sigh. "You're really hurting my ego here. But yeah. And I'm sorry about what I said at Mo's that night. I was out of line. I was just in a weird place, I guess. Lonely."

The sincerity of his words touched her. "You're forgiven," she said. "And I hope you find the right woman for you. I really do." Danny was a good guy—he hadn't been right for her, but she appreciated that he was her friend.

"Let's head out," Tony called.

"How long have we been hiking?" Hannah asked Danny as they prepared to set out once more.

He pressed a button to illuminate the face of his watch. "About three hours. It's going faster than I thought. It helps that a lot of this trail is in the sun during the day."

For a while the trail wasn't as steep, and they followed a series of cairns across what must have been a scree field in summer, the loose rock and gravel frozen and for now at least, stable beneath a blanket of snow that Ryan and Eldon had packed down for them. The moon bathed them in a soft, white light, adding to the otherworldly feel of the expedition. If not for the struggle to carry the heavy pack, the uncertainty about what awaited them at the top of the mountain and the need to place each step carefully on the uncertain terrain, it would have been a glorious hike. As she trudged along, forcing herself to put one foot in front of the other, to keep going in spite of pain and fatigue and worry, she promised herself she would return in the summer to hike the trail to the top.

She and Jake could come here together. He would be great to hike with—he wasn't a complainer, and he wasn't the type who turned every activity into a competition. He didn't mind taking time to admire the sunset or contemplate the stars. Thinking about him made her smile. She was glad of the darkness, which prevented the others from seeing that smile, which she was sure was the look of a woman who was completely gone for a man she had only known a little more than a month. She and Jake had scarcely been apart since she had spent the night at his apartment. She had been sure at least one of her parents would caution her about not rushing into a new relationship so soon after her split with Danny, but when she had slipped into the inn before breakfast after her first night at Jake's, her mother had only smiled and said, "You look like you had a good time last night," which had both embarrassed and pleased Hannah. Her father's only acknowledgment that something might be going on between his daughter and the new deputy was to remark that he certainly liked Jake and hoped he decided to stay in town.

Hannah hoped so, too. The only shadow in the picture of happiness she was painting with Jake was the knowledge that he didn't see Eagle Mountain as his long-term residence. He had made it clear he intended to move on and move up. Which wasn't to say she couldn't follow him, but everything she loved was here—not only her parents, but her job and her work with Search and Rescue. She could always find another job, but replacing the two sets of people who were truly her family wasn't so easily done.

She gave herself a mental shake. No need to rush things. Her motto from the beginning of this relationship was to take each day as it came. She would enjoy being with Jake but she wouldn't put pressure on him or on herself to make this long-term. Only now that she was a couple of weeks into being with him did she realize how foolish that philosophy could be. It hadn't worked with Danny, and she feared it wasn't going to work with Jake.

But for now, she was stuck—too besotted with him to break up and too fearful that he would leave her to completely lose herself in loving him.

Love. A powerful four-letter word. Neither of them had used it with each other and she didn't intend to. But when she was being completely honest with herself— here, on the side of a mountain in the dark—she could admit she was falling in love with Jake. That felt about as thrilling as walking a ridge of rock with a steep drop-off on each side, and every bit as dangerous.

"ALL I CAN tell you is they haven't made it to the top yet." Ted, the SAR volunteer, was huddled in the front seat of the rescue vehicle, the engine running and the heater on. When Jake had arrived at the trailhead, Ted had invited him to sit with him. "I wouldn't mind the company," he'd said. "This is the most boring part, waiting for the action to begin."

"What happens when they get to the top?" Jake asked.

"If he can get a cell signal, Tony will call me." Ted picked up the phone he had propped in one of the cup holders between the seats. "He should be able to get a signal. The climber's partner called from there."

"How are they going to get up there in the dark, with all the snow?" Jake asked. He couldn't see the mountain from here, but he had a memory of a sharply jutting peak frosted in white.

"They'll figure out a way," Ted said. "A lot of this work is figuring out things as you go along. I mean, we practice and train for everything we think we might encounter, but there's always something new. It's what makes it exciting and keeps it interesting. And of course, people are always figuring out new ways to hurt themselves, so that keeps us on our toes."

"You haven't seen anyone else around, have you?" Jake asked.

"You mean like lookie-loos? That happens in summer sometimes, but when it's dark and cold the onlookers tend to stay away."

"You really get people who show up at the scene of a rescue to watch?" Jake asked.

"It can be pretty exciting when we're, say, pulling someone up out of a canyon or doing a whitewater rescue on the river."

"How do they know to show up?" he asked.

"They listen to the emergency channel. Anybody can do it. Used to be you had to have a special scanner or radio. Some people still keep those, especially in remote areas of the high country, but most places you can listen in with an app on your phone."

Jake nodded. He knew people listened to police channels but he hadn't thought about them following search and rescue calls. Was that how Charlie Cutler had known where Hannah would be, those times he had left those items at her car? "You haven't seen anyone else, have you?" he asked. "Anyone on the trail?"

"It's not really the time of year for hiking," Ted said.

"How did the man who was hurt get up there?" Jake asked.

"He and his buddy climbed up the back side of the mountain, hiking over on the saddle that connects Mount Baker and Peak 14. It's pretty narrow and there's a lot of scree in summer and ice in winter, but with proper precautions and good skills, it's doable. Then you can ski down the west couloir all the way down to a big snowfield that comes almost to the state highway. If you park a vehicle at both ends it makes for a long day trip."

"But Search and Rescue didn't go in that way?"

Ted shook his head. "Too risky in the dark, carrying all that equipment. Tony thought about sending a couple of people over there, to try to get to the injured man ahead of everyone else, but he was afraid they'd get caught in the dark. And we don't know why this man fell. Maybe there's rotten snow up there or something. This trail is slower, but safer."

Ted offered Jake a piece of gum and he accepted. "If you're worried about Hannah, don't be," Ted said. "She knows what she's doing and our motto is to always take care of ourselves first. We're not going to be able to help anyone if we're injured ourselves. We'll push ourselves and do things a person without proper training should never attempt, but Tony won't hesitate to call off a mission if he thinks it's too risky."

He didn't ask how Ted knew he might be focused on Hannah. They hadn't been hiding their relationship and there were no secrets in a tight-knit group like Search and Rescue. "That's good to hear," he said.

"Is that the only reason you came out here?" Ted asked. "To check on Hannah?"

He hesitated. He wanted to warn Hannah and the others, but he didn't want to spread information that wasn't true. "There's a possibility Charlie Cutler didn't go to Utah after all," he said. "I wanted to warn Search and Rescue to be on the lookout for him."

Ted nodded. "I'll let Tony know when he calls."

"You don't sound surprised to learn that Cutler might still be here," Jake said.

"I saw both the men he killed. Professional work. He was evading capture, but he wasn't running scared. And he seemed at home in conditions other people would find hostile. I thought he might stick around here at least until snowmelt."

"You talk like someone with law enforcement background," Jake said.

"Special Forces," Ted said. "Afghanistan. Let's just say I've dealt with men like Cutler before."

His tone of voice sent a shiver down Jake's spine. He'd been all wrong about Ted when he thought he was just an easygoing old-timer. Right now, with Charlie Cutler out there somewhere, Jake was glad to have Ted on his side.

"Okay if I wait here with you until you hear from Tony?" Jake asked.

"Suits me. Like I said, I'm glad of the company."

They didn't say much after that, and when the phone rang, it startled them. But it wasn't Ted's phone; it was Jake's. "Hello?" he answered.

"Jake, it's Dwight. Thought you'd want to know about a call that just came in. Folks out on county Road 11 got home late from an out-of-town trip and their cabin had been broken into. The burglar took food and a pistol and a bunch of ice climbing equipment."

"Okay." He waited for Dwight to tell him why he should be interested in this.

"Are you at the Mount Baker trailhead right now?" Dwight asked.

"I am."

"Then you're only a couple of miles from these people's cabin."

"You think this burglar might be Cutler." A chill settled over him.

"I don't know. Ice climbing gear is easy to sell and can bring a lot of money, so maybe it was just a garden-variety break-in. But if it is Cutler, maybe he doesn't want to sell the equipment. Maybe he wants to use it. Tell the SAR crew to keep a lookout."

"I will." He ended the call, and held the phone in his hand.

"I heard most of that," Ted said. "You think Cutler is headed up there after Hannah and the others?"

"I think it's something we have to consider."

"What are you going to do?"

"I have to go into town. There's someone I need to talk to." He opened the passenger door. "Tell Tony what you know. He can decide how to handle things from his end. One thing we know about Cutler is he avoids groups of people. As long as everyone stays in groups, they should be safe. And whatever you do, don't leave Hannah alone."

"We won't," Ted promised.

Jake sprinted to his Jeep, then headed back to town. He hoped he was making the right decision, leaving like this. But he needed help if everyone was going to come out of this safely.

HANNAH COULD NOT GAUGE time or distance in the dark, so she was startled when the line of hikers came to a halt and word was passed back that they had gone as far as they could go. They began unloading gear and Tony summoned her and Danny forward, where an anxious-looking man greeted them. "This is Vick," Tony said. "He was skiing with Jeremy when Jeremy fell."

"One second he was fine and the next he was falling," Vick said. "I thought he was gone, but when I looked over the edge I saw he'd landed on a ledge. Down there." He pointed off in the darkness. "I've been lying here for hours, calling down to him, trying to keep him talking." His voice broke, exhaustion and fear in every syllable.

Danny patted his shoulder. "It's okay," he said. "You did everything you could to help your friend."

"Does Jeremy have any health conditions we should know about?" Hannah asked. "Any chronic illnesses? Does he take any medications?"

"Nothing," Vick said. "He's super healthy."

"Was he complaining of anything before he fell?" Danny asked. "Any shortness of breath or unusual pains?" There was always the possibility that some physical ailment had triggered the fall.

"No. We were having a great time," Vic said. "He was skiing ahead of me, doing great. I don't know what happened—all of a sudden he just went over and kept going." His face contorted, reflecting the horror of the memory.

"You've done a great job staying with him, keeping his spirits up," Danny said. "We've got him now, and we're going to take good care of him."

What might have looked like chaos to someone who just happened upon the scene erupted on the mountaintop as everyone set to work, the many parts of an intricate dance coming together. A team set up flood lights to illuminate the shelf where Jeremy Prather lay on his side, half-curled into a fetal position. He wore black ski pants and parka and a black helmet. One of his skis and his ski poles lay a few inches from his right leg, while the other wasn't visible.

A trio of rescuers began rigging lines to secure Jeremy, the various rescuers who would be assisting him and the equipment needed. Hannah harnessed in and climbed down to the ledge where Jeremy lay. She was glad of the darkness now, because it prevented her from seeing how close to the edge she was standing, and how far the drop would be if she fell. Danny followed, but the ledge itself was so narrow they scarcely had room to examine the injured man. At one point, Hannah stood with her feet on the edge of the rock shelf, the rest of her leaning out into thin air, trusting in the safety harness and ropes to support her.

"Jeremy, my name is Hannah. I'm a paramedic and this is Danny. He's a nurse. We're going to make you a lot more comfortable, very soon."

Jeremy, a heavy growth of black beard standing out sharply from his pale, pale face, stared up at her with sunken eyes and tried to smile. "That sounds good," he rasped.

Carefully, aware there was no way to do this without causing Jeremy more pain, Hannah and Danny examined their patient. "Closed displaced fracture of the left femoral shaft," Danny diagnosed. "At least three broken ribs, but no lung puncture. His left knee is swollen, but hard to tell if there's tendon damage."

Hannah recorded Jeremy's blood pressure, pulse, and oxygen saturation, and they fitted him with a mask and portable oxygen. She drew up a syringe of morphine and administered it, then watched as some of the tension gradually eased from his face. "We're going to need to move you into a litter," she said. "It's not going to feel very good while we're moving you, but once you're secured in there, you're going to feel so much better."

The next thirty minutes were spent fitting the vacuum mattress into the litter, securing the litter to lines, then lowering it to the shelf, where Danny and Hannah carefully maneuvered Jeremy into his new bed. She adjusted the mattress to fit around him, immobilizing the fractures and providing a much more comfortable resting place than the frozen rock on which he had spent the past seven hours. Then they tucked in chemical heat packs and covered him with blankets. "How's that?" she asked when they were finished.

Jeremy smiled up out of his cocoon. "Good. A little too warm, even."

Hannah looked across at Danny, who was hugging himself, shivering. "Should have brought some of those hot packs for us," Danny said.

Her radio crackled. "How's it going down there?" Ted asked.

"Good," she answered. "Jeremy is doing great and we're all secure."

"Great. I've had a conversation with HAATS, along with avalanche forecasters, plus Ryan and I hiked up and had a look ourselves. We think we can bring a helicopter in at first light to lift Jeremy off the mountain. There's not as much snow up here as I thought, and what there is is stable. It will be safer for everyone than trying to bring him down in the dark."

"That's great." HAATS was the Army National

Guard's High Altitude Aviation Training Site. Those soldiers were the best in the world in maneuvering in this terrain and SAR had worked with them before. Hannah hadn't relished the idea of carrying Jeremy—who was a big man—down that steep trail, not to mention the suffering he would have had to endure from the constant jostling on the way down.

"I'm leaving Sheri and Ryan up here to monitor all the lines and ferry down any supplies you might need," Tony continued. "I want you to stay on the ledge with Jeremy, monitor his condition and administer pain meds to keep him comfortable. Are you up for that?"

"Of course."

"I could stay," Danny said.

"You could," Tony said. "But you're six-four and Hannah is five-six. She'll be a lot more comfortable on that ledge than you are."

"I'd manage," Danny said.

"You can stay up top with Sheri and Ryan," Tony said. "Relieve Hannah if she needs it, and help with transport tomorrow. Depending on the weather, that could be tricky."

They had all trained last summer with HAATS on airlifting patients, but the idea of having to repeat the exercise in a real-life situation made her stomach hurt. It took real muscle to wrangle the lines from the helicopter's hoist, and a few extra inches of height wouldn't hurt, either. "Good idea," Danny said. "I'm on it."

Things gradually calmed down after that, as the rest of the crew headed back down the mountain and the four who remained behind—Hannah with Jeremy on the ledge and Danny, Ryan and Sheri two hundred feet above, settled in for a long, cold night. Hannah gave Jer-

emy a couple of energy gels and some water, and one of
the team up top sent a flask of hot soup down to her on
a line. That soup was one of the best things she had ever
tasted and went a long way toward easing the chill. She
settled herself on the few inches of ledge next to the litter, and wrapped a space blanket around her shoulders.
The low murmur of conversation from above provided a
soothing backdrop, and she was close to falling asleep.

She roused herself to check on Jeremy. His pulse was
steady and he slept heavily, exhausted and aided by the
morphine. By this time tomorrow, this would all be a
memory—an exciting story to tell in the future, when
he had cheated death on a mountaintop.

She looked up at the full moon. At this elevation it
seemed close enough to touch, and she could make out
the shadows of valleys and craters on its surface. She
wouldn't forget this night, either, one in which she had
pushed herself to her limits, overcome fear and doubt to
help save a life. The hardest part was over now. In the
morning they'd load Jeremy into the helicopter, then head
back down the trail, tired and sore but victorious. She'd
go back to the inn, take a long shower, eat scrambled eggs
and bacon and toast, and sleep for twelve hours. Then
she'd see Jake, and tell him all about her big adventure
and make love until she fell asleep again. A good end
to a good couple of days. Only a few more hours and
she would be there, safe and warm and comfortable and
stronger than she had been before.

Chapter Fifteen

"Jake! Is everything all right?" Jake had pictured himself walking calmly into the inn and explaining what he wanted to Hannah's father, but something in his expression must have alarmed Thad. The older man hurried from behind the front counter. "Is it Hannah? Has something happened?"

"Hannah is fine," Jake said. "Search and Rescue is headed to the top of Mount Baker to rescue a climber who fell."

Thad searched Jake's face. "There's something else, isn't there?"

"It may be nothing, but I don't want to take a chance it's something."

"What is it?"

"Charlie Cutler may not have gone to Utah at all," Jake said. "The man the FBI thought was him turned out to be a cousin."

"You think he's still here," Thad said.

"There was a break-in on County Road 11 this afternoon. Someone stole some food and a bunch of ice climbing gear."

"The trailhead for Mount Baker is on County Road 11," Thad said. "What do you think Cutler is up to?"

"The skier who was hurt—he and his friend got to the top of Mount Baker by crossing the saddle from Peak 14 and hiking up a short ways. They were skiing down when he fell. I think Cutler may have a scanner he uses to listen in on emergency calls so he knows where Search and Rescue is headed. He may be planning to intercept them up there."

"Because he wants Hannah." Thad's voice remained steady, though he was very pale.

"I may be wrong," Jake said. "I hope I'm wrong. But I need to go up there and see." He took a deep breath. "And I need ice climbing gear to do it."

"You can't go up there alone," Thad said. "That'll only get you killed. Especially since you don't know what you're doing."

Jake had expected him to say as much. And he was right. "Someone has to do something," he said. "It will take hours to get up the trail Search and Rescue took. We can't get air support up there until morning. I'm afraid if we wait it will be too late."

"I'll go with you," Thad said. "I've traversed that saddle before. It's not that difficult if you know what you're doing."

"I can't let you do that," Jake said, alarmed. Hannah would never forgive him—and he'd never forgive himself—if he took Hannah's father up on a mountain and got him killed.

"I'm older, but I'm not washed-up yet," Thad said. "I can do this to help my daughter. But we're going to do this right."

Jake nodded. Some of Thad's enthusiasm was infecting him. "I'll do whatever you say."

"Then first thing, we call the sheriff and talk to him. We don't do this without him signing off on it."

"That was my next step, after I talked to you."

Thad put a hand on Jake's shoulder. "You call Travis. I'll go get my gear."

He left and Jake moved to an alcove off the lobby of the inn and dialed the sheriff's direct number. "Hello, Jake," Travis said. "Dwight told me the latest developments regarding Cutler. Do you have something new?"

Jake summed up his theory about Cutler's next move, and his plan to try to intercept him on the saddle between Peak 14 and Mount Baker. "Thad Rogers is coming with me. He's climbed in that area before and I don't have the skill to do it by myself."

"It's too dangerous," Travis said.

"Yes, sir. It is. But I think it's more dangerous if Cutler attacks the SAR team up there on that mountaintop with no sort of law enforcement support."

"Let me talk to Thad."

Jake found Thad in a storage closet just off the front desk. "The sheriff wants to talk to you," he said, and handed over the phone.

Several minutes of intense conversation followed. Thad's half of the conversation consisted mostly of "Yes, sir" and "I'm sure" repeated over and over. Finally, he handed the phone back to Jake.

"Now that you've put the bug in his ear, Thad's determined to go up there without you," Travis said. "Short of arresting him and locking him in a cell, which I can't really do, I can't stop him. So you have to go with him to look after him."

"Yes, sir." Something Thad had said must have changed the sheriff's mind about letting Jake attempt to intercept Cutler. Maybe because he, like Jake, saw that it was their best chance.

"There's something else you should know," Travis said. "We had a report come in a few minutes ago from another house on County Road 11. One of their snowmobiles is missing off a trailer parked beside their garage. They heard the engine fire up at seven o'clock, but by the time the owners got outside, all they could see was the tail light disappearing into the woods. Dwight drove out there, but didn't see any sign of the machine."

"Cutler could have taken it to get to the trail across the saddle," Jake said. "I understand there's a road leading up there."

"Maybe," Travis said. "The machine that was stolen is a 2019 Polaris Switchback, black."

"I'll be watching for it."

"I'm sending three officers up the trail SAR used to rendezvous with you at the top," Travis said. "If you do spot Cutler up there, avoid him if at all possible. Your job is to protect civilians, not to initiate a confrontation."

"Yes, sir."

"Good luck. And do everything Thad tells you. He has all those climbing medals for a reason."

Jake pocketed his phone. "We're going to do this, then," Thad said.

Jake nodded. "We are."

Thad handed him a pair of heavy coveralls. "Wear something warm and easy to move in under these, but you'll need these for the ride up there."

"My Jeep has a heater, Thad."

"You can't get up that road in a Jeep—not this time of year. We'll go by snowmobile."

Cutler had known that, even if Jake hadn't. Jake was

more sure than ever that he was right and Cutler was headed toward the SAR team. "Do you have a snow-mobile?"

Thad grinned. "I do. You get dressed while I let Brit know what's up, then we'll get going."

Despite knowing that Thad was an award-winning mountain climber, Jake had not pegged the older man as someone with a daredevil personality. Only when he was riding behind Thad as they raced up the forest service road toward the summit of Peak 14 did he realize he was riding with a wild man. Thad opened the throttle wide and they hurtled up a steep trail marked only by tall orange plastic poles at intervals on either side of the road, a rooster tail of snow flying up behind them. The light on the front of the snowmobile illuminated only a tunnel of landscape, making their path seem impossibly narrow, trees crowding in on either side. But he had to trust Thad to know what he was doing, so he gritted his teeth and held on so tightly his muscles ached.

By the time Thad swung the snowmobile around in a wide, level area near the top of the peak, Jake was shaking with both cold and nerves. He braced himself with one hand on the machine as he climbed off, and waited for his legs to steady. Thad showed no such hesitation. He moved to the back of the snowmobile and began un-strapping equipment. "Leave the coveralls here," he said. "Get into this harness. Here's your pack. Don't forget your ice ax. Do you remember everything I told you?"

"I think so." Thad had given him a quick and dirty crash course in climbing procedures, and had ended the lecture with, "Don't worry too much. I'll do the heavy lifting. You just follow orders and hang on."

"You'll be amazed what you remember when you get in a bind," Thad said.

Jake felt steadier now. He looked at the gear piled at his feet, then around the parking area. "I want to look around a little," he said. "See if anyone else has been up here ahead of us."

Two snowmobiles sat under a tarp at the far edge of the parking area. He guessed these belonged to the injured skier and his friend. But a circuit of the entire parking area revealed another set of tracks in the rougher snow at the far edge of the clearing. An attempt had been made to brush snow over them, but the tracks cut deep in the hard-packed snow. At first, he thought they might be old tracks, made days ago, but when he followed them beneath the trees, he found a black Polaris snowmobile half-hidden behind a large boulder.

Jake took out his pistol and double-checked that the magazine was fully loaded and there was a bullet in the chamber. He hoped he didn't have to use the weapon, but he would do whatever it took to protect Hannah and the other members of her team. He returned to the snowmobile where Thad was waiting, already harnessed and pack in place. "I think Cutler is up here," he said. "I found a snowmobile hidden over in those rocks." He gestured into the darkness. "From what I can tell in the dark, it matches the description of the one that was stolen."

"He won't be expecting anyone to have followed him in the dark," Thad said. "If we're lucky, he'll be so focused on his destination that he won't look behind him and see our lights."

"If he does, and he's still got that rifle with him, we'll be easy enough to pick off," Jake said. The thought made him queasy, but he pushed it aside.

"Hard to climb with a rifle," Thad said. "Hard to aim steady up there, too."

Jake didn't add that Cutler had trained for missions like this, and that he had a marksmanship medal. Better that at least one of them not realize how much the odds were stacked against him. "Let's go," he said.

Thad checked his phone. "There's a signal up here," he said. "Anybody you want to call?"

Jake hesitated, then said. "Yeah. Yeah, there is."

HANNAH WAS STARTLED when her phone rang. Vick had told them he had to climb up the mountain to get a signal strong enough to call for help. The team had been communicating via radio, and she hadn't thought to check her phone. Everyone she knew should be asleep at this time of night. She was going to be really annoyed if some spammer was interrupting her on the top of a mountain in the middle of the night. But when Jake's name flashed on the screen, she smiled. Leave it to him to be thinking about her. "Hey," she answered. "What are you doing up this late?"

"How are things going up there?" he asked. "Everything okay?"

"Calm as can be," she said. "My patient is stable and cozy and I'm enjoying the view, safely roped in on a ridge a couple hundred yards from the summit."

"Who is with you?"

"Danny, Sheri and Ryan. The National Guard is sending over a helicopter at first light to airlift our patient. Then we'll have to hike down."

"I don't want to frighten you," Jake said. "But we think Charlie Cutler may be headed your way."

Her breath caught at the name she hadn't expected to

hear. "He's supposed to be in Utah," she said. "He's supposed to be in custody by now."

"The man the FBI thought was Cutler turned out to be his cousin. Someone stole a snowmobile and some climbing gear this evening. We think it was Cutler, and he's headed your way."

"How would he know where to find me?" The idea was incredible—and horrifying.

"I think he probably listened in on a scanner," he said. "One of the cabins he broke into probably had one—some of those emergency radios with weather bands have police bands, too."

"I can't believe this is happening."

"I'm going to call Tony and tell him, but I wanted you to hear it from me first. I'm on my way across the saddle between Peak 14 and Mount Baker. I don't think I'm that far behind Cutler."

"Jake, you can't make that climb by yourself! Especially not in the dark."

"It's actually really bright up here, with the full moon, and I'm not by myself. I have a very experienced guide with me."

Something in his voice made the hairs on the back of her neck stand up. "Who?"

"Your dad. He's the most experienced climber I know and he insisted on coming with me."

"Nooooo," she moaned.

"I have to go now. Let the others know what's going on. If you know Cutler is coming, he won't be able to sneak up on you. And he's always avoided groups before, so you have that in your favor."

"Jake?"

"I'm still here."

"Promise me you'll be careful. I... I don't want anything to happen to you."

"I'll be careful. You, too. Remember I love you."

The call ended before she could reply. Her heart pounded, his words echoing over and over. *Remember I love you.*

"I love you, too," she said, then keyed the mic button of her radio. SAR trained for all kinds of situations so that they'd be prepared in the case of a real emergency. But having a serial murderer headed toward you through the darkness wasn't the kind of thing anyone could prepare for.

THE MOON ON the snow was so bright Thad declared they didn't need their headlamps. "That will make us a little less obvious if Cutler does look over his shoulder," he said, as he double-checked Jake's harness. "Though if we were doing this like the 10th Mountain Division in World War II, we'd dress all in white. Then we'd be invisible against the snow."

"Let's hope Cutler didn't think of that," Jake said. Though the murderer had supposedly gone through the same training that had been developed for the original Tenth Mountain Division troops in World War II, he didn't think Cutler had access to winter camouflage.

"White's not a popular color for outdoor gear," Thad said. "People want to be visible, so it's unlikely he found any to steal." He tugged on their lines. "I'll lead the way. We won't hurry. Follow in my footsteps. If you fall, self-arrest with your ice ax like I showed you."

Jake's stomach heaved at the thought of falling, but he merely nodded, and followed Thad out onto the icy ridge between the two mountain peaks. The first few yards were much like walking any icy trail, and Jake gained confidence as his crampons bit into the rough surface of the ice. But as they progressed farther, the trail narrowed to less than a foot wide, the ice whipped into rough peaks by the wind, so that every step was at an angle. He stared down at his feet and gripped the ice ax in his right hand, suddenly fearful of dropping it and seeing it spin out into the void on either side of the trail.

"Breathe." Thad's voice drifted to him, soft and clear. "This looks a lot scarier than it is."

Jake nodded and tried to do as instructed, though his breath caught in his throat, his lungs refusing to completely fill.

"I think you were right and someone is ahead of us," Thad said, again speaking softly. "There are fresh tracks."

"Can you see him?"

"No. The terrain is pretty uneven. Don't worry about him right now. Worry about getting across this middle section. It's the trickiest."

Jake decided that no one who wasn't desperate or had a death wish would voluntarily cross that icy ridge. The rough, crusty surface crumbled at every step, and he felt his ankle wrench as he flailed to keep his balance. "Easy," Thad called back to him.

When Jake felt steady again, he looked ahead to find the older man regarding him calmly. "You're doing great," Thad said. "Come to one of my clinics at the ice festival and I'll show you some really exciting stuff."

"This is excitement enough for me," Jake said. Movement beyond Thad's shoulder caught his attention. "Down!" he hissed, and crouched low. The small, dark figure was at least a hundred yards ahead, moving swiftly across the ridge. So far, he didn't appear to have noticed his two pursuers.

"I don't think he's seen us," Thad whispered.

Jake shook his head. He squinted, trying to bring Cutler's figure into sharper focus. He didn't see the outline of a rifle. Did that mean Cutler had, indeed, left that weapon behind? He wouldn't go unarmed, but he had stolen a handgun from one of the houses on County Road 11, so maybe he had that with him. "We need to get closer." Close enough to be within shooting range of Cutler. Jake would give the man a chance to surrender, but he wouldn't let him get within striking distance of Hannah and her friends. Cutler had proved he was ruthless—Jake would be just as ruthless.

Chapter Sixteen

"What are we supposed to do—just sit here waiting for this maniac to take us out?" Even over the radio Hannah could hear the tremor in Sheri's voice.

"Is there somewhere up there you can take cover?" Hannah asked. "Behind some rocks? Anywhere you're less visible?"

"We're already in a kind of niche between some boulders," Ryan said. "We settled in here to be out of the wind."

"Then stay there," Hannah said.

"What about you?" Danny asked.

"He's not going to see me down here," Hannah said.

"All he has to do is follow all the ropes," Danny said. "You should come up here with us."

"I'm not going to leave Jeremy." The idea of leaving this seriously wounded man to whatever Cutler decided to do, while she ran and hid, appalled her.

"He's stable and sleeping, right?" Danny said. "He won't even know you're gone."

"I'll know I left him," she said. "And I won't do it. Besides, his pain meds are going to wear off in the next hour or so and I'll need to give him more."

"I'll come down and stay with him then," Danny said.

"Cutler doesn't give a rip about me. You're the one he's fixated on."

"No." She couldn't shake the idea that giving up her post here would put the others in more danger. She didn't want Cutler to find them first and take his anger and frustration out on them.

"What have we got that we can use as a weapon?" she heard Sheri ask in the background.

"Rocks," Ryan said. "Rope. Hey, I have a grappling hook. That would make a good weapon."

"Not against a gun," Danny said.

"If we see him first and take him out we'll be fine," Ryan said, with more bravado than Hannah could have managed.

"We need to stop talking, in case he hears us," she said. "You know how sound carries up here."

"What is Jake doing about this?" Danny asked.

"He and my father are hiking over across the saddle," she said.

"Are they out of their minds?"

"Dad thinks they can do it safely."

"Maybe twenty years ago. Thad isn't a kid anymore."

"Don't tell him that. He'll say he can still outclimb you any day of the week."

"He'd be right," Danny said. "But I'm not much of a climber. And Jake isn't a climber at all, so what's he doing risking his life that way?"

"You'll have to ask him when he gets to you." Jake and her dad would reach the others, she told herself. She wasn't going to entertain any other possibility. She signed off and checked her watch. Three fifteen. Another three hours before the beginning of sunrise. How long after that before the helicopter could be here?

And how long until Charlie Cutler arrived?

"Is something wrong?"

The question, from Jeremy, surprised her. "Hey." She knelt beside him. "How are you feeling?"

"Hurting again." He licked dry lips and she found the water bladder she'd placed under the blankets to keep it from freezing and directed the bite valve to his mouth.

"I can give you another shot in about forty-five minutes," she said. "Can you hang on until then?"

"Yeah." He frowned. "I heard you on the radio. What's wrong?"

How much to tell him? There was nothing he could do to help. "We're just coordinating personnel movement," she said. "Your ride to the hospital should be here in another four hours or so."

"You people are amazing," he said. "I've never seen anything like it."

"You're pretty amazing yourself," she said. "A lot of people wouldn't have survived the fall you took."

"Where's Vick?"

"We sent him down with the rest of the crew. He didn't want to leave you, but he was exhausted."

"He's the best. He kept me from panicking, and then talked to me while we waited for you guys to arrive. I don't know what I would have done if he hadn't been there." He laughed, which turned into a cough. "I'd probably be still lying here, freezing to death," he said.

Maybe. Or he might have hung on until morning, when someone missed him and called for help. In her short time with Search and Rescue, she had seen some miracles. She had also seen people who didn't make it. That was the part she hadn't considered when she signed on with the group—that there were days and weeks where the job was more body retrieval than life saving. She always reminded herself during those times that those bodies were important to their families, so what they were doing was also important, if not nearly as satisfying.

"You must be tired yourself," Jeremy said.

Physically, she could feel exhaustion pulling at her, a heavy weight around her shoulders and ankles. But she was far too keyed up to let sleep overtake her. Especially after that phone call from Jake. "Tell me about skiing down mountains like this," she said. "Have you done it before?"

"I've skied this mountain before," he said. "Two years ago. Everything went perfect that time."

"Have you been hurt before?"

"Never. I guess I was overdue for my luck to run out."

"Do you think you'll do it again?"

"Ask me again in a few months. Or ask my wife. I guess I wouldn't blame her if she insisted I stick to lift-served terrain from now on." His voice grew thick. "She's pregnant, with our second child. Maybe it's past time I started playing it a little safer."

They talked about his little boy, his job as a systems analyst, his wife and how they met. He was in a mood to talk, and Hannah didn't mind listening, though one ear was always attuned for other sounds—the scrape of a boot on rock, the rattle of debris raining down from above. The stealthy approach of someone who shouldn't be up here.

At four o'clock she administered another injection of morphine and Jeremy drifted off. She checked the vacuum mattress and adjusted his blankets, then settled back, one hand wrapped around the syringe in her pocket, the empty hypodermic needle the only weapon at her disposal. If Cutler was set on slitting her throat, as he had his other victims, she was determined to fight back.

JAKE SPENT LESS time focused on his feet now, and more time watching for glimpses of Cutler ahead of them. "He's moving really fast," he said.

"Faster than I'm comfortable going," Thad said. "We're going to catch up with him soon enough."

What would they find when they did?

They had progressed only a few feet farther before Thad pitched forward. The sudden hard tug of the rope that linked them made Jake stagger, and brace against the strain. He stared as Thad grappled at the slope with his ice ax. "What can I do to help?" Jake called.

"Just...stand there. Don't move."

A few moments later, Thad staggered to his feet beside Jake. "Are you okay?" Jake gripped the older man by the shoulders.

Thad nodded, breathing hard. "It's good to know I still know how to do that," he said after a moment.

"What happened?" Jake asked.

"I think our friend up there knows we're following him after all."

"Why do you say that?"

Thad switched on his headlamp and turned to train the light down on an abrupt dip in the trail. "I think he hacked out a section of the trail," he said. "I didn't notice in time and slipped. Probably took a year or two off my life, but I'll be okay."

"Can we get around it?" Jake asked.

"Just step carefully. We'll be fine. But be on the lookout for other booby traps."

They found the second trap fifty yards farther on—a

slick sheet of ice four feet across, glinting in the moon-light. "He must have dumped all the water he had down here," Thad said.

They traversed this section on hands and knees, cram-pons and ice axes providing traction. "How much farther to the summit of the mountain?" Jake asked when they were upright again.

"That's it up there." Thad pointed ahead, to an uplift of bare rock that reminded Jake of a broken shark's tooth.

"How long will it take us to get there?" Jake asked.

"Half an hour. Maybe forty-five minutes?"

"How far ahead of us is Cutler?"

Thad looked ahead at the dark figure that slipped in and out of view. "I'd say he's almost there," he said. "Then he'll have to climb down to the SAR team. Didn't you say they're a couple hundred yards below the sum-mit?"

"Yes."

Thad nodded. "The down climb will take more time. We'll get closer to him then, maybe catch him in mid-climb, when he's more vulnerable."

It was hard to think of Cutler as being vulnerable. Since his escape he had assumed mythic proportions. *He's just a man*, Jake reminded himself. *He's made mis-takes before, and been caught. He can be caught again.*

Jake only hoped no one else died before Cutler was back in custody.

SOMEONE WAS MOVING around above. The crunch of cram-pons on ice was faint but clear in the still air. Careful not to tangle her safety line, Hannah levered herself up on hands and knees and climbed over the litter and pressed herself into a narrow space between the litter and the mountain, the chill of the bare rock seeping through the layers of her clothing like an icy finger tracing her spine. She waited, holding her breath, ears straining. The silence was so complete she might have believed she had suddenly lost her hearing.

Suddenly, a scream rent the air, and sounds of struggle. Heart in her throat, Hannah strained her ears to make out what was happening. Her radio crackled and she groped for the transmit button in the dark. "What's happening?" she whispered.

"He's here," Sheri gasped. "He got Ryan. Oh God, Hannah, I'm sorry."

The radio went dead. "Sheri! Sheri!" Hannah tried again and again to raise her friend, but the only reply was ominous silence.

Chapter Seventeen

"Help! Oh God, please help!" At first Jake thought the woman who slammed into him was Hannah, but when he was able to pull back enough to look at her, he realized it was her fellow SAR member, Sheri.

"It's okay," he said. "You're okay."

"Sheri, what's happened?" Thad asked.

She looked from one man to the next, her eyes growing a little less glazed. "Charlie Cutler's here," she said. "We'd been watching for him. Listening for him. We were hiding and didn't think he could sneak up on us, but he did." Her words became more rushed, her voice higher pitched. "He came out of nowhere, and he had a knife. He slashed at Ryan and Danny and just…just *shoved* them off the mountain. They were clipped into safety lines, which should have saved them, but Cutler looked right at me, then he…he…" She shook her head, the words choked off by sobs.

Thad pulled her close and held her. "It's all right," he said. "You don't have to tell us."

But she did. Jake needed to know everything Cutler had done since his arrival on the mountaintop. "What did he do?" he asked, keeping his voice gentle.

"He cut the safety lines," she said. "He just bent down

and cut the lines, then kicked the ropes over the side. He was watching me the whole time he did so and I'll never, ever forget the evil in his eyes." She buried her face against Thad again.

"Did he hurt you?" Jake asked.

She shook her head. "He took a step toward me and I ran. I didn't look where I was going or anything. I just unclipped my own safety line and ran. I remembered Hannah had said you and her dad were headed this way, so I ran this direction."

"Cutler let you go," Jake said. If the killer had wanted Sheri dead, Jake was sure Cutler would have followed her. "He wants us to know for sure that he's here."

"I tried to warn Hannah," Sheri said. "I radioed her but then I dropped the radio. She's down there on that ledge with Jeremy, who's too injured to do anything to protect her. Oh God, Cutler will probably kill him, too." She began sobbing again.

Jake patted her shoulder. "Stay with her, Thad," he said.

"What are you going to do?" Thad asked.

"I'm going to try to stop him." He drew his pistol. "Where is Hannah, exactly?" he asked Sheri.

She raised herself and sniffed, pulling herself together. "You'll see the ropes we rigged, and a pile of gear and stuff. She's over the edge on a ledge maybe a hundred feet down."

"There's nothing to stop Cutler from picking her off with a gun," Thad said, his voice strained.

"He's never shot any of his victims," Jake said. "He's used a knife on all his other victims." He would try that with Hannah, too, but to do that he had to get close to her. He'd have to climb down that ledge. But he wouldn't make it to her if Jake had anything to say about it.

"DON'T THINK YOU can hide from me. I know you're down there." Hannah had never heard Cutler's voice before, but she knew it was him. He didn't sound anything like she expected. Instead of the deep, menacing growl she had given him in her imaginings, he had a higher pitched, pinched sort of voice.

"I've been looking forward to meeting you," he said when she didn't answer. "I can't wait." He chuckled and she closed her eyes, willing herself not to be sick. She gripped the syringe more tightly in her hand, wishing she had thought to fill it with a very large dose of morphine. Enough to knock him out. That was completely against regulations, but surely she could be forgiven.

She stifled a gasp of hysterical laughter. How absurd to be thinking about licensing regulations at a time like this.

"I hear you," Cutler said. "Are you laughing or crying? It doesn't matter. I'm coming down. But first, I need to get rid of a few obstacles." A few seconds later a length of rope slid down, pooling on the litter where Jeremy lay, snoring lightly. A second coil of rope followed. "There," Cutler called. "You won't need those safety lines anymore."

A shower of rock followed, then a boot appeared, and Cutler was climbing down another length of rope with the ease of someone moving down a stepladder. She shrank further into the shadows, aware she was trapped, hemmed in on one side by a wall of rock and on the other by the litter, and beyond that the fall into a deep gorge, from which her body might never be recovered.

Cutler smiled at her, an expression that sent a shiver through her, his eyes so lacking in warmth, so distant even as he stared right at her. She turned her head, not wanting to see those eyes anymore. "Just give me a minute," he said. "Let me make a little more room." He bent down and shoved at the litter.

"No!" she shouted, realizing he intended to push Jeremy off the ledge.

Cutler straightened and turned to her once more. "She speaks." Again, the awful smile.

"Don't hurt him," she said. "I… I'll cooperate with you, but don't hurt him."

"You will cooperate," he said. "You won't have any choice. But if you like, I'll leave your patient for later." He beckoned. "Come here."

"How did you get here?" she asked. "How did you know I'd be here?" She didn't care about the answer; she only wanted to keep him talking. Jake was on the way. All she had to do was keep Cutler talking, keep him focused on her, until help arrived.

"I listened to the scanner," he said. "Once I knew your location, I made sure I had what I needed to get up here."

"You've been stealing from summer cabins and the ski huts," she said.

"People are very careless with their belongings," he said. "And far too trusting. A couple of those cabins didn't even have locks on the doors."

"You left that bandanna on my car," she said. "And the candy wrapper."

"I wanted you to know I was thinking about you. Were you frightened?"

Did he want her to be frightened? Would saying no enrage him? "I was frightened," she admitted.

"Come here," he said, his voice more forceful now.

She looked down. There was nowhere else to place her feet.

"Step on him. It won't matter to him after a moment."

She wasn't going to step on a man with a broken leg. Instead, she stepped on the edge of the litter, closer to Cutler, but still out of his reach.

"We need more room," Cutler said. He bent and grasped the side of the litter again.

"No!" She screamed the word, which echoed across the canyon below.

"Cutler! Freeze!"

Her heart lurched as she recognized the voice behind the command. Cutler looked up. "Go away, Deputy," he said, the calmness with which he spoke chilling. "Unless you want to see this woman die."

"I have a gun trained on you," Jake said. "Make a move and I'll kill you."

"And risk putting a bullet in an already injured man? Or in Hannah?" He lunged and grabbed her wrist and yanked her forward with such force she might have been a rag doll pulled along by a child. He wrapped a powerful arm around her and held her to his chest.

"Let her go!" Jake sounded more desperate than forceful now.

Something stung Hannah's neck and she closed her eyes, realizing she was feeling the very sharp blade of a knife. A knife like the ones Cutler had used to slash the throats of his other victims. The knife he intended to use on her. She curled her hand around the syringe in her pocket, which she had not let go of since this ordeal began. If she stabbed Cutler with it now would he use the knife on her? And how would she get one small-gauge needle through the layer of winter clothing he wore? She sagged, her knees suddenly jelly.

"Don't faint on me," Cutler said, hauling her upright against him. "It's so much better if you're awake for the whole process."

Process? He thought of murder as a process? The rage this idea engendered banished her weakness.

"Are you still there, Deputy?" Cutler called.

No answer. Cutler hugged Hannah more tightly. "I guess he left," he said. "I can't see him anymore. Looks like it's just you and me." She shivered as his lips brushed the side of her cheek.

"Cutler!" Jake's shout echoed across the canyon. Cutler jerked his head up as a heavy grappling hook hurtled toward him. He tried to dodge the missile, and brought the hand that held the knife up to shield his face. He still held Hannah, but his grip loosened enough for her to half turn in his arm, and bring the needle up, burying it in his eye.

With a cry of rage he released her. The grappling hook caught him in the shoulder, snagged in the fabric of his parka and held. Hannah grabbed hold of the rope Cutler had climbed down on and began to haul herself up, even as Cutler tried to drag her back.

A shot rang out and Cutler roared again, but released her. Then Jake was pulling her up, into his arms. He held her tightly with his free hand, the other still holding the pistol. "Are you all right?" he asked.

"Yes." She nodded. "But we have to get Cutler away from Jeremy. He was trying to push the litter off the ledge."

Thad and Sheri ran up to join them. Jake indicated the rope the grappling hook was attached to. "Hold on to that and don't let go," he said. He holstered the pistol and picked up the rope Hannah had climbed up.

"What are you going to do?" she asked.

"I'm going to arrest Cutler."

"Jake, no!" But he was already climbing down.

JAKE KNEW THAT Cutler was pinned by a grappling hook in the shoulder, with a gunshot wound in the other shoulder. And he had a hypodermic needle in one eye. The combination ought to have disabled him enough for Jake to get handcuffs on him, but he knew better than to count on it. If he had been able to choose, he would have waited for help to arrive before confronting the murderer, but Hannah's insistence that Cutler wanted to push the litter with Jeremy Prather aboard into the canyon forced him to take action.

His boots touched the ledge, but he held on to the rope until he was standing steady and had his bearings. The light of his headlamp illuminated Cutler, crouched against the rock less than five feet away, clutching his shoulder, blood staining his parka. He had managed to remove the hypodermic from his eye, and free himself from the grappling hook, which hung between them, the sharp, curved tines of the hook hanging at eye level, menacing.

Jake stared at the hook, fear climbing his throat. He forced his gaze away and met Cutler's eyes, shining in the beam of his head lamp. "You're no match for me, Deputy," Cutler said, the nasal whine of his voice like fingernails on a chalkboard.

Jake didn't answer, but raised the gun. "Don't move or I'll shoot."

Cutler sprang to his feet and lunged for the hook as

Jake fired, but the shot went wild, the bullet flying out into the emptiness over Cutler's right shoulder. Cutler clawed at the hook and Jake dropped the gun and grabbed hold of one curved prong with both hands as it swung toward him. He staggered as Cutler pulled back on the hook, and had the terrifying sensation of one foot struggling to find purchase in thin air.

"One shove and goodbye, Deputy," Cutler said.

Jake kicked out, hard, and caught Cutler square in the chest, sending him staggering back. While Cutler struggled to regain his balance, Jake crouched and retrieved the gun. He trained it on Cutler, one hand holding the weapon steady, the other clutching the grappling hook. "Don't move," he said. "You're under arrest."

Cutler's eyes were wild with fury. Jake was sure the other man would rush him again, and tightened his grip on both the pistol and the hook. But Cutler turned, not toward Jake, but away, and just as Jake pulled the trigger Cutler leaped off the ledge. He disappeared without a sound, but the thud of his body hitting the rocks below was unmistakable, and sickening.

Jake's legs gave way and he sat, his back against the rock, and stared at the man in the litter in front of him. Jeremy Prather opened his eyes. "Who are you?" he asked.

"Nobody important," Jake said, and closed his eyes. He was suddenly very tired, and determined to wait here and not move until someone else arrived to take charge.

"Jake!"

Hannah's voice roused him. "Jake, are you all right?"

He struggled to his feet, realized he was still holding

his pistol, and shoved it back into the holster. "I'm fine," he said. "And Mr. Prather is fine."

"What happened to Cutler?" This question was from Thad.

Jake swallowed. "He jumped." The sound of Cutler's body hitting the rocks would haunt him for the rest of his life.

"I should come down and check on Jeremy," Hannah said.

"Come down, then."

"We need to set new safety lines," Sheri said. "Jake, you need to help Hannah with the ropes. She'll show you what to do."

Later, he would try to come to terms with what had just happened, but for now it helped having something to focus on that required his full attention. They fixed the new safety lines, Hannah checked her patient, who was fine, then Jake and Hannah embraced. They didn't say anything for a very long time, just held each other. He breathed in the scent of her hair and tried to memorize this sensation of her in his arms.

They could have stood that way for hours, but screaming from above startled them apart. "Sheri!" Hannah called. "Sheri, what's wrong?"

"It's Danny! He's alive!"

Jake and Hannah scrambled up to the others, to find Danny, obviously battered but standing upright, with one arm around Sheri. "He just came climbing up the backside of the ridge," Sheri said, tears streaking her face.

"What happened?" Hannah asked.

The others filled her in on Cutler's earlier attack, relating how he had shoved Danny and Ryan off the mountain and cut the safety lines. "I landed hard in a big snow-field," Danny said. "Had to swim my way out, then got pretty beat up on the rocks climbing back up. I was still attached to the other end of the rope he cut, so I managed to tie a rock around it and throw it around a jagged out-cropping and use that to help me climb up. I tried yell-ing but I guess everyone was so focused on Cutler they didn't hear me."

"Don't you ever say you're not a very good climber," Hannah said. "You're an amazing climber."

"But what happened to Ryan?" Sheri asked.

The question cast a pall over their celebration. "I don't know," Danny said. "I called for him and looked around the snowfield where I landed, but he wasn't there."

"We'll have to look for him as soon as it's light," Han-nah said.

"When the helicopter flies in for Jeremy, we'll ask them to look," Danny said, his expression grim. "Maybe they'll be able to spot him from the air." He didn't say "spot his body" though Jake thought that was what they were all thinking.

"What time is it?" Hannah asked.

But before anyone could answer, a phone rang. Sheri pulled out her cell phone. "Hello, Tony," she said. "You're missing all the excitement."

She listened a few moments. "Okay," she said. "We'll be ready." She ended the call and tucked the phone away. "The helicopter is on the way," she said. "ETA thirty minutes."

"You didn't tell Tony about Ryan," Hannah said.

"It didn't seem like the kind of thing to mention on the phone."

"Come on." Danny put a hand on each of the women's shoulders. "We've got work to do."

"Anything I can do to help?" Jake asked.

"No offense," Danny said. "But stay out of the way. I'm not being rude. When that Blackhawk lowers that cable it's the most dangerous part of the whole operation. That thing can take a man's head off."

They heard the helicopter long before they saw it. It came at them from the west, a speck the size of a fly hovering in the distance and gradually growing larger, the sound of its rotor rising to a roar so that they had to shout to be heard. Jake did as instructed and remained well out of the way on the summit, watching as Hannah, Sheri and Danny maneuvered the cable and attached a tag line, dodging the menacing hook and fastening the litter with a finesse he was sure looked much easier than it actually was.

The helicopter lifted up and away from the mountain, and the litter rose up into the belly of the aircraft, then the chopper swung away, headed east. "While I was in radio contact, I asked them to look for Ryan," Hannah said.

No one said anything for a long ten minutes as they contemplated the potential loss of their fellow volunteer, or perhaps the ordeal that had just passed. Then Sheri's phone rang again. "Hello?"

She jumped up, her face transformed. "They spotted Ryan!" she shouted. "And he's alive. Hurt, but alive." She listened again. "Yes, sir, but…yes, sir." She hung up the phone. "There's a fresh squad coming up to handle Ryan's rescue. Jeremy is stable, so the Blackhawk is going to hang around to help."

"What do we do now?" Jake asked.

"We collect our gear and head back down," Hannah

said. She looked to Danny. "Are you okay to make it down? I noticed you're favoring your ankle."

"I'll be fine," he said, and began coiling rope.

Twenty minutes later they had almost everything packed up when Sheriff Travis Walker, Deputy Jamie Douglas and Deputy Shane Ellis reached the summit. Travis looked them over. "Everybody okay?" he asked.

"Yes, sir," Jake said. "Everyone but Cutler."

"What happened to him?"

"He jumped. I guess he was serious about never going back to jail."

Travis shook his head, but said nothing else. Jake would provide a full report later. Sheri explained they were expecting another rescue squad to arrive shortly to set about taking care of Ryan, and the sheriff and his deputies agreed to stay until the new rescuers arrived, in case they could be of assistance.

Then Sheri, Thad, Hannah, Danny and Jake started down, moving slowly, carefully. No one spoke for a long time, then Sheri tilted her head to the sun. "I feel like I should go to church and light a candle," she said. "I've never seen so many miracles in one day."

"We should have a new motto," Danny said. "Eagle Mountain Search and Rescue—Miracles at No Extra Charge."

Hannah looked over her shoulder and smiled at Jake, and suddenly, he didn't feel as tired and sore. Maybe finding her hadn't been a miracle, but it had been an unexpected blessing, one he would never take for granted.

Epilogue

Ryan hadn't fared as well as Danny in his plummet from the mountain, having broken his ankle and his shoulder in the fall. But the second rescue squad got to him quickly and was able to effect a second lift with the Blackhawk, which carried its double load of the wounded to a trauma center in Salt Lake.

Search and Rescue conducted a third mission near Mount Baker three days later, to retrieve the body of Charlie Cutler, which had been located in a ravine on the mountain's west side. Austen and Ted rappelled into the ravine and secured the body to the hoist of a helicopter that lifted it out. Hannah was just as glad to be spared that duty. Instead, she received a call from Vick Balin, who told her Jeremy had undergone surgery to put a metal bar in his leg, was healing well and expected to make a full recovery. "You people were angels up there," Vick said. "Absolute angels."

"It was an amazing experience for all of us," she said, and Vick didn't know even half the story. Danny and Ryan surviving being tossed off the summit of Mount Baker would go down as a SAR legend, and already the bad jokes were circulating about not trusting Hannah with a syringe.

Word was that Jake was in line for a commendation for his bravery on the summit, though he modestly dismissed the idea. "The SAR volunteers were the true heroes that day," he said. "And Thad Richards. I never would have made it across that ridge without him."

When told he would receive a commendation, too, Hannah's father was speechless. The reporter had chosen that moment to take his picture, and this newspaper clipping had been added to the wall beside the checkout desk at the Alpiner Inn, along with the image of Hannah riding the stretcher out of the icy gorge. The picture showed Thad standing between Hannah and Jake, an arm around each of them, looking a little stunned.

Even though Jake dismissed the commendation as "no big deal," Hannah insisted they celebrate, so he took her to dinner at a new steakhouse in town, situated in a new building that had been made to look old, which featured lots of antiques on the walls and a bar full of exotic whiskey. "I hope the steaks are as good as they seem to think they are," Jake said after studying the menu.

Hannah laughed. "They have homemade pie, too. You deserve a splurge, don't you?" she asked.

"I know you do, and that's good enough for me." He set aside the menu, avoiding her eyes. He'd been acting a little distant all evening, and it was beginning to ruin her appetite.

"Is something wrong?" she asked. "You've been acting strange all evening."

He picked up his fork and turned it over. "Nothing's wrong, exactly," he said.

She swallowed, and tried to steel herself against whatever was coming. The expression on his face didn't portend anything good. "What is it?"

"I got a call from Colorado State Patrol today," he said. "They offered me a job."

She caught her breath. "That's good news, isn't it? Isn't that what you wanted?" Her voice broke and she blinked rapidly, but not fast enough to hold back the tears.

"Hey." He leaned over and took her hand. "What's wrong?"

She shook her head, then picked up her napkin and dabbed at her eyes, noting the black streaks of mascara on the white linen. "I don't want you to leave."

"Who said anything about leaving? I'm not going anywhere."

She looked up, stunned. "You turned them down? Jake—"

"I told them I'd only take the job if I could stay in Eagle Mountain."

"Why is that?" she asked.

"Because this place feels like home. I have friends here. I have an apartment I like, and I have Gus." He squeezed her hand. "I have you."

"But that was your dream job," she said.

"It's still my dream job." He shook out his napkin and spread it in his lap. "I start next month. The reason they offered me the job was because they want another officer on this side of Dixon Pass. One of the supervisors saw an article about what happened on Mount Baker and thought I was a good candidate for the job, familiar with the locals and the country around here." He grinned. "I didn't bother mentioning I've only lived here three months."

She laughed, as much from relief as amusement. "You've made the most of those three months," she said. "Making all those friends and adopting a dog. Finding that great apartment."

"Finding you," he said. "All of that other stuff I could replace, not you."

"Gus is irreplaceable," she chided. Now that he'd had some training, Gus was shaping up to be a great dog. Jake was even talking about teaching him search and rescue work.

"Okay, maybe that's true. But you're the reason Eagle Mountain is home for me now." He brought her hand to his lips and kissed it. "I love you, Hannah," he said. "Everything that happened on Mount Baker just made me realize how much."

"I love you, too, Jake." She stood and leaned across the table and kissed him.

That was how the server found them, clinging to each other over the table. He cleared his throat and they sheepishly pulled apart. "Something to celebrate?"

"We have a lot to celebrate," Hannah said. A whole future of adventures together, and a chance to fall even more deeply in love.

* * * * *

SMALL TOWN VANISHING

NICOLE HELM

To anyone who preserves the history of extraordinary ordinary people in all the small, weird ways.

Chapter One

Kate Phillips was no stranger to being alone. When your father disappeared the same day as your sixteen-year-old friend, an entire town who had once treated you like a cute eccentric could decide you were pariah by association.

Her mother hadn't helped. Marjorie Phillips had blamed *everyone* in the town of Wilde, Wyoming, for the disappearance of her husband—in dramatic, screaming theatrics for a decade now.

Which, yet again, made Kate guilty by association. Or at least, someone to avoid.

Kate could have withstood that, she was certain, if she hadn't lost her best friends in the process. The problem was that Kate's only friends growing up had been the Hart triplets. Different though they were, the four of them had been an inseparable group. Constantly in each other's pockets.

Then Amberleigh had disappeared the same day as Dad, and Hazeleigh and Zara had treated her differently ever since. Hazeleigh had slowly come around. Hard not to when both Kate and Hazeleigh worked at the Fort Dry Historic Site, Wilde's historical landmark. Hazeleigh doing research for the supervisor at the fort, Mr. Field, and Kate as a living history interpreter and tour guide.

But Zara had *not* come around. Pointedly so.

So, Kate's life had come down to two things: her angry

mother and her job. At least Kate loved the job. She knew Wildeans tended to pity her when they weren't suspicious of her, but this job was the one thing that felt...normal in a life that had changed a decade ago.

Normal to be alone, doing some work dressing mannequins, the day after Christmas. In a drafty old historical building that likely wouldn't have visitors until the summer months.

Still, she liked to change out the displays. Focus on the past, rather than her present.

Mr. Field was in his office, so she wasn't *totally* alone. He might shut himself up in there and not say two words to her, but that was still more companionship than she had in her small attic room with Mom. Mostly, despite living in the same sprawling house, their paths rarely crossed. Mom's choice. Insistence, really.

It was for the best. Kate had been happier since they'd nonverbally agreed to keep their distance—as long as Kate did all the errands and everything that was expected of her. But happier didn't negate the loneliness. She'd get some kind of animal if she weren't allergic, but everything hypoallergenic gave her the creeps.

Kate sighed. She could do lonely. She was *good* at lonely. But lonely at Christmas—a holiday Mom hadn't celebrated in ten years—was a different kind, a deeper kind of lonesome, and she couldn't wait for the calendar to switch over to the new year. Put the ten-year anniversary behind her.

She heard the door squeak open and finished tying the apron on the mannequin, telling herself not to run to see who the visitor was like a desperately sad inmate.

"Did you hear?" came Hazeleigh's voice, a few seconds before she appeared—all pastel layers and wild curly brown hair. "They found Eli Mayfield."

"Really?" The missing boy had disappeared from Wilde some time the night of Christmas Eve, at least that's what Kate had read in the paper. According to the sporadically updated town Facebook page, the police had begun to get desperate last night due to the frigid temperatures and the boy's young age, and Kate had been reminded of all the awful ways a disappearance could strangle just about everyone in town.

"Safe, and sound, and not a moment too soon," Hazeleigh continued, unwinding a fluffy pink scarf she no doubt had knitted herself. "The doctors are saying he could have been dead from exposure if he'd been out there another few hours."

"Thank goodness." Kate meant it, though she wasn't sure she sounded as relieved as she should have. A seven-year-old didn't deserve to just disappear, or worse. But Kate couldn't help but think of her own father. Dead? Alive? Gone on purpose? Gone against his will?

It had been ten years, and she knew she should move on. Give up. Wasn't that what her mother always told her? But Kate never could bring herself to.

And finding out last week that it was very possible Amberleigh's same-day disappearance had very little to do with her father brought up new questions.

"How…how was he found?" Kate asked, trying to find the right way to handle this. She was *relieved* the young boy had been found. Not jealous someone had been found when her father hadn't.

"It was Jake's brother Brody who found him," Hazeleigh said. The six Thompson brothers had bought the Hart Ranch and had been working it for the past almost two months. Kate didn't know all of them by name, but she knew Jake as he'd been instrumental in helping get

Hazeleigh cleared of the murder charge that had been leveled against her.

December had been a busy month in Wilde.

"Jake was telling Zara that if something is lost, Brody's always the one to find it. I'm not sure how Brody managed, but apparently he was out all last night and found the boy. I'm so glad he did. Apparently poor Eli just got turned around trying to prove to his friend he could climb Mount Hopkins higher than anyone."

Kate nodded. "I suppose it's a relief to everyone he just wandered off." *Wasn't stolen. Wasn't like when Art Phillips went off with a* teenager.

"I'm going to go tell Mr. Field."

Kate nodded as Hazeleigh wafted over to Mr. Field's office. Kate looked at the mannequin she'd been dressing, but for once she wasn't thinking about the frontier. She was thinking about her *own* past.

Where something had been lost.

Jake was telling Zara that if something is lost, Brody's always the one to find it.

Well, maybe the mysterious Brody Thompson was someone she should get to know.

"It had to be done." Brody looked at Cal, scowling in the driver's seat. After spending a few hours with the police and a very grateful Mayfield family, Brody wanted quiet, something hot to eat and maybe a beer. But as many questions as the police might have asked him, he knew it was only a precursor to this.

Getting chewed out by his *brother*. "We're talking about a missing kid here."

"I know what we're talking about," Cal returned, his grip on the truck's steering wheel tight enough to make his knuckles white. "I just don't know how you all seem to expect me to be able to keep us here if you and Jake are constantly getting your name in the papers."

Because somehow Wilde, Wyoming, still depended on the local paper for its news. It was like stepping back in time, this new life Brody found himself in.

He was surprised to find he didn't hate it, and much like their *brother* Jake, Brody wanted to stay.

"You were part of the search, Cal," Brody reminded the man who'd once been his commanding officer, but these days had to pretend to be nothing more than his ranching brother.

Cal didn't do *blending in* as well as he thought he did. He also wasn't as hard as he fancied himself. Though he'd tried to keep it on the down low, Brody knew that Cal had stood up to the boss when Jake had found himself in some trouble.

Brody wasn't comfortable thinking about how much trouble Jake had gotten himself in, or how jumping in front of a bullet meant for Cal had almost cost him his life. Jake was alive, and the boss was off their backs.

Perhaps not now that Brody had gotten a little local notoriety—even if Wilde local meant about fifty people.

The issue was that Brody would have his name in the paper so closely after Jake's. No time for the town to get bored of the Thompson brothers. Which meant attention and perhaps poking into their pasts. Which was a no go.

Because the men of Team Breaker—who didn't exist anymore—were supposed to move to Wilde and disappear. Not make a name for themselves.

But it was a *kid*. "The boss is going to have to accept that anywhere we live, we're part of the community. It's ecosystems, plain and simple."

Cal grumbled some intelligible words but didn't otherwise mount an argument.

Who could argue against ecosystems?

Cal turned off on the gravel road that would take them to the ranch. Brody had been born and bred in the Chicago suburbs. He might have had more awareness of the existence of agriculture than his friends from New York City, but that didn't mean squat in the face of the reality of a ranch.

But he'd learned. He'd tackled the task of learning how to be a rancher like he'd taken to the task of becoming an army ranger. Ordinary didn't suffice for Brody Calhoun—Thompson these days. No, his parents had been so below ordinary and capable that Brody did everything in his power to stay as far above the pack as he could.

He was always the first to volunteer for whatever task their ranch hand, Zara Hart, had to teach them. It was winter, so the learning curve wasn't too steep. Come spring, they better know what they were doing.

Come hell or high water, Brody would know what he was doing. And exceptionally well.

They drove under the archway that still read Hart Ranch, though the Harts didn't own it anymore. Zara Hart had stayed on as ranch hand, and she and her sister Hazeleigh still lived in a cabin on ranch property, but the ranch was now the property of Team Breaker.

Known in Wilde as the Thompson brothers.

Cal drove the winding lane toward the house. Brody appreciated the Wyoming views. They were pretty, as grand and picturesque as everything he'd been told about the Wild West as a kid, but it was the house that did something to him.

Brody had grown up in apartments, spent months on the street when his dad had gone through a "rough patch" and Mom had disappeared. The big rambling house situated in the rolling hills, bracketed by far off mountains was…beyond a dream. Brody's dreams had been excellence in the military.

This was something else, and he still wasn't comfortable with the way that something else swelled inside him like a storm. A wild howling thing that would die if it ever got taken away.

Dramatic.

"Who the hell is that?" Cal grumbled as he pulled up to the house. A woman paced the big wraparound porch, something clasped in her hands.

Brody frowned. Something about her was familiar but he couldn't put his finger on it, so he and Cal got out of the truck at the same time and surveyed the woman from afar.

She stopped pacing, staring right back at them, but she neither approached nor offered a greeting until they walked up to the porch.

She stood on the top stair like she belonged there and was greeting strangers to her house. But when they both came to stop at the bottom of the stairs, she attempted a smile. It frayed around the edges.

"Hi."

Brody and Cal exchanged glances.

"I'm… K-kate. Kate Phillips? I work with Hazeleigh. Uh, the last time we met I was dressed up like a pioneer."

Brody knew laughing wasn't the polite thing to do, but it was a hard-won thing. She *had* been dressed like a pioneer at that crazy little fort where Hazeleigh worked. When Jake had begged him to go along with Zara and Hazeleigh to some living history Christmas thing, Brody had done it simply because Jake had been shot, and that and Christmas had softened Brody enough to agree.

This woman *had* been there, dressed up in pioneer clothes, lecturing the small group on Christmas in Wilde, Wyoming, something like centuries ago. He remembered finding himself a little interested against his will. Brody couldn't say he hated the way she'd been dressed either. There was something...endlessly interesting about all those layers and what they might be hiding underneath.

But Kate Phillips looked just as prim and pretty in jeans and a big puffer jacket standing on his porch.

Funny how it could feel like *his* porch.

"I brought cookies," she blurted out, shoving a plastic bag at him.

"For Jake?" Cal asked, clearly confused.

"Not exactly." She sucked in a deep breath, and she didn't look at Cal. She stared right at him, brown eyes deep and a little heartbreakingly desperate. "I have someone I need help finding."

Brody didn't wince, he'd been in the military too long to outwardly react. Besides, Cal reacted enough for the both of them.

"I'm sorry, that won't be possible."

Kate's entire expression fell, like a building taken out by an inside explosion. But she managed to stop the crumple right before it destroyed everything. She straightened her shoulders and looked at Cal coolly. "I wasn't asking you."

Cal was clearly taken aback by how quickly she'd changed from nervous stutter to cold put-down. It made Brody smile.

"Why don't you go on inside, Cal? I'll handle this."

"Yeah, I just bet you will." He glared at Kate. "Look, miss, you might be friends with Hazeleigh, but this isn't some—"

"Cal, it's only *neighborly* to hear her out. You go on inside. Think ecosystems."

Cal turned his glare on him, shook his head, but didn't say another word before stalking inside, the door slamming behind him.

Kate frowned after him. "He's charming."

Brody didn't say what he wanted—that she should see him supervising a deadly mission in the Middle East—because here he wasn't Brody Calhoun, army ranger, and Cal wasn't Cal Young, lead on a secret mission to take down a terrorist target.

They were just ranchers. From here on out.

So he smiled at Kate and went for sarcasm instead. "Devastatingly so." Brody studied the cookies in the bag she'd shoved at him. He'd been up all night looking for the Mayfield boy and he'd barely eaten. He pulled one from the bag. "Is someone missing?" Brody asked.

"In a manner of speaking. Hazeleigh said Zara said Jake said—"

"Maybe you shouldn't take everything you hear fourth-hand so seriously."

"Technically it was only third-hand."

He held up his fingers and put them down with every point. "Jake. Zara. Hazeleigh. You."

She mimicked his position. "Jake told Zara." She put down one finger. "Zara told Hazeleigh." Another finger. "Hazeleigh to me. That's three."

Brody laughed. He knew humoring this woman wasn't going to make his life any easier, but he couldn't help it. Someone needed help—and it had been seared into his bones to help where he could.

He was well aware of all the places he couldn't help.

He popped the cookie into his mouth. Good. No, not just good. Exceptional. "You can bake, Kate Phillips. Are these supposed to be a bribe?"

"Yes," she said solemnly. "Did they work?"

"We'll see. Why don't you come inside, and we'll talk it over where it's warm?"

She pulled the coat she wore tighter around her. "I'm fine out here."

"Cal won't bite. Promise."

"No, but Zara will."

"Uh, well…" Brody didn't know what to say to that. Zara might live in the cabin on the property, but ever since Jake had come home yesterday, Zara had been a constant presence in the house, repeatedly telling the *likes of them* that men were terrible at caring for the wounded.

No one had dared argue with her.

It was a strange phenomenon Brody hadn't fully worked out, considering the six of them had stood up to a lot worse than a mouthy ranch hand.

But Jake was in love with Zara, whatever that meant, and Jake was hurt, and…

Bottom line was Brody had gotten himself into enough hot water. Time to slow things down. "I'd like to help, but…"

"But you won't. Because of Zara."

"Listen—"

"No, I get it. Believe me," she said, pushing past him, "I get it."

It was the glimmer of tears in her eyes that just about killed him. Brody could withstand a lot of things. But he was a sucker for tears, even ones that didn't fall.

"You haven't even told me who's missing," he called after her.

She stopped at the little sedan that seemed so out of place in this harsh Wyoming winter. "My father disappeared ten years ago," she shot at him. "With Zara's sister, at least that was the rumor. That…speculation has been my life for ten years. Now we know Amberleigh Hart is dead, and she wasn't with my father. I want to find him, but if Queen Zara is in charge here, then—"

Brody heard the screen door squeak behind him, and he knew without looking Zara would be standing there. Just by the shocked, guilty, then back to furious expressions that stormed over Kate's pretty face.

"What am I queen of?"

Kate stood there for a moment, somehow looking both furious and deeply wounded at the same time before she got into her car and slammed the door. She didn't *peel* away, but she certainly drove off in a hurry.

"What was that about?" Brody asked, turning to face Zara.

Zara shrugged, her eyes on the retreating car. "Let me guess. She wants you to find her father."

"Yeah."

"You should."

"Huh?"

Zara blew out a breath. "Look, I don't know if I really believe her dad didn't have *anything* to do with Amberleigh's disappearance, but he didn't kill Amberleigh." Zara frowned at where Kate had disappeared. "Trying to find closure sucks, but Kate deserves some."

"I don't think I'm the one to give it to her."

Zara turned her dark gaze on him. "You find things, Brody." She smiled faintly. "That's your expertise, isn't it?"

He supposed it was, and the need to live up to it had him taking the address Zara gave him and following Kate home.

Chapter Two

It had been a long time since Kate had felt fully paranoid. That first year after everything had imploded she'd found herself looking around every corner, over her shoulder, constantly holding her breath and waiting for her father to step out of the shadows.

Her schoolwork had suffered, her *life* had suffered, but she'd made it through somehow. Mostly by focusing on taking care of her mother and spending whatever free time she had finding her father.

Eventually, as her job at the fort had begun to fulfill her, she'd let some of the search obsession fade away. She had a job and Mom still needed looking after. She'd tried to step away from the one giant mystery of her life.

But ever since Amberleigh's body had been found on the Hart Ranch a few weeks ago, Kate had felt like she had at sixteen.

Edgy. Paranoid. Desperate. She'd started poring over her old research. Trying to reconstruct what she knew. Trying to tell herself new leads might help her to...

She went into the market and picked up a few things Mom needed. Things *were* different, ever since the news of Amberleigh's death had spread. The stares were back. The whispers. And because Mom tended to yell, accuse and melt down when those things happened, everyone kept their distance.

No one asked how she was. No one...

She swallowed. She couldn't let the things that had happened this month change all the personal progress she'd made. She didn't *need* anyone in town to care about her. She had her job and her responsibilities. She had coworkers she could ask a favor of as long as Mr. Field wasn't busy and Hazeleigh didn't have to think too hard about why they'd grown apart in the first place.

Everything was *fine*. Who cared if people watched her get into her car? Who cared if Mom was likely to yell at her for being late when she got home? Who *cared?*

She had built walls around the hard things and given herself some good things and *that* was what she cared about. She drove down Main Street and then up the curving drive to the house that stood on the top of a hill, above the town like the Phillips were better than everyone.

The house, the grounds, none of it had been well taken care of since Dad left. They should have sold it before it had gotten this dilapidated, but Mom refused, and Kate only had so much access to money to accomplish repairs.

But the house stood, and it was something of a legacy. Wasn't that more than Zara and Hazeleigh had? Maybe they got to stay on the Hart Ranch, but it wasn't *theirs* anymore.

Kate just wished she could feel any kind of pride in her legacy.

She had to get these downer thoughts under control before she went inside though. Kate needed to build back the wall the past few weeks had crumbled.

She got out of her car, grabbing the overly-full grocery bag. It was too heavy a weight and she should probably switch it to one of the canvas bags she had in the back, but—

The bottom gave out, the cans hitting the driveway with a *clank, clank, clank*. Kate managed to catch a few before they fell, but a few went rolling down the driveway, gathering speed. Kate lurched to grab as many cans as she could and upend them so they didn't roll away. But one slipped through her grasp, picking up speed as it went, until it landed with a thud against the bottom of a boot.

A cowboy boot. She looked up, surprised to see Brody Thompson standing there. She hadn't seen his truck, hadn't heard him approach. She supposed because the truck was at the bottom of the drive. He'd walked up and...

"What are you doing here?"

He bent down and picked up the can from under his foot, then crossed to her and held it out. She took it, but she didn't know quite what to do with it.

His eyes tracked around the array of cans of soup on her driveway. Then he looked straight at her, something like...she wanted to call it pity, but it didn't *feel* like any pity she'd ever gotten, and boy, she'd gotten her share.

"I'll help you, if I can," he said quietly. Seriously.

She studied him for the longest time, trying to understand his change of heart. Trying to understand... But then it dawned on her. She was so pitiful even Zara—who *hated* her for what her father had supposedly done with Amberleigh—had given Brody the okay to help.

She wished she were too proud to take it, but she wasn't. Ten years in, she was still as desperate for answers as she'd always been. If she got answers—even if they were the bad kind—she could close that chapter of her life. Maybe leave Wilde. Maybe...

If she could find the answers, her life could finally change.

She glanced back at the house. Mom would not be okay with any of this. They couldn't have this conversation here.

Just because Zaza might have given Brody the okay did not mean Kate had to hang out at the Hart Ranch like she was a little girl again.

"Maybe we could talk about this at the fort? Tomorrow morning?"

He frowned a little, looked at the big, rambling but run-down house behind her. "Someone you're hiding from?"

How to explain? There was no easy answer.

"If it's a husband, or boyfriend, or whatever, I'd make sure to let him know—"

"A...boyfriend," she repeated. The word felt foreign. Like it belonged to a different universe. Certainly not one she was a part of.

Brody flashed her a grin, "If I lived with a pretty woman, I wouldn't want her hanging out with a strange man at some isolated fort."

Pretty...woman. She was truly and utterly speechless. *Pretty woman* said with that hint of some kind of regional accent she couldn't place. And that grin. Which she might have characterized as flirtatious if it were aimed at anyone else.

"I live with my mother."

He nodded, as if that was also an acceptable answer. "Yeah, I'm not popular with moms."

"She doesn't... She wouldn't like..." Kate blew out a breath. If she expected help, she needed to get a hold of herself. "I'd prefer to discuss all this away from her. It upsets her, understandably. Besides, I keep all my research in my office at the fort."

"Research?"

"I've been searching for my father for a decade. I have plenty of research."

Brody frowned at that. "It's been a long time. You've

done a lot of work. You have to know that even with my help, the chances of finding him are slim."

"I know. Believe me, plenty of people haven't been able to. I'm not expecting miracles. I just can't seem to…" She struggled to find the words. *Let go? Get over it? Move on?* "I just have to use whatever I can to try and solve this." And she had to focus on practicalities not the complex tangle of emotions battering her insides. "I can't really pay you, so if that's a deal-breaker—"

He gave the house a look, totally inscrutable. "I don't need payment. Except maybe in cookies. We'll just consider it a favor for a friend."

"I'm not your friend."

"Zara is…something like a friend, but mostly I mean Jake. He's all gaga over Zara, so…" Brody shrugged.

She wished she knew what that kind of loyal friendship was like, but that wasn't the point. "Tomorrow morning? Is eight all right?"

"Sure." He looked at the cans littered around them. "You need some help?"

Help. She wanted to laugh. When was the last time anyone had offered something like help? "No, I've got it."

BRODY DIDN'T TELL anyone what he was doing. He figured Zara would mention it to Jake, but with Jake relegated mostly to bed, and Zara hovering over him like a private nurse, Brody wasn't too worried about what Jake knew.

When Cal asked about that Kate woman, Brody changed the subject.

Best to see what was what first. Finding lost things people didn't want found *was* his expertise after all, not anybody else's. Back when Team Breaker had received their assignment, Brody had been the one to find the terrorist cell's home base.

Too bad some of their intel had been faulty.

He pushed that thought away and parked his truck in the lot of Fort Dry Historic Site. Snow was piled up around all three buildings that made up the fort, but the walks were ruthlessly cleared. Salt put down to keep the ice at bay. The site was surrounded on all sides by flat snow-covered land, the mountains far off in the distance.

A door opened and Kate stood there, waving him over. She was dressed in jeans and a sweatshirt when he'd kind of expected her to be in her historical getup.

The odd feeling spiraling through him was disappointment. He rather enjoyed her all dressed up, looking like some ghost from the past. "Thought you'd be in your costume."

"We don't officially open until ten," she said primly, having to look up at him as he approached. She wasn't short exactly, but he was tall and so he towered over her a little bit.

She didn't seem all that concerned about his size and being alone together, whereas Hazeleigh was *just* getting used to not jumping a foot when he or his brothers approached. Kate didn't seem at all *afraid* of him. Her nerves all seemed to stem from the topic at hand.

She led him into the small building that seemed more offices and storage than historical facility. Her office was small, and he hesitated following her inside, considering they'd be basically on top of each other.

And he was a little too intrigued by the prospect.

He hung by the door, but she marched in and pulled a crate from under her desk. Then she moved to a filing cabinet and pulled out an entire arm full of folders. She put them on top of the crate. "This is just what I've got in print. I keep some things on my computer too."

He looked at the sheer volume of information. She had more on her father's disappearance than he'd had on the leader of the terrorist organization Team Breaker had been after.

"Kate…"

"I know, you think because I did all this you won't be able to find him."

"It's not that exactly." He *excelled* at finding people, even when the circumstances said no one would find them. This was more about all the work and hours she'd put into this disappearance. All the hope she clearly had that her father could be found, and probably with a happy-ending kind of result.

In Brody's mind, happy endings didn't come after all *this*. "Maybe he doesn't want to be found."

"And maybe he's dead," she said flatly, putting to words what he'd really wanted to say. "I know the possibilities. I know that the chances of me finding something that makes me feel better is slim to none. I don't need happy endings, Brody. I just need answers. Closure."

He nodded. "All right. I'll see what I can do. Do you mind if I take this back to the house?"

She studied the information and chewed on her bottom lip, a slightly distracting movement because she had a very *interesting* mouth.

Yeah, it had been a while since he'd been in the consistent, solitary company of a woman. And Kate was the… fragile kind. Well, fragile wasn't the right word. She'd held up under losing her father and trying to find him. She was vulnerable maybe, and a little naive. Not his type.

His body wasn't getting the memo.

"I'd rather keep everything here. It's safer here. We

could just look through stuff and I could explain anything to you. I know you have a ranch to run. I don't expect you to just… I don't know."

She sighed and lowered herself into a rickety-looking chair. "I didn't really think this through. Hazeleigh said Zara said Jake said…" She trailed off, smiled up at him a little. "Yes, I know, third-hand and all, but when she said you knew how to find things… Maybe if I'd heard that a month ago, it wouldn't have mattered, but with Amberleigh's body being found…"

She shook her head. "She was my friend too, you know. Maybe not my sister, but my friend."

"You were close with all of them." It didn't need to be a question. The palpable *emotion* was evidence enough.

"Yes. But it was Zara and I… We were best friends." Kate shrugged as if shrugging away that emotion, but it lingered. In her eyes. "I was close with the triplets. We grew up together. My father was a teacher at the high school. Very well respected. My parents were sort of a golden couple. Mom from a well-to-do family, my father from a wrong-side-of-the-tracks family who'd pulled himself up by his bootstraps to get an education, then come back and serve the community." She shook her head. "Neither here nor there, I guess."

"It all helps when you're trying to find someone. You never know what might help."

She blew out a breath. "One day Dad didn't show up to work. And Amberleigh didn't show up to school. There was never any evidence they disappeared together, but they both disappeared the same day and, well… I suppose it's natural what people came to believe."

"That they had an affair?"

Kate shrugged again, but it was jerkier.

"Was there any evidence of an affair?"

"Nothing concrete. But enough that looking back over it, people wondered. Amberleigh liked to hang out at my house, even though we had more freedom at the Hart Ranch. She took violin lessons with me and my father, and Dad gave her private lessons for free—presumably because her father wouldn't have paid for them, but people put…other reasons behind it."

Yikes. Brody wasn't sure what to say to that.

"My mother denied it vehemently, and so did I. Amberleigh was… She liked to shock people. Men especially. She'd said a few things that I'd never thought twice about, but the police really liked that angle. Which meant all that was left was for the town to shun the entire family."

"Guilt by association?"

"Pretty much."

Brody didn't know how to outwardly react given the sensitive situation. He changed the subject instead. "But Zara didn't blame your father. She blamed you?"

"It isn't that simple. And like I said, neither here nor there." She picked up a folder. "These were the initial missing persons reports for my father and Amberleigh."

Brody took the outstretched papers and skimmed over them. Nothing connecting the two beyond circumstantial sorts of things. Nothing left behind—no note, no hints. Just one day they were there, and the next they weren't.

He looked up from the papers to see her standing there, hands clasped so hard her knuckles were white. A brittle expression on her face that suggested she was working very hard to hold herself together—and was definitely old hat at it.

He couldn't quite work Kate Phillips out. She didn't fit into any neat box. At turns awkward, nervous, bitter, determined.

"You've certainly had a rough go of it, haven't you?"

She startled, looking arrested, big dark eyes meeting his. "Me?"

"Well, sure, you were the one caught in the middle."

Chapter Three

Kate had to fight back the emotion that threatened to swallow her whole. She didn't know Brody Thompson, and he didn't know her. She supposed that was why he could look at this with such a lack of bias.

Caught in the middle?

She shook her head. "Not that simple."

"Seems simple to me. Your dad and your friend disappeared. I'm assuming a good half the town blamed your father and you by default. When bad things happen in a small community, everyone has something to say about it and the people involved."

"Are you well versed in small towns?" she asked, because it hit too hard, too close to the bone when all that scar tissue she'd built up was supposed to keep her safe.

He smiled enigmatically, but there was something very…deep behind that smile. Not humorous, at least to him. "Something like that." He hefted the boxes easily. "You've got somewhere with a little more surface area for us to work?"

"There's a conference room in the back."

He nodded, then jerked his chin as a sign for her to lead the way. He carried *all* of it like it were nothing. Which gave Kate a little flutter low in her stomach.

For a moment Kate had the strangest sensation she'd

stepped into a dream world. This couldn't be real. Help from a very nice-looking man. Who was friendly and polite and was supposed to know how to find people.

Ten years, no one had helped. No one had been *polite*.

She blinked when he raised an eyebrow at her. *Right*. She exited her office, skirting him with as much room as she could—a little afraid if she got too close, looked too hard, he'd disappear in a puff of smoke like the mirage he must be.

She led him to the conference room and turned on the lights. It was frigid. "I can go grab the space heater from my office."

He waved her off. "I'm fine." He dropped the crate on the long table and studied them, even though he couldn't know what was in them. But it was like he was doing some kind of mathematical calculation.

"Day of information here." He pointed to a spot on the table. "Police reports and the like from then on out." He moved a little ways down. "Anything leading up to the disappearance." And so on until he expected her to make five piles of the information.

"That's not how I've been organizing things."

He shrugged. "It's how I need to organize things." Then he just stood there…waiting for her to get to work. She couldn't say she *liked* being ordered around, but she was used to it, wasn't she? Reorganizing her life, reshaping *herself* to suit the needs of everyone around her. Her mother, the town.

And you survived by doing all that. So she moved forward and began to organize in the way he'd instructed her. But Brody didn't sit idly by. He helped, creating a human chain. She told him what something was, he put it in the appropriate spot.

They'd gotten through almost all of it when Kate

glanced up at the wall clock. "I have to go get ready for my shift."

He waved her off. "Yeah, go ahead."

"You want to…stay?"

"I just got started. I'll let you know before I go."

"All this has to be put up and away. I don't think we have any groups who've rented the room, but—"

He waved her away again. "I'll handle it."

I'll handle it. Had anyone said that to her since that fateful day ten years ago? Because it seemed like she had been stepping up to handle *everything* since Dad disappeared.

But Brody Thompson was going to *handle it*, and Kate didn't have the first clue what to do about that.

Once Brody got everything set up the way he needed, he started going through all Kate's files. She'd kept meticulous records—not just police reports and credit card statements, but notes on people she'd talked to or people who'd talked to *her*.

It was impressive, really. Obsessive, possibly, but Brody wasn't a stranger to being obsessive himself. And as it made his task easier, he was mostly grateful for it.

He got lost in it all, building a picture in his mind of what that day looked like. He made his own notes, began compiling his own theories, and yes, came to some conclusions.

Like, there would have to be some pretty amazing explanation for why these two people disappeared on the same day if it wasn't together.

A crick began to form in his neck, reminding him he wasn't as young as he used to be. When he looked up to stretch out his neck, he found her standing there in the doorway. She was dressed in her getup—all layers of fabric, big skirts, even a bonnet.

His heart thumped once, *hard* against his chest. Some out-of-body premonition before everything went back to normal.

He'd felt that thing a time or two—usually before some *really* bad things went down. But he wasn't in the military any longer. He was in a tiny town in the-middle-of-nowhere Wyoming under an assumed name.

Helping a woman dressed like she belonged in a covered wagon find her father who—by all accounts—had left of his own accord.

But *why*.

"I have to close up the building." She was frowning at him, as if she didn't understand what was going on in front of her even though she knew exactly what he'd been doing. She'd *asked* him to do it. "You've been at this all day. I…"

Brody looked down at his watch. The break with his concentration made him realize he was *starving*.

"Did you even eat anything?"

Brody ran his hand through his hair. He'd been deep in it and it was taking a few seconds for him to emerge from the facts of the case to refocus his brain on the present. "Ah, no. Got kind of lost in the research."

"Well, I certainly know that feeling, but you should eat." She studied the table, but didn't say anything else. She wasn't going to ask if he'd found anything. Somehow that made him feel sympathetic, when it wouldn't do either of them any good for him to try to make her feel better.

"I think I've got a line to tug."

"A line… Really? That quickly?"

He shrugged, not wanting to get her hopes up, though he could practically see the way she was trying to hold herself back from hope. A woman who'd been burned a few too many times.

Which meant he was playing with fire. Something he'd promised himself not to do anymore, but… Old habits died hard. "Did you ever really look at the financials, Kate?"

"Of course. I pored over his credit card records. His bank statements. But nothing out of the ordinary."

He wished he could agree. "Unfortunately, there are a few charges on that credit card that don't add up."

"That's impossible."

Brody didn't say anything. She didn't want to believe him, not his problem. So, he just waited.

She closed her eyes and sighed, pushing her fingers against her temples. "Not impossible, of course. I just… I spent so much time on them."

"There were multiple charges to a place called Stanley Music."

"My father was a music teacher. Charges to anything music related make sense."

"But they don't. There's a pattern to the payments he made, and to the private lessons Amberleigh took."

"It could have been sheet music. Supplies. Private lessons would necessitate some personal cost, even if he wasn't charging her for the lessons. We could afford it."

"Sure. But I looked up Stanley Music. I couldn't find one. Not in Wyoming. Not in the entire United States that fit the information on the statement."

"Maybe they went out of business."

As if Brody didn't look that up too, but he could see she needed her suggestion to be a possibility so he just shrugged. "Maybe."

"But you don't think so. You think it means something."

"I think it's a lead to tug. That's all."

She let out a slow breath. Then tried a very sad attempt

at a smile. "All right, then we'll tug on it. But first, you must be starving. I owe you a meal."

"You said you couldn't pay me."

"I can't. But I can feed you."

Chapter Four

There was a small kitchen in the back of the main fort building. Mr. Field looked to be gone for the day, so Kate didn't have to worry about explaining Brody to him.

"You just make yourself comfortable. I'll change, then I can whip something up in about ten minutes."

"You don't have to do this."

"I'd feel a lot better if I did. And it's nothing. I just keep a few things here on the off chance I get caught in the snow."

"With that tiny car, I'm surprised you don't have to stay here all the time."

"A truck would be more convenient." And expensive. "But I don't mind staying out here when I have to. It's like…" She trailed off, feeling heat creep up her cheeks. Brody was nice and all, but that didn't mean she needed to confess every history nerd aspect of her lonely life. "Well, it's just fine. Be right back."

She left him there, went and changed quickly into her modern clothes, then returned to him on his phone.

He didn't look up, so she got out a skillet, precooked chicken breast slices and some frozen vegetables to put together in a quick little stir-fry.

Deep down, she liked to get snowed in here. It meant she didn't have to go home to the ghosts of her father, the anger of her mother coating every inch of the house even though they kept their distance. Here she could pretend she'd chosen a life of adventure and possibility out on the prairie and being all alone was simply a necessary component of that westward dream.

"What about that Mr. Field or Hazeleigh? They never stick around to drive you home in bad weather?"

"Oh, Mr. Field doesn't live far off. In the winter he usually just snowmobiles over. Or stays home if he's a mind to. Hazeleigh doesn't drive much, and the truck is Zara's. Besides, she's just Mr. Field's research assistant, so she's more beholden to him than the fort." She shrugged. "I don't mind. Really."

"I thought rural folks were supposed to be all neighborly and helpful."

"They are." She moved the food around in the pan. "I'm...complicated."

"I don't think you're the complicated one, Kate."

"No, but if you ever meet my mother, you'll know why people would rather keep out of it."

Brody frowned at her as she scooped the food from pan to plate. She didn't meet his gaze, but she could feel it all the same. He was trying to size her up. Make sense of her. *Good luck, buddy.*

"My mother was no prize, so I understand that I suppose," he muttered, watching her with such intense study that Kate kept her gaze on the plate as she slid it in front of him. Before she could retreat, maybe make excuses about needing to clean up and leave him to eat, he reached for her wrist.

That should probably be alarming rather than a little thrilling. *You really have absolutely no life.*

"You're going to sit down and eat some of this yourself. Go on and get yourself a plate."

"I'm not really—"

He raised an eyebrow at her.

"You're very used to telling people what to do, aren't you?"

"*Very,*" he said, but with a smile so it felt…friendly. Like they were sharing a moment rather than she was getting bossed around. He let go of her wrist, and because she was nothing if not a biddable soldier, she got herself a plate and let Brody serve up some of the food she'd made on it.

He gestured to the seat across from him at the tiny table, and she took it. He was doing her a favor after all. Without pay. Why not do as she was told?

Besides, she *was* hungry. She took a bite and then looked up at him. The Thompson brothers were Wilde mysteries. No one had a clear idea where they'd come from, what brought them here or why they all looked and sounded so different.

"How'd you wind up in Wyoming?" Kate asked casually. She was rather used to trying to get to the bottom of mysteries.

Brody stared hard at his plate before flashing a smile. "Oh, this and that. Cal's sort of the de facto leader. I go where he goes."

"You talk differently than he does."

"Do I?" He shrugged. "We weren't raised together. We're a motley crew of brothers—half, step and adopted. Maybe that's why we stick together now."

"That's…sweet."

His eyebrows shot up for a second and then he relaxed into another smile. "Not something we're accused of being all that often."

She thought of the six brothers. They were all big and intimidating looking, no matter how some of them smiled and clearly tried to lend a friendly air to their interactions in town. There was something…different about them, and it wasn't just that they weren't from around here.

"Well, if you keep cooking for me like this, I might just have to marry you."

She tried to laugh, but it came out strained to her own ears. She did not know what to do with anyone making *marrying* jokes, let alone a man that looked like Brody Thompson. He was just so…tall. And muscular. Most of the men she knew were more a rangy sort. Or had that older rancher paunch that seemed to settle over them all eventually. But Brady was *built*. Like an actor in one of those superhero movies. Then there were his eyes, which were an intriguing maze of hazel.

None of which is very applicable to your life, Kate. Get it together.

They finished eating, and Kate quickly cleaned up. She felt Brody's eyes on her the whole time, and while she might have indulged in one quick fantasy that he was looking at her because he liked what he saw, she knew better.

He was trying to figure her out. She was a puzzle for him to solve. That and pity were the only reasons he was helping her.

But, without being asked, he stepped in to help dry the dishes.

"I should get back to the ranch, but I'll look into this Stanley Music mystery more. Maybe there's an innocent explanation."

And maybe there's not. "If there's any kind of answer there, I want it. Good or bad. I can handle it."

He looked down at her, and she felt a careful study. Like he was determining for himself if she could.

After a moment or two, he nodded. It was as much agreement as she could expect, she supposed.

She led him back through the building again and out

the front door. They stepped out into the frigid dark. Kate locked the door, and when she turned, she noticed big fat snowflakes fell from the sky. The walk was already covered by the new snowfall. His truck windshield was dusted as well.

"Why don't you let me drive you home?" Brody said.

"You don't have to worry about that."

"No trouble. Easy in my truck."

"I'll stay here tonight. No worries." She motioned to the smaller building. "I've still got some cleanup to do."

"I—"

"Thank you for all your help today." She stuck out her hand. This was business, wasn't it? Maybe she wasn't paying him, but he was doing her a service, and she'd find ways—meals and whatever else she could think of—to at least make some of his time up to him.

His mouth curved ever so subtly, like he understood the clear dismissal, but it amused him rather than frustrated him. He took her hand in his, shook, but didn't let go.

"I'll be back tomorrow to look through the rest of your research," he said.

Kate could scarcely concentrate on the words with her hand completely engulfed in his. A heat so incongruent to the cold winter night around them.

He released her hand back into the cold. "But I'm staying right here until you're safely inside."

She rolled her eyes, though she didn't…hate that he was being a gentleman. It was like someone caring about her. She knew he didn't. He was basically a stranger. This was common courtesy or something.

But even that was rare in her life.

"Bye, Brody," she said, turning away and marching toward the office building.

"Bye, Kate."

AFTER WATCHING KATE walk quickly to the smaller building where her office was located, and arguing himself into his truck rather than going back inside and demanding to drive her home, Brody drove back to the ranch.

It didn't sit right. Something about little Kate Phillips spending the night out at that old fort in the middle of *nowhere* felt beyond wrong. Unsafe.

You're not in Chicago, and you're not in charge of her.

But she'd seemed…resigned to be this lonely, solitary figure. When she was so…so… Well, he couldn't quite figure out what she was just yet. Probably best if he didn't, and just focused on the task at hand. Helping her figure out what happened to her dad.

He had a lead. A line to tug. That was the only thing he needed to be concerned with.

The snow increased and by the time Brody made it to the ranch, he was glad he'd left when he had. Of course, if he'd waited, he'd be stuck there, and Kate wouldn't be out there all alone.

He scowled at himself. He didn't need to go saving every damsel in distress. Or he'd end up like Jake with a bullet to the gut.

He parked, walked through the blustery snow, stomped his boots on the mats outside, then stepped into warmth.

Home, something inside of him whispered. Cozy glow, the low drone of voices from the kitchen. His family—not the one he'd been born to, but the one that had been forged in the heat and danger of a Middle Eastern desert.

He took off his winter gear, hanging and putting everything carefully away, not because he was so inherently clean, but because he'd quickly learned if he didn't he'd have damp boots and layers the next morning when the chores needed to be done.

He stepped into the kitchen. Everyone, including Zara,

was huddled around the small farmhouse table. They needed a bigger one, and good Lord, they needed someone who could cook something beyond frozen dinners.

He had a sneaking suspicion Zara was more of a cook than she let on, but had no desire to feed all of them.

The pan of frozen lasagna looked like it had been through a battle of its own. Only a small sliver remained.

He was inherently thankful Kate had included vegetables in his meal.

"Better get in here quick if you're going to get any," Landon offered. Tech expert and the only one of them who grinned or joked with any regularity, Landon often acted as the face of the Thompson brothers, when Cal's uptight frowning didn't fare well.

"Already ate," Brody returned.

"You did? Where?" Cal demanded.

"Did you need my minute-by-minute itinerary, Sergeant?"

Cal scowled. As that hadn't been his real rank even when they had been deployed and active Team Breaker members.

There was the scrape of chairs, mutterings about things to do. Zara helped Jake to his feet. He was still hobbling, but he was looking better. Getting better. And he had the pretty little ranch hand to nurse him back to health.

Brody didn't know why that seemed *lucky*.

Brody certainly wasn't lucky, because after two minutes it was clear to see everyone had deserted him so Cal could lecture him.

Brody found he didn't have the stomach for it tonight. So he thought he'd cut it off at the pass. "Cal, I get it. I'm not doing this to make you mad."

"Aren't you?" Cal still sat at the table. Brody wondered if his father had been the normal sort if this might remind him of a teenage dressing down. Was Cal the kind of father figure Brody would have wanted if they weren't all about the same age?

No easy answer for that. But there was for Cal's question.

He grinned. "Just an enjoyable happenstance."

Cal snorted.

"They took us out," Brody said, low and letting some of his frustration simmer through. He gripped the ancient kitchen counter, needing something to steady himself where he was. "They plopped us in the middle of nowhere."

"To keep us alive, Brody."

"Sure, but did we sign up for erasing our old lives to keep us alive? I didn't. I signed up for helping people. Now, I don't have a death wish, particularly at the hands of some terrorist lowlife, so I'm happy to be here, laying low, but I can't… She needs help. An easy kind of help. An easy kind of help I happen to excel at."

"You're already in the paper. You want every townsperson with a problem to solve to come to you?"

"Sure, why not?"

Cal groaned.

"I didn't sign up for this life. I'll accept it, but I won't turn my back on people who could use my help. That's my line in the sand. It should be yours, too." And because if he stayed he'd only get madder, Brody turned and left Cal to do the dishes on his own.

Zara was coming down the stairs as he approached the bottom.

"Headed home?"

She shook her head. "Probably stay."

"You ever not here?" he asked, meaning for it to come out like a joke, but he still had a little bit more edge in his voice thanks to Cal, so it landed all wrong.

She paused on the stairs, blocking his way up. "Rarely. You got a problem with that?"

Brody sighed, feeling like a jerk. "No, I don't."

"Good." But she didn't move. She frowned down at him. "You know, Kate shouldn't…" She shifted, uncomfortably, something he rarely saw from Zara, who always seemed so sure of herself. "If you want a space to work, Kate shouldn't feel like it can't be here."

"That's exactly what she seemed to feel like. Wonder why?" Brody had no idea why he was standing up for Kate. He'd known Zara longer. Hell, he *liked* Zara. But Zara was so…strong, and Kate was all alone.

Zara's entire demeanor changed, she charged forward, brushing past him to get off the stairs. "You don't know anything, Brody. Keep that in mind."

"I know one thing, Zara. She seems like she could use a friend, and she doesn't have one. You, on the other hand, have plenty." Brody didn't watch to see if that comment hit its mark. It was none of his business, anyway.

One of these damn days, he'd learn how to mind his own.

Chapter Five

Kate whistled to herself as she made a quick microwave oatmeal breakfast. The snow would be enough to keep everyone away this morning—visitors, Mr. Field. Everyone would be hunkered down or shoveling out.

And she got a morning to herself at the fort to enjoy. Lonely? Maybe, but at least today she was alone with a lot of things she loved.

After she shoveled the walks, she'd finish the new exhibit, maybe digitize some of the records for the fort's website. She'd have all that history all to herself, and *that* was something to whistle about.

As she set to walk back to the office building with her oatmeal, the sun was finally beginning to peek its way above the mountains. Kate tramped through the snow around the back of the buildings where she could get a better view. Maybe stand in the cold, eat her warm oatmeal and watch the sunrise.

Gorgeous. She almost felt content, but as the light began trailing over the world around her, she saw something odd.

Snowmobile tracks. That went all the way up to the office building she'd slept in. Weird. Maybe Mr. Field had come by last night and forgotten his key? But surely he would have seen her car in the lot and known she'd stayed over. Surely he would have knocked.

Kate pulled her phone out of her pocket and checked for messages. If he'd snowmobiled all the way out here in the dark, come straight to the office building rather than the main building, wouldn't he have tried to contact her?

She looked around the vast gorgeous white of a Wyoming winter, and felt a shudder of unease, no matter how beautiful the sunrise was.

Silly, of course. Thinking about her father's disappearance always gave her that paranoid watched feeling. But she couldn't enjoy the sunrise now, so she turned and headed back for the front door.

Which she'd left unlocked when she headed over to the main building. She stopped in her tracks. If someone had come out this way, they could be in there now.

Don't do this to yourself again.

Kate closed her eyes and focused on her breathing. She wouldn't go back to being that girl she'd been when Dad first disappeared. She could not allow herself to fall back into those old fearful traps that made her miserable.

"Kate."

She screamed. Then immediately winced when she recognized the voice. She didn't want to open her eyes and face the owner of that voice, but she could hardly run away. She sighed and opened her eyes.

"Are you okay?" Brody asked, concern etched all over his face.

Kate tried to smile, but she knew it failed. "Of course. You just scared me is all."

"I thought you would have heard me come up."

She couldn't have possibly heard anything over the heavy pounding of her heart. "Lost in thought. Pretty morning." She gestured to the sun, the mountains far off in the distance.

Brody looked, but she saw him take in the snowmobile tracks, the footprints. He studied the landscape with a cold assessing stare that left her mesmerized for a second.

Then he moved forward so swiftly she didn't have a chance to ask him what he was doing before he took her by the arm and started pulling her toward the front. "Come inside, Kate."

She didn't argue with him. Didn't know why or what he was even doing. He wrenched open the door and muttered about small towns and locking doors.

"What on earth?"

"What on earth is right? What's going on around here?"

"Well, I was trying to eat my oatmeal and watch the sunrise."

"And presumably found those snowmobile tracks, the footprints of at least three people and yet you were still standing outside in an open field, all while the door to shelter and possible safety is unlocked."

Kate blinked. *Three* sets of footprints? She hadn't really thought they'd be…different people's footprints. But that still didn't mean… It couldn't mean…

Kate cleared her throat and tried to look imperious. "There are quite a few explanations if you'd like to listen to them instead of overreact."

He looked taken aback. "I do *not* overreact."

"Could have fooled me."

He gaped at her, and she couldn't fight back a smile. She'd made a man like Brody Thompson speechless? Not a bad way to start the day.

"It was probably Mr. Field. I'll call later to make sure, but he often comes by just that way. And he's the forgetful sort. If Hazeleigh wasn't here to keep him organized, he probably forgot his keys. Or maybe he got distracted. You can never tell with him."

"You were scared," Brody pointed out, his voice oddly flat.

"I was…jumpy. Digging into my father's disappearance always makes me jumpy. But I'm safe here."

She had to be.

"Three sets of prints isn't one Mr. Field."

"Would you like me to be scared?" she returned, with a little too much snap to her tone, considering Brody was helping her. She took a deep breath and struggled to find a smile. "Look, it's fine. I promise. I'm fine. Why are you here?"

"To look through the rest of your research. I told you I'd be back."

"I know, I just assumed with the snow… The roads couldn't have been good."

He shoved his hands deep into his pockets. "They weren't so bad."

She didn't believe him, but she also couldn't figure out why he would have braved the roads to help her. But here he was. Maybe he was just a man who really felt committed to following through.

"I appreciate your dedication," she said, maybe a tad primly.

"Do you store anything valuable here?"

She resisted the urge to roll her eyes since he clearly was determined not to let it go. "Probably not in the way you mean. We have one-of-a-kind documents and artifacts, but not the type that are going to go for big bucks. Trust me, it was Mr. Field, or maybe some lost hikers looking for shelter. There's nothing here anyone could want."

Brody looked down at the crates of research she'd spent ten years compiling. "You so sure about that?"

Kate's stomach sank.

BRODY WASN'T PROUD of himself. She went pale right there before him.

What was it about people who couldn't lock their damn doors? People bound and determined to let threats get the better of them, rather than fight them off at the first sign.

"I've…been doing this for ten years. I've talked to every cop, every private detective in a fifty-mile radius. Nothing in here has ever given anyone any clue where he might have gone. What he might have done."

"You don't know what Stanley Music is."

"It's a music company!" she practically yelled. "There are *invoices* with an address and phone number. It made all the sense in the world."

"Invoices." Brody frowned and thought over everything he'd gone through yesterday. "I didn't see any invoices."

"They were with the credit card statements. I paper clipped everything together. Any receipts or invoices that went with the charges. They were there."

"There were no invoices with the statements. Not for Stanley anyway."

"You're wrong." She straightened her shoulders, temper giving her pallor some color in her cheeks. She turned on a heel and marched back to her office.

Brody followed, leaving a healthy distance between them. He'd been through everything in the finance pile. Not everything entirely. It was possible she'd misplaced something, but Kate didn't strike him as the careless type.

She began to flip through the files. Finding the one she wanted, opening it, pulling out the credit card statements. She flipped through all the receipts and invoices clipped to the first. Then the second. Then the third, with increasingly jerky movements.

"I can't find them. I must have… I must have done something with them." She took a slow steadying breath, clearly trying to keep from panicking. But it was there in her eyes, darting around the office. "I'll just have to go through everything. It'll be there."

She blew out a breath, very slowly, very carefully. "I must have misplaced them. Left them somewhere. You might have put them in a different file with your organizing. They're..." She spoke softly, almost to herself. But then on another deep breath in and out, she looked up at him. "They *were* here."

"I believe you," he said, both because he did and because she seemed to need the reassurance. "Let's spread it all out again. Check the room I was in."

She nodded her head, a little bit too vigorously.

They spent hours going through every folder, every last shred of paper. Brody took a break to go pick them up some food from town. She didn't touch her sandwich except the few times he'd remind her to take a bite.

The single-minded focus she had made him a little uncomfortable, because it bordered on...well, a lot of behaviors that weren't conducive to solving a problem. But she wasn't in the military. She didn't have to worry about personal investment—this was her life. Her father. It *was* personal, and he couldn't tell her to be calm or detach herself from it.

He'd have to take that on for her.

After they got through all her files, she tore her office apart. Sure they must have fallen behind a drawer, or desk, or got stuck in a book.

"Maybe they're at home," she said, sitting in the middle of her little office, the entire contents all but exploded around her. "They must be. They have to be."

Brody thought about her compact car and all that snow. The plows had been out, but the roads were still bad. It was clear she wouldn't rest until she could check her home, but Brody was pretty sure they were gone. And she was going to have to deal with that, but not until she was ready. "I can drive you."

She started to try to put her office to rights, then stopped abruptly. "No. No, this is insane. I'm letting you make me insane."

He didn't point out it was hardly his fault her invoices were missing. She was teetering on the verge of a meltdown. He was impressed she hadn't fallen off that edge yet, but he was pretty sure any commentary from him would push her.

"I can't do this again," she muttered to herself. "I won't."

"Do what?"

She looked up at him, blinked as if surprised to find him actually there. "Nothing. It's not important." She sucked in a breath. "I mean, this is just an overreaction. Clearly they got misplaced. What other possibility is there?"

"Snowmobile tracks, unknown footprints, you don't lock doors out here apparently."

She looked at him, mouth hanging slightly open. "You think someone *stole* them?"

"I think someone *could* have stolen them."

"They went through my things, stole just these, what was it, three invoices? Out of all those papers? All that work?"

"Maybe the three invoices were the only incriminating thing."

"This is insane. No, I'm sorry. I can't get on board with that. I appreciate your help, Brody, I do. And when I'm home next, I'll check out my room. I'm almost certain they're there. It will all check out and…" She was getting ahold of herself, but it was a hard-won thing. "I can't let myself do this again. I have to let it go." She wrapped her arms around herself, continuing to nod. "I finally have to let it go."

"You want to just give up?" Brody asked, surprised that would be her go to. He didn't think it'd last, but to even try to give it up seemed incongruous to everything she'd ever done up to this point.

She let her arms fall and began cleaning up again. Bustling around busily. "Like I said, I really appreciate the help, but it was a…" She stopped, clearly trying to come up with a word. "Well, I appreciate the help. I'm sure you have more important ranch work to be doing."

She was dismissing him. Brody laughed, maybe with too much of an edge to it, but if there was one thing that got under his skin, it was people not taking the proper precautions. "You are not staying here alone."

She stopped what she was doing, straightened. "I beg your pardon."

"Call Mr. Field."

She fisted her hands on her hips. "Don't take that tone with me."

"Call Mr. Field and ask him if that was his snowmobile. His *three* sets of footprints. Your father disappeared, Kate. Maybe you and the town would like to believe that was voluntary. Hell, maybe it was, but I know when things aren't right. Things aren't right."

"You are paranoid," she whispered, like a shocked accusation.

"You aren't paranoid enough."

"No, I went down that particular road. I played that game, and…" She shook her head violently and squeezed her eyes shut. "This is too much," she muttered to herself. Eyes opened, she stared him down. "Brody, I appreciate your help, but I can't… My father left. I didn't handle that very well when it first happened. I thought everyone was out to get me. I thought I was being followed. I had a very bad year or two, but—"

Everything inside of him stilled. "Someone was following you when you were sixteen?"

"That isn't what I said. I said I *thought* someone was. I was delusional—with grief, and worry, and all sorts of things. I was alone and unbalanced. I would have gone to a therapist, but my mother said I would be fine if I just let it all go."

"You didn't," Brody pointed out, gesturing to all her work.

She surveyed the mess, and just looked so sad. "I tried. It took a while to create some balance. No, I didn't fully let it go, but I stopped letting it rule my life. I can't go back to that."

"And I can't walk away from this knowing you might very well be in danger."

Chapter Six

Kate wasn't sure how long she stood, staring at Brody with her mouth hanging open. She hadn't been sure what she'd be getting when she asked for Brody's help, but definitely, *definitely* not this.

"You…must be joking."

"Why would I be joking?"

"Why would I be in *danger*?"

He sighed, as if she were a child who couldn't understand a very complex problem. And he didn't have the words to explain it. "I'm well versed in analyzing situations, acknowledging threats and picking up on cues that danger—"

"How?"

He clamped his mouth shut for a moment, stood there looking like something frozen. Then he scowled. "Trust me."

Which seemed like the most absurd thing to say. Trust? A man she barely knew who was just supposed to be helping her *research* her father's disappearance. "Why?"

"Are you always this difficult?"

"No. I'm very rarely difficult. I am biddable, and normal. This is not normal. This is… You need to leave now."

His expression didn't really change. It…melted. Or

just…blanked. There was nothing there now except a very stoic man blocking her exit.

Kate swallowed, not sure what her next move would be if he refused, but eventually he let his crossed arms fall.

"Fine," he said.

"So, you're going?"

He turned and began walking away. "Not exactly."

Not exactly. Kate scrambled after him. He was already opening the door to the building.

"What do you mean *not exactly*?" she called after him.

He stopped and turned. "I'll sit in my truck if you don't want me in here. But I'm not going anywhere as long as you're determined to be all alone, in the middle of no-where, with three people snooping around where you slept last night. Alone. Without any damn protection."

Then he let the door close behind him, leaving Kate with the echo of a door slam and complete and utter disbelief.

"I am not in any danger," she muttered to herself. How could she be in danger? There had been years she'd pored herself into this. Nothing had disappeared. No strange men, no cops, no private investigators had noticed the Stanley Music thing. They'd had the invoices.

And who would have looked into those? Kate herself hadn't, because it made *sense*. Maybe they were missing, but it still made sense Dad would have spent money at a music company.

Someone was following you when you were sixteen?

It had been her imagination. Everyone had said so. And nothing had ever happened to her, so they were right. They were right and Brody was… Well, he was overstepping.

Brody was off base. Maybe something was wrong with him. Maybe Zara had sent him here to mess with her. Okay, that was a bit far-fetched. Maybe Zara had stopped being her friend, but even angry Kate couldn't imagine Zara being *mean*.

He needed to…back off. Go away. Most certainly not stick around. She had to go tell him to leave. Make it clear.

She grabbed her coat and walked outside. It was snowing again, which meant she'd have to spend the night here again. Now, thanks to Brody being a *lunatic*, that thought left her with dread.

No, he did not get to ruin her peace of mind *and* sit out there in the parking lot like some kind of misplaced babysitter.

He'd be a really hot babysitter.

That unbidden thought made her even madder as she marched up to his truck and knocked on his window. He looked up, rolled the window down with a pleasant smile on his face. "Help you?"

"I could call the police."

"And tell them what?"

"That an insane person is insisting I not be alone. You're…you're stalking me!"

He grinned. "I'm just sitting in my truck in a parking lot, Kate."

She opened her mouth to say something to him, but she had nothing. *Nothing.* He was just going to sit here. Even if she called the cops?

"What is wrong with you?" she demanded.

He shrugged. "I get it. You feel like I'm overreacting. But I don't feel like I am, and if something happened to you because I went home like you demanded, well, I wouldn't be able to forgive myself. I'm sorry if that puts a wrench in your life, but I plan on only doing things I can live with for the rest of mine."

Which kind of insinuated there'd been a time and place when he'd done something he wasn't living very comfortably with. She almost softened toward him, even knowing she shouldn't. She really shouldn't.

"I can drive you home," he said earnestly. "I can drive you to Hazeleigh's and you could stay with her until the roads are clear and she can drive you back here. I can do a lot of things, but I can't leave you alone when everything I've observed tells me there's a high statistical chance you or your information is a target of some kind."

"You sound like a cop."

His easy smile didn't fade, but something in his eyes shuttered. "I'm not."

If he drove her back to Mom's, she'd need someone to drive her back to the fort for work tomorrow. But she'd have time to look for those invoices.

You know they're not there.

She sighed, the snow swirling heavily around her. She did know that. She was very careful not to take things back to the house that Mom might find and get upset about. She was very careful to keep everything together and organized. She was very careful.

Those invoices were missing. "I don't understand how or why someone would have taken three slips of paper. Even if they were incriminating. How?"

"I don't quite know, Kate. But I'll help you find out."

He seemed so earnest. So competent. No one ever wanted to help her find out *anything*. She knew she should be smart and resist it, but she just wasn't strong enough to do that.

"All right. Let me call Hazeleigh and make sure she's…" Kate trailed off as Brody's smile deepened. "You already talked to her."

"Just as a precaution."

A precaution. He was unhinged. She was going to get

in his car and let him drive her places? She sighed. "I've got to get my things. I'll be right back," she muttered.

BRODY WAS QUITE pleased with himself. Less pleased with the way the snowfall kept increasing. When Kate reappeared with a backpack and a purse, she was covered in snow by the time she jogged from the building to his truck.

She clambered in, tossed the bags in the back. "Going to get bad again."

Brody eyed the sky, the quickly disappearing parking lot around him. "Looks like." He reversed out of the parking spot, his windshield wipers going at full blast. "Did you ever call Mr. Field?"

"No."

"Afraid of the truth?"

He couldn't look at her to parse her reaction. His eyes had to stay on the road—if what little he could see would be considered a road. They hadn't gone a mile when he'd regretted his decision.

"Brody, this is bad."

"Yeah." Whiteout bad. "I'm thinking I should probably just turn back and we both stay in your little office building tonight?"

"Yes, but be careful. You don't want to get stuck in a di—"

There was the squeal of tires, Brody barely caught it over the roar of the wind. He couldn't see anything, but he felt the impact. Someone had crashed into them. They jerked forward. Brody tried to slam on the brakes, but they got bumped again, so even though he had his foot stomped on the brake, they went forward on the slick road.

Brody kept a death grip on the steering wheel, but the truck was skidding. No, it wasn't skidding—it was being *pushed*. Whatever car had run into them was still trying to drive forward? Whoever had hit them must have lost consciousness with their foot on the gas? Or maybe were so confused by the storm, didn't know to stop.

Or...

Brody didn't let his mind immediately go to nefarious, purposeful crashes. In a whiteout like this, an accident was all but inevitable. But he'd still take precautions. With his foot still on the brake, he tried to see what was going on.

He couldn't see anything. Not headlights, but maybe the slight outline of another truck? He had to bring his focus back to his windshield. The other truck was pushing his truck from the side. If he hit the gas, maybe he could dislodge them from the truck trying to push them off the road. They'd risk skidding in the snowy conditions, but Brody figured he could handle that best.

Kate was being too quiet, but he had to get them to safety before he could risk looking at her.

"Hold on," he said. He punched the gas, and the tires squealed, but they didn't propel forward.

They were stuck. In the snow, or maybe ice underneath. There was no way to get out of this. He heard the crunch of metal and then *thankfully* the other vehicle seemed to reverse and hopefully—

Another painful jerk of the car, metal screeching. A purposeful, painful ram that sent the truck tipping into a ditch.

"Hold on," Brody yelled as the truck fell—hard, and mostly on its side. Glass shattered as something impaled the driver's side window. Brody managed to hunch forward to avoid being skewered himself, though he felt something scrape against his back, pain searing with it.

White was all around them, pain radiating down his back. Brody struggled to unbuckle himself with his limited range of mobility. He could see what had impaled his truck window—a twisted, rusted mile marker made of metal.

He swore, viciously, because the narrow miss left his bones feeling a little jellied. Swearing, breathing, acting brought his composure back.

He looked at Kate. She was hanging limply, the seat belt the only thing that had kept her from falling into his seat. A little trickle of blood dripped from her chin.

Brody swore again as he leaped into action. He struggled with his seat belt—eventually pulling the pocketknife from his pocket and cutting the straps off. He wouldn't be able to get out of his door, so they'd have to get out of Kate's.

"Kate...."

"Hurts," she muttered.

"I just bet. Can you open your eyes?"

She groaned, but eventually blinked her eyes open. They widened, in surprise or understanding. "Brody."

"Can you get your door open?"

She winced, closed her eyes again, but kept moving. Turning toward her door. She managed to pull the handle and push the door open, but it only immediately fell back closed.

Brody tried to leverage himself closer. "Try again," he said, gritting his teeth against the pain in his back and the discomfort from contorting his body this way.

She did as she was told, and he managed to hold it open this time. "Okay, climb out if you can."

She struggled, first to get her buckle undone, then to get up and over and onto the ground. Brody's arm was shaking by the time she was finally free of the door. He had to drop it, let it slam shut.

Swearing, he gave his arm a bit of a rest by trying to gather up everything he would need. He grabbed the gun from the glove compartment, made sure the safety was on, and then shoved it in his pocket. Cal was going to be *all* kinds of ticked off about the truck, but Brody figured he had to survive this before he worried about Cal's anger.

He reached into the back and pulled out Kate's bags. Who knew what they were going to do next, but it might pay to have whatever she had packed away on them. He shoved the door open, and tossed the bags out.

Kate was standing, but bent over like she couldn't quite handle being upright. Still, when she heard him grunt, she looked up, then shuffled through the snow to reach out and hold the door open so he could get himself free of the truck.

He let out a vicious streak of curses as the pain worked its way through his body, and seemed to stiffen every last inch of him. But he looked at Kate. She had a nasty knot on her temple with blood dripping from it.

She must have knocked her head on the door when they'd been run into. "I don't suppose you have a first-aid kit in your bags?"

"No," she said, shaking her head, but the movement had her knees buckling.

Brody managed to scoop her up before she fell to the ground. "Gotcha."

"Dizzy," she grumbled.

"Yeah, concussions'll do that."

Brody looked around. The world was white. The wind howled and the snow kept falling. There was no sign of anyone. There weren't even tire tracks because the snow had already covered them up. He couldn't ask anyone to come out in this. Even emergency services would struggle in this mess.

"We'll have to walk back to the fort. I don't even think we got a mile down the road, so it's doable." He wished he were dressed a little better for the weather, but he'd manage.

"You can't carry me," Kate mumbled into his shoulder.

"Of course I can." He'd carried his brother Dunne farther, when Dunne had been seriously injured in a dust storm. He could carry a petite woman in the snow.

He just had to make sure he knew which way they were going. Where they were. He pulled the pocketknife from his pocket again. He had a little compass on the center of it. They'd been traveling westbound on the road, but he couldn't *see* the road.

"Brody, I can stand."

"I can carry you. You don't happen to know which way we need to go, do you?"

She turned her head, then groaned and closed her eyes.

He'd take that as a no. He scooped up her bags, hissed a little as he slung them over his shoulder and the straps hit the scrape on his back. He studied the truck. It would mostly be facing the direction they'd been driving. Maybe a little off course, but if he could find the road at the back of the truck, he could shuffle along and follow it as best he could back to the fort.

The road *had* been plowed, so there wasn't as much snow on it. All he had to do was follow that edge along the plowed snowbank.

"You just hang tight," Brody murmured, when Kate tried to mumble something, but it didn't sound like actual words. "We'll get you warm and all fixed up."

He'd have to find a way.

Chapter Seven

It was cold. Bitterly, bitterly cold. Her face hurt. Her temple *really* hurt. Her arms hurt from clutching Brody's neck. Her entire body hurt from being rammed and jostled.

She couldn't open her eyes. Every time she did, a wave of nausea went through her and she thought she might throw up right there on Brody's shirt.

So she kept her eyes shut. And tried to keep her mind blank, but all she could think was...

He was walking them to their death. He wasn't *from* here. He clearly didn't know anything about survival. They should have hunkered down in the truck. There was heat there, even if they had crashed into a ditch.

How had they crashed into a ditch? She understood someone had run into them—though it was some kind of bad odds to have a car accident in a blizzard in the middle of nowhere—but where had the other vehicle gone?

She played it back. It was fuzzy. She was pretty sure she'd passed out for a little bit, which was beyond terrifying. She'd never really had anything wrong with her. She'd never even broken a limb. Never been put under anesthesia.

And she'd lost consciousness over a bump to the head. "Going to die."

"Don't be dramatic," Brody said, and he sounded so... sure. So strong. Even as the cold air soaked deeper and her whole body throbbed with aches and pains, and she was certain he couldn't be walking in the right direction, that certainty in his voice soothed her.

Maybe he *did* know what he was doing.

Wouldn't that be funny?

"There we are."

She managed to open her eyes, though it was a hard-won thing, like her eyelashes had frozen together. All she saw was white. Even Brody was covered in white.

"Impending death?"

"Ha. Ha," he replied, though she hadn't really been making a joke.

Then she saw it. The flagpole. Right in front of her face. Brody moved around it and she saw the lump she was pretty sure was her car, because there was a little antenna coming up out of it.

"I'm dreaming. Hallucinating. Psychotic breaking."

"You are fine," Brody said through gritted teeth. "Aside from being a little overwrought."

She laughed, which she supposed proved his point. "Overwrought. Of *course* I'm overwrought. I have invoices missing and people stalking me and you, *you* some stranger I barely know, insisting on helping me and instead getting us into an accident."

"*I* did not get us into an accident. Keys?"

"What about keys?"

"Keys to the building, Kate."

Keys. Keys? "Oh, keys. Purse. But I didn't…"

He set her very carefully on her feet, and he didn't let her go. He positioned her so she was still leaning against him. Which was good, because she couldn't seem to find her balance. The world kept tilt-a-whirling around. She had to close her eyes to make it stop.

She heard the howl of the wind. Felt the cold sink deeper

and deeper now that she wasn't all pressed up to Brody's warm body, and wasn't that a shame.

"Kate."

"I want to lie down."

"I'm sure you do, but unless you want to freeze to death—not a fun way to go I'm almost certain—you'll stay standing for another few minutes. Now, open your eyes and tell me which key."

On a heavy sigh, she managed to open her eyes. He held her keychain. She looked at the door they were in front of. Main building. Her arms felt heavy, sluggish, but she managed to point to the one in his hand that would open the main building.

He opened the door, still holding her weight, and then once it was open, he scooped her up again.

It was weird because it wasn't the most comfortable position in the world, but it was kind of nice. To rest her head on his shoulder. To know he was going to take care of things.

When was the last time anyone had taken care of anything for her?

He was flipping the light switch back and forth, cursing under his breath.

"You sure swear a lot."

"Yeah, I'll apologize later."

"Must have lost electricity. Happens sometimes during blizzards."

"Fantastic." He muttered some more things under his breath, but she didn't catch them all. Finally, he set her down on a bench. He crouched in front of her, staring her in the eye. "We need to bandage up your head. Get some water in us. Then we'll figure out what to do."

"We should call someone."

"Not until the worst of this is over," Brody replied. "I don't want anyone coming out in this, do you?"

"No, I suppose not."

"First-aid kit?"

"Under the front desk. I'll—"

She tried to stand, but Brody's arm on her shoulder held her still. "I'll get it. You sit tight. Eyes open. Seated upright. Understood."

"Yes, sir," she said, attempting a mock salute but listing a little to the right.

"God help me," Brody muttered, then he turned on his phone flashlight and disappeared behind the desk. He returned with the first-aid kit. He moved quickly, efficiently, like he was used to such things.

He washed out the cut on her wound, murmuring reassurances when she hissed out a breath of pain. Gently, even though his hands were large and rough, he smoothed a bandage over her head where it hurt the worst.

"Water?"

"Mr. Field has a little fridge in his office."

Brody disappeared again, then returned with two bottles of water. He'd already downed half of his and handed her the other one. "Drink some of this. No painkillers till we know the extent of your concussion."

"I've never had a concussion."

"That's good."

She sipped the water, watched as Brody studied the building. The quiet, the lack of being jostled and the water was a bit like coming back to earth. Her head hurt viciously. Her body was stiff and sore. This was bad, and the full reality of that began to settle on her shoulders.

They were going to have to *do* something.

"The third building," she said, figuring it was their best chance at a warm night, with food, shelter. It would require roughing it, and using the historical artifacts, but it would keep them warm and safe through the night.

"What about it?"

She lifted her hand to touch where her head hurt, but then thought better of it. "It's an old cabin. We use it for living history and demonstrations. We can build a fire. I can heat up water on the stove. There are bed frames and old blankets. Nothing great, but it'll get us through the night. There might even be some supplies to make bread."

"Bread," he echoed.

"You should grab some water, maybe some perishables from the fridge. There should be sacks behind the front desk to help carry some things." She tried to stand. He was by her side in a second.

"I'm still dizzy, but I can walk. Really."

Slowly, he released her and she managed to prove her point. She could stand on her own, take a few steps. He studied her for a good minute before he apparently decided to be satisfied.

"All right. Don't move. Don't carry anything. You don't want to mess around with a concussion. Just stand here until I get everything ready."

Kate agreed, and then had to swallow down the lump in her throat. *Get everything ready.* He'd carried her through a *blizzard.* She didn't know what to do with any of it, but she knew she owed him…everything.

BRODY GRABBED ANYTHING he thought might be useful overnight. They were quickly losing whatever light could be found amidst all that snow, and he wanted to get settled— not just so Kate could rest, but so he could fortify this building they'd be staying in against whatever threat might be out there.

Someone had knocked them into that ditch. It might

have been the middle of a blizzard, but Brody knew what it was like to be under attack. What it meant to be a target.

Somehow, Kate had become a target. After ten years—no, she'd said weird stuff had happened in those first years before she'd backed off. She must have been close then, and he was close now.

Brody wouldn't have thought a small town in Wyoming would be the kind of place threats and purposeful accidents would happen, but he also hadn't expected dead bodies and murder—which they'd dealt with earlier in the month, leading to Jake's gunshot wound.

Bad things could happen anywhere, and when people did bad things, they often went to great lengths to cover them up.

Brody returned to where he'd left Kate. She was far too pale, but she was still standing. Her eyes were focused and open now. She definitely had a concussion, of that Brody had no doubt. But she didn't seem to have any other serious issues beyond bumps and scrapes and bruises.

He wouldn't be able to carry her *and* the supplies over to the other building—not because he was incapable, but because he simply didn't have the right kind of bags to transport everything in and keep his hands free enough to carry her.

"Why don't you wait here while I—"

She shook her head, then winced and pressed a palm to her forehead. "I'm not saying I'm great. But I can walk over to the cabin."

He didn't like it, but it was either that or leave her alone, and he didn't like that either. He hadn't seen a sign of anyone on the long hike over, but that didn't mean threats weren't looming.

"Okay. Lead the way."

"I can carry—"

"I'll carry everything," he said firmly. "You get us there."

She didn't seem satisfied, but eventually she clasped her hands together. "Okay."

Brody grabbed her bags he'd carried from the truck, the bags of food, first aid and water bottles he'd taken from this building, then followed her back into the cold, blinding white.

He hadn't realized how damn cold that wind was until he'd been out of it.

He waited for her to lock the door, then looked to where the third cabin would be. He couldn't see it in the white—not really.

"We just walk straight," she yelled over the howling wind. "Stay right behind me. We get turned around, we're in trouble."

Brody wasn't too worried about it. He could find things in worse conditions than this, but he let her feel like she was in some charge. He followed her slow shuffling steps, biting back the frustration both at the slow pace and how much pain she must be in. He had to repeatedly talk himself out of dropping his bags, scooping her up and getting her to that cabin himself.

But they finally reached the building, covered in white until Kate brushed snow from the padlock, undid it and then shoved the door open. She waved him inside, but he nudged her in front of him.

He closed the door behind him and looked around. Too dark to make out much of anything. He put the bags on the ground, pulled out his phone for a flashlight.

"Point it this way," Kate said, moving his arm to angle the light toward what he supposed was a kind of…kitchen. She began to move around the cabin and it took him a few minutes to realize she was lighting old-fashioned lanterns.

Then she knelt next to the big hearth in the middle of the room and began to work at starting a fire.

Eventually, she'd filled the place with enough light they could move around and see well enough. It was a big open space, though different areas had clearly been made into the kitchen, bedroom, living room. There was furniture, but all old. Probably historically accurate.

They were protected from the wind, but the place was still cold. Though warmer if he stood closer to the fire.

He needed to do a bit of a perimeter check, bolster the doors. But he wanted to be sure she wasn't going to collapse on him before he left her alone for even a second.

"Why don't you sit down," he said as she continued to putter around the cabin. Hell, she'd filled a big kettle with snow and now had it boiling on the old stove. "Rest a little."

"Are you going to sit down and rest a little?"

"I don't have a concussion."

She wrinkled her nose at that. "Do you know anything about concussions?"

"Enough. You don't want to push yourself." He pulled the rocking chair from the corner to be next to the fire and pointed at her to sit. "If you haven't developed any new symptoms in a few hours, you can take some painkillers if you've got the right kind. Maybe we should eat something."

She sat gingerly. "Didn't you get hurt at all?"

"Just a few scrapes," he replied. "I'll get you a snack and some water and—" He turned to go to where he'd left the bags, but she leaped to her feet.

"You're bleeding."

He waved her off. "I'm fine."

"Brady, that's an awful gash." She grabbed his arm in an attempt to keep him still. She peered at his back. "It cut through your coat, your clothes, your *skin*. You have to let me clean and bandage it for you."

He tried to twist his head enough to see, but it was across his back. He doubted it was as bad as she thought— he'd survived quite a bit worse—but it probably would be best to get it cleaned up. Infections were no fun—he'd dealt with his share of those too.

"For heaven's sake. You sit your butt down and let me put something on that." She gave him a little shove toward the rocking chair, but he stayed firm. There were things to do—protections to make.

"I am serious, Brody. I will…" She looked around the room, clearly looking for some kind of suitable threat. "I'll tie you to that chair if I have to," she said. Seriously. As if she could.

He shook his head. "No, you won't."

"After you fell asleep, I could—"

"I'm not saying you can't. I'm saying you won't. But if it means that much to you…" He walked over to the chair. Sat down, angled so his back was to her rather than the back of the chair. "Bandage away."

She scowled at him, but went to the bags and found the first-aid kit. She stood behind him and studied his back for a moment. "You're going to have to take off your coat, and shirt, and everything," she said at length.

He shrugged out of his coat, pulled his sweatshirt and thermal up over his head. When she did nothing, said nothing, he looked over his shoulder at her.

She was staring at his back with a kind of wide-eyed shock he didn't think meant his injury was *that* bad. She didn't look horrified, or even scared.

She looked interested.

He tried not to grin to himself. "Is it that bad?"

She startled a little. "Oh, no. Probably not. I mean, it's bad." She bustled over to the stove. "I need to wash it up a bit before I disinfect it." She started carrying the kettle back over to them and the fire.

He jumped to his feet. "You shouldn't be—"

"I feel much better. Really. My head hurts, and I feel a little nauseous, but my vision isn't fuzzy anymore. I don't feel that dizzy. Sit."

He frowned at her, but she was…lucid, moving fine, capable, and it would probably be best if he was bandaged up. He sat.

She got to work. She had some kind of towel—he hoped from this century instead of the last—and poured the water on it, then began washing his back.

The room got very quiet. He could still hear the howl of the blizzard outside, but they were insulated. The fire was doing its job and warming them up.

"You…have a lot of scars," Kate murmured, the whisper of her breath floating along the bare skin of his back.

Uh-oh.

Uncomfortable with that and the way she touched said scars so gently, Brody had to fight back the urge to shrug her hands off him. "Yeah, so?"

"What from?"

"Life, Kate." A life that had never been as kind and gentle as she was being.

"I imagine this will be another one. It might need stitches. I don't really know…"

"Just bandage it up for now. It'll be fine. I'm sure of it."

She sighed, her breath once again moving over him, having a very unfortunate reaction. He tried to think about anything else. The gaps in the plank floor. The way the windowpanes rattled. Someone lived here, without electricity or a phone, over a hundred years ago.

She smoothed the bandages—she had to use more than one due to the length of the cut apparently—and Brody kept his eyes focused on that gap in the floor between his boots.

"There," she said, apparently pleased with her efforts. "The worst of it should certainly be over by morning, and then we can call someone and get you to a doctor."

"I'm sure it's fine." He got to his feet—away from her soft gentle hands. He picked up his shirt off the ground. It was dry thanks to the heft of his coat, but there was a bloody rip in the back.

"I don't suppose you've got any large men's shirts lying around here, do you?" He glanced at her.

She didn't meet his eyes. Her gaze was fixed straight on his chest. She also did not answer his question. Just stared.

He knew he needed to say something. Pull his shirt on. Do *something* other than stand here, letting his brain go in directions it absolutely could not. Particularly when she had a bandage on her head and a concussion and…

Yeah, Kate Phillips was off-limits. He pulled his shirt on, trying not to wince as pain lanced his back.

She blinked, finally raising her gaze to meet his. Her cheeks turned an appealing shade of pink.

Do not. Do not. Do not. He cleared his throat, stepped back. "I'm going to check the perimeter."

Chapter Eight

He disappeared before she could think of anything to say. Out into the howling white.

"Check the perimeter." Long after Brody had disappeared, Kate found herself saying those words out loud. Over and over again. Who said *check the perimeter?* What was there to check?

She considered it as she tidied up from bandaging him. She fretted a bit about the size and depth of that scrape on his back, but that led to thoughts about his back…which led to thoughts about his front.

She blew out a long breath. She had never been that up close and personal with a man's body before. He was just so…big. And strong. And there were all different shapes and sizes of scars—like he'd been to war and back.

That stopped her in her tracks. Maybe he'd been a soldier of some kind. She knew a few guys from her high school class who'd joined the military. It would make sense. But why hadn't he just said that?

Well, perhaps he'd had a terrible time. If he'd seen combat, perhaps he had PTSD. Poor man. He wanted to avoid the subject and—

She probably should focus on getting through the night and a lot less on Brody Thompson.

She studied the cabin. She wished she had more blankets out here, especially since Brody's coat was torn. And bloody. But if they took turns and kept the fire going through the night, surely someone could come dig them out by morning.

Brody's poor truck might be totaled, which was going to be a problem of its own. But his problem, not hers. Though she should probably offer...something? He'd been driving her. But only because he'd insisted. *She* would have stayed put if he hadn't been around...messing with things.

Of course, she'd been the one to approach Brody in the *first* place.

The door swung open and Brody stepped in, once again covered in snow. Though the warmth from the fireplace quickly set to melting it.

"Still going strong. I'm going to have to call my brothers and let them know where I am and convince them we can stay put for the night. You don't think your Mom would try to come get you in this storm, do you?"

Kate was caught so off guard she laughed. When he frowned, she managed to swallow down the rest of her laughter. "Uh, no. She'll just assume I've hunkered down."

"You're not even going to give her a call?"

"No, it won't matter."

He gave her such an aghast kind of look she felt herself explaining even though she didn't want to. "Look, we're not your typical...mother–daughter... I don't live with her because... It's...complicated. She won't be worried about me. The end."

"You sure?"

"Positive." She gave a smile and a nod. Because she was sure, and fine, and that was...her life. "Call your brothers. I'll see what I can put together for dinner."

His eyes darted to her temple, where the bandage was. It ached, throbbed and she doubted she'd be able to sleep tonight if she couldn't take something for the pain, but she really was capable of moving around and doing things.

"Don't worry. I'm fine." *No one ever worries about me, and I am always just fine.*

He seemed to take that at face value and pulled his phone out of his pocket. He walked over to the far corner and greeted his brother. Kate puttered about the kitchen. She had a lot of the ingredients for the different frontier foods she demonstrated making for visitors, but it seemed like a bit much to drag it all out for some ash cake when Brody had grabbed some of the nonperishables she kept in the office. Canned soup over the stove would be the easiest.

"Yeah, look, had a little fender bender so I'm stuck here. I'll have to deal with the truck once it clears up. I'll keep you up to date," Brody was saying into his phone. When she glanced at him, he rolled his eyes and mimed the scolding he was likely receiving from the speaker.

She tried to smile, really, but it was hard to find humor. Truth be told, she would feel pretty good if someone was worried enough about her to yell at her on the phone. She frowned down at the soup.

A few minutes later, she could feel Brody approach. "Soup should be heated through in a few."

He studied the old wood-fire stove she was using. "You know how to do all this pioneer stuff, huh?"

Kate nodded. "I've always liked history, and I always liked the fort. There's an ancestral connection." She shrugged. She didn't really want to see the glazed-over look in his eyes most people got when she talked about history and genealogy. "So, I studied what interested me."

She scooped soup into the replica historical bowls, as the originals were under glass in the museum proper. She carried them over to the rickety table. It felt a little strange to do all of this in her modern clothes, but it was still mostly old hat. "Dad always wanted me to be a history teacher, but this suited me better than trying to wrangle teenagers. I get to live out my prairie fantasies and go home to indoor plumbing and the internet."

"Best of both worlds." He went over to the bags, plucked two bottles of water from them and sat one down in front of her before taking a bowl of soup across from her.

It was…teamwork. It was *strange*. But Brody dug into his soup and it felt kind of…nice. Cozy, almost. Aside from the injuries and what not.

She figured she should keep the conversation going. A pleasant back and forth would make the time pass faster. "Hazeleigh says you were all new to ranching and Zara had to teach you."

"Mmm. Mostly city boys."

"So, what brought you to Wyoming?"

"Oh, like I said. Cal's deal. We just follow." He waved it off like that was an answer, but it wasn't much of one. Maybe he thought she'd be bored, like she always assumed people would be bored if she told her stories.

"Were you a soldier before you all decided to ranch?"

His face went very carefully blank, and there was a strange…coldness to his gaze she'd never gotten from him. "Excuse me?"

"I just thought maybe… The scars…and you said *perimeter*." She stopped herself from stammering out any more explanations. "Never mind."

"It was a long time ago."

"Right. Sure. None of my business." She forced herself to smile at him, then look down at her soup and ate. Eating she could do. And if her mouth was full, she wouldn't say anything stupid.

After an oppressive silence where it was an effort to swallow past all the discomfort, Brody spoke.

"I was in the army."

She looked up to meet his gaze over the table. "You don't have to talk about it. I just… I was trying to make conversation."

"I know. I just don't particularly care to relive."

"Yeah, of course."

They finished their soup in utter silence, and Kate felt like a moron. This, among all the other reasons why she was a pariah in town, was why she didn't date. Not that this was a date, just that she was bad with people. Conversations. Normality.

She quickly scooped the last bit of soup in her mouth and then stood. "Done?" she asked brightly. "I'll wash up." She reached forward to take his empty bowl, but he grabbed her wrist before she could finish the movement.

His grasp was gentle, but firm enough to anchor her there. "I just…need you not to tell anyone that. The army thing."

She blinked. "It's a secret?"

He seemed to consider that word. "In a way."

"Okay. Sure. Lips are sealed."

He slowly released her wrist, the pads of his fingers trailing down the top of her hand. Did he really have to be *so* good-looking? And did she really have to be so *her*?

NORMALLY, BRODY WOULD have offered to clean up since she'd made dinner, but he needed to do some other things he didn't want her to pay too close attention to. Like setting up signals at all the entrance points. If someone tried to get in through the windows, they'd knock over something that would crash.

"I figured we'd take turns sleeping," she offered, pointing at the "bed" in the corner. Brody had slept in a lot worse conditions, but that still didn't make what he could only assume was a straw mattress a *real* bed.

"Ah, so you *do* believe me about being in danger." He studied the locking mechanism on the front door. Not nearly secure enough. How would he fix that? He turned to study their surroundings for an answer and caught her staring at him like he'd grown an extra head.

"Why would I think we're in danger?" She pointed to the hearth. "I was worried about the fire."

"Oh." *Whoops.*

"You don't honestly think we're in danger," she said, with a hint of incredulity to her voice.

He could let her live in her little fantasy world. Let her believe she was perfectly safe, but it wouldn't really serve her, would it? Better to know there was a threat out there, so she might actually protect herself. Lock doors. Be safe.

"What do you think happened back there when we crashed?"

Her frown deepened, but then she rubbed her head as it clearly hurt her wound. "I... You slid off the road into the ditch. Because of the weather."

He raised his eyebrows. "How did you hit your head?"

"That part is a little...fuzzy, but you slid into a ditch. Why wouldn't I hit my head?"

"Not that side of it. Not the way we fell. We were hit, Kate. By another car. Easy enough to do with the snow that bad, though a bit strange out here in the middle of nowhere. Still, I was willing to believe it was an accident. Until the other driver kept going, and rammed us again straight into that ditch."

"But... Why?"

He knew she was smart and capable, but he supposed what she *was* was frightened and out of her depth. Everyone around her had convinced her that she was always just overreacting, though she had probably been right about her suspicions of being followed or watched when her father first disappeared.

Maybe someone had even wanted her to *believe* she was overreacting, to stop looking into things. There was a lot still to uncover—not just about her father's disappearance, but about those early months after.

"You said you thought someone was following you back when this all started."

She shook her head. "Brody. Honestly, you have to understand. I was bereft. I couldn't sleep. I kept bugging the police and… I wasn't myself. I wasn't in control."

"Maybe not, but that doesn't mean someone wasn't watching you as you poked and prodded at the case. And what happened when you let up? Or hid it better?"

She looked taken aback.

"You're trying to act like you let it go. But all that research wasn't done in the first few years. And you came to me. Maybe you dialed it back, maybe you kept it on the down low, but you've never stopped looking for your father. You were just doing it quietly. Then I came in and did it not so quietly."

She still didn't say anything. She stood there, looking like he'd punched her. He wanted to take it all back. Reach out and soothe her somehow. But Brody didn't know how to sugarcoat the truth. Not when she'd be in more danger if she didn't accept it.

"There is something about Stanley Music that someone doesn't want you to know, Kate. It's too much of a coincidence otherwise."

"But…" She clearly couldn't think of any way to refute that, though she wanted to. "I'm sorry, you want me to believe after ten years of everything I've done, you come along and in a few hours find the one thing that…" She trailed off, looking pained.

He went over to the first-aid kit and went through everything until he found some painkillers it would be safe for her to take with that concussion.

"Sometimes an investigation needs someone who knows nothing. You knew your father was a music teacher, so the invoices made sense to you. The police too. And probably any private investigator. They were looking for irregularities, and that wasn't one."

"So, why did it stick out to you?"

He handed her two of the pills and then a water bottle. She stared at both with some distrust. "Your head hurts. You'll feel better if you take them."

She heaved out a sigh, but took the pills and the water. She swallowed both down. She lowered herself into one of the rickety chairs at the kitchen table. "You're trying to avoid the question," she said after a few minutes of silence. "If the police were looking for irregularities, what was it that you were looking for that made this stand out to you—and you alone, after years of cops, investigators?"

"And years of your own research?"

"I never knew what I was looking for. I was just… searching."

"You should give yourself more credit. I can't think of too many people who would have put together the kind of organized, comprehensive information you have. And it just might lead to answers, if we're careful. If you let me—"

"Stop avoiding the question," she snapped. "Why you?"

He didn't have to answer her. He didn't owe her any damn thing, but he *felt* like he did. Regardless of what his brain tried to tell him. "I was trained to look beyond the obvious, beyond what people want you to see. It's not like police work, where you go off the facts and the evidence. It's…more complicated than that."

"Trained," she echoed. She looked up at him with those soft brown eyes. "In the army?"

"Yeah." He had the strangest desire to tell her everything. Everything he'd been. Everything he'd done. It was impossible, but he *wanted* to, and he was more shaken by that need than he cared to admit.

"Why not threaten me back when I was sixteen? Why not crash my car or whatever when I was little more than a sad, desperate teenager?"

"Well, the timing might have made things all the more suspicious. By waiting, they take any heat off. Keep it separate." But they could have attacked Kate when she was alone. She seemed to be alone and isolated an awful lot. Instead, they'd stolen the invoices, presumably. Then waited until she was with someone else to try and cause some damage.

"You don't think that," Kate said flatly, as if she could see into the inner workings of his brain. "You think something else."

Brody sighed. "Your father might have left, but he's still your father. He might not have wanted you hurt."

"You think my father…"

"I just think there's a possibility the man who disappeared is involved in…whatever this is to try and cover up whatever Stanley Music is."

Chapter Nine

"I'm very tired," Kate said, because she was. Because the exhaustion burrowed so deep she wanted to cry. Not deal with any of this.

Her father. Alive. Stealing invoices? Warning her, but not hurting her? But not *not* hurting her, because her head throbbed. Her body just ached. Everything was off and wrong.

And this man standing there, looking at her with *pity* in his mesmerizing hazel eyes. It was all wrong. This was *not* her life.

"Take your boots and socks off and I'll try to dry them by the fire. Sleep for a bit. Probably not more than two hours. You seem pretty good for a concussion, but we can't be too careful."

We. That felt so very strange. But she nodded and got to her feet. She felt like dead weight and everything was far too complicated to sort through. Maybe if she went to sleep, she'd wake up and things would make any kind of sense.

She took her boots and socks off. They weren't too bad, but having them nice and warm when she woke up would be nice.

She crawled into the bed—for all the living history she'd done here, she'd never actually crawled onto the bed with its straw mattress, grass-stuffed pillow and old scratchy blankets. Much as she loved history, she was rather a fan of modern comfort. But she was so tired she thought she could have slept in the middle of a snowbank.

Brody crouched down next to the bed, so that he was almost eye level with her.

"I'm not going anywhere," he said, making it sound like a grave promise. "I'm going to help you until you have answers."

She laughed, wondering idly if she was delirious. "Why?"

He studied her, then reached out. He gently smoothed the stray strand of hair that had fallen over her face and tucked it behind her ear. His fingertips just barely brushing the skin behind her ear. If she'd been standing, her legs would have given out.

"It's the right thing to do."

She wished he wouldn't have said that. It meant too much to her. Made all those jangled, scared feelings inside of her soften too much.

But then he stood and she closed her eyes, and it felt like not two minutes later she was being shaken.

"Come on, Kate. Wake up now."

She groaned. She wanted to roll over and pull the covers over her head, but he tugged them away instead.

"Sleepy," she muttered.

"I just bet. But you need to get up for a bit. I made coffee."

"Coffee." She managed to blink her eyes open. Brody was sitting on the bed, pushing her up into a sitting position next to him. She blinked blearily at the wood stove. "You made coffee on that?"

"I'm very resourceful. Practically a pioneer myself." He

pulled her to her feet. "Kind of amazing what they managed to do with how little they had, isn't it?"

"That is exactly what is amazing." She had the same thought, day in and day out at work. She loved finding all the ways people had persevered with so very little. She loved trying to impart that knowledge to people.

Because humans had been surviving the unthinkable since the beginning of time, and finding ways to live and love throughout that darkest of it.

Brody hauled her to her feet. She wavered. Though her feet were steady underneath her, her vision twirled for a moment.

Brody held her by the elbows, keeping her upright. "You let me know when you're steady."

She stared at him. He'd woken her up because of the concussion. He was holding her up, waiting for her to be steady. There was a growth of dark whiskers—darker than his brown hair—all over his chin. He looked vaguely disreputable, but he was holding her like she were glass.

She reached out and touched his chin before she could think better of it. "Prickly."

His eyebrows raised, and his mouth curved, and somewhere in the back of her head she had the thought this was probably inappropriate. But she was too tired to work up any embarrassment.

"Coffee," she said. When he tried to help her over to the chair, she pulled one arm free and patted his shoulder with it. "I'm steady now."

He let her go, but she noticed he hovered right behind her as she made her way to the kitchen table. Once she was seated and he was certain she was steady, he went to the coffeepot.

He poured the coffee into one of the tin cups they kept in the cupboard. The coffee looked a little thick, and she much preferred cream and sugar, but they didn't have any of that. So, she'd have to choke it down black.

He set the cup in front of her, studying her. "How do you feel?"

"Like death," she replied, blowing on the coffee.

He chuckled. Then poured himself a cup.

"You probably want to sleep."

"No, I'm good." He sat in the chair across from her. The only light came from the fireplace and the lanterns she'd lit last night. But the cabin was now warm and cozy against the howling world outside.

It couldn't last. She might be tired—heck, she might be delirious—but she understood this was nothing but a respite from what came next. If Brody was right, and someone had crashed into them on purpose, she was in danger.

Danger.

It was hard to wrap her mind around, and yet… She looked at Brody, sipping his hot black coffee without even a wince. She had no doubt he'd know how to handle danger. And he seemed determined to help her. No matter how little she understood *that*, she believed it.

"So, what comes next, Brody?"

He didn't pretend to misunderstand her. He put his cup down, leaned his elbows on the table and considered. "Once it's morning, I think we should go back to your office. The invoices might be gone, but we still have the credit card statements. I'm going to have to find a way to look into Stanley Music that doesn't raise any suspicions. Once we can get out of here, I think… Kate, I don't think you should be alone until we know who hit us."

"But I'm always alone."

He frowned. "I thought you lived with your mother."

"Well, yes, but…"

"I understand if you don't want her to be in danger, but—"

"I can't decide if you're purposefully misunderstanding me or if it's just so incomprehensible to you, you can't wrap your head around it. Didn't you say yourself your mother was no prize?"

"Yes, I said that."

"Then you should understand that we are not…that way. My mother and I might live together, but in separate wings. She doesn't like me. She doesn't spend time with me. We exist…in parallel universes. She does what she wants—I take care of everything as long as it's carefully out of sight."

"That's pretty cruel, Kate."

"She would agree with you."

He frowned even deeper. "I meant her. *She* is pretty cruel. At least my mom just took off whenever she didn't want to be around. I certainly didn't have to look after her."

Somehow, despite the fact that he was this big strong ex-soldier of a man who'd carried her through a blizzard, and promised to help her figure this out because it was the right thing to do, it was far too easy to picture him as a little boy without a mother.

"I don't know why we're talking about this." She rubbed at her temple, under the bandage. "I'm not myself."

"Seems to me you're being exactly yourself, instead of hiding it all under some biddable exterior, but that's not you."

She laughed. Bitterly. "Oh, yeah, how?"

"If you were biddable, you'd have friends. You'd have a framework. An ecosystem." He waved the room around them. "But you have this job you love, and you've made some kind of manageable life for yourself in the wreckage of what had to be pretty devastating."

SHE STARED AT HIM, and Brody didn't really know what she saw. He wished he could…make this easier on her. But the only way out was through. This might be *her* problem, but he had a feeling something he'd done had kicked off the renewed interest in her. Snowmobiles and car accidents.

Part of her being some sort of target was his fault, and he'd see this through to the end. Make sure she was safe.

"Maybe I should be a little more biddable so I'd have an *ecosystem*," she said at length. "Who says ecosystem?"

"Someone who's made a study out of people and groups and how they work." Brody tried not to bristle. She had a head injury and had been thrust into something she didn't—couldn't—understand. "I know you're overwhelmed." He stilled her tapping hand by putting his own over hers on the table. He tried to ignore the stab of gratification that she stilled at his touch. "This is a lot. But we'll figure it out. I promise you that."

"If…" She swallowed, and she didn't tug her hand away. She let it lay there, under his. Small, but not fragile. She met his gaze. "If my father stole those invoices, he's here. Close. If he's hiding something bigger than disappearing…" She closed her eyes. "I just wanted to find him. To have closure. To understand what he'd really done—to Amberleigh, to anyone else. That's all I wanted. Instead I'm opening up a can of worms."

"Maybe. But there might be closure in that can of worms."

"I feel like I'm sixteen again. Losing *everything* I thought I knew. Alone."

Brody squeezed her hand. "But you're not alone. Not this time."

She shook her head, opened her eyes and fixed him with a heartbreaking look. "Why?"

"You asked for my help."

"That doesn't guarantee someone is going to help, Brody. I definitely learned that lesson."

"It does when you ask me. Besides, I like you, Kate. You might not see it in yourself, but I see someone who built the life they wanted and that suited them with what little they were given. Kind of like those pioneers you like so much."

After a moment of stunned silence, she pulled her hand out from under his. He had to resist the urge to hold fast, and he wasn't at all comfortable with that urge, so he folded his hands behind his head.

"I'm starting to believe you're too good to be true," she said, studying him suspiciously. "What secret are you hiding? Do you keep corpses in your attic? Kill animals? Have bird pets?"

"What's wrong with bird pets?"

"I don't know. They're creepy."

"I have none of those things." But he did have a secret, one he hadn't been so adept at hiding. He'd figured back when they'd been sent here that it'd be easy to pretend to be someone he wasn't. Hadn't he made a career out of that?

But it was different when it wasn't a mission. When it was just life—even if it wasn't your own. He was still himself, even if himself was this Brody Thompson, rookie rancher. But he wasn't playing a role, or trying to keep his country safe.

"I know it's not morning, but you grabbed some flashlights, right?"

"Yes." And he needed to focus on this little mission he'd made for himself, rather than...anything to do with his past.

"Then let's go over to the office building. Get the files now. What's the point of sitting here, sipping coffee, feeling sorry for me?"

"Not a good idea. We don't know who's out there. Going

out in the dark with flashlights is like a shining beacon of *please kill me.*"

"You can't really believe..." She trailed off. "Someone really...purposefully crashed us into a ditch?"

Brody nodded. "I'm sure of it."

"But they didn't kill us."

"No. Though leaving us crashed in the middle of a blizzard wasn't exactly a kindness. Who would have thought I'd have the skills to get us to safety?"

"Carry me to safety," she muttered. "Certainly not me." She sighed. "Then what are we supposed to do all night? Sit here and knit?"

He opened his mouth to say something—something he absolutely should *not* say, or think, or allow his brain to even form words for. He pushed it aside. "I think I'll take a little nap, if that's okay with you?"

She studied him quizzically, but she nodded. So he got up and went to the strange pioneer bed. It'd be good to rest while they had nothing to do. Come morning there'd be plenty, and clearly he needed a little more mental clarity.

He situated himself on the rickety bed, half feeling like his large frame would break it. Worse, the pillow smelled like her. Something vaguely flowery the snow and head wound should have dulled before she laid down.

But he closed his eyes, used all his old army tricks for falling asleep even in stressful or uncomfortable conditions and was out within seconds.

When he woke up, Kate was quietly moving around the stove. It looked and smelled like she was putting together some kind of breakfast. Though the fire and lanterns were giving off most of the light, he could tell that even if it was still dark outside, it was starting to brighten.

He sat up, and though Kate didn't look over her shoulder at him, she had to have heard him move.

"You talk in your sleep," she said, her tone carefully devoid of any kind of inflection that might give him a clue to what kind of things he talked about. In his sleep.

He sat on the bed, scratching a hand through his hair. "Oh, yeah? About what?"

"I couldn't understand all of it," she said carefully. She turned, put a plate of food on the table and gestured him for it. "But you mentioned Cal *a lot*."

Brody winced as he walked over to the table. His stomach rumbled. "That is a look into my psyche I could do without," he grumbled. "Are those homemade biscuits?"

"I had all night. I could only entertain myself reading for so long." She gestured to a book on the table. It was a diary of some kind. "I've read it a million times. Practically memorized it. So I figured cooking would be the next best thing."

He flipped open the cover. "Good reading?"

"For some. It's the journal of the first owner of this cabin. Well, a photocopied replica. We have to keep the original in better archival conditions. But the writer was Sarah Marks. I show it on some of the tours or read little parts to give them an idea of what the day-to-day was like."

"And what was it like?"

"Hard," she said with a laugh. "Lonely," she added, a little more seriously. "Sarah had a rough life. She left everything she knew back east, then lost her husband, her baby."

"Sounds depressing."

"I suppose. More melancholy than depressing." She took her own plate and sat across from him. "There's something comforting about… Well, it's hard to feel sorry for yourself too much when you know struggles are just part of it."

"Part of what?"

"Life."

He couldn't argue with that. "This is amazing, Kate."

"You're just hungry."

"The cookies were amazing, too."

She looked down at her plate, but she couldn't quite hide the smile of pleasure. "I like to cook," she said simply. "I had a look outside. I'm not sure we're getting out of here today."

"That bad?"

"I can't remember this much snow. Not in the past few years. And likely even if your brothers could get out here, they've got their hands full dealing with the cattle."

"I suppose as long as we can hike over to the office building and do some research, all's not lost. Maybe the weather will keep anyone after you at a distance."

But they'd definitely be taking some precautions before they walked over.

Chapter Ten

It was kind of nice to eat breakfast with someone. And Brody didn't force the conversation to stick to her father and the missing invoices. He asked about Sarah and the cabin, like he had an interest.

She knew better than to go into one of her long involved lectures only she and maybe Mr. Field and Hazeleigh cared about, but he asked good questions. Interested questions. It gave her warm fuzzy feelings—ones she should put a stop to.

They cleaned up breakfast, Brody standing hip to hip with her as they used boiled snow to wash everything. She fumbled things a few times, but didn't dare look at him to see his reaction.

He was being nice. He had some sort of misguided superhero complex. Save the little lady. And she needed the help, so she'd take it. And not get any ideas. If he *liked* her as he claimed, it was the friendly sort of like. Probably thought of her as some kid sister.

"How old are you?" she asked before she could think better of it.

She didn't dare look at his expression, and his voice didn't give anything away as he answered her. "Thirty. How old are you?"

"Twenty-six."

"Not so far off."

That response shocked her enough to look up at him, and he was looking down at her and... She darted away, putting the dried plates and cooking utensils back where they belonged, creating some much needed distance.

"Sun should be up well enough now," she said brightly.

He agreed and they piled on all the layers they had, even fashioning blankets to act as scarves. Brody emptied out her backpack carefully, then strapped it on in case they needed to bring back any more supplies.

She opened the door and winced at both the brightness—even of dawn's light—and the cold wind.

"I don't suppose you know how to shoot a gun," he asked conversationally.

"Sure I do. You know, presuming it's a nineteenth-century era gun."

Brody laughed, which made her frown.

"What on earth are you laughing at?"

"Sorry, I just had a very clear image of you in your pioneer garb, skirts blowing in the wind, pointing one of those rifles at some dirty lowlife. Like an old Western."

"And that's funny?"

"It's far too appealing, Kate."

Which shut her up, because what was she supposed to say to that? Appealing? Who thought *any* of that was appealing?

"I don't suppose you've got any weapons lying around?" he asked.

"Up at the main building. Locked up, of course. You don't really think we'll need..." She trailed off when she saw his gun. From *this* century. "Oh."

"Just a precaution."

"Of course."

"Make you nervous?"

"Not the gun so much as the reason you're holding it." She looked around at the bright, blinding white world. Was someone really out there, wanting them dead? He had to be overthinking.

"I want you to stay put—just for a minute, while I take a quick look around."

"Brody…"

"Just a precaution. You can leave the door open, just don't step out yet. I'm going to walk around the cabin, look for tracks, signs of anyone."

"Okay," she agreed, reluctantly. He nodded, then stepped out into the cold morning. The snow reached his knees, and she watched him as he disappeared around the corner of the cabin. The gun in his hand looking both menacing and like it belonged there.

She heaved out a breath, watched the fog of it swirl and then disappear. She squinted out over to the main fort building, and then the office buildings. It was a short walk, though it'd take longer in the snow.

It struck her, in these random quiet moments, how insane this was. Surely her father wasn't stealing bits of her research. Surely no one was trying to get them killed. And surely Brody Thompson—former soldier, current rancher, too hot for anyone's own good—wasn't helping her and saying things about liking her, finding her *appealing*.

She'd had a psychotic break.

But after a few minutes, Brody reappeared. Still holding that gun. Still far too attractive bundled to the hilt. "Looks to be clear. Let's go."

"You didn't see anything?" she asked, stepping forward into the white. She tested the snow, hoping for a hard pack, but her foot sank up to the thigh.

"No sign of anyone. Which was about what I figured.

The blizzard was too much. Whoever hit us had to have retreated back to wherever they have shelter."

When Kate struggled to pull her leg out of the snow to make the next step, Brody chuckled.

"I could carry you again," he offered.

"I can do it," Kate muttered. And she did, but it was slow going. She had to hold onto Brody's arm at times, to leverage herself up and out of the practically waist-deep snow.

But they got to the office building, and she fished her keys out of her coat pocket and opened the door. They stepped into the dark building. She flipped a switch and nothing happened. "Electricity is still down, which means no internet."

"Damn," he muttered. "Until we can get more information about Stanley Music, we're kind of at a stalemate."

Kate blew out a breath. "Maybe I've got something about them in the paperwork that we just missed the first time around." She doubted it, but she headed for her office anyway. She'd spent ten years on compiling all her records. Maybe she didn't remember everything, but she'd have remembered that or looked twice at it. "Or maybe it used to be a business and we have some record of it…" They didn't keep Wilde records in the fort that weren't directly *related* to the fort, but she had access to digitized records and…

Her thoughts stumbled to a stop as she looked at her office. It wasn't messy exactly, but she could just tell it wasn't as she'd left it.

You were mad at Brody. You weren't paying attention. Don't go down this paranoid road again.

It was her mother's voice in her head, and it was right of course. She'd had a concussion at this point. She wasn't thinking clearly. Brody wasn't helping with his stories of being run off the road or…

"What is it?"

Kate inhaled sharply, because she hadn't been breathing. She'd been spiraling. She hated that feeling. *Hated* it.

"I just left in such a rush. Didn't realize what a mess I'd left." She tried to think. Really think. Past the car accident. Past all the ideas Brody had *put* into her head.

Brody laid his hand on her shoulder. A gentle, but anchoring pressure. "Kate."

She looked up at him, and she wanted to be able to tell him that everything was fine. As it should be. But he looked…concerned, and all those times her mother had told her she was losing her mind, convinced her she was paranoid, it wasn't concern.

Kate had tried to convince herself it was. Mixed up in grief and betrayal that she'd taken out on Kate through no fault of her own.

But Brody was showing more care than her mother… ever had. It had always been Dad who was the compassionate one. Any warmth or happiness in her childhood had come from him, and then he left.

"Stuff's been moved around," Kate said, very quietly. Very carefully. If Brody told her she was making things up, she might just crumple.

But he held her gaze, very serious. "What exactly?"

"I don't know. Little things. My chair should be pushed into my desk. My computer monitor isn't usually pulled forward like that. Maybe Mr. Field…" But she trailed off. Because, of course, Mr. Field hadn't been in. No one had been in. There'd been a blizzard.

"Come with me." He didn't give her the opportunity to agree or disagree. He was already pulling her along, back to the front door. He released her and swung the door open.

He studied the door, front and back. Crouched, practically got nose to nose with the knob. "Someone broke in,"

Brody confirmed. "But took great pains to make it look like they hadn't."

Kate lowered herself into a chair. This couldn't be... But why would Brody lie? Why would he be trying to confirm all her worst thoughts? Unless they were true.

Unless they were always true.

"I wasn't paranoid. I wasn't unhinged. This whole time. This *whole* time, someone has been paying attention to me." Kate let her face fall into her hands. Her body ached, her head throbbed, but the idea that she had never been wrong, never been off base...

It wasn't closure, but for the first time in ten years she felt...lighter. Surer.

She'd been right. All along.

"It couldn't have been about Amberleigh, or at least just about her. We know he didn't kill her, that somewhere along the line they parted ways—*if* they left together. He's not covering up a murder, but he—or someone—is trying to hide *something*. And have been, for ten years."

Ten years. She wished she could race home and tell her mother right now.

I was right. I was right all along.

She wanted to laugh, but that wasn't what bubbled up inside of her. It was much closer to a sob, and her eyes filled and... *Oh, hell.*

Anguish just poured out of her. She couldn't stop it. Ten years of the mental gymnastics of talking herself out of things, and to know she had been right. Maybe there were still things she didn't know, but at the heart of it she hadn't been clinging to a fantasy.

"Hey, hey. It's all right. It'll be all right. We'll get it all figured out. Don't cry." Brody patted her shoulder awkwardly, which *did* make her laugh. She wiped her face and tried to find some control.

"It's not a…worried, sad cry, exactly." She inhaled deeply and let it out. "Just ten years' worth of relief."

"You were right."

She looked up at him and managed a smile, though she knew her face must be a mess. "I was right. When everyone convinced me I was wrong. It doesn't untangle everything that's been tangled, but some things, I guess. It's like a relief. After all this time. Part of a weight lifted off my shoulders." But there was still a weight there. "You think it was my father."

"I think it has to involve your father in some way. Someone has kept their eye on you, without harming you in any way—at least until I got involved."

"Or Stanley Music got involved."

Brody nodded. "Fair point. We need to figure out that piece of the puzzle, but I guess the world is currently against us in that respect."

"It's waited ten years. I suppose it can wait another few days."

"Look, it's up to you, but Landon's got a way with computers. If they haven't lost power, if they've got time to spare beyond the cattle, I can ask him to look into it while we're stuck here."

Kate bit her lip. "Will that make him some kind of target?"

"He'll be able to keep it on the down low. Better than I would. I would have asked him in the first place if I'd thought digging into it would unearth anything other than…well, old information."

"I can't imagine they have power, but if you think he can help, that's fine."

Brody nodded, pulled his phone out of his pocket. "I don't have much battery left. What about you?"

Kate pulled her phone out of her pocket. "Plenty. You want to use mine?"

"Yeah, thanks." He took her phone and called his brother.

While Kate stared at the door, wondering what happened now that she was right.

"CAL WON'T LIKE IT."

Brody scowled into the phone. "What does Cal like these days?"

Landon chuckled. "Fair enough. I'll see what I can do once the power's back. Zara's putting us through the paces with all this special blizzard cattle care. I won't be back at the house for another couple hours. And I can't imagine coming to get you guys today. Roads are toast, and you've got our best vehicle."

Brody winced at that, but he didn't let on that the best vehicle was currently *toast*. "We can survive another day or two out here. I'd just like to get somewhere a little more…" Brody looked out the window. They were sitting ducks. Whoever had hit them was somewhere out there, and maybe they'd retreated thanks to the blizzard, but that wouldn't keep them away forever. Especially knowing those snowmobile tracks outside Kate's office yesterday were probably theirs. "Well, I'd like Kate to have a doctor check her out. She's got a nasty bump."

"We'll get someone out to you by tomorrow, for sure," Landon said. "Even if we have to call some kind of emergency services. But you know how to look after a bump."

"Yeah, I do."

"Enjoy ringing in the New Year stuck in 1895," Landon said with a laugh.

"*The New Year…*" Brody echoed.

"Yeah, have you lost track of time? Today's December

thirty-first. See you next year, bro," Landon offered. "We'll check in again tomorrow, see where we're at."

"Yeah. Tomorrow. Later." He pressed End on the phone, then turned to Kate. She was pale, the bandage on her head probably needing redressing. Her eyes were red from her crying jag, and he couldn't imagine what it would be like to just…carry all that grief and anxiety around for ten years.

And she'd never given up. Even when she'd clearly told herself she had. It was kind of a miracle. He'd lost that kind of faith in just about everything. Except his brothers.

"Well, I guess we're spending New Year's Eve together, Kate."

She laughed. Which he didn't quite understand, but she looked genuinely amused by the notion.

"Missing out on a big party?"

"Oh, yes, that's me. Big party plans on New Year's Eve. It's never just me alone, watching the ball drop and eating an entire cake by myself."

"Alone? Really?"

"I'd get a cat, but I'm allergic."

"Kate…"

"Have I given the impression I have friends? Hazeleigh is the closest thing I've got and that's complicated. Certainly too complicated for New Year midnight countdowns." But she didn't sound like she was complaining, or that she felt lonely. "What about you? Big New Year's traditions?"

Traditions? Most of his adult life had been spent deployed or in army barracks. He'd never had much reason to take leave. That's why he'd become part of Team Breaker. "I can't remember the last New Year's Eve I wasn't with my brothers. That's about it."

"I always wanted a sibling. Like the Harts. They always had each other." For the first time she sounded wistful.

It made his chest hurt. All the ways she was alone that mirrored in a lot of ways his own…isolation growing up. Much like her, he'd found a purpose in his profession. But he'd also found a family.

"I don't suppose you've got any champagne around here, then?"

Her mouth curved, some of that wistfulness leaving her face. "I very much doubt it, but we can raid the kitchen and see what we can come up with." She sighed. "What were they doing in my stuff, Brody?"

"I don't know, but I'd say you still have—or had— something someone wanted. We could go through and see if you notice anything else missing?"

She sighed heavily, but got to her feet and nodded. They went back to her office and she surveyed everything with a critical eye. She sat at her desk chair, rifled through the folders. "Something is missing," she muttered to herself.

Brody let her work and studied the office from a stranger's eye. It'd be easy to pick out the things that didn't connect to her work at the fort. She kept everything organized and labeled. But why now?

He truly believed something he'd done to look into Stanley Music had prompted whoever was out there to make a move, but either she had something about Stanley Music in there they hadn't seen, or there was something else as well.

"I looked into the other invoices, music stores and the like, right? But maybe we need to focus on anything relating to music."

"Okay."

She handed him a couple folders and he began looking through with a critical eye. Anything relating to music he set to the side. They worked in silence for a while.

"That's what's missing," she said suddenly. "I had an appointment book in here of Dad's that had lists of all the lessons—dates, people, how much they owed and if they paid."

Brody leaned against the doorframe and considered this new information. "They don't know exactly what they're looking for or they would have got it the first time."

She chewed on her bottom lip as she surveyed the little piles they'd made in the cramped room. "So, it's probably not my dad. And they might be back."

"Both possibilities." And it all connected to lessons and music. "Something wasn't on the up and up with your dad's music lessons."

She looked up at him. "He did teach music, though. I learned to play the violin and so did Amberleigh—even if something else was going on, there was something legitimate there."

"Makes it a better cover."

"For what?"

Brody considered. "I don't know how much you heard about Amberleigh's murder, but she was involved with a group that ran and sold drugs. That doctor might have killed her, but it was all because she was messed up in this group involved in drug running."

"But wasn't the group all arrested after shooting Jake?"

"Supposedly. But all it takes is one of the higher-ups not getting caught, or even more likely, it's a system of groups."

"An *eco*system?"

He glared at her, but it was hard to hold when she was smiling at him. Teasing him. "Something like that," he returned. "Let's get all the music stuff together. We'll take it with us, but leave this looking the way it was so if they do try to come back, they might not notice that we've taken some things."

They worked for another few hours, separating and

compiling. Brody turned over the question of *why now* in his head, and at the end of the day, he had to believe whoever was doing this hadn't been aware of just how much information Kate had. Until looking into Stanley Music had tipped them off.

Once they'd gotten through everything, and put what they didn't need away, Brody glanced at his watch. "We should head back to the cabin. We'll be losing daylight soon. Let's go raid that kitchen."

She nodded and they put the layers of clothing they'd taken off back on. When they stepped outside, the sky was a deep, vibrant pink. The clouds were lighter shades, giving dimension and little wisps of fiery gold. The mountains seemed to absorb that gold and practically throb with the color of it.

Kate breathed out and stopped for a moment, and Brody found himself stopping, too. Transfixed by the beautiful sunset.

"This is why they stayed," she said, and he had a feeling she was talking more to herself than purposefully trying to tell him anything. But he listened all the same. "Hard day, terrible blizzard. You're tired, you're hungry, but you came this far, and at the end of the day, you see something like this to remind you that you came here for a reason."

There was a truth to her words that echoed inside him, but only for a moment before he remembered they were targets. Anyone could be out there, lurking in this beautiful world of hers. "How'd they celebrate the New Year on the frontier?" he asked, pulling her forward so they could get moving.

"Not much differently than any other day," she said, gripping his arm to help her leverage her legs over and through the snow. "It was hard to get anything special out here, or visit with neighbors. Most efforts had just been done for Christmas, and with the winter weather, travel was less likely. They'd have chores at the crack of dawn, so staying up till midnight wasn't very popular. Different traditions might have been brought depending on where you came from, but for Sarah Marks it was just another day, mostly."

Just another day. He could certainly relate to that. But it seemed wrong to treat it that way when Kate didn't go to parties, or have friends, didn't even have a mother who cared enough about her welfare to spend time with her. She was alone.

He knew from experience that even when it was more comfortable to be alone, it wasn't always the easiest thing. She pulled her keys out and pushed them into the lock. She twisted, and then she stilled.

"Brody." She looked up at him, holding her keys in the door, not pushing it open. Her eyes were wide, concerned. "It wasn't locked."

Chapter Eleven

Brody's expression changed completely. Right before her eyes. Yet it didn't seem like he moved a muscle. But everything got harder. His eyes narrowed, and his hand very carefully moved through the air to close over hers on the keys.

His other hand held the gun.

Nerves jittered up Kate's spine, but she breathed through them. Whatever was going on, she could be brave. She could be like Brody. Stoic and certain.

"I don't see any tracks, do you?"

They both surveyed the snow around them, but though the wind wasn't whipping around like yesterday, it was certainly still blowing the snow into drifts and peaks that would obscure footprints. Even as she looked back at their own just walking over from the office buildings, they'd been obscured. Visible indentations, but harder to determine how many people, what size.

"I don't see anything."

Brody frowned, staring at something around the corner. "Don't move, okay?"

She nodded and he took his hand off hers. He moved carefully over to the cabin, peered around, then immediately pulled his head back. He stalked back to her, grim and blank.

"Go to the cabin," he said, his voice barely above a whisper. "Quick as you can. Lock whatever you can, barricade the rest."

"But you—"

"Have a gun and fighting experience. You don't, Kate. If someone is in there, I will be able to handle it. If no one is in there, I'll come get you."

Kate struggled with the order. After all, Brody was only here because of her. But he *did* have experience she didn't have. Fighting and guns. He'd been a soldier. He knew how to deal with a threat.

"What did you see?"

"Not sure, but it could be snowmobile tracks. Go to the cabin."

Kate looked across the long yard to the cabin. Where it had felt safe. And warm. She did want to go there, but not without him. She turned to face him. "Be honest with me, isn't alone more dangerous than together?"

"No. I promise, if anything is in there, it's a threat I can handle. But only if I don't have to worry about you."

Kate inhaled. She wanted to listen, because going to the cabin sounded much safer than trailing after him. But what if he got hurt? That scrape on his back was bad enough, if he went in there alone—

He put his hand over hers again, pulled the keys out carefully. He moved her fingers so she curled them around the keychain. He squeezed. "Now, Kate."

She could argue. Say she could hold her own. She could listen to her conscience and not let him handle this alone, but all of those were dumb choices. It put both of them in danger, and had more to do with her wanting to be seen as brave when she wasn't than with common sense.

She had to trust him. "Just be careful. Don't take any

unnecessary chances. We just want to be safe. You don't need to be a superhero."

Something in his expression changed—she couldn't read it, but there was something softer in it. "Go on. Fast as you can. I'm not going in till you're safe inside."

She nodded and started out. The high snowdrifts made running impossible, but she moved as quickly as her body and the snow would allow. She told herself the whole way that this was *precaution*. Brody would open the main building, and maybe someone had been in there, but they'd have to be long gone by now.

They would have heard a snowmobile. In the office building, for sure, they would have heard the engine puttering up to the main building. Maybe if it had come last night in the blizzard when they'd been hunkered down at the cabin they wouldn't have heard it, but this morning?

There was no way anyone had snuck up on them. No way anyone was in that building.

And there's no way someone came out here last night in the middle of that storm?

She looked back at Brody. He was still waiting by the door. His hand was on the knob, and he held the gun in his other hand. As much as that gun was a sign of all the bad things, he looked completely right somehow, standing in the middle of all that white, his hand clasped around his weapon.

He'd been a soldier. She reminded herself of that over and over again as she returned her focus to the cabin. He'd been a soldier, and knew how to fight. He had all those scars, and yet he was all in one piece.

Because he knew what he was doing. This wasn't just about protecting her. It was about protecting them. Finding the truth. She'd asked for his help, and in Brody's mind that meant...helping until the problem was solved.

She didn't know men like that. She hadn't believed they existed. Not since her dad had left her and shattered any illusion she had about... Well, everything.

She finally made it to the front door, panting heavily but here. She unlocked the door. She gave Brody one last look. He was just a figure now at this distance. She couldn't make out his expression, only the shape of him.

She swallowed down the anxiety, the fear. For the first time, she fully put her trust in someone and prayed it wouldn't come back to bite her in the butt.

She stepped inside the cabin. Brody had told her to lock and barricade everything, but she wanted to leave the door open for the time being. If Brody came, she wanted him to be able to get in quickly. So, she started at the back. There were only windows to worry about here, but they were low enough to the ground and big enough to be entrance points if someone broke the glass.

She couldn't exactly board them up. It would ruin the historical integrity of the cabin and—

Are you really standing here worried about historical integrity under the current, potentially dire circumstances?

Okay, well, even if she had the supplies to board up the windows, it would take too long. She surveyed the room. If she put the table on its side, it would cover most of the window. It wasn't very heavy, but if she reinforced it with some heavier items, it would definitely be difficult to get through.

She set about doing all of that, trying not to fret about Brody. Just focus on the tasks. That was how she'd gotten through a lot of her life.

She got the windows mostly covered, or at least as good as it was going to get. For the front door, she could drag the stove over, maybe. It would be hard, and she wouldn't want to put it in front of the door quite yet. She'd wait for Brody. But she could get it closer.

She turned to study the stove and determine how hard it would be to move on her own. Then screamed when a man stepped out from the corner between the wall and stove—a gun in each hand.

"Don't move," he said. She didn't recognize him. Nothing about the weather-beaten face covered in black-and-gray whiskers and long hair was familiar to her.

But that voice. She knew that voice almost as well as she knew her own. "Dad?"

He pushed the hat he was wearing back enough so she could see his eyes. The dark brown of her own. Eyes she'd spent her entire childhood looking into.

She couldn't seem to breathe and tears filled her eyes. It was all wrong. He couldn't be here, holding guns, and yet... It was her dad. He was here. Ten years and she was standing in the same room as her father.

"Kate, you have to stop this."

"Stop...what?" Crying? A few tears had slipped down her cheeks, but that didn't seem fair. She hadn't seen him in ten years. And he was standing so far away, still holding those guns even if he was pointing them at the ground.

"All of it. The investigating. That friend of yours poking into things. I've kept you safe all this time, but I won't be able to if you keep this up. They'll kill you. They'll kill him. If he comes after us, he'll beg for death."

They and *us*. Kate couldn't make sense of it. Of any of it. "You disappeared without a word. Without a trace."

"Yes, and I thought that would solve everything. But you didn't let it go. So, this was the last resort. You have to stop, Kate. This is your last chance. Your only warning."

"Dad, you're here." *Here.* Her father was *here*. She could reach out and touch him. Hug him. But he held two guns and she didn't dare. It wasn't even out of fear exactly. She could just feel this…wall between them. Ten years and tons of secrets.

"You let this go, Kate. You don't tell *anyone* you saw me—not even your friend out there. Do you understand me?"

"No. I don't understand *any* of this."

"I have to go. I'm sorry. I am." He moved for the door, so quickly she reached out to stop him, but he'd already left the cabin.

She scurried after him. "Dad."

He walked with long purposeful strides in the opposite direction of the main building. "Dad!"

But he didn't look back.

She took two steps and then stopped herself. He didn't want her to follow. He didn't want *her*.

He just wanted her to stop.

BRODY DIDN'T HEAR the scream, the shouts. He was already in the main building. It was silent as a tomb, what with the electricity out. But someone had jimmied the lock. Maybe they'd already left, but Brody had to be sure.

The building didn't have the best lighting, so despite the bright sun bouncing off the white snow outside, the interior was dim.

He did his first sweep of the main room, studying the array of mannequins. They were particularly creepy in the heavy silence, alone. Faceless. Brody repressed a shudder. It was hard to notice if anything was different. He didn't know the room well enough to notice subtle differences, and at the end of the day he didn't know what these people were looking for if they'd already been through Kate's office and papers—and more than once.

Still, he looked, determined not to leave any stone uncovered. He poked into closets, corners, behind exhibits. He was glad he'd been through the compound last night so he had a basic idea of the lay of the land. But he didn't really know what would be off or wrong.

Maybe he should have kept Kate with him. He shook his head. Sending her off to the cabin where she'd be safe. Protected.

Unless…

The cold grip of fear was no stranger. Brody had dealt with that every moment of his deployed years. Even more so when they'd been Team Breaker, and one mistake could have cost any of his brothers their lives.

But fear could cost as many lives as it could save. He'd watched Kate walk to safety, and if they wanted her, they would have stuck around after the car accident. They would have taken or threatened her in the ten years she'd been living this—whatever it was.

The smart thing was the thing he'd chosen to do. He knew that in his gut. Even as he worried for Kate.

When you let yourself care, worry was a natural response to danger. Somehow…he'd allowed himself to care for Kate.

He snorted quietly. *Allowed* himself. It had hit him out of nowhere. Maybe that first moment he'd met her, giving a prim lecture in her pioneer costume. And everything he'd learned about her since didn't help that initial glimmer of interest. Attraction.

He'd always had great timing, hadn't he?

Grimly, Brody moved forward into the back of the building. The kitchenette and some changing rooms were here, and a back exit. Presumably, they'd chosen to break in to the front exit only, but they might have left through the back.

He poked his head into the changing rooms, then stilled.

The hairs on the back of his neck stood up and he stopped breathing—focusing all his energy on listening.

He'd heard something. A very, very faint something—could have been a mouse, the wind—but it was *something* enough to be on extra alert.

He moved through the two changing rooms, making absolutely no noise. He kept his gun gripped at the ready, his breathing even, and his ears and eyes alert to every possible nuance around him.

He heard it again. The creak of a floorboard, not loud—muffled almost. But definitely made by something heavier than a mouse.

He moved toward it. The kitchenette was a small, cramped room—Brody knew that from yesterday. It was also the room that housed the back exit door. He edged toward the opening that would allow him to see into the room. He paused after every step, careful to be noiseless. Careful to have his gun ready and his instincts sharp.

He angled his body just so he could see a sliver of the room. The sliver with the door. It was closed. He didn't see anyone. So he inched forward.

Someone was in the room, shoving something into a backpack. Carefully, Brody raised his gun.

"Don't move," Brody ordered, holding his gun pointed directly at the man's back.

But the man whirled on Brody, his own gun out and pointed, pulling the trigger during the whirl.

Brody had to dive back behind the refrigerator as some kind of shield. The man kept shooting and Brody huddled there, inwardly cursing. He hadn't wanted to shoot first, but he could have debilitated the guy before saying anything. Maybe his instincts were getting rusty.

Not going to fly.

Brody crouched and waited for the man to appear so

he could take him down, but he never did. Eventually, the gunshots stopped but still the man didn't come at him. Carefully, Brody eased his head out to survey where the gunman was, but there was nothing.

The door hung open.

He'd…run. Brody moved for the door, still careful and alert to make sure it wasn't some kind of trick or trap. But when he looked out the backdoor, there the shooter was. Zooming off into the blinding white on a snowmobile. Brody had no hope of catching up. The engine roared through the air—and another vehicle seemed to come out of nowhere to meet up with the first. In a few more seconds, they were gone and the world was quiet again.

Brody sighed. They were gone—more intent on escaping than on hurting him, which he supposed was a positive all in all. He'd need to get Kate up here to see if they'd taken anything.

Kate.

He practically vaulted back to the front of the building, whipped the door open. Took a few steps out into the snow to see the cabin.

And she was standing outside of it.

Chapter Twelve

Dad had disappeared. She'd stood there, sure he'd come back. Sure something would happen. But he'd disappeared into the vast world around them and…

She jumped about a foot when a loud *bang* pierced the air. "Oh, God." Her vision whipped to the main building. Brody… Dad had said…

If he comes after us, he'll beg for death.

"No, no, no." They couldn't.

Bang. Bang.

If they hurt Brody… She had to… Something.

She squeezed her eyes shut. *Stop panicking. Think.*

She couldn't go running in there. She didn't have a weapon. She didn't have anything. She had her phone. She would call for help. Maybe the roads were bad, but if people were *shooting,* someone would have to come *help.*

She fumbled in her coat pocket for the phone, her hands shaking as she drew it out, but before she could dial anything she heard a different sound. Like a door slamming, opening. She looked up and across to the main fort.

There was Brody. She couldn't make out his expression across the vast yard between them, but he immediately began to move for her. He didn't appear to be hurt.

Thank God. She ran for him as he stormed toward her, and when they met, she couldn't help but throw her arms around him. He was okay. In one piece. No visions of him bloody in the middle of her mannequins had come true. "I heard gunshots. I thought…"

He pulled her away from him, holding her by the elbows. "You should have stayed put. You should have stayed damn put."

There was a fury in his voice, in his eyes, but his hands were gentle, and she had the distinct impression he wanted to physically shake some sense into her. But he didn't.

"I heard *gunshots.*"

He sighed. "None of them mine," he muttered, scanning the world around them. He was all *soldier* in that moment. Remote. Capable. "Let's get inside."

He let go of one of her arms, but not the other. There were enough tracks now that she didn't need as much help through the snow, but still he didn't let her go. They walked back into the cabin.

It had grown cold again, so many hours without a fire. Her pants were wet. Her heart was jittering in a million different ways.

She'd seen her father. She desperately wanted to tell Brody, but Dad had warned her not to. For his own good.

"I have no idea what's going on," Brody said, moving toward the fireplace. To her surprise, he set to restarting the fire with practiced ease. "You'll need to look around the main building to see what they took. The gunman had a backpack of some kind. He put something into it."

Brody stood, frowned. "He wasn't here alone. Two men on snowmobiles."

Had one been her father? Should she tell Brody… She looked up at him. He was so strong and sure and he'd been in the military. Maybe he could handle whatever her dad was mixed up in.

But she thought about the guns Dad had held. The things he'd said.

They'll kill you. They'll kill him. If he comes after us, he'll beg for death.

It had been her father. Alive. Here. Protecting her, so he said. She swallowed. She couldn't put Brody in the middle. This wasn't his family. His fight. He could get hurt or worse if he helped her and she had to…

She had to protect Brody.

The emotions swirling around inside of her were too much, but she had to control them. Swallow them down. She couldn't tell Brody she'd seen her father. She had to somehow…get out of all of this.

"I don't suppose there's anything we can do about it now. It's getting dark and they…just shot at you and left?"

"Yes," Brody confirmed, his frown so deep it created creases around his mouth. "Just ran off. Like cowards."

"Maybe…" Kate swallowed. "Maybe they just wanted whatever it was they got and that's it. They clearly don't *really* want to hurt us."

Brody's hazel gaze focused in on her, intense and not at all interested in her suggestion. "They drove us into a ditch, and while those bullets just now might not have hit me, they were plenty real. You're going to need a new refrigerator for your kitchenette."

Her stomach dropped out. Presumably the refrigerator was the only thing that kept those bullets from hitting him. "Brody…" She almost reached out. She couldn't have even said what she wanted to do. Hug him? Touch him? It was all so silly.

She just had to put it all to an end. That's what Dad had said. "This is…too much. If it's this much trouble, this much danger to look for my father, to look into Stanley Music, we should stop."

"Stop?" Brody echoed, like he didn't understand the word.

"If we let it go…" She didn't want to let it go. She wanted to know and understand what was happening. Why her father was here and had left her. Standing there. No real explanation. No teary greeting on his part. A terse warning with *guns* and then gone. "I don't want…" She stopped herself from saying *I don't want you to be caught in the crossfire.* It was true, and she knew, deep down, he would never accept that as a reason. He wouldn't consider himself in danger.

But she believed her father, that Brody would be, if he pushed this. It was her problem. Her mystery. Her father. Even her threat.

"I don't want to be in danger for these answers. That's not what I signed on for. I just wanted to know where he went, but if it's going to put me in danger, I don't want answers. It's been ten years without them. Better to just… let it go."

He stared at her for a very long time before he spoke. "Is that really what you want to do?"

She met his gaze. She had the horrible feeling she was disappointing him, which was absurd on a number of levels. Number one, she was saving him so it didn't matter what he thought. Number two, why should his opinion matter? She'd had to stop caring about what everyone thought a very long time ago.

He sighed before she could answer, put his hand on her shoulder. Oh so gently. "I know you're afraid, Kate. You have every right to be, and it's certainly nothing to be embarrassed about."

She wanted to laugh. She felt plenty of embarrassment over a lot of things, being afraid of this situation was hardly one of them. Car crashes and gunshots? Yeah, she wasn't embarrassed to be scared.

Still, better he read it that way than to understand what had really happened.

He squeezed her shoulder. "I promised I'd protect you, and I don't break my promises."

Now she really was going to cry. No. *No*. She'd already cried in front of him today. She was going to be strong and figure this out. She forced herself to smile. To put her hand over his and pat it in a friendly manner. "I'm sure you don't. You're a very good man." It physically hurt to say the next bit. "But I'm not your responsibility, Brody. I don't want this. It's more than I bargained for." She sucked in a breath, let it out. As she did, she took a step away from him, so his hand fell off her shoulder. She maintained eye contact no matter how much it hurt. "I'm done. I quit."

Brody was sure it took a full minute, maybe two, for the words to penetrate enough to make sense. *Quit?*

"Without answers? Without closure?" he said, because surely…surely that wasn't who she was. She was just scared. Shaken up. She'd find her backbone again and see this through.

Something flickered in her expression. "Yes." She said that so certainly, but her eyes told a different story. Conflict.

She wasn't sure at all. He wanted to press her, but he forced himself to keep his mouth shut. He'd just been shot at. He was used to that kind of thing, and honestly it wasn't so bad when it was just a coward trying to escape. Much worse when someone was determined to end your life.

But Kate wasn't used to gunfire. She was sheltered. He'd back off for tonight. Let her think they'd called it all off and that she was safe. If they could get home tomorrow, get her head checked out, they'd have a new discussion.

Or he'd tuck her away somewhere safe and handle it.

She couldn't possibly let it go. She just needed some time to accept or believe he'd keep her safe. That was all right. He had to remember he was dealing with a civilian, not a soldier.

"All right, Kate," he said at length, struggling to find a neutral tone. "If that's what you want."

She nodded firmly. "It is."

He tried to smile, but wasn't sure the movement of his face muscles made it even halfway there. He felt a bit frozen and awkward. Strange feelings for a man like him.

"Well, we're still stuck here tonight," he offered, searching for something to say. Some way to distract himself from the strange, crushing disappointment that had wound itself around his lungs. "New Year's Eve."

"I'll make some ashcake," she said, just a shade too desperately.

"No offense, but that doesn't sound very appealing."

She laughed, still that desperation in her tone, but he let her lecture him about ashcakes and she seemed to settle back into herself. He left the cabin as it was—table upended in front of the window with an assortment of heavier objects weighing it down. The front door was locked, not barricaded, but he'd keep an eye on it. He didn't plan on sleeping tonight.

Maybe the men today had run away. Their interest seemed to be information over hurting anyone, but that didn't mean things would stay that way. Still, he'd make sure it seemed like he'd put it away. Like it wasn't weighing on him.

He smiled as she handed him a plate with this…ashcake on it. "Well, it doesn't look like ash."

She rolled her eyes at him as she sat in a chair next to him, close to the fire, her own little cake on a plate in her lap. "I told you it's not *ash*. It's completely enclosed and *cooked* in the ash."

"Right, right."

Despite the rickety old construction—the snow and the fire worked to keep the cabin cozy. It didn't feel half as rustic as he'd anticipated. Much nicer than sleeping in a desert hunting a terrorist leader, that was for sure.

He studied her out of the corner of his eye. She was... fidgety. In a way, it was a positive. She wasn't acting like she was in a lot of pain or that she was dizzy or feeling any other adverse effects from the concussion. He needed to change her bandage, but he figured he'd let her eat her cake first.

Maybe he could find some way to put her more at ease. "I know that people shooting guns off isn't exactly a day at the park."

Her gaze went very...*imperious*, and she straightened in her chair. "A day at the park? No, we call gunshots and break-ins and all that..." She waved her hand in the general direction of the fort building. "We call *that* a day at the movies."

"It was just an attempt to get away. If they'd really wanted to hurt me, they would have—"

"Is this supposed to make me feel better?" she interrupted on a shocked demand.

She had a point, and since she did, he grinned and went for a joke. "Care about me, Kate?"

"I'm very grateful," she said solemnly, holding his gaze.

Not quite the answer he wanted, strangely enough. But probably best for both of them. "Probably be a good idea to switch out that bandage on your head."

"New bandage to ring in the New Year. *Woo*." She wiggled her fingers unenthusiastically in the air, which made him grin.

He got up from the chair to retrieve the first-aid kit.

"I should look at your back, too. I should have looked before all this. Oh, Brody, you're probably in pain. I'm sorry, I—"

He put his hand on her shoulder so she didn't jump out of her chair to start fussing over him. "I'd let you know if it was a problem. No point in taking unnecessary risks out of pride. Now sit still."

She frowned, but did as she was told while he gently removed the adhesive holding her bandage in place.

She nibbled on her bottom lip and he had to work very hard to keep his mind focused on the task at hand. Her cut. Her bump. Her *concussion*. The cut had scabbed over, but the bump was still awfully big. "No headaches, dizziness, or anything else out of place?"

"Not really. My head hurts, but it's more a throbbing right there on the bump rather than something I'd call a headache."

"Good." He put on a new bandage, wondered if he should have had her ice that bump. Too late now. Get through tonight and ideally they'd get her to a doctor tomorrow. "All set."

She stood. "Your turn, then," she said, firmly, pointing at the seat.

"It's—"

"You can't ring in the New Year with a bloody old bandage. It's bad luck," she said, managing to keep a straight face despite the fact she was making stuff up. She looked at her watch. "You've only got ten minutes left."

He supposed there was no point in arguing. He'd make it fine another day or so with the same bandage, but if it made her feel better. He'd shrugged out of his coat earlier as the fire had warmed up the cabin, so he only needed to pull off the sweatshirt and thermal layers and sit so she could reach his back.

She made a distressed sound. "Brody." Her fingertips gingerly touched his shoulder—much higher than that scrape. "I should have done this this morning. Hours ago. You've bled clean through—even your thermal."

"But not my sweatshirt."

She let out a frustrated breath. "Stay put." She moved around the cabin—boiling snow again, coming up with some kind of rag. He couldn't tell if she was more irritated at him for being this bad off, or more irritated at herself for not thinking to change the dressing on his wound.

He was betting on more irritated with herself, which made him feel…guilty, he supposed. "I'll get checked out tomorrow." If it really did need stitches, Dunne would no doubt stitch him up whether he wanted to be or not. "I promise you, it's fine."

"I promise you, I can see it better than you can and it isn't *fine*. Maybe it's not going to kill you, but it's not *fine*. Now sit still. I'm going to wash it up and then re-bandage it."

"Yes, ma'am."

She was quiet for a while, washing his back with her little rag, while one small hand rested on his back as if for balance. As if he was her anchor.

Clearly, he'd lost too much blood if he was thinking in such ridiculous metaphors.

"Did you get *all* these scars in the military?" she asked softly, with that same note of distress. Like she was worried for him, when those scars were so old he hardly remembered which ones came from where. At least the ones on his back.

He opened his mouth to make a joke about her undue interest in his scars, but in the end he found he really just wanted to tell her the truth. "Most. I was a boy left to my own devices, so I managed to scrape myself up some before I joined."

"How many years were you in the military?"

"Enlisted the minute I could. Deployed as often as I could."

"Didn't want to be home?"

"Not in the least, and it was a cost-free way—more or less—to get the hell out and do something worthwhile."

"So, why'd you stop if you were doing something worthwhile?"

The urge to tell her the truth was surprisingly strong. He couldn't, of course, but it was strange to come to the moment and *want* to. He'd always figured it'd be an easy enough secret to keep. After all, everyone important in his life knew, because everyone important in his life had been there.

Kate wasn't…important, exactly. *That* wasn't why he wanted to tell her. Not at all. It was because…. Well, if he told her, surely she'd trust him to handle this situation with her father. She'd understand he wasn't your average soldier. Or even above average. He'd been exceptional in every way. The only reason he was here instead of bringing down more terrorist groups was because he'd become too much of a target for doing just that. All because some idiot had pushed the wrong button.

Regardless of the whys, he was a target the military couldn't risk—not because of his life, but because of what he knew.

That was why he wanted to tell her. Because it would help. Not for any other reason.

But he couldn't, and now he'd waited a very long time to answer, which meant he needed something stronger than, *I guess I just felt like I was finished.* "Dunne was hurt."

Which he supposed was the simplest, most truthful way he could explain it. "For the first time it made more sense to be stateside and civilian than enlisted and deployed."

"I don't understand how you can be so close to your brothers if you were alone as a kid."

He smiled a little. "That's because you don't have brothers."

She sighed, and it sounded sad, but she smoothed the bandage down on his back and then patted his shoulder. "All done."

He stood and turned to face her. She picked up his shirts. "You've ruined your shirt," she said, holding the gray thermal that now had a bloodstain on it—more blood than he would have anticipated—around the tear. No doubt Dunne would get some joy out of stitching him up, which Dunne could use.

"It'll do," he said, plucking the shirt out of her hands. He didn't wince as he pulled it on, only because she was studying him so intently.

With *interest*. If nothing else, she liked the look of his body and he found himself far too pleased that she did. But then she frowned. "You shouldn't be moving so much. You'll bleed through another bandage just overnight. Here." She took his sweatshirt and opened the neck hole and held it out to him—like he was a small child who needed to be dressed.

It was…sweet. A mothering kind of gesture he'd certainly never been offered in all his life. So, he bent forward and let her settle the sweatshirt over his head and then pull his arms through the sleeves.

"There," she said, giving a firm nod as if she was trying to convince herself all would be well. She gave his chest a pat, and then her hand just kind of *rested* there. And she stared at her hand on his chest like she wasn't quite sure what to do about it.

He covered it with his own. She inhaled sharply and then just sort of held her breath. He should let her hand go, certainly not turn it so he could read the time on her watch. Certainly not let the pad of his thumb stroke the inside of her wrist while he did so.

She let out that breath she held, a shuddery sort of sound. She didn't pull her hand away and it *was* New Year's Eve. Almost midnight.

He could kiss her. It was tradition. Good luck. Nothing more.

She looked up at him, the rise and fall of her chest a mesmerizing cadence to the moment. It was just New Year's Eve, that was all. And she didn't back away. If anything she leaned toward him.

So, he took the hand she was still holding and settled it on his waist, slid his own arm around her, pulling her closer. He took his sweet time—because it was enjoyable, because it gave her the chance to back away if she should want to.

But she didn't. So, he lowered his mouth to hers. He'd meant to make it simple. A brush of lips. Nothing more. Something that wouldn't reach inside him and rearrange everything, but that seemed to be all Kate was capable of when it came to him.

Because he lingered there at her mouth—soft and sweet, like spring in the middle of all this winter. And she held onto him, like she didn't want him to go anywhere. Which was fine with him. Right here was *more* than fine with him.

He slid his hand down her back, pulling her closer, so their bodies could touch, mold, melt. But she jolted there in his arms—in surprise more than alarm, because she didn't pull her mouth away from his. But it was enough of a lurch that Brody found about two brain cells to rub together and eased his mouth away from hers.

She was staring up at him with those big brown eyes like she didn't know *what* to do. *How* to react. Clearly, she felt very out of her depth, and Brody didn't really know how to make that right.

"Happy New Year," he managed, because he didn't have the slightest idea what to do about this except create some distance.

"Yeah, right. Happy…" she said, her voice just a faint echo.

He very carefully eased her back. "You should get some sleep, Kate. I'll watch the fire."

She nodded, blinked, then turned away and crawled into that sad little bed. He settled himself into his chair for a very long *uncomfortable* night.

Chapter Thirteen

Kate didn't sleep well. How was somebody supposed to sleep well after they'd been kissed like *that*? Surely not every kiss in the world would rock a person off their axis.

Not that she would know as that was the one and only time she'd been *really* kissed. Tim Fletch had put his overly moist mouth on her in the sixth grade, but Zara had pulled him off and punched him for her.

Always have someone else fight your battles, don't you, Kate? Not this time. Kisses or not. Confusion or not. She would not allow Brody to be caught in the crossfire of her own problems. If she had any New Year's resolutions, that was it.

Which meant she couldn't kiss Brody again. Not that he probably would. He'd just kissed her because it was New Year's. That was all. He wasn't really *interested*.

What if he is really interested?

Her stomach swooped because lonely girls who'd been isolated and shunned since the age of sixteen *had* to develop excellent imaginations, and Brody felt like some culmination of every fairy tale she'd ever dreamed up. Strong and handsome. Gentle and kind. Good all the way through. Protective and self-sufficient. She wasn't sure how he could be real, but she had to get it through her head that no matter how real he was, he wasn't for her.

Most especially *now*. She had to keep him far away from anything to do with her father.

When it was finally a decent hour to get up, she tried to creep out of bed, assuming he'd fallen asleep in his chair. But he was sitting there, eyes tracking her movements in the murky dark of morning in the cabin.

She blinked at him, her thoughts fracturing in a million different directions. Except the one she really couldn't entertain. *Couldn't we kiss some more?*

"You didn't sleep," she said, sounding strangled even to her own ears.

"Here and there." He smiled and held up his phone. "One of my brothers should be here any minute. They drove Zara's truck over, far as they could, then used a snowmobile to get the rest of the way. They'll take us back to the truck and then we'll head back to the ranch."

The ranch. Then home. This whole…thing was over. Which was good, what with his severe cut and her concussion. Doctors and home. Her mother. Life, back to normal.

And somehow finding a way to keep Brody out of her family drama. Because he wouldn't. He wouldn't just back off. She'd really have to convince him he needed to let it go.

She swallowed. It figured, didn't it, she finally had a man in her life—sort of—who she'd like to keep there, in a variety of different ways, but she had to push him out. For his own good.

"That's great. You really need to get your back checked out."

He stood, slowly. Somehow, even though he'd just sat in that uncomfortable chair all night, he looked perfectly rested. Even though he had that awful cut on his back, which she kept forgetting because he moved as if it didn't bother him at all.

And he'd kissed her. Really kissed her. Of his own free

will. Not only to make her feel better. Even if he did it because of New Year's Eve, it was still at least kind of because he wanted to.

"We should pack up," he said gently.

Which was when she realized she was just standing
there, staring at him. "Right. Yes." She jumped into action,
moving probably more quickly than she needed to. But she
could feel his eyes on her as she flitted about, packing up
her stuff, putting the cabin back to rights.

Once she was satisfied, and had her bags over by the
door, she slapped her hands together. "Well, I hope you
enjoyed your trip back to 1872." She smiled up at him like
she would to any fort visitor. Or tried. He was staring at
her a little too intensely, standing a little closer than she'd
thought.

"I did," he said, very seriously. So seriously her heart
fluttered and she didn't look away from him like she
should.

"Gunshots notwithstanding, I suppose."

"Seems in keeping with the frontier vibe," he said with
a shrug. He stepped closer. So they were almost toe to toe.
And she should step back. Look away. Because he was
holding her gaze the same way he had last night and she
knew what came next now.

But she *wanted* it.

No matter how her rational brain told her to stop, she
didn't. When he lowered his mouth to hers, she kissed
him back. Wound her arms around his neck. If last night
had been an introduction, a test, this was something like
a detonation.

He held her tight against his body. His mouth did things
to hers she'd only ever *read* about. It was as amazing as
all those romance novels said. So, she held on for dear life,
and met all that fire with her own—as untested as it might

be. Dimly, she realized the door behind her back was… vibrating. Someone was…knocking.

She pulled back a little, trying to blink herself back to reality. But Brody's mouth had moved down her neck and, *oh, wow.*

But someone was pounding on the door and yelling Brody's name.

Kate cleared her throat, gave him an ineffective push. "Brody."

"Hmm?"

"I think your brothers are here."

His head came up, his eyes cleared and he scowled at the door—someone was definitely on the other side, pounding on it and calling out his name.

"About the kind of timing they'd have," he muttered darkly, then gently moved her to the side so he could pull the door open.

Landon was on the other side. He took in Brody's thunderous expression, then looked at her. Kate didn't know what he saw, but his mouth curved into a grin.

Kate didn't even have it in her to be embarrassed. Brody had kissed her. No countdowns to midnight in sight. Like he wanted to. Like he *liked* to.

It left her dazed at best.

"Well, let's get y'all loaded up," Landon said. He had the hint of a southern drawl, looked nothing like Brody. Or Cal, for that matter. Or Jake. Landon was fair—blond-haired and blue-eyed. He had a similar sturdy build, but his frame was lankier, less compact.

Even though Brody had said they weren't fully biologically related, Kate had to wonder if all this *brother* talk was something born of the military. At least for Brody. What he'd told her about her childhood sounded lonely and bleak.

Familiar.

People showing up to help this way was *not* familiar.

But that's what was happening. Brody and Landon carried everything and waited for her to lock up. There were two snowmobiles waiting—one empty, presumably Landon's. And one with a driver covered from head to toe in winter gear. If Kate had to guess, she'd say it wasn't Cal. And since it couldn't be Jake, it had to be Dunne or Henry. Based on Dunne's injury, which she knew nothing about except that he walked with a limp, she'd guess the driver was Henry.

Brody helped her onto the snowmobile behind Landon. "We'll talk at the house," he said in her ear.

Talk.

Talk about *what*? But he was climbing behind Henry and then they were zooming off. The white was so blinding Kate had to close her eyes until they slowed to a stop. Waiting for them was a truck.

Kate blinked at the driver.

"I know it's a hardship, but you're going to have to let go, sweetheart," Landon said good-naturedly.

"Sorry," Kate muttered, her eyes still on Zara as she managed to climb off the snowmobile. The men were handling her bags and loading the snowmobiles up on the trailer the truck was pulling. Kate stood in the middle of it, not sure what to do or say.

Zara had been her best friend, but Zara had always had a very clear sense of wrong and right. What should be done and what shouldn't. Amberleigh and Dad's disappearance had meant Kate was *wrong*. For ten years, she had been *wrong* in Zara's eyes.

Kate was tempted to tell her to shove her help where the sun didn't shine. But Zara would probably laugh at that, not be offended.

"Come on," Brody said, taking her gently by the elbow. "You okay?"

Kate nodded and let him pull her to the truck. Zara climbed into the driver's seat without a word, and Kate and Brody climbed into the back. He was comically cramped in the narrow back seat, knees practically at his elbows once Landon got in. Henry climbed in the passenger and then they were off.

In silence, they drove to the Hart Ranch. Kate got the feeling Landon *wanted* to say something, but didn't have a clue where to start with all the different kinds of tensions layering the air.

The roads were clearly still bad. Zara drove slow and carefully, skidding a few times but holding the truck on the road with white knuckles and gritted teeth.

When she pulled up to the ranch, there was a sense of relief that they'd made it. Kate knew she should thank Zara as they got out of the truck, but honestly the only thing she could concentrate on was escape.

She stepped into the bitterly cold snow and gritted her teeth against it. She moved around the truck, finding Brody and Landon taking her bags out of the truck like they were going to take them inside. She couldn't let them do it.

"I really appreciate everything, Brody, but I should head home. I don't have a car, and I know the roads are bad, but the truck got through all right. Or I could maybe snowmobile over. I could ask Zara if you'd prefer, but—"

Brody was shaking his head. "You can't go home, Kate."

"But—"

He nodded at Landon and Landon headed inside after Zara and Henry, leaving her and Brody alone in the yard. Brody put his hand on her shoulder.

"I think you should stay with us for a day or two, just until we can be sure those guys aren't coming back. Zara spends the night a lot since Jake got shot, and Hazeleigh could spend the night, too, if it'd make you feel more comfortable. But… I can't let you go home just yet. Not until we know who was shooting at us."

"We don't *have* to know that," Kate said, and knew she sounded overly desperate. "If they don't shoot anymore."

"But we don't know they won't," Brody said earnestly. Sweetly, almost. Protectively, definitely.

Of course she'd somehow find her way into kissing a guy who was earnest and protective, and her father's disappearance would get in the way. Or reappearance in this case. That *was* the story of every relationship in her life, wasn't it?

And she couldn't argue with Brody. Because in order to really prove that she was safe, she'd have to tell him the truth about talking to her father. Then he might believe she wasn't in direct danger anymore, but she didn't really think he'd back off. No matter what he did with that information, it would put him in a danger she couldn't stand the thought of him being in.

So, she had to go along with this. Force herself to lay low at the Hart Ranch for a bit, and when no one came after them, he'd let her go. He'd let *it* go. He had to.

BRODY CHALKED UP the wary way Kate looked at the house to all her history with Zara. He couldn't help but think maybe some close quarters had the potential to heal that rift or soothe it over. Zara had been the one to encourage him to help Kate, after all. There were clearly some unresolved feelings between the two women, and if Kate stayed put a few days, maybe these were ones she could resolve.

As a bonus she'd be safe, and maybe he could find the answers for her. She was scared to get them, that much was for sure. But that didn't mean she was safe if she *didn't*. He didn't want to scare her with that fact, so he'd handle it.

He led Kate inside, took her up to his room. "You can sleep in here tonight."

"Is this your room?"

"I'll take the couch." He put her bags down. "I'm going to go see about a doctor doing some kind of virtual appointment with you, and—"

"What about your back?"

"I'll have Dunne check it out. He has some medical experience."

Kate's frown deepened. "Some doesn't sound very reassuring."

"It is. I promise. Why don't you rest? It's been a long few days."

"You didn't sleep last night."

Last night. Which brought back thoughts of that kiss. Then the one this morning. Which wasn't why she was here, and it wasn't what he could allow himself to focus on right now.

No matter how much he wanted to.

The color rose on her cheeks and her eyes were on his mouth. She was thinking about it too.

He had to get out of here. Quick. "Just lie down for a bit," he said. Or instructed. He wasn't sure, because he got the hell out of there before he did something that would distract him from his mission.

Because figuring out who'd shot at him and what was going on with her father was definitely his mission.

He went to find Landon to discuss anything he might have found on Stanley Music. He'd get around to Dunne and his back eventually.

Kate wanted to back off, and he understood. But she didn't understand Landon could find things without anyone knowing he'd found them. She didn't realize the lengths he and his brothers could go to keep her safe.

And he couldn't let her know, but he could help her. Even if she thought she didn't want his help.

He grimaced, because he felt a bit like Cal. High-handedly making decisions for her, without her knowledge. He wasn't going to keep her in the dark forever. Just…until she was ready to face this.

He didn't feel any *better* about it, but that didn't stop him. He found Landon in the kitchen, drinking coffee.

"Headed back out to help Cal with the cows," he said. "Zara's talking to some doctor in town to see if he can come out and take a look at Kate."

Brody nodded. "Anything on Stanley Music?"

"Haven't had much time, but I did some poking around. Whatever it is, it's got the kind of security walls that don't make sense for a *piano* company. I'll be able to dig further once I've got some more time."

Brody nodded. He wanted to push, but a blizzard meant other things came first. "What can I do?"

Landon's eyebrows raised. "Have yourself checked out."

Brody frowned. "What do you mean?"

"I've known you too long, seen you hurt too many times. I also saw that wreck of yours—I played down the damage to Cal. You're welcome. But I know something's wrong with you."

"Just a scrape on my back."

"So, you're basically bleeding to death?" Landon returned with a grin. He nodded to the door to Dunne's bedroom that also served as a mini medical center as needed. "He's waiting for you."

Brody hedged. "Got a few things yet to take care of."

"I'm sure you do. But you're going in there if I have to

wrestle you in. And since I know you're injured, I know where to hit."

It *would* be a draw usually—a wrestling match. He and Landon were evenly matched, and rarely got the better of one another.

But Landon could be mean when he wanted to be, and he'd use Brody's injury against him to get what he wanted.

Brody sighed and went to Dunne's door. He knocked, then stepped inside.

The room was bright for a change, curtains drawn back. It was a sparse room, military clean as Dunne was a lifer—his father had been military too.

In the corner of the rather large room that Brody assumed had once been some kind of parlor, was a medical setup. Clean, efficient and prepped.

"Sit," Dunne said.

So Brady sat.

Out of all of them, Brody worried about Dunne the most. Or maybe it was a tie with Cal. They both held tight to the idea they could control *everything*. When everything about their lives these days made it very clear they could not.

When Dunne ordered him to take off his shirt, Brody did so.

The cursing he heard Dunne utter was the most he'd heard him say in almost six months. So maybe he'd bless the injury, even if he didn't bless the pain.

"Needs stitches," Dunne muttered.

"I figured," Brody said on a sigh.

Chapter Fourteen

Kate didn't do resting well. Especially here in Hart house, a place she'd spent many a childhood hour with her friends. All of whom were either dead or not so much friends anymore.

She didn't want to be here. She wanted to be home. Alone. Where she could deal with everything. On her *own*. Like she'd been doing for the past ten years.

But there was no way to get home.

Maybe if she asked Zara, Zara would drive her. Surely Zara would want her gone. Yes, that's just what she'd do. She plugged in her phone and changed her shirt since she had an extra sweatshirt in her bag.

Before she could do anything else, Zara barged in. No knock. Typical.

She had a phone to her ear. "Are you dizzy?"

"What? No."

"No dizziness. Swelling, but lucid. What day is it?"

"What?"

Zara rolled her eyes. "What day is it?"

"New Year's Day," Kate replied, crossing her arms irritably. So like Zara to just barge in and make demands.

"Yup, she's good. Okay." Zara made a few more assenting noises, offered a thanks, then put the phone in her pocket. "Doctor says you're good. Rest. You can take acetaminophen if your head hurts. Any development of new symptoms, or if that swelling doesn't go down in a few days, you should either go in or call, depending on the road conditions."

"Fantastic," Kate muttered.

"Yeah, I saw that truck. You're pretty lucky."

"I feel like the end of a damn rainbow."

Zara *almost* cracked a smile. "I'm, uh, going to make dinner. You want to help?"

"*You're* making dinner?"

"I can cook."

"I know you *can*. You hate to, though."

Zara shrugged and waved Kate to follow. "The guys all take turns, but I've been picking up Jake's since I've been spending most nights here. Most of the time I have Hazeleigh come over and take my turn for me, but she's eye-deep in some project for Mr. Field she can do from the cabin."

"Right, well, how about you just drive me home instead? Then I won't be a burden."

Zara studied her at the top of the stairs. "You were shot at."

"No, *Brody* was shot at."

Zara rolled her eyes and headed down the stairs. "Brody can handle that."

"I know he was in the military, but——"

Zara stopped suddenly, sent her a quizzical look. "He told you that?"

Kate winced. He'd told her no one could know that, didn't he? She hadn't thought Zara would count, or maybe she *hadn't* thought.

"I mean, I *know* because Jake told me," Zara continued, leading Kate to the kitchen. "So, don't feel bad that you said it. I'm just surprised he told you as they don't really like telling anyone."

"He certainly didn't tell me much."

"No, he wouldn't." Zara moved to the fridge and began pulling out ingredients. "Sit down, concussion girl, you can chop."

Kate was by far a better cook, but she didn't see much point in arguing with Zara, who set a cutting board and some vegetables in front of her. "Chop away."

Kate just grunted and went to work. They worked mostly in silence, Zara standing at the counter, Kate sitting at the table. When someone broke the silence, Kate was just as surprised by Zara speaking as she was by what she said.

"I can't make up for ten years."

Ten years. Kate fought back the wave of sadness and focused on anger. "Probably couldn't hurt to *try*," Kate muttered.

Another silence followed, and Kate figured that would be that. But Zara sighed.

"I never hated you, Kate. I hated…everything that happened."

Kate looked up at Zara, who was frowning down at the chicken she was cutting into pieces. "You had a funny way of showing it."

"Well, I've never been any good at grief, or sympathy, or… Well, you know me." She shrugged and dumped the chicken into a skillet.

Kate sighed and got to her feet. She went to where she knew they kept the spices, pulled out a few and began to season the chicken standing shoulder to shoulder with her ex-best friend. Who was putting out an olive branch for the first time in a decade.

Kate wanted to be harder. Angrier. But she knew Zara,

and olive branches weren't frivolous. She wouldn't—couldn't—offer one unless she felt really miserable about what had happened.

"I didn't try either," Kate muttered.

"You shouldn't have had to."

"No, but… Look, we were sixteen. We sucked."

Zara laughed. "Yeah, we did. And so did it. But… I still should have been there. Your mom was difficult even before this, and I…left you to her. Same as leaving you to the wolves."

"Maybe," Kate agreed. "But you had your own wolves."

"Yeah, well…" Kate went and got the vegetables and brought them to the skillet. She handed the full cutting board to Zara and Zara slid them into the pan.

"Find me a lid."

Zara did as told.

Then they stood there and watched the meal cook. Kate couldn't say they'd just absolved ten years of hurts, but it was a step, she supposed.

"Look, do you think you could drive me home? I know Brody thinks I'm in danger, but I swear I'm not."

"Car accidents and shootings aside?"

Kate blew out a frustrated breath. "I don't want to be his responsibility. I don't want him… Even if he could handle whatever, I don't *want* him to."

Zara frowned at her. "Brody's a good guy."

"I know he is." Way too good, in fact.

"If anyone can help you, Kate, it's him. It's the whole lot of them."

"Maybe I don't want any help."

"I guess that's fair." Zara studied her, and she shouldn't be able to have any insight after ten years of distance, but Kate had a bad feeling she understood all too well. "But do you not want it because you don't, or because after ten years of getting the shaft, you don't trust help when it's offered?"

Kate stared at Zara, because that statement caused an awful pain in her chest. She wanted to protect Brody, she *did*, but maybe…maybe in part because she just wasn't sure his help would go right. Maybe she was a little sure it would end in disaster because, yes, for ten years no one had tried to help.

"Been there. Done that. So I recognize the signs," Zara said quietly. "But Jake just kept being there, helping me out. Because… I don't know, they just have to. It's who they are. They *have* to do the right thing, even when it's not *their* right thing. I don't know how else to explain it."

Kate knew Zara didn't have any clue how much that twisted the knife of guilt she was already impaled by.

"I can't take you home. I trust Brody's judgment on this. You aren't safe."

"Maybe *he* isn't safe."

Zara blinked, studied Kate with a scrutiny Kate did *not* appreciate, but couldn't avoid. Because she wasn't that mysterious. She hadn't changed *that* much.

"First, I think you underestimate what Brody is capable of. I've seen it firsthand, and you know not much impresses me. Second, he wouldn't want you protecting him, for a wide variety of reasons." Zara reached out and touched Kate's shoulder—not something Zara was much on doing even when they had been friends. "If you have any feelings for Brody, any at all, you need to tell him the truth. Whatever the truth is. He deserves the truth, and he can handle it. The truth *and* whatever this is."

Kate pulled back from Zara's hand. "The truth is we'd all be a lot better off if I stopped looking into my father's disappearance."

Zara nodded. "Then you need to tell him that, and tell

him why. Because trust me, no matter what Brody says out loud, he's going to get to the bottom of this for you. The only way to stop him is the truth."

Kate blinked, her entire body going cold. She wanted to deny what Zara was saying, but Brody had given in so easily. He was also making her stay here. Zara was right.

He'd say he'd given it up. And keep going. Not in a duplicitous kind of way, exactly. But because of whatever it was inside of him that made him need to protect. Help.

She should be irritated by that, instead of feeling even more tangled up about how much she liked him. "I need to talk to him."

Zara nodded behind Kate and Kate turned to see Brody and Dunne standing in a doorway that Kate knew went to the main floor bedroom.

Kate sucked in a breath, then marched over to him and grabbed him by the arm. "Come on." She pulled him out of the kitchen, ignoring the fact Dunne and Zara were likely watching them go with avid interest.

It didn't matter. The only thing that mattered was getting him to stop. She dragged him all the way back to his room. She closed the door behind her.

"You're still looking into it, aren't you?"

Brody's eyes widened, but he stuck his hands into his pockets and rocked back on his heels. "Well…"

"I told you to stop!"

"I know, Kate. But you have to understand, until we get to the bottom of this mystery, we don't know what that car accident or shooting was about. We don't know you're safe—no matter how much you want to be or insist you are."

She wrung her hands together. Maybe she could find a way to tell him the truth that would get him to back off.

Get him to understand. She believed Zara. A lie wouldn't work. He'd get to the bottom of it.

So she had to go with a deeper truth. "You've made me an awful lot of promises, Brody. You shouldn't. I'm nothing to you."

"That isn't true. At all." He crossed to her, took her wringing hands in his and held her gaze. "I told you, I like you, Kate." So serious. So honest.

"I know." Her hands stilled under his and she wanted to lean into him. She wanted to kiss him like they had this morning. See where it went—where it could go. She wanted to, far more than she should.

But she had to ignore the flutter in her heart. It would change her mind, and she couldn't. If he kept pushing, he would get *hurt*. No matter how strong or smart he was.

I think you underestimate what Brody is capable of, Zara had said. Zara, who never thought anyone was as strong or stubborn or determined as her. Maybe she could tell him and get him to back off and maybe... Maybe Brody knew what he was doing.

She blew out a shaky breath. She didn't want to take that chance—she didn't want *him* taking that chance.

He liked her...? He kept *saying* he liked her, and there was no reason to lie. No reason to kiss her the way he had. She couldn't manage a reason to make his kisses false, which only tangled everything more. "I almost wish you didn't like me," she managed.

He grinned, pulled her to him. "Almost."

She wanted to sink into that acknowledgment, but she couldn't allow herself. It wasn't right to let him kiss her and like her when she'd lied to him. She pushed at his chest. "Brody, there's something I have to tell you." She didn't know how else to do this. She knew he wouldn't want to kiss her anymore. And he also wouldn't let the thing with

her father go. She got nothing she wanted if she told him
the truth.

But she just *had* to. Because, like Zara had said, he
wouldn't let up. Moreover, like Brody himself had said
back at the cabin, it was the right thing to do.

KATE LOOKED SO DISTRESSED, it ate at him. Brody let her go,
let her start to pace. She muttered a few things to herself,
but Brody waited. She had something to say, so he waited.

No matter how he itched to touch.

"You can't go after my father. You can't look into Stanley Music. I know you want to. I know you think it's the
right thing to do." She turned to face him, so heartbreakingly desperate. "Can't you trust me that it isn't?"

He didn't understand her fear. He tried, really, Tried to
put himself in a civilian's place, where random gunfire
might in fact scare them enough to back off. But she'd
been so tenacious for ten years. He couldn't reconcile that
with this.

Or the expression on her face. Scared and desperate. She
had a right to be scared. More than a right. But he didn't
understand the desperation. Like there was a very specific
threat lodged at them when Brody wasn't even sure anyone *really* wanted them dead. Scared, yes. Hurt—maybe,
and certainly if they wanted them hurt, that could lead to
inadvertent death. But her behavior still didn't fully make
sense to him.

The answers weren't written on her face, so he placed
his hands on her shoulders. "It's not that I don't trust you,
Kate. It's that I don't understand what's going on. What
is this about? Really?"

Her face crumpled. Not into tears. More like she couldn't
hold the weight of something. She pulled away from his

hands. She didn't start pacing again, but she backed away from him slowly, once again wringing her hands.

"Kate—"

"I saw my father," she blurted out, squeezing her eyes shut like she was afraid of a blow that would come after that confession.

But her words didn't make sense. "What do you mean?"

She sighed, opened her eyes, which were shiny with unshed tears he also didn't understand. "When you told me to lock myself in the cabin, he was there."

Brody thought there must be some kind of earthquake under his feet—it was the only explanation for feeling so suddenly off-kilter. "There. In the cabin. *With* you?"

She nodded.

"Why… Why wouldn't you have told me that? Where did he go?" He stepped toward her. He didn't know what emotions were swirling through him. Anger, and frustration, and a hurt that was out of place, for sure. "I could have followed. You should have yelled. You were *alone* with him?" he demanded.

"He just… He was there and he told me to stop looking into things. To let it all go."

"Oh, well, then let's give *up. Naturally*," Brody said sarcastically. He felt guilty for being so scathing, but that only made him angrier. Why should he feel guilty? He'd been trying to help her and she'd… She'd just give up because her father showed up after a decade and out of nowhere and told her to?

"He said…." Kate cleared her throat. "Brody, he said he'd been protecting me, but he couldn't if I kept pushing. He said if you kept going after them, you'd *beg* for death." Some of that indecision, and sadness, and uncertainty hardened into sparks of anger. "How could I have told you knowing that you would have absolutely still gone after them even with a *death* threat leveled against you?"

Those words, unexpected and unique, stopped him in his tracks. Leaked all the anger, and frustration, and confusion out of him. "You're… You're trying to protect me." It was a very strange feeling, and it took him a moment—or maybe a few—to wrap his head around how out of sorts that made him feel.

He'd been fighting side by side with his brothers for years. They had each other's backs, and they'd certainly jump in front of a bullet for each other. In fact, had done so. But that wasn't…protection. That wasn't this.

She'd wanted to give up on ten years of looking for her father, not just because her father had said he wouldn't be able to protect her anymore if she kept pushing. No, the way Kate had said that made it seem secondary. Made it seem like the most important thing, the thing that would make her give it all up, was the death threat leveled at *him*.

"I'm sorry," she said, though it was a little stiff. "I just thought… He was very specific, Brody. Not just that you'd be killed, but that it would be…messy. He had two guns, and all this gear, and… I know you probably think you could handle it. Zara thinks you could handle it. Everyone thinks you could handle it and maybe you could. What do I know? Not a darn thing, except I couldn't live with it. You shouldn't be risking any of it for *me*."

He crossed the room. Maybe he should have kept the distance. He was off balance enough to make a mistake, but she looked so miserable and worried and he… He had to touch her. Assure himself this bizarre change of events was *real*.

"Why not?" he asked, taking her hands in his.

"What?" she asked, looking at their hands as if she didn't understand why he was touching her.

"Why shouldn't I risk it for you, Kate?"

She looked up at him, and he knew no one had really backed her up before. Her mother sounded terrible. Her friends had backed off. She'd been alone and surviving in her own way for a decade.

He knew what that was like, and how hard it could be to believe someone might want to stand by your side. To fight with you. He hadn't become *brothers* with his friends overnight. They'd all slowly had to learn to trust and believe in each other.

Because he knew, and understood, he wanted to give her…everything. Maybe if he stepped back and analyzed it, it didn't make any sense. But he didn't want to do that. He touched his mouth to hers, thinking it could be something light and sweet. Reassuring.

But he couldn't pull himself back. He wanted to hold onto her. To drown himself, and her, in this and in them. She melted into him, pliant, and he couldn't imagine anyone else ever belonging here in his arms the way she did.

He tangled his hands in her hair, and her hands wrapped around his biceps, clutching him closer to her. The kiss was a perfect, sweet world distinct from everything else going on around them, and he'd have been happy to stay here. Right here. Rather than deal with everything else.

But everything else always came calling, whether a person wanted it to or not. He sighed against her mouth, pulling himself slightly back. They needed space. They needed to focus on the task at hand.

But when he looked at her, all he could think about was how much he wanted her in his bed.

"I thought you'd be mad at me," she said, looking up at him, eyes clouded with desire even amidst all that confusion. "For lying."

"We all lie, Kate." He ran his hands down her arms.

Wasn't he lying to her now, more or less? If he told her everything he'd done in his military career, wouldn't she believe that he could handle whatever her father leveled at him? But some lies were…necessary. Maybe. "I've just never had anyone lie *for* my safety before."

She still clutched his arms, looking up at him. But her expression went imploring. "If we stop, he'll just leave us alone. He's alive, that's enough for me to know. We don't need to know what bad thing he got himself caught in. I'm safe. You're safe. That's all that matters."

He wished that were true. Wished he could let her believe it were true. Agree and take her to bed.

But she was dead wrong, and if he didn't do something about it, they could both wind up dead.

"Kate, they keep taking information *you* have." He ran his hand over her hair. "At some point, they're going to wonder what you can prove even *without* the evidence they've stolen."

Chapter Fifteen

Kate wanted to drown in the warmth Brody's body provided, but his words were a cold reminder that her real life
was something…twisted and ugly and confusing.

The only way she'd been able to survive it had been to
withdraw into herself. Now she had Brody kissing her,
and Zara apologizing. People rallying around her to help.

Brody kissed her temple. "Come on, let's go eat dinner."

She tried to smile as she nodded agreement, and she let
him hold her hand on the way down to the kitchen. It was
a reassurance she supposed. He hadn't taken any relish in
telling her they'd come after her eventually, and he hadn't
dropped the bomb and left.

He was here. He wasn't mad she'd lied. He'd been
bowled over that she cared enough to protect him.

Maybe they were more alike than she'd thought, and
maybe…that should give her some hope. Brody had grown
up feeling alone, solitary. He'd made that clear. But he'd
made a life with his brothers as an adult. Clearly excelled
in the military. And when Dunne had been hurt, rallied
together with his brothers to move here.

They took turns cooking, and apparently they all ate
together. When Brody pulled her into the kitchen, all five
other brothers were in the room. Zara was still back by the
stove, hopefully not ruining the dinner Kate had helped

her start, while Henry stood next to her, filling cups with milk. Dunne and Jake were both sitting. Landon was sitting as well, but he had a computer in front of him he was tapping away on. Cal stood by the back door, looking grumpy—which Kate wasn't sure she'd ever seen him look anything but.

"How's the head, Kate?" Jake asked.

She managed to smile. "Good enough."

Brody ushered her into a seat, and he took the one next to her. Zara put the skillet on a trivet and a bowl of fruit next to it. Henry doled out glasses of milk, and Cal eventually sat next to Landon.

"You're in my seat," he muttered.

Landon grinned at him. "First come, first serve, buddy."

Zara handed out plates and silverware, then moved to sit next to Jake. Her hand trailed across his shoulder, and he scooted the chair next to him out for her. She handed him a napkin, he handed her the serving spoon from the fruit. It was an oddly mesmerizing dance. Zara had always been so fiercely independent. So resistant to any help. She'd done everything for everyone.

Now she was holding a man's hand under the dinner table.

Kate snuck a glance at Brody. He was looking at Landon's computer screen with a frown, but there was an ease to him here. Surrounded by his brothers, cramped together around a kitchen table Kate had eaten at as a child before the triplets' mother had died.

There'd been a similar vibe then. Family. Warmth. Chatter. Much different than Kate's own house, even before Dad's disappearance.

It was kind of amazing Zara had found a way to bring that back.

They ate, and Landon didn't put the computer away. Instead he pointed out things he'd found about Stanley Music, making Kate's stomach twist with anxiety.

Was she putting them all in danger?

"The security set up around any mention of this place is high tech. It's definitely not a music company. The piano thing is a front, but it'll take me some time to dig under the front without anyone figuring it out." Landon frowned at the computer screen while he took a bite of dinner.

Kate opened her mouth to tell him he didn't have to stick his neck out for her, but Brody silenced her with one clear disapproving look.

"I'll handle your chores tomorrow, give you more time."

Landon nodded, but Dunne shook his head. "You've got to give those stitches a few days to heal, cowboy."

Brody scowled.

"Welcome to the wounded crew," Jake offered, holding his glass up in mock salute.

"At the very least, Kate should stay here until we can be sure she's not in danger," Brody said firmly.

All eyes except Brody's turned to Cal. He was scowling, but based on what little Kate had seen of Cal Thompson, he was *always* scowling.

But there was something like an…ingrained chain of command, she supposed. They weren't waiting for permission, she didn't think. She couldn't imagine Cal refusing and Brody just shrugging and saying *okay, go home, Kate*. But they were waiting for…well, a fight.

As if sensing that, Cal changed his scowl. She thought maybe he was trying to smile, though it wasn't a very believable one.

"Of *course* she should stay. At your service, Kate."

Dunne snorted, Landon grinned and Brody looked torn between irritation and amusement.

This was the kind of family she'd always imagined during uncomfortably silent dinners with her parents. Not all happiness and light, but…real interaction. Connection. It was what she'd had with the Hart triplets. Before.

They ate the remainder of dinner, much of the conversation revolving around ranch chores—which had always been a Hart dinner-topic staple. Though Kate supposed this wasn't the Hart house or Hart Ranch anymore. It surprised her how well Zara had eased into that transition.

But she supposed it had something to do with the man who's hand she was holding under the table.

"Well, I've got a few things to go over. Thanks for dinner, Zar—"

Cal was already on his feet, but Zara was shaking her head. "You can't go yet," Zara said, standing. "Dessert." She turned her gaze to Kate. "Kate knows what she has to do to earn us dessert."

Kate's jaw dropped. "You can't be serious."

"Mom's rules. I *always* abide by Mom's rules."

It was strange how easy it was to fall into who they'd been before with each other—even though neither of them were who they'd been before. "Your mom would not be cool with you living with a guy before marriage."

Zara's grin widened as she lifted a shoulder. "I never minded a little of my mother's disapproval. *You* on the other hand…"

"Just what exactly are we witnessing here?" Landon stage-whispered.

"Kate has to play for us," Zara said. "Her choice of instruments, since she can play them all."

"Do we…*have* instruments?" Jake asked, genuinely perplexed.

Zara rolled her eyes. "You should really pay more attention to your own house, Jake." She pushed back from the table and Kate kept shaking her head.

"We are not little kids anymore."

"Fine. Enrage my mother's ghost. See how well you sleep tonight." Zara grinned, and Kate felt a matching one tug at her mouth.

Bittersweet, yes, but the sweet was starting to drown out some of that bitterness. Which was how about fifteen minutes later she was situated in the living room, Zara's late grandpa's fiddle in her hands. All the men gathered around for an impromptu concert.

Kate hadn't played in front of anyone in years, but music had always been her solace. She expected to be nervous, but once she started the song, it was like she was the only person in the room. Until she finished, and everyone applauded.

She gave a silly little bow, accepted the many compliments, flushing with the simple pleasure of sharing something she loved. Much like her job at the fort when she got to lecture people about her interests, but this was...different. More intimate.

As she walked upstairs, tired and ready to just *sleep*, she realized that thanks mostly to Zara, but also the Thompson brothers, for hours there, she'd forgotten about her father. About concussions and stitches and gunshots. She'd enjoyed her life, enjoyed other people.

She stepped into Brody's room—what had once been Amberleigh's when they'd been ten or eleven, before she'd made Hazeleigh switch with her so she had the room that could be easier to sneak out of.

But Kate didn't think of Amberleigh or Hazeleigh. She thought of herself. Kate Phillips. Who she'd always been, but had lost parts of. She liked this Kate, and the...future she seemed to have now.

She turned to face Brody who stood hesitantly in the

doorway, and for some reason his uncertainty in this moment gave her courage. And a sense of…purpose.

"We really don't have to push this—the whole thing with my dad. Not just to protect anyone, Brody." She looked at him as he studied her. "I… Tonight was nice. It could just be…like this."

He nodded, and some of the tension in her shoulders unwound as he crossed the room to stand in front of her. "We can do that," he agreed, putting his hands over hers. "But how long does that last, Kate?"

She closed her eyes. "I don't care," she said, even though it was a lie.

He squeezed her hands like he knew her words were a lie. "You deserve answers, and I think you have the right to be sure none of this comes back to bite you later. If we see it through to the end, we get all that—and at the end of it all, I promise you, it can still be just like this."

She opened her eyes and looked up at his hazel ones. He really was *so* good, but she didn't think he understood how much she didn't want to ruin what she'd had tonight. "Do you know what it's like to feel like yourself for the first time in ten years?"

His expression took on an arrested look that softened into an understanding. "Yes. I do."

He understood, and that was just another thing she'd had too little of. And he was something she'd never had. Why shouldn't she take, while she could?

"You should get some sleep," he said, sounding raspy. Backing away, though he didn't turn for the door. Just took a step away from her.

She didn't want that. She took the step he'd retreated, reached out and touched his chest and held his gaze, filled up with all this old and new confidence. "Stay."

He froze, and she almost smiled at how carefully he held himself. "I can take the floor or…"

"Brody," she said, shaking her head. "Don't be thick-headed."

"I'm not. I'm trying to be…noble."

She grinned, because for a little bit of time today she'd felt like who she used to be. Before she closed up, closed in. She felt like… Kate Phillips. Not a pariah, or a loner. Just herself.

"Don't."

BRODY WOKE UP in the familiar bed of the Hart Ranch. He hadn't gotten used to calling it *his* bed, but if he woke up with Kate every morning, maybe he'd get there.

She was still fast asleep. Hair in disarray on his shoulder. He thought maybe there should be some guilt here, but he couldn't find it. Probably because he cared. Deeply. And he knew, no matter what, he'd do everything it took to give her answers, to keep her safe. To give her that same glow she'd had last night playing the fiddle.

Then again in his bed.

He slid out of bed, hoping not to wake her. She muttered something, rolled over and then was back to being fast asleep.

In his bed, in this new life he'd been building for himself. Outside the military.

Did he know what it was like to feel like himself for the first time in a decade—over a decade for him? More than he'd ever be able to put into words. And while some of that was the ranch, and the lack of structure the military had provided to constantly measure himself against as proof he was better than all he'd come from, the final piece, the *key* had been Kate.

Dressed, he crept out of the bedroom. He needed some

coffee and a chat with Landon about Stanley Music, and Kate needed her sleep. He'd fill her in on whatever he found when she woke up.

Besides, he didn't have the first clue what to say to her if she woke up. It all felt a little…overwhelming. Too big for only the short time they had been together. He needed to be careful. They both needed to be careful. If they were, maybe something with some longevity would work out. But too hot, too fast was bound to scorch them both.

Coward.

Probably so.

He entered the kitchen, irritated with himself. Landon was at the kitchen table, his computer in front of him, a mug of coffee at his side. He smoothed out his expression and greeted Brody with a, "Good morning."

Brody poured himself some coffee, then took the seat next to Landon. "Anything new?"

"Bits and pieces, but nothing concrete. Stanley Music is definitely a front. For what and who? Still digging."

"You're sure no one knows you're digging?" Landon glared, clearly affronted. Brody held up his hands. "Kate's the one in danger of getting caught in the middle. We can't be too careful."

Landon's expression went surprisingly shrewd. "What's going on there?"

Brody shrugged, looking at his coffee rather than the odd air of disapproval on Landon's face.

Landon grunted. "You and Jake are as subtle as sledge-hammers falling for—"

Brody whipped his gaze up, all warning.

Landon rolled his eyes and sighed. "Lovely young women."

"I live for the day you do anything with subtlety, Landon."

There was a moment—so quick, Brody wondered if he'd

imagined it—where Landon's expression went grave. Then he grinned. "What's the point in being subtle?" He tapped his laptop. "Unless it's hacking related, of course. Look, I'll focus on this today. Zara said they're pretty well dug out of the blizzard. Looks like the roads are better today. Cal can't get too mad at me missing a day of chores."

"Except it's you, me *and* Jake missing chores."

"You know he's only grumpy because you both got hurt on his watch."

"His watch," Brody grumbled. "At some point he's going to have to learn we aren't his to watch anymore."

"Aren't you the one always telling me to give him time?"

"Yeah, yeah, yeah."

"There is one thing you could do, as long as the roads really are up for it and Dunne clears you to drive. I called the county office yesterday to check in on a business license, but they said I'd have to come down in person. If you can get a look at that license, there should be a name or maybe a shell company we can follow up on. You do that, I'll put in some chores so Cal can unclench."

"Yeah. Absolutely." Brody was already on his feet, ready to move.

"Make sure Dunne says driving's okay."

Brody nodded. He didn't *want* to, but he supposed it wouldn't hurt to ask. And if Dunne said no? Well, at least Brody would know he needed to sneak around.

But first, he needed to tell Kate… Well, maybe not everything. Enough. Something. She was enjoying feeling normal again, and if he could figure out her whole Dad thing himself, without her having to worry over it, well… Wouldn't that be good?

He found a clean mug, filled it and then retraced his steps back upstairs. When he slid into his room, Kate was sitting up in bed, running her hands through her tangled hair. She looked over at him sleepily.

"Morning. Brought you some coffee. Didn't put any cream or sugar in it, but I figured a pioneer woman knew how to take it black."

She smiled. "You'd be wrong, but I'm desperate enough not to care this morning."

He moved over and carefully handed it to her, then because he couldn't help himself, dropped a quick kiss to her mouth. He would rather sink into kissing her, coffee be damned, but he wanted…to fix everything for her too. The sooner he got to work, the sooner he could.

"I'm going to do some chores this morning. Ranch is kind of slammed from the blizzard."

Her eyebrows drew together. "I thought Dunne told you not to do any chores."

"Cal found me some lighter assignments that won't mess with my stitches."

"How can I help?"

"Sit tight."

She frowned. "I didn't grow up on a ranch, but I know a thing or two and…"

"Best if you sit tight," Brody reiterated. "You've still got to be careful of that concussion," he said, drifting his fingers over her bandage. "And Cal can be a grumpy SOB. Just rest. Maybe tomorrow you'll be up to some light chores. In fact, I'll work on him today. He'll have stuff for you to do tomorrow and he'll even think it's his idea. Nothing puts Cal in a better mood than something that's his idea."

"What am I supposed to do then?"

"Whatever you want. Rest. Relax."

Kate grimaced.

He took a seat next to her on the bed. "I wish I could

take you to the fort so you could work, but it isn't safe. Not yet."

"No, I know." She shook her head and gave him a smile. "I'll figure something out. Maybe make a big lunch for you guys."

He took her hand and pressed his mouth to the top of it. "You'd be considered a god among us lowly mortals."

She snorted a laugh. "All right, then. Goddess it is."

Brody got up, wanting to get on the road. He had a good hour's drive to the county clerk's office.

"Brody, about last night…"

He froze, a strange dread creeping through him. Did she have regrets? Was this where she let him down easy?

"That was good, right?"

He turned, cupped her face with his hands, careful not to jostle her into spilling her coffee. "Last night was great."

She grinned. "You'll spend the night with me again tonight?"

"Any night you want."

Chapter Sixteen

Kate was so bored she could scream. She'd managed to keep herself occupied daydreaming about Brody for a good hour. Then she'd gotten restless, and cleaned the kitchen, and made soup, which now simmered on the stove. She'd preprepared sandwiches to go with the soup. She'd even peeked in on Jake, who she *barely* knew, to see if he needed anything while Zara was out working.

But nothing really needed to be done, and she was in not-her-house with not-her-things. She messed around with the old fiddle, but even that couldn't hold her interest.

She needed a trip home. A few changes of clothes. Different shoes. Her laptop. She had most of the things to get her through a few days away from home, but a few days was up and she needed a refresher.

Besides, she never let herself go too many days without asking her mother if she needed anything. Maybe Mom wouldn't notice her absence, but Kate…felt guilty anyway.

She looked around the kitchen, then decided now was as good a time as any. She pulled her phone out of her pocket and called someone she hadn't called in ten years. Zara.

"Hey, Kate. What's up?" Zara greeted.

Kate could hear the wind whipping in the receiver. Zara was out working, and Kate was *jealous*. It made this choice even more necessary. "Can I borrow your truck? Just going to run home and get a change of clothes and stuff. Maybe run into town for some dinner supplies. I made sandwiches for lunch because there wasn't anything really defrosted, but I'd like to make a hot dinner."

"It's Cal's turn to cook," Zara replied. "So if you're willing to take over so I don't have to have half-baked frozen pizza, I'm in. Brody okay with you taking off?"

Kate knew she shouldn't lie, but the fib came out of her mouth before she could stop herself. "Of course."

"Extra set of keys hanging up in the mudroom."

"Thanks."

"No prob."

Kate hung up, grabbed the keys, and then her purse, and was headed out for Zara's truck in no time. The crew would come back in for lunch in about two hours or so, so she had plenty of time. She'd be back to check on her simmering soup and set out the sandwiches before everyone was back.

She hummed to herself as she got in Zara's truck. This could be normal. This could be real life, and no matter what Brody had said about answers, Kate finally realized she didn't *need* them. Maybe it was seeing Dad that had done it. He was alive. He'd made a choice to leave.

Now she knew, and no matter what he was mixed up in, he'd made his own choice.

It was closure. Sort of.

Kate turned the key in the ignition, then sighed, a little kernel of guilt eating at her. What if Brody came in early and she was gone? Zara would know where she was, but he would worry first. Worry too much.

Which was nice, actually, someone to worry over her. But it meant she owed him…an explanation.

A text. A quick to-the-point text. Picking up some stuff

at my house, and some groceries at the Mart. Be back before lunch.

She read it back to herself. Considered. Maybe she should just stay put. Wait for Brody and...

Oh, for heaven's sake, no one had tried to hurt *her*. They'd tried to hurt him. He was the one who should be worried. Maybe it would be like high school when she felt like she was being followed, but no one was going to shoot her for driving home.

She hit Send and began to head off the Hart Ranch. Her phone rang not two seconds later. She sighed and answered.

"Hello," she offered brightly.

"Damn it, Kate," Brody's voice growled. It echoed through the speaker. She even liked his voice. So low and commanding, regardless of the situation.

She kept her tone light and breezy. "Brody, it's just home. A trip to the Mart. I'll be back in no time."

"No trip to the Mart. Absolutely not. Go home."

She didn't know why it warmed her that he was treating the Hart place like *her* home. "Just a change of clothes. Pop in and say hello to my mother, and make sure she doesn't need anything. Brody, you can't keep me prisoner. I have to be able to do *something*."

There was a long fraught silence. Kate drove, and she paid attention. Waited for someone to jump out. A car to appear and follow her. Shots. But nothing.

"You can't treat me like I'm a frail doll," she said seriously. "Or in mortal danger *all* the time. That's overkill, and I think you know that. They've stolen from me, yes, but they haven't done more than that and follow me around a bit here and there."

"Here and there," he muttered disgustedly. "They ran us off the road."

"Us. Not me."

"Kate…"

She knew he wanted to argue more. She also knew he couldn't stop her, but she wanted him to understand. She needed him to. So, even though it was embarrassing to admit, she had to tell him.

"I spent an entire year of my life anxious and paranoid. In and out of the counselor's office. I wanted to see a therapist, Brody, because I couldn't control my thoughts. Mom wouldn't let me, so it was a hard-won fight to find some peace. I can't go back to that place. I can't do it again. I have to be able to live the way I've been living."

His silence took on a life of its own and Kate held her breath. This would be a sticking point. She couldn't constantly be babysat. She wouldn't constantly be fearful. Her father was out there, doing something shady, maybe, okay probably, but he'd been protecting her. Brody was protecting her by being careful looking into Stanley Music.

She just couldn't be sixteen again. She couldn't *feel* like that again. She wasn't sure she'd be able to crawl out, even as an adult with help available to her now. People who cared. Whatever therapist she wanted. She didn't know how to survive it twice.

"If you feel anything is wrong, you're being followed at all, *anything*. You call me," Brody said, sounding pained but he was giving her the space she asked for. "You call the police. I don't care, you do whatever you have to do to stay safe," Brody ordered.

Which was fine enough. She didn't want to die or be attacked. She just wanted a change of clothes. Some time alone to think. In her own space. "All right."

"Promise me."

"I promise. I don't have a death wish, Brody. I have plans tonight."

Het let out a low chuckle. "They better be with me."

"Of course."

Then he sighed. "I should probably confess something."

Kate parked Zara's truck on the road. Her mother would pitch a fit if a rusty old truck was parked in the drive, and it hadn't been shoveled anyway. She should do that. "What should you confess?" she asked, climbing out of the truck.

"I'm running an errand for Landon, trying to look at a business license for Stanley Music."

Kate stopped in her tracks. "Brody!"

"It's nothing."

"It's poking into things. They threatened you as much if not more than me. Turn around and go home now."

"How about this? We both do the thing we've set out to do that we lied to each other about, and then tonight we show each other just how sorry we are."

It was absurd. She should absolutely be furious with him, not walking toward her house, *smiling*. He'd lied.

Then told her the truth when she fessed up too. He hadn't had to. She would have never known the difference. Maybe that was a low bar, but it was her bar. She'd done the same more or less, hadn't she? "I hope you're very sorry."

"The sorriest. I might be sorry two or three times."

Which had her smiling all over again. She was probably pathetic, but she didn't *feel* pathetic. She felt as happy as she'd been in *years*. "All right, but you have to promise me the same thing—if anything feels wrong, you call for help."

"Yes, ma'am."

She sighed and tested out the words he'd said himself. "I'll see you at home."

"Soon enough."

She ended the call and slid the phone back into her pocket. She looked up at the house on the hill. It looked as dark and abandoned as it ever did. She'd learned to accept that she existed in a weird kind of living mausoleum to her father's memory—or disappearance or *whatever* went on in her mother's head.

But cohabitating with Brody in the historical cabin, and then the Hart house packed to the brim with people, she realized how *sad* it all was. Zara had said she'd left her to the wolves, because Kate's mother had always been cold and distant.

But the truth was, her mother had felt safe. Mom's disapproval and detachment had felt so much safer than friendship and caring about anyone when her father and friend could disappear seemingly of their own volition. Possibly even together.

She hadn't just been *left* to this life, she'd held on to this life because it was all she'd had.

She didn't want to anymore.

Which filled her with a sense of purpose. *Get your things.* She needed to get back to the Hart Ranch. Maybe they'd find some answers on what her father was involved in. Maybe they should. The guns, the warnings. He certainly wasn't involved in anything *good*, and he seemed to be… Well, he wasn't in control, was he? He'd said he couldn't stop them from coming after her if she kept poking.

Worry curled in her gut. She really wished Brody would stop digging, but he'd had a point. She'd always be looking over her shoulder if they didn't create some closure, and she knew from experience that was no way to live.

She blew out a breath as she considered the two entry points to the house. The side door would lead her to her room, and her side of the house where Mom almost never went.

But if she went in the main door, she could find her

mother and ask if Mom needed anything. She didn't *want* to do that, but guilt propelled her.

She didn't know why she felt guilty. Mom never seemed to feel anything. But there was some latent need in Kate to take care of her mother, even if Mom never returned the favor.

So she unlocked the front door, then frowned. She could hear voices from the room off the foyer. A man's and a woman's. Recollection and dread skittered down her back, but she had to be imagining things. She had to.

But when she stepped into the parlor, both her parents stood there. Arguing, clearly. For a moment Kate wondered if she'd stepped back in time.

But then she saw the guns in her father's hands.

BRODY WASN'T USED to impatience. It was something that had been drilled out of him in the military. Things took the time they took. A soldier needed to be patient. An elite soldier didn't let tension and adrenaline distract focus.

He didn't feel very elite, waiting for the sleepy county clerk to get his butt in gear and fulfill Brody's request. He felt like jumping over the counter and taking care of things himself.

But instead he sat in a hard plastic chair, in a small building that smelled of industrial cleaner, and waited. After eons the older man behind the counter shuffled back into view, holding a flimsy piece of paper. "Went ahead and copied it for you. It's owned by an LLC," the man finally said. "Stanley, Inc. LLC." He showed Brody the paper. Which told him nothing, but he supposed it gave Landon another avenue to investigate.

He slid the paper over the counter. "That'll be fifteen dollars."

A bit steep, and Brody hadn't *asked* for a copy, but he

still counted out some cash and handed it over. "Thanks." He took the paper and stepped back out into the early afternoon sunshine. Blinding with all the snow on the ground, but not as frigid as it had been.

Brody walked back to his truck and got in. He called Landon and put him on speaker before pulling back out onto the highway.

"Owned by an LLC. No names of people, but the LLC name is just Stanley, Inc."

"Weird I couldn't find that online, but something to go on. Take me two minutes to figure out."

Brody drove as Landon typed away. "Owned by a Jonas Lantsey." More silence except for the clacking of computer keys. "Who's been dead for twenty years, so that doesn't wash. But I'll dig deeper on him. Might have something to go on once you get back."

"Kate back yet?"

"Don't think so."

Brody frowned. She'd been right. He couldn't keep her prisoner, and there'd been no specific threat against her. Brody did truly believe her father was keeping her safe. But he still didn't like the *potential* of mistakes. A man with a gun had shot at him. Someone in a truck had run them off the road.

Even if she wasn't a target per se, she wasn't *safe*. And he needed her safe.

"I'm on my way back. Call if you find anything truly interesting."

"Sure thing, boss."

Brody rolled his eyes at Landon's send off before he hit End on the phone. Then he typed in Kate's number.

If she wasn't headed back to the ranch by now, he'd just stop by the Phillips house and pick her up. Well, she had

Zara's truck so maybe he wouldn't pick her up so much as follow her home. Keep an eye out.

It was better to be overcautious than careless. Something he had a feeling Kate needed to learn. Or maybe just accept his temporary protectiveness until they got to the bottom of everything.

He wasn't going to let something happen to her just because she didn't understand the full threat. He couldn't. And she had to know that, considering she'd been willing to give it all up to protect *him*.

Something that still leveled him, humbled him, made him feel awkward and far younger than a man who'd seen what he'd seen should feel. So he'd act. Rather than sit in all that feeling.

He hit Call on her number and waited while it rang. Her voice came over the speaker, encouraging him to leave a message.

She hadn't answered, which had a cold pit of dread forming in his stomach. But before he could truly panic, and start speeding toward Wilde, a text message from Kate dinged.

Just having lunch with Mom. Will call soon.

He supposed that was a good enough reason to not answer his call, but why was she having lunch with her mother who hadn't even known she was away from home the past few nights?

He chewed that over on the drive back home.

Chapter Seventeen

Kate was in a little bit of a daze. She'd been shocked to see her parents together, and then...she wasn't sure what had happened. Her head pounded and she opened her eyes, realizing she was in a sitting position.

Tied in a sitting position. To a chair. She'd passed out. No...no, something had happened. She willed her mind to part the fog that seemed to encompass it. She had been standing there, staring open-mouthed at her parents. Both of them. Calmly in the same room. Then Mom had stepped forward and...

Something had hit Kate in the head. Hard. Right where she was already hurt. Then everything had gone black.

She tried to reach her hand up to touch her head, but the lack of movement reminded her she was tied up. To a chair. She looked around the room. Still the parlor. Still her...parents.

Together. Standing in the same room, like ten years hadn't passed. Like Dad had never disappeared.

"You shouldn't have hit her so hard," Dad was saying to Mom.

Her mother had hit her? Her *mother*. And her father wasn't saying *you shouldn't have hit her* or expressing any sort of outrage. He was just scolding Mom about the *strength* of the blow.

"It got the job done, didn't it?" Mom replied.

"What's going on?" Kate rasped, surprised at how raw her throat felt.

They both turned their gazes to her. Mom looked furious. Dad looked...like he had back at the cabin. Angry, worried, frustrated. He was dressed in some bizarre tactical gear, guns strapped to him. Her father. The kind, warm music teacher.

But it was him. Somehow, it was him, and her mother had *hit* her, and she was tied to a chair.

"You came home at the wrong time. Figures. Making my life complicated like always."

It sounded like her mother. Like everything she would normally say. But Mom had hit her where she was already hurt and tied her to a chair. "I don't understand." *Any* of it.

Mom rolled her eyes. "No one asked you to, Katherine."

Kate closed her eyes. Everything swirled and nothing made sense. She wanted to just...sleep. Give in to whatever this was. Let whatever happened happen.

Her phone ringing jolted her painfully out of the daze she'd been falling into.

"Brody," Mom said, frowning at her phone. "Is that who she was with at the fort?" she demanded of Dad.

Dad shrugged. "Didn't get a name, but she doesn't talk to very many people."

They both looked at her again. "Well, who is he?"

Kate didn't even open her mouth. She'd give them nothing, because while none of this made sense, her mother had hit her. One of them had tied her to the chair. No one was trying to help her or save her. She was, essentially, their prisoner. Both of them.

Neither of them needed to know who Brody was. Ever.

Brody. He knew where she was. He would come looking for her when she didn't answer. Relief swamped her.

She'd been afraid for him, but she knew he could take her parents. No matter what was going on, he could save her from this bizarre turn of events. Not just could, *would*.

"What's that smile for?" Mom demanded.

"I'm not smiling," Kate said, sounding like a guilty toddler even to her own ears.

"She never did learn to lie. A problem from the start," Mom muttered, still holding Kate's phone and pondering the screen. "He must know where she is and she's stupid enough to think he'll come for her."

"Must be the same guy then," Dad said, sounding tired. "Best to keep him away if we can. He's not your average loser."

Mom nodded. "We learned that lesson with the others, last month."

The others? What on earth?

Mom typed something into Kate's phone. Then she held it in front of Kate's face. "That'll buy us time, don't you think?"

Just having lunch with Mom. Call soon.

Kate was very afraid it would buy Mom the exact kind of time she was referring to. And nothing good would come out of that time. "Time for *what*?" she demanded. Nauseous. Her head hurt so much she wanted to cry.

Her mother had assaulted her.

"Don't worry about it," Mom said, with a smile. "You've wrecked my plans for the last time." She turned to Dad. "We have to kill her."

Kate knew she made some kind of noise, but her parents acted like they hadn't heard it. While they discussed *killing* her. Like they were discussing what to make for dinner.

"She doesn't know anything," Dad said, shifting on his feet uneasily. He rested his hand on one of the guns connected to his vest.

"She knows enough. She's got to be gone. Which actually solves this Brody person problem. We'll frame him for the murder. Should be simple enough. Then they're both out of the way."

"Marjorie, you cannot kill our own daughter."

"Of course not. Killing is *your* job."

Dad lifted his chin. "I won't."

Mom raised an eyebrow. "Interesting rebellion, Art."

"This is a line."

Mom shrugged. "Not my line. I suppose you'd rather ruin fifteen years of work? I suppose you'd rather die yourself?"

For the first time Dad looked over at her. There was conflict on his face, but that didn't warm Kate's heart any. The conflict wasn't over whether he'd save her or *not*. It was over whether he was going to kill her or…it seemed, let Mom do it.

Whoever he was now, these ten years later, however he'd maybe tried to protect her from afar these past ten years, he was *conflicted* about the *manner* of her *murder*.

He was not her hero. Beginning and end of story.

Kate wanted to cry, but knew she couldn't. She'd *finally* found a life in the aftermath of what had happened ten years ago, and she simply wouldn't give in. If she did, it wouldn't just be her life over. They'd frame Brody. Maybe he'd be able to prove he hadn't hurt her, but she wasn't about to be party to putting him through that.

She needed a plan. No matter how her head hurt. No matter how much it felt like she might throw up.

"She could join us," Dad said, but even Kate knew by the way he'd said it that it wasn't an option.

Mom laughed. Way too loudly and way too long. "*Join* us. That wasn't an option back then and it's hardly an option now. She's always been so depressingly straitlaced."

Mom looked at Kate with a mix of scorn and disgust. "She *never* could have given us what we wanted."

"I'm not killing her, Marjorie. I've killed plenty, but I'm not killing my own daughter."

Mom raised an eyebrow at Dad. "You know what happens then."

"So be it."

Her father had...killed? The man who'd taught her to play the violin? Who'd put her up on a horse when she'd been a little girl at the county fair. Who'd driven her to school singing along with The Beatles?

I've killed plenty.

It was a nightmare. She was just having some very realistic dream. This was too much to take in.

Funny, how her mother's behavior wasn't all that shocking. Maybe *murder* was a little over the top, but Kate had never expected her mother to care about her. She'd made that mistake enough times as a child that even once Dad had left, she hadn't expected Mom's reassurance.

Mom picked up her own cell phone and held it to her ear. "We're going to need you," she said. "Art's refusing to do the job." There was a beat of silence. "Main house," she said, then pushed the phone back into her pocket. "Now, we wait."

Kate looked at both her parents. Wait. To die? No. She was going to find a way out of this.

She had to. For herself. For Brody. She *had* to.

BRODY RETURNED TO the Hart Ranch and frowned when Zara's truck was nowhere to be found. He'd hoped that Kate had returned it and Zara had taken it elsewhere, but a sinking suspicion in his gut made him very much doubt it.

He sat in the idling truck. He was low on gas, and he still needed to go check on the truck that had crashed and see when they could go about getting that towed and repaired. Having one truck between the six of them, with only Zara's truck and Hazeleigh's temperamental car as emergency backup wasn't going to work for long and Kate had said she was having lunch with her mother.

He should give her space.

Every instinct he'd ever honed in the military told him to ignore *space*, but he wasn't in the military anymore, was he? Even if Kate was in danger, it wasn't from terrorist groups bent on destroying entire cities and countries. It was from her father, who was maybe dealing with something shady. But small-town Wyoming shady.

He needed to ratchet down his theories. This wasn't the military. He forced himself to get out of the truck and walk inside. He'd check in with Landon on this Jonas Lantsey character, and then…

Then he'd check on Kate. If she didn't answer her phone, he was going over to the Phillips house. He didn't want to make her paranoid or fear every bump in the night.

But he had to keep her safe.

Zara and Hazeleigh were in the kitchen when he entered, and Brody realized that for all the issues the women had been through, they knew Kate. Who she was and how she acted.

"Would Kate ever have lunch with her mother?" he demanded. She wouldn't lie. Could it have been code? What kind of code was that?

Zara and Hazeleigh looked at each other, then back at him with surprise.

"She might," Zara offered. "Mrs. Phillips always had a way of making Kate feel guilty."

Brody wanted that to make him feel better, but all it did was lower his opinion of Mrs. Phillips, which was already about as low as his opinion of his own mother.

But Hazeleigh was frowning deeper and deeper. "That was true when we were younger, but not really lately. I mean, Kate *would* have lunch with her mother out of guilt. But I don't know the last time Mrs. Phillips did anything *with* Kate. Usually she just orders her around and keeps her distance."

"She texted me that she was having lunch with her mother."

"I guess if she texted you, it must be true, but—"

Hazeleigh was interrupted by Brody's phone chirping. He took it out of his pocket. A text from Kate.

A few errands to run for Mom. I'll text you when I'm on my way back to the ranch.

She ran errands for her mother. He knew she did. He didn't want to feel paranoid, and what would following her around do? Make her fearful. She was keeping in contact with him, and she'd promised to call for help if she suspected anything.

"I guess I'm overreacting. She's going to run some errands for her mom."

"But you think something's wrong?" Zara pressed.

"I don't know." Which was a hard thing for him to admit. He could go into town, follow Kate around, make sure she was safe.

But he knew that wasn't what she wanted.

Landon walked into the kitchen. He nodded at the Hart women, then turned to Brody. "Got you a full mockup on this Jonas Lantsey. Not sure it'll help any though. He died long before Stanley Music was created—LLC or the fake piano company."

"Jonas Lantsey?" Hazeleigh asked.

"You know him?" Landon returned, surprised.

"I did. Sort of. He was Kate's grandfather. Mrs. Phillips's father. He died when we were kids. Right, Zara?"

Zara nodded. "Yeah. I remember that. Kate wasn't really close to him, but he was one of the richest guys in town. Owned the bank and a bunch of things. The funeral was a big deal for Wilde."

"I guess that lines up with what I found. I got a name on the wife, but didn't look too closely at the family. Just his business dealings."

"He's connected to Kate's parents. That seems…" Brody trailed off, thinking it through. Kate's father was the one who disappeared. He could have easily used his late father-in-law's name to start whatever shady dealings he was into.

The question remained why?

"I don't like this," Brody muttered. "This is far more complicated than some small-town crime."

"So was what Amberleigh was caught up in," Zara pointed out. "She disappeared the same day Mr. Phillips did."

"But the men involved in killing Amberleigh were arrested."

Landon tapped the counter thoughtfully. "Drug rings can have more than one branch, especially when you're dealing with low-population areas like this. They'd need to run to a bigger city to really make enough money to make it worthwhile. Let me pull on that thread."

Brody nodded and Landon left, likely headed back to his room and his laptop. He'd get to the bottom of it, and with that information Brody would be able to keep Kate safe. Permanently.

Zara was studying him and Hazeleigh was twisting her fingers together. Neither of them looked any more settled or comfortable than he did.

Zara looked at her sister, then back at him. "If you think

something isn't right, maybe it isn't. Sometimes feelings are right." She gave Hazeleigh another enigmatic look.

"She told me she didn't want to feel paranoid again," Brody said. "I go around checking up on her every five seconds…"

Zara nodded and Hazeleigh studied him, which was odd. Usually she was a bit too skittish to look any of them in the eye. "Do you have anything of Kate's?" she asked. "Anything she touched recently?"

"Her bag is up in my room."

"Sometimes… Not always, but sometimes I can… I can just kind of feel if something bad is going to happen." She grimaced over at Zara. "I knew Zara was going to find something bad that day she found Amberleigh. It's the triplet thing, sort of, but sometimes it can be deeper. Kate could be… I just…"

Zara put her hand on Hazeleigh's shoulder. "Just get her something Kate might have touched today, and we'll see if Hazeleigh has a feeling."

"Don't get your hopes up," Hazeleigh said, making a pained face. "I can't control it. It doesn't always mean things. I just…"

"I'll go get something," Brody said. He'd seen men with a sixth sense about things in the military. He'd never fully bought into it, but sometimes he'd seen a guy know something bad was coming. A gut feeling. An instinct. Brody didn't know what to call it, but at this point, he'd believe whatever might assure him Kate was safe.

Chapter Eighteen

Kate wasn't sure how much time had passed. She didn't allow herself to worry about it. She just focused on her restraints and thinking through all the different ways she could get out of them.

The ones around her hands were looser than the ones around her feet, which could work in her favor.

She hoped with everything she had inside of her that *anything* would work in her favor.

It would. It had to. Brody had said it himself. She was like those pioneers she loved to study and tell people about. She was resourceful and scrappy. She would hold on to their example.

Hopefully there were no more ugly surprises. She kept her gaze on her mother as she tried to loosen whatever had her hands tied behind her back and to the chair. It wasn't rope. It was some kind of bendable plastic. Like an old jump rope she would have had as a girl. It was thick enough that the knots weren't completely incapable of being untied.

Eventually.

Of course, even if she did untie her hands, she wouldn't be able to untie her feet without arousing suspicion, and her father had guns. She did not.

Weirdly, neither did her mother. Who seemed…in

charge of this whole incomprehensible thing. If her father really wanted to save her, he could simply turn those guns on her mother.

Which told Kate everything she needed to know about being saved.

She knew Mom had been texting Brody every once in a while with a new excuse why she wasn't home yet, but eventually... If she could stay alive until tonight, there was no doubt Brody would come for her.

There was something empowering about that. Knowing she had someone she could depend on. She didn't want him to risk himself for her, certainly didn't want him being framed for her murder any more than she wanted to die, so that only made her more determined to handle this herself. Or at least get accomplished what she could, and if he came in the end and saved her—well, it would be like they had done it together.

Doing whatever she could, however she could, would make him proud. It would make herself proud, and she wouldn't have to feel afraid anymore. If she managed to get out of this, she wouldn't be afraid of any damn thing.

She blew out a breath, the sick feeling in her stomach had ebbed a little bit, but the effort she was putting into untying the knots without drawing attention was making her hot. She felt flushed and unsteady. No doubt her mother— her *mother*—had given her another concussion. Kate didn't know much about that, but she knew it couldn't be good.

Of course neither was her mother wanting her dead.

Mom was sitting calmly on the antique couch Kate had never been allowed to sit on. Dad stood in the corner, arms crossed, looking angry but...resigned.

Every once in a while Mom studied her, then checked her watch. Kate had no idea what that was about, so she just stilled and waited for the moment to pass.

Then, once Mom's gaze went elsewhere, Kate got back to work on trying to undo the knots tying her hands behind her back. She was definitely getting somewhere, but she had to stop until she could figure out what to do with her untied hands.

Mom stood abruptly. "He's here."

Dad's hands dropped from their belligerent pose, and his expression blanked. Mom…fixed her hair, of all the incomprehensible things.

Kate could hear the loud halting steps of someone deep in the house.

After a few minutes of waiting, an elderly man stepped into the room. He was shorter than Mom, or maybe just a little stooped. He looked like he'd at one time been a little heavier-set and was still wearing clothes from that time. They hung off his almost sickly frame, and a big black cowboy hat swallowed what seemed like his entire head.

Kate could only see his chin and his gnarled hands. Not a young man, by any means. Not a strong man. He also didn't seem to have any guns on him.

Mom looked at him with a cool kind of…awe, or respect, or something very rare for Marjorie Phillips. Dad looked at him with a wariness that did not help Kate's nerves.

"Do you know what a risk I've taken coming here?" the man rasped, taking off the overlarge black cowboy hat.

Kate gasped at the face revealed to her. She even shook her head. She couldn't believe it. This had to be… She couldn't even access what this had to be.

The man in front of her had died twenty years ago. He looked older now, but she'd never forget that imperious scowl her grandfather had *always* worn. It was on his face now as he took her in.

"Honestly, Marjorie, I told you years ago she wasn't

suitable," he said, looking at Kate with unveiled distaste. "So *emotional*."

"She hasn't been any trouble. She's never been any trouble."

It was the strangest thing, her father standing up for her. Like he always had. She'd always cast him as the hero for that.

But he had guns. Mom and her supposedly *dead* father did not. Whatever he was, even standing up for her, Dad was not the hero.

"Honestly, him too," Jonas Lantsey said with the wave of a hand. A very-not-dead hand. Kate stared at it, mesmerized. She'd gone to his funeral. She'd watched her mother grieve…in her mother's way.

The entire town had come out for his funeral. There'd been talk of a statue.

Now he was here. Alive. Apparently part of this whole her-mother-wanted-to-kill-her thing.

"He's been a very effective enforcer otherwise." Mom sighed heavily. "I suppose it's understandable. He's a little too attached to the child."

Child. She was twenty-six years old. And *her* child.

"Should have had a boy," Jonas said.

"Well, clearly I've had a break with reality," Kate said. Out loud. Because honestly. This was…beyond insane. She'd been having trouble believing Brody—all perfect knight in shining armor—could be real, and interested in *her*, but he'd *felt* real enough. She'd accepted every moment up until this one, more or less.

But no. She'd actually died when she'd had that concussion. Or maybe earlier. Oh, she was in a coma. That would really make the past week make so much more sense. A very delusional coma.

"Would you shut up."

It was only her grandfather's sharp command that had her realizing she'd been speaking all those thoughts out loud.

Then she laughed. She couldn't help it. She was losing her mind. That only made her laugh harder, and harder, no matter how much everyone ordered her to stop laughing.

Then her grandfather—her *dead* grandfather whose funeral she'd gone to—stepped forward and backhanded her across the face.

Hard.

That stung. And grounded her in the fact that no matter how incomprehensible, this was reality.

She had to get out of here ASAP, because she was going to wind up dead, no matter how closely she was related to all these people.

"I told you to shut up." He gripped her chin, surprisingly hard for his thin frame and the fact she knew he was eighty-three. "You are a pathetic little girl and no one is going to come for you. We'll make sure of it."

Kate smiled. It was reckless, but she couldn't help it. "We'll see about that."

He reared back again, a look on his face very familiar and she realized how many times when she'd been a child that he'd wanted to hit her. Just like this. But he hadn't.

She saw the way his gaze flicked to her bandage. He was going to hit her there again, just like Mom had. She'd lost consciousness, and she couldn't afford that again.

When his hand came down, she angled her head a little so he hit a slightly different spot. It still hurt. Desperately, enough to have her eyes stinging with tears and a gasp of pain to escape her mouth, but she allowed her eyes to close and her body to go limp.

Hopefully they thought he'd knocked her out. If they left her alone for even five minutes, she'd find a way to escape.

BRODY BROUGHT KATE'S backpack to Hazeleigh, not bothering to force himself to be calm. He hurried. He thrust the bag at Hazeleigh, and he waited impatiently while she took it and closed her eyes.

She frowned. She moved the bag from hand to hand, ran her fingers over seams. Her frown deepened and deepened, regret suffusing all her features. She looked at Zara first.

"It's okay, Haze," she murmured.

Sad eyes turned to Brody and she held the bag back to him. "I'm sorry. I really am. It's hard to force it. I thought maybe I could, but I don't feel anything one way or another."

Brody set the bag on one of the chairs and then thrust his hands in his pockets. "I'm sure it's fine. I'm sure." Of course the more he repeated *sure*, the less *sure* he felt or sounded.

"You know what? I'll text her that I need my truck back," Zara said, already pulling her phone out of her pocket. "Ranching emergency. If she doesn't say she's coming right home, we go get her."

Brody stood very still, fighting every last instinct inside of him. Because she'd asked him to give her space. Because she wanted to feel like her life was normal. He remembered the way she'd smiled last night, feeling like she'd found herself after a decade.

If he went barging in, he ruined that.

Unless she's in danger.

Zara hadn't waited for his approval. She sent the text with a flourish, and then they all stood there, still and waiting.

"She's typing," Zara said. Then frowned. "She stopped." Zara peered at her screen, and Brody had the sense they were all urging her to answer. Answer that she was on her back home.

Zara chewed on her lip, Hazeleigh twisted her fingers, and still no message came.

"Screw it," Brody muttered. "I'm going."

He swept out of the kitchen. He didn't have a clue what the Hart women's response was, because he was focused on only one thing.

Making sure Kate was okay.

He felt guilty, even now, getting into the truck. She wanted space, and freedom, and not to be thrust back into a bad mental place. He understood that, more than she probably thought he did. He knew how important finding a way to deal with the hard parts of life could be.

But he couldn't give her the space she needed now. Which was a terrible rock and a hard place, but he just… It wasn't who he was. To wait. To feel this uncertain, this torn.

If she hated him for it…

He paused for a moment, but only a moment. Because he'd take her hate over her blood on his hands. Someone had run them off the road, shot at him. Her father had warned her to back off and Brody hadn't. Maybe it wasn't the military, but it wasn't normal life either.

If someone had gone after her, it was his fault. He'd pushed, even after the warning. Landon was smart enough with computers to know how to cover his tracks, but maybe Brody's going to the county office had set off something.

Brody had to be *certain* he hadn't put her in danger. That was on him. His mindset. He'd deal with it, once he knew she was okay. He'd deal with anything if she was okay.

He was about to stomp the gas, but Cal appeared in front of the truck, looking disapproving and angry.

Brody clenched his teeth together and rolled down his window. He wouldn't have a fight with Cal. Not now.

"We need the truck," Cal said.

"Too damn bad." Brody jerked the truck into Drive. But Cal didn't get out of the way, and Brody couldn't back up because there was a tree behind him.

"I know you want to solve Kate's little mystery, but we have a ranch to run. You can't just—"

"Kate went to get some things from her house, and she hasn't come back yet. She won't answer my calls. I'm going to go make sure she hasn't been *killed*."

Cal studied him, eyebrows drawn together, lines digging around his mouth. Lines that hadn't been there a year ago. This year had put him through hell, and he still hadn't clawed his way out.

Brody wanted to soften, but he just kept picturing Kate back in the truck. Her head bleeding. Unconscious. He'd carried her through a blizzard, and she'd...

"Stay put. Three minutes," Cal said.

"Cal—"

"Okay, two. Do not go anywhere." Then he disappeared, reminding Brody of too many deserts to mention. He supposed that's what kept him sitting there in the idling truck. It wasn't so much just that muscle memory of Cal being the superior officer. It was... Cal.

Where he led, the rest of them followed. Fought. And won. They were a team. A unit. They had to move together, or they were just disparate parts, not sure where they belonged.

But there were no fights left. No missions. This was just life. At some point he'd have to stop overreacting.

But when Cal reappeared with Landon and Henry, Brody supposed he'd stop overreacting some other day.

Cal got in the passenger side, Henry and Landon squeezing into the back.

"You don't all have to come. She might not be in any trouble, really."

Landon shrugged. "And she might be. In which case, you'll need us. You're a *terrible* shot."

"I hope to God there's no shooting." Brody squeezed his hands on the steering wheel and tried to access who he'd been once upon a time. "I am *not* a terrible shot."

"Compared to Henry, you are."

"Compared to Henry, everyone is," Brody muttered, hitting the gas pedal.

Henry only tipped his cowboy hat he'd grown overfond of in the months they'd been here. Because it hid his face, and discouraged conversation.

"This is probably overkill," Brody kept muttering. Trying to talk himself out of it. But he kept just driving toward the Phillips house. When she was probably in town. At the Mart. Or talking to her mother. Maybe she'd gone by the fort to pick up her things.

She was fine. He was an idiot.

"Your instincts are telling you it isn't overkill," Cal said firmly.

Brody might have thought it strange, Cal encouraging him to do something that wasn't laying low, but he understood things he thought Cal hadn't come to grips with yet. So he said it, gently as he could.

"We aren't in the military anymore, Cal. This is just normal life."

"Tell that to Jake who got shot trying to save this one just a few weeks ago," Landon said, jerking a thumnb at Cal.

"No one else is getting shot on my watch," Cal said grimly, squinting up at the Phillips house as it came into view. "Not us. Not anyone."

Brody concentrated on the snowy road, and it felt like

a mission again. The four of them. Danger. Worry. But the cool determination to see things through without any loss of life.

They simply wouldn't allow it.

Chapter Nineteen

Kate listened, trying to file away all the information being passed from her mother to her father to her grandfather.

If she thought too deeply about it, she wanted to laugh again at the absurdity of it all. Or maybe cry. Either way, she had to keep her breathing even, her body limp and her eyes closed.

No matter how much her neck was starting to hurt.

They'd discussed *how* to kill her, which was surprisingly cold-blooded and easy. Shoot her in the head.

Kate could almost believe they were talking about someone else. In fact she tried to picture someone, *anyone* else.

But they were struggling to figure out how to coordinate framing Brody. That was buying Kate some time.

"You've been contacting him with her phone," Jonas was saying in his cold rasp. "We'll kill her in her bedroom, get him to come over."

"We could do murder-suicide," Mom suggested. "Cleaner."

"You'd have to time it right. The police can figure out all those time-of-death things, and God knows people don't think you leave this house."

"I'll take a sleeping pill. If Art won't do the deed, you'll have to."

Jonas grunted, clearly irritated by that. "Might as well kill him too while we're at it."

"You're going to kill all these people over some money?" Dad asked.

"You've been killing people for over ten years for some money and power, Art. How is this different?" Mom demanded.

"She's our *daughter*."

"You didn't care so much about our daughter's feelings when you were sleeping with her friend when they were teenagers."

Kate's fingers seemed to go numb and she tensed against her will. She waited for her father to refute those words. It had always been a rumor, one she'd even believed for a while, but when Amberleigh had shown up dead last month—with Dad having nothing to do with it—she'd believed it was a mistake.

A misunderstanding.

"Amberleigh has nothing to do with this," Dad said flatly.

"No, she doesn't. You're lucky you didn't have anything to do with her death. That would have been ugly. For you. We're not going down for any of this. I believe my father and I have always made that abundantly clear."

Kate wanted to throw up. Or maybe cry. Anything but sit here with her head lolled to the side, her neck aching. Her whole body in pain. She wanted this over.

"We could let her go. You know, Kate. She's not going to tell anyone. She'll do what we say. She's always done what we say."

Mom scoffed. "You *are* delusional."

For once Kate agreed with her mother. Maybe she'd listened to her father, but she'd never been all that biddable. Maybe she'd *thought* of herself that way, because she could be guilted into things. But Brody had pointed out to her that she'd set up exactly the life she'd wanted in the ways she could.

She had to believe she could keep doing that. So she went back to work on the knots keeping her hands tied. She was so close, and she didn't want to listen to anymore of the callous way they talked about ending her life.

So she focused on her. On the knots. On some kind of freedom.

Kate managed to get a knot untied and nearly made a noise in delight and couldn't quite keep her body still. Not only did she move, but the plastic rope hitting against the chair made a noise.

Kate kept her eyes shut, lolled her head and moaned. She didn't blink her eyes open. She kept her breathing even. Everything depending on them thinking she was out of it. She moaned one more time, quieter this time, then stilled again.

And hoped with everything she was that they fell for it.

"Maybe you've killed her already," Mom said, sounding hopeful.

Kate had to keep her face utterly still, no matter how much she wanted to frown at that.

"She had that head wound before she came here. Then I hit it. Then you hit it. Perhaps she won't come back around."

"Perhaps," Jonas agreed, sounding unsure. "But we can't leave that to chance. Shooting is simpler, and easier to pin on someone. Particularly if we can kill him as well. I'll take care of Kate. You, Art, will take care of the man. Or we'll take care of you."

"Fine," Dad muttered.

Kate had to remind herself, over and over, not to react.

Not to let that lance of hurt and all this confusion and *grossness* tense her features or make a sound. She had to make them think she was really, really out of it.

If they left her alone for even two minutes, she could get her feet free and then she could fight. She knew what she was against now. She wouldn't be taken by surprise. Unless her dead grandmother walked through the door, she supposed, except she half expected that now.

There was nothing left to surprise her. Her father had slept with a sixteen-year-old. He'd killed people. Mom wanted her dead. And her late grandfather was alive and pulling the strings. She still didn't know what they'd been up to for the past ten years, but she didn't care.

She just had to save herself. The police could handle the rest. She'd gladly leave it up to the police to handle the sickening rest.

"We'll need to get everything set up in her room," Jonas said. "Then get a message to the man. Get him here. Kill Kate. Kill him. It'll need to be close together but not too close together."

Kate wondered how she could come from all these people who were just coolly planning a murder like they were planning a family vacation.

"We'll map it out," Mom said. "Let's go see what kind of space we're dealing with in Kate's room."

She heard the sound of feet moving. Would they all leave? Would she really get her chance?

"You too, Art," Mom said sharply.

"What about Kate?"

"What about Kate?" Jonas replied. "Even if she wakes up, she isn't going anywhere."

Kate kept utterly still, but deep inside she was smiling. *That's what you think.*

BRODY PARKED OUTSIDE behind Zara's truck. It was parked on the street rather than in the drive, but Brody didn't know if that was a sign or not that something was wrong.

"Maybe I should go up, knock on the door. By myself. See what's up."

Cal nodded. "What if something *is* up?"

"It's not like someone is going to shoot me on the doorstep. Be a little tricky to get away with that." But he looked up at the gloomy house with an uncomfortable chill running down his spine.

"Way to tempt fate," Landon drawled.

"All right, we all get out. But you guys stay behind. Spread out, maybe?" Brody shook his head and let out a harsh laugh. "This is insane. We are back in the real world. I can't go treating my life like a military mission."

"Why not?" Cal returned. "Military missions and life have a lot in common."

Brody didn't have the time or the wherewithal for a debate on *that.* So he got out of the truck. If he was struggling to deal with reality, at least he wasn't alone. His brothers were here.

Henry studied Zara's truck, poked around the snow it was parked on. "If she ran errands, she's been back a while. Truck's cold and looks like it hasn't moved. So either she only parked once or she parked in a different spot the first time around."

Brody looked from Henry and Landon up to the house. It was dark. A little rundown. When he'd first come here to tell Kate he'd help her, he thought it looked like a haunted house from a movie.

His opinion on that hadn't changed any.

He couldn't say it felt like they were being watched,

but there was something about the house. Deep, and dark, and secretive.

Appearances could be deceiving. This house could be as nonthreatening as any middle-class suburban neighborhood house.

But this was Wilde, Wyoming. And this was Kate, and it was the feeling deep inside that things weren't as they should be.

Brody looked at his phone, then went ahead and dialed Kate's number. Her last chance to assure him things were fine before he barged in. He swore. "Straight to voice mail."

"We'll fan out. See if there's anything to see."

Brody shook his head. "I'm just going to go up to the front door. Kate or her mother will answer and tell me I'm overreacting."

"We'll be flanking you, out of sight, to prove it," Landon said, clapping him on the shoulder. His cheerful, unbothered demeanor at odds with his words.

"Since when do you agree with Cal?"

Landon shrugged. "Since we found a dead girl on our property last month. Since Jake got shot. Since you got run off the road. Should I go on?"

Brody blew out a breath. "Fine. See what you can find. But it's going to be nothing." Nothing at all. He stomped toward the front door while his brothers melted away.

It didn't escape Brody's notice they were all armed.

There was going to be a reckoning coming for them all, when they stopped flinging themselves into dangerous situations and started accepting that ranch life in middle-of-nowhere Wyoming was their lot.

But for now he had to be certain there was no danger. Then deal with the embarrassing fallout when Kate answered and yelled at him for invading her space.

God, he hoped like hell he would end up embarrassed and yelled at and not just a few minutes too late.

The walk up to the door was long and winding. Strange the estate was so nice and so… He didn't want to say it was poorly taken care of. There was some visible effort—but like it was just too much space for whoever was expending the effort to truly accomplish anything.

He had a feeling he knew exactly who the person giving any effort was.

When he finally reached the front door, he hesitated. This was a new feeling. Hesitation. Uncertainty. It reminded him too much of being a child. Of wondering who would be home, or who wouldn't. Wondering what grandparent, or aunt, or uncle would take him in. Uncertain he'd ever have a chance to take the reins in his own life.

But he had, and maybe the military had been taken away from him, and maybe that had been his identity, but he didn't *need* it to be. He needed Brody Thompson to be his identity, and Brody Thompson needed to be a man of action.

His phone chirped before he could ring the doorbell. It wasn't a text from Kate like he'd hoped, but a text from Cal.

Two vehicles back here. A snowmobile and a Cadillac. With the text was a picture, dim and hard to make out as it was clearly through some kind of garage window.

Brody frowned at the picture of the snowmobile. It was a common belonging in these parts, but he'd think if Kate had one, she would have suggested using it. From what he knew about her mother, he couldn't imagine she used one.

The Cadillac seemed even more out of place. Maybe it had been twenty years ago when the house had been nice, but it was a newer model—which meant it hadn't been sitting there like the house.

Brody looked up at the door.

Something was definitely not right here.

Suddenly all his uncertainty was gone. He was going to get to Kate right now.

But before he could act, the front door opened, just a hair, then stopped. Brody moved to the corner, out of sight, and listened.

Chapter Twenty

Kate waited, counting in her head. She had to at least get to five hundred before she dared move. Though she'd heard their footsteps leave, it was hard to differentiate three different people. Someone could have stayed behind.

She carefully opened one eye. The room seemed to be empty. She looked around. *Careful, careful.* She had to be both fast and careful.

When she was sure the room was empty, she got the ropes off her arms and reached down to untie the ones around her legs. Her fingers fumbled and her neck and head ached, her stomach heaved but she couldn't allow herself to throw up. That would be too loud. Even if all three people were in her room on the other side of the house. They'd know.

They'd come back.

Careful, hurry.

Once she had the ropes untied, relieved tears threatened. But she wasn't out of the woods yet. She jumped to her feet, then nearly tumbled over. A wave of dizziness coupled with legs that had fallen asleep. She managed to catch herself on the coffee table.

The slap of her hands onto the surface of the table was loud, but not echoing. Not as loud as falling would have been. She held herself there, willing her vision to stop wavering. Trying to get her breathing under control.

But she knew she didn't have this kind of time.

She pushed herself back upright, then closed her eyes. The world was spinning. Her legs were tingling, but at least that was feeling over numbness. She carefully took one step forward, still with her eyes closed, just testing, slowly, to make sure her legs would hold her up.

She blew out a breath and then opened her eyes. Her legs were holding her up. The world hadn't stopped spinning, but if she could reach out and hold onto things for balance, she could make it.

She reached for the chair she'd been tied to, then managed a few unsteady steps to the wall. She leaned against it, breathing too hard. A few tears had leaked out of her eyes, but nothing mattered except getting out of this house. To Zara's truck.

She couldn't call for help. Mom had taken her phone. But if she could get to the truck…

Kate managed to use the wall as support and get out of the parlor, but as she was telling herself she just had to make it to the truck, she realized she didn't have her purse. Which meant no truck keys.

"Damn it," she swore softly, then winced. No talking. No nothing. If she couldn't drive away, she'd just have to run. If she kept walking, maybe the dizziness would cease, and she could run.

She'd *crawl* if she had to. She would not stay here and let her family kill her.

She could see the front door now. She was almost there. Outside was freedom. Within her reach.

She heard nothing but her own heart beating hard against her chest. Her breath raggedly going in and out.

Too loud. Her body was too loud, but she only had to get to that door.

She nearly cried out when her hand closed over the doorknob. She wanted to sob, and though tears began to fall in earnest, she blinked them away. She turned the knob, but before she could pull it open, she heard footsteps.

"Don't."

Kate slowly turned to face her father. He was at the other end of the wall. He had one gun in his hand.

Pointed at her.

Kate looked beyond him. No Mom. No Jonas. Just Dad.

"You have to let me go, Dad," she said, and though tears kept falling, her voice sounded strong. Commanding.

He took a few steps forward, and there was an uncertainty in him that gave her hope. Maybe he'd let her go. He didn't want to kill her. He was her only chance.

"You don't have to do anything, just turn back around and let me go."

But Dad shook his head, slowly moving closer and closer. "They'll kill me if I do."

"It sounds like maybe you deserve it." Maybe that wasn't the smartest thing to say, but honestly. He'd slept with a minor. He'd killed people. He was willing to let his own daughter die. He was not a good man.

"Don't make me do this, Kate. Come back in. Maybe I can talk them out of it, but I can't let you go."

"*Make* you do it?" There was a little pang inside of her, a desire to *want* to believe him, help him. Her father who she'd desperately missed and tried to find for ten years.

But he was lying. He had his finger around the trigger. He wasn't letting her go. He wasn't talking anyone out of anything. "I'm not making you do anything."

She wouldn't go back in there. She'd simply have to make a run for it. If he shot her…it was better than waiting for what they were planning. It would be harder to frame Brody if she tried to escape this house.

If she died, it would damn well be on her own terms. If she could get out of the door before he shot, maybe the door could... Well, she doubted it would block the bullet, but maybe slow it down enough that it didn't kill her.

Of course that would put a crimp in her escape plans, but again, it would make it harder for them to frame Brody. And there was always a chance she survived.

There was *always* a chance if she fought.

So she said no more, she jerked the door open and ran. Or tried to.

BRODY COULDN'T HEAR what was being said, but he recognized the cadence of Kate's voice. He crept back out, carefully eased the door open another inch.

"Don't make me do this, Kate. Come back in. Maybe I can talk them out of it, but I can't let you go." It was a man's voice. A man who sounded at the end of his rope.

Never good, and certainly not the lunch with her mother or errands she'd been texting him about.

He sent a quick text to Cal to bring everyone around front. He wasn't sure what trouble there was, but it *was* trouble. And whoever was speaking was damn well not going to let Kate go.

But before Brody could act the door flew open, Kate barreling right into him and nearly knocking him over.

Because she was running. Instinct took over and he manage to grab her and pivot so they didn't fall, even as a gunshot exploded from within the house. Missing them both.

"Brody," Kate said on an exhale. She grabbed onto his arms, eyes wild and unfocused. "You're here."

"What's going on, Kate?"

"We have to run. They're going to kill me. We have to…" She tried to pull him away from the door, but she trailed off as Cal, Henry and Landon appeared.

"You brought everybody," she said, and she didn't sound mad. She sounded awed.

"Not everybody—"

"Down," Henry shouted, and out of pure instinct from having worked with his brothers for a very long time, Brody pulled Kate onto the cold snowy ground as gunshots went off.

Brody looked up in time to see a man step out of the house, but before the man could get a good shot off on any of the three men with guns, Henry shot the hand that was curled around his gun. On a wail of pain, and a spurt of blood, the gun clattered to the porch below.

Pushing Kate back and out of the way, Brody dove for the gun. He managed to get a grip on it, but the original owner kicked him hard in the stomach. The shot to the hand certainly hadn't taken him out because the blow knocked the wind out of Brody.

Still, he held onto the gun as the man reared back to kick him again, but Brody wasn't about to let that blow land. Brody managed to jump to his feet and deliver an elbow to the gut of the man. He swept the man's feet out from under him, and then nodded to Cal's approaching form. "Get that other gun off him. Got something to tie him up?"

"Yeah. Called the cops. They should be on the way."

Brody looked at Kate. She was too pale. Blood dripping from that wound on her head like she'd been hurt there again. She leaned up against the side of the house like it was the only thing keeping her up.

Before Brody could ask if she was okay, a shot sounded from somewhere else. Henry started shouting orders to Landon and they huddled behind the trucks in the street.

Cal, Brody and Kate were protected by the overhang of the porch, but that meant Brody couldn't see where the shooter was, and he was too far away from Landon and Henry to communicate easily.

Brody heard sirens in the distance, but they were still far away. Another shot sounded from the shooter and the truck window exploded.

Kate let out a yelp of surprise. Brody went to her side.

"Oh my God. They're going to kill them. All of us." Kate's knees buckled, but Brody held her up. Held her to him.

"No, they're not. How many?"

"What?"

"How many people are in the house?" Her eyes still looked dazed, but she furrowed her brow as if in thought. "Just two as far as I know. They… My whole family. I don't know what they were doing. Something bad. Mom and my grandfather…my *dead* grandfather. They wanted to kill me. Dad didn't want to, but he would have. He would have." Tears were streaming down her face, and she wasn't making any sense.

The cop cars were getting closer. They had gear. Tactical training. They were capable of handling this, Brody knew.

But he and Cal were more capable.

He looked over at Cal. He'd finished tying up the man who'd shot at Kate. Was that her father?

No time.

"We can take them out before the cops even get here," Cal said.

"Read my mind." He turned to Kate. "Kate. Look at me."

Her eyes didn't really focus, but she turned her head to him.

"Where are the people shooting?" he asked gently.

She blinked once. Twice. "I don't know unless I see what window they're shooting from." She blinked once, her eyes finally focusing. "Brody, you should let the police handle it." She looked past him to Cal. "The police can handle it."

Brody pressed a careful kiss to her cheek. "We can do it better, Kate. Promise." He pulled back. "Trust me, okay?"

She swallowed, then nodded. "I have to know what window. Let me—"

"You'll stay right here where you're safe." He pulled his phone out of his pocket, but before he could text Landon, the man Cal had tied up spoke.

"They're in the attic. Third floor, door at the end of the hall, stairs go up to the attic."

Brody looked at him and couldn't stop the sneer of disgust. He'd been ready to *kill* Kate. Brody wanted to crush him.

"Can we trust him?" Cal asked.

Brody looked back at Kate. She looked hurt, incomprehensibly destroyed, but only for a moment. Then she shored herself up. "Trust? No. But he wouldn't want them getting away and him taking all the blame."

"All right. You stay put, okay? Do not move from this spot. Landon or Henry will come move you when they can, or you can go with the cops if they get here. Do not come inside."

"I know the house."

"We can figure out how to get to the attic."

"It's a big house. Take me with you."

"You're hurt. You—"

Another gunshot went off, blasting out another window on Zara's truck.

"We don't have time to argue," Cal muttered.

"I'm only going to follow you," Kate said stubbornly, no trace of the confusion or tears from before.

Brody didn't like it, but they didn't have time. Every gunshot from above was doing damage to the truck Landon and Henry were hiding behind. There was nowhere else for them to go, and until Henry had the vantage point for a good shot, they were sitting ducks.

"Okay, let's go," Brody muttered.

"Wait. Give me his gun," Kate said, pointing to the man on the ground.

"Do you know how to use his gun?" Cal asked suspiciously.

"I'll figure it out."

Cal shrugged and handed it to her. Then they stepped into the house as a team.

Chapter Twenty-One

Everything felt surreal, but Kate followed Brody and Cal into the house she'd grown up in. A gun in her hand.

She wasn't as dizzy as she had been, and she had her feet under her now. Shock had been replaced by anger. By *fury*.

She'd been deemed unworthy by her family, disposable even. They had been callously ready to end her life.

Well, they were going to pay. In jail. Where they clearly belonged. All three of them.

Though Cal and Brody had led her inside, they didn't know where to go. Yes, they could have figured it out. She wasn't *necessary* to this mission, but she could help make it faster. Get Landon and Henry safe, and those local cops who might not be ready for a shooter from the attic.

She slid in front of Brody, keeping her footsteps light. She'd snuck around this house enough to know how to move through it silently. Like a ghost. She'd always been little more than a ghost here.

Now she understood why. Well, understood wasn't the right word. She didn't *understand* any of this, but she at least knew what she had to do.

Up the first set of stairs, then the second. All the doors on the third floor were closed, except one in the middle. Which was unusual. As far as Kate knew, the third floor was usually locked up. Mom claimed she didn't use it, and Kate rarely came up here these days.

She turned to Brody and Cal and motioned them to come closer. "It's usually locked tight up here. That room is open."

Both men studied the open door, then nodded. Brody reached out and pulled her behind him. They were in charge now.

They crept forward, in a kind of crouch, both holding guns as if they were simply extensions of themselves. It was like watching a movie. Except she'd been intimate with one of the men doing all this.

She crept behind, trying to model the way they held their guns so she could be ready. So she wouldn't be a liability.

No, she refused to be that.

Cal swept into the room, Brody behind him. It was something like a dance. Since Kate didn't know the steps, she waited at the door.

They both crept around the room, utterly silent, looking in the closet and under things. Brody shook his head as he returned to the door.

Something creaked above them, followed by another gunshot. The shooter was definitely in the attic.

Brody and Cal moved forward again, toward the attic door. It was closed, and Kate knew it would screech when they had to open it. But if the floor creaked above every time they got ready to fire their gun in the attic, then they only had to time it right.

She gestured Brody to move closer, and she whispered just that in his ear. He nodded. Then pulled his phone out and tapped a text to someone.

She assumed Landon and Henry outside. When she

heard the faint echo of a gunshot outside, then the groan of the floor above, she understood.

He'd had Henry shoot at them even though he couldn't get a good shot. Then, when the gunshot rang out just above them, Cal jerked the door open.

"You stay here," Brody whispered in her ear. "Watch any entry point. Someone appears you don't recognize? Shoot."

Kate blinked. But then she nodded. Because she could do this. She *had* to do this. Not just for Brody, but for herself. To prove something... She wasn't what she'd imagined herself to be all those years of plodding along, alone, researching her father's disappearance in a sad bid to prove that it wasn't what it looked like.

No, she was strong. She'd built the life she wanted. She'd escaped, and now she was going to help bring her family down.

BRODY HAD BEEN in enough rickety buildings, particularly with Cal, to know how to navigate a loud staircase without letting anyone above know they were coming. It was about being light-footed, knowing where to step, and despite being a big man, knowing how to be graceful and agile.

He and Cal took their time. No matter what was going on outside, they could only focus on the inside. The here. The now. A silent surprise arrival.

Cal was in the lead because Brody had been talking to Kate, but as they reached the top of the stairs, they came shoulder to shoulder as best they could. To assess and enter the room at the same time.

They looked at each other, nodded, then stepped forward, guns at the ready. But Brody only saw one man. Crouched next to one window. The attic was full of bits and pieces so Cal peeled off to search, while Brody stayed on the shooter.

Who turned, eyes wide in surprise.

Which matched Brody's. The shooter was an elderly man. He barely looked like he could walk without assistance, even though he clearly held the gun that had been shooting at Henry and Landon.

It shocked Brody enough not to shoot. But the man's eyes went cold, and Brody knew a stone-cold killer when he came face-to-face with one. Which cut through the shock.

Brody shot. Though it was a strange feeling, he reminded himself that no matter how old the man was, and how difficult it might be for an elderly man to recover from a gunshot wound, he'd wanted to kill Kate. Her supposedly dead grandfather.

Cal moved forward after the man crumpled to the ground and took the gun. "Easy enough," he muttered. There were groans coming from the writhing man, but Cal set the gun aside.

"On this score, but Kate's mother is in here somewhere. You take him down to the cops if they're here. I'll go find her."

KATE FOCUSED ON keeping her breathing even. Cal and Brody were taking care of the dangerous bit. She had led them where they needed to go, and now she was just sort of the lookout.

Nothing would happen. She wouldn't have to shoot. Everything would be fine.

For just a second she closed her eyes. Because even when this was all over, her life was irrevocably changed. *Fine* was going to be something she had to work hard for again.

When she opened her eyes, nothing had changed, but she still felt…on edge. Something in the air. Something around her. She felt…watched. She frowned, looking down the length of the hall. Nothing.

But the silence was oppressive, and her pulse skittered. She glanced back at the attic door. Cal and Brody had left it slightly ajar, but not enough that she could see their progress.

Kate blew out a breath. She was just getting paranoid. They were rounding up Mom and her grandfather and she was just the lookout. That was all.

A door at the opposite end of the hall creaked open. Kate readjusted the grip on her gun and pointed it in the direction of the room, heart suddenly galloping in her chest. But she would remain calm. Had to.

Maybe it was… Well, she didn't have a good answer for that. But she was the only one here. She had to deal with it. Carefully she moved closer to the cracked-open door, keeping her footsteps light, avoiding the places she knew would creak.

A head peeked out, just barely, just enough to see the perfectly coiffed brown hair Kate recognized as her mother.

"Stop," Kate ordered. Because *she* was in charge now. With a gun.

Mom's face slowly turned toward Kate. She sneered, then boldly stepped forward into the hall, as if the gun in Kate's hands didn't scare her at all.

"You won't shoot me."

Kate blinked in surprise. Her mother wasn't afraid. At all. Despite the fact Kate had a gun and she didn't appear to.

"You're a weakling and a coward. Put the gun down, Katherine. Before you hurt yourself." Mom just kept walking toward her and the thing her mother had never understood about her was that calling her names, telling her what she was or wasn't only made Kate more determined in exactly what she was. Who she was. Herself.

Kate did *not* do as she was told. But she nodded. "You're right," Kate agreed. "Not about the weakling and coward thing. The fact I'm standing here proves that you're wrong there, but you are right that I probably won't shoot. I'm not a good enough shot to know how to shoot you without killing you. And unlike you, I don't want to kill anyone. Actually, you don't want to kill anyone either. Dad and Grandpa had to do all the killing for you, didn't they?"

Mom's disdainful expression turned into a smile that had Kate's blood running cold.

"You know why?" Mom reached inside her jacket and pulled out a very small gun, pointing it in Kate's direction. The smile was terrifying without the gun, but now—Kate couldn't breathe.

"I enjoy it too much." Mom lifted her gun and Kate knew she had to save herself. She had to shoot first. But she *really* didn't want to kill anyone. Even the cold-blooded woman who'd birthed her and still wanted her dead.

A gunshot went off and out of pure instinct Kate flung herself onto the ground. But it wasn't her mother's shot. It was from upstairs.

Oh God.

Kate knew she didn't have time to panic about Brody and Cal. Mom was looking at the ceiling and this was Kate's only chance.

She regrouped, set herself up lying there on the ground and aimed as Mom's gaze came back down to her. As Mom's own grip on her gun tightened, aimed.

Kate didn't know who shot first.

A GUNSHOT FROM just below exploded before Cal had even carried the old man to the stairs.

"Kate." Brody jumped in front of Cal, practically scaled the entire staircase and burst out the door. Kate was sprawled on the ground, and he leaped forward and lifted her up with one hand. "Kate. Where are you hurt?"

"Brody." She let out a rush of breath. It might have been a laugh except nothing was funny. "I'm fine." She pushed at him, and he had to slowly get it through the haze in his brain that she was all right. He loosened his grip on her.

She looked down the hall. A woman was crumpled on the floor. Still.

Kate swallowed. "We shot at each other. She missed. I didn't." Kate was beginning to shake, so Brody slid his arm around her.

"Did I kill her?" she asked weakly.

"Here. Sit down." Brody helped her into a sitting position, then popped his head in to the attic stairwell. "We're good," he told Cal. "We'll get the cops and a paramedic."

Cal nodded. "I'll do a field dressing up here."

Brody turned his attention back to Kate. "You sit right here."

"Did I kill her?" she repeated, starting to go pale.

"Don't move."

Brody walked down the hall to the crumpled woman. He kicked the gun back toward Kate. A tiny thing that couldn't have done much damage from that distance. Kate's gun on the other hand had been of the high-powered sort.

Blood was beginning to seep out onto the floor. Brody couldn't tell where the woman had been shot, but he took a limp hand and tried to find a pulse. He breathed out a sigh of relief when he found one, though he wasn't sure how long that would last. "She's still got a pulse. We'll go on downstairs and find a cop. Get them up here. We'll need an ambulance."

Kate was by his side even though he'd told her to stay put. Still pale, still shaking, but very clear. "We can't leave her alone."

"Kate."

"Not because I care. Or maybe I still care, I don't know. The point is, she left me alone unconscious, and I managed to get away. Someone needs to watch her just in case."

"All right." He nodded. "I'll stay. You go get the cops."

She nodded. She looked at the puddle of blood slowly growing next to her mother. "I don't want to kill anybody, but if she dies… I know I had to do it."

"I know you did."

She nodded again, then turned for the stairs. By the time she reached the top, she was moving at a jog.

Brody blew out a breath and found himself in the very strange position of hoping a woman who'd tried to kill her own daughter survived.

For Kate's sake.

Chapter Twenty-Two

Everything became a bit of a blur after Kate ran downstairs. She found a cop. An ambulance showed up. Mom, Dad and her grandfather were taken away in one. Brody insisted on driving her to the hospital, though she felt fine. Maybe weak and a little dizzy, but she'd survived.

Turned out survival was a powerful healing force.

The hospital was even more of a blur, especially when they insisted Brody couldn't accompany her and she was on her own. Doctors and nurses poked, and prodded, and asked questions until everything around her felt like a buzzing cacophony of noise.

She'd passed out, which had earned her a CT scan and an overnight stay at the hospital. Once she was settled into a room, a parade of different kinds of police officers started to come in. She was asked questions, all sorts of nonsensical questions, over and over, by different officers. Some she recognized, some she didn't.

She knew she didn't have the answers they wanted. All she knew, even now, was that her family had been willing to kill her to hide whatever it was they'd been doing for the past ten years.

A nurse ushered in her next visitor, and though she was routinely disappointed it wasn't Brody, she managed to smile at someone she actually knew.

Thomas Hart was a deputy for Bent County, and cousin to the Harts. She'd grown up with him, and even though they weren't close, she knew he would give her some answers others wouldn't.

"How are you holding up, Kate?"

"I'm okay. What can you tell me?"

He itched a hand through his hair, looking a little sheepish. "It's a bit complicated as of yet."

"I know my family are bad people. You don't have to spare my feelings. They wanted me dead. Message received."

Thomas nodded, somewhat apologetically. "I can't tell you everything. Some federal agencies came in and they won't tell *me* everything. But Zara called me and asked me to give you a rundown on what I could."

Zara had called him. Zara cared. Maybe Kate had lost her family, but she'd gotten Brody and regained her best friend.

"It seems the Lantsey family, your grandfather and your mother in particular, have been creating a kind of drug-selling center. Multiple rings. Amberleigh was involved in one—the one we took down last month, but there were more. Your father was involved in almost all of them, and apparently his disappearance was tied to a tip coming through back then that he was involved in drugs. So he had to disappear or face an investigation from the feds."

Kate understood all the words, but it was still like it was happening to someone else. About someone else. "My grandfather—who faked his death—and my mother and my father were all selling drugs."

"More or less. Running the organizations that sold drugs. They amassed quite a fortune doing it. We're working on search warrants that will help us bring down the remaining rings, but at the end of the day, you brought down a major drug operation, Kate."

"I didn't do much." Just shot her mother. She kept waiting to feel guilty about it, but too many mixed emotions prevented her from getting all the way there.

"All that information you collected for the past ten years? That's a whole heck of a lot. We've got years of stuff to go on, because of you. Which means the chances of them actually getting charged and convicted is higher. Be proud of yourself, Kate."

Proud. She didn't know how to be, but she appreciated Thomas coming on Zara's behalf. Now she had some answers. "Can I see Brody?"

"That's up to your doctor, but I'll see what I can do."

She managed a little smile, then settled back into the uncomfortable hospital bed. She wished she could...well, not go home, but go to her *new* home. She wanted to settle in Brody's bed at the Hart Ranch and bury her head in the sand for a few hundred years.

When the door opened next, exhaustion settled in her bones. But it was *finally* Brody. Who looked as exhausted as she felt.

Still, she asked him the one thing she hadn't been able to bear asking anyone else. "How's my mother?"

"She's alive still. From what information I could finagle, she made it out of surgery."

Kate nodded. "I don't want to ever have anything to do with her ever again, but I don't want to be the reason she's dead. I suppose that makes me weak."

Brody slid onto the bed next to her, wrapped his arms gently around her. "I think it makes you incredibly strong."

She smiled up at him. "Brody, you saved my life."

"*Helped* save your life. You did the vast majority of that."

She leaned against him and sighed. "You came. I was worried she'd convince you not to with all her texts."

"I talked myself out of coming a million times, so don't thank me too much."

She reached up, cupped his face. "But you came. No one else has ever showed up for me. Not like you have."

"I always will."

She didn't think it made any sense to believe him, but she did. So much. "Yeah, I think you will."

"You should probably stay at the ranch for a while, with me. Until things fully settle down. The feds will be crawling all over that house for a while."

She smiled to herself. "Are you asking me to move in with you?"

He stiffened a little, but it was kind of sweet. She'd seen him in action now, multiple times. He was this big strong military guy who knew how to carry her through blizzards and take down bad guys, but he still wasn't quite so sure about all this relationship stuff.

"I guess I am," he muttered. "Share a room, anyway. It comes with five annoying brothers, though."

"I always wanted siblings."

He kissed the top of her head. "You got them. And me."

"It's a pretty good deal," she said, snuggling in. No matter what happened with her family, she *had* gotten this pretty good deal. Through her own strength and determination, and a little help from a military man.

THE NEXT DAY, Brody was allowed to bring Kate home to the Hart Ranch, what was becoming the Thompson Ranch, he supposed. She was definitely a little worse for wear, but the doctor had been pretty positive about the prognosis. She might suffer from headaches for a while, but as long as no further brain injuries happened, there shouldn't be any lasting effects.

Brody was determined to make sure of it.

She was quiet on the drive home, and he didn't press. She had a lot to work through. A lot to deal with. It didn't surprise him she was handling this better than he might have imagined. He'd stopped being surprised by her strength and simply learned to be in awe of it.

Brody parked and helped her out of the truck. She leaned her head on his shoulder as they walked up the shoveled path. "I always loved this house."

"Well, it's yours as long as you'd like."

They stepped inside and everyone was there. There was a big banner on the wall that that said Welcome Home, Kate, and streamers.

Kate laughed. "You guys. This is too much." She looked up at him, but he shook his head.

"Don't look at me. I had nothing to do with it."

Her gaze roamed over the small crowd in front of them and then she moved forward and wrapped Zara and Hazeleigh in a tight hug. Zara looked uncomfortable, but she patted Kate's back awkwardly while Hazeleigh sniffed and murmured a few things Brody couldn't hear.

"Stay as long as you'd like, Kate," Cal said, as if he spoke for all of them. "Especially if you keep cooking for us on Brody's turn."

"Here, here," Landon readily agreed.

"Thank you. Really. All of you. For…everything. Cal. Henry, and Landon, and… You put yourself in some danger for me, and I…"

"It's nothing," Henry said gruffly.

"Part in parcel when falling in with the Thompson brothers," Landon drawled with a wink.

"All right, I'm going to have to break this up. Doctor's orders. She's got more resting to do," Brody interrupted.

"Good, you lazy lot are behind on ranch chores," Zara said good-naturedly, as she began to shoo them in different directions.

Brody helped Kate upstairs. She was definitely dragging.

"I don't know how," she said through a yawn as he followed her into his room, "but I am tired."

"You've been through a lot. I can't imagine you slept well last night in the noisy hospital. You should sleep now and get all caught up." He nudged her into the bed, pulled the covers up over her. She smiled sleepily up at him, patting the small sliver of bed next to her.

"I know you've probably got a million things to do but stay for a few minutes."

Minutes seemed so paltry, and she seemed so...perfect. Just lying there, smiling up at him. How she'd come through all this, he didn't know. He only knew that the powerful feeling that swept through him wasn't going away.

"I love you, Kate."

Her eyes had been drooping sleepily, but now they popped wide open, something like shock slackening her features. "Oh," she breathed. "Are you sure?"

He wouldn't have thought anything she could say would have made him laugh. Not when every muscle in his body felt like it had turned to heavy metal. Not when for so long he believed love couldn't be real.

But he loved his brothers. And he loved Kate. He was exceptional at many things, so he'd figure out a way to be exceptional at loving her. No matter how it scared the hell out of him.

He took that seat next to her on the bed. "There isn't

a thing I don't like about you. You're smart and funny. Every time I think I've got you pegged, you turn out to be something else. You've got all those shy trappings, but at the end of the day you're so determined you never let your fear stop you. You've been dealt all these blows, and you keep fighting. Trying to make a place for yourself. You stopped depending on anyone else to make it for you and I don't know, I guess that makes me want be the one you depend on. So, yeah, I'm sure."

She pushed up into a sitting position and flung her arms around him. "I love you too. No one's ever seen me the way you do, and you make me see myself the way I am. I don't know how I could have done all this without you."

He held her tight. Kissed her cheek. He felt a little off-balance. For a lot of reasons, but…she was right.

She pulled back, tears in her eyes but they didn't fall. "I know it'll take a while to really process what they did, what losing them means, but I have you. And Zara and Hazeleigh. And brothers, I think. So, it'll all be good. No more lying, and secrets, and all that. Just…normal life."

Secrets. Brody practically winced. He had some of those. Ones he wasn't supposed to tell.

But how could he keep them from her after *that*?

"There's something I have to tell you."

Her face didn't fall exactly, but a wariness crept in. "Oh."

He took her hands in his, tried to find the right words. The right balance. He couldn't tell her everything. It would be a dereliction of duty—not to the military, but to his brothers.

"Kate… There are things I can never tell you."

She tugged at her hands, but he held firm, looking up at her. Maybe a little desperately. "Hear me out. Give me a chance.... They're military things. Reasons we ended up here..." He shook his head and knew he was already botching it. "We were a military group. All of us who moved here. From different branches and backgrounds, recruited to do dangerous missions because... Mostly because we were elite soldiers who didn't have any family to hold us back."

Kate chewed on her bottom lip, but she stopped trying to withdraw her hands.

"Our job was to find, research and ultimately stop and take down terrorist organizations. We did that for years, and successfully. Our team got quite a reputation, which meant that we were targets. There was an intelligence breach and our identities were found out. Long story short, the military killed us, on paper, and gave us this new life."

Her eyebrows were furrowed, and she was clearly considering his words.

"So, your name isn't Brody?"

He managed a small smile. "Adam Brody Calhoun. I always went by Brody though. But I'm not him anymore. He's dead. That probably doesn't make sense to you, but it's the only way..." Brody shook his head. "I'm sorry, Kate. I should have told you sooner. Or..."

Kate touched his cheek. "I'm glad you told me so I can understand." She smiled at him when he finally looked at her. "That's the kind of secret that doesn't matter all that much because that was your past. I'm glad I know it, but you're right. I don't need the details unless you want to give them. I just need you. Here. This is your future."

He looked at her for the longest time, half convinced she couldn't possibly be real. But she was here. And his.

"I never really thought about my future, but this is more than I could have dreamed."

"I think we both deserve a little more than we could have dreamed."

Yes, they did—and they'd have just that.

* * * * *

COMING SOON!

MILLS & BOON

THE HEART OF ROMANCE

A ROMANCE FOR EVERY READER

MODERN

Prepare to be swept off your feet by sophisticated, sexy and seductive heroes, in some of the world's most glamourous and romantic locations, where power and passion collide.

HISTORICAL

Escape with historical heroes from time gone by. Whether your passion is for wicked Regency Rakes, muscled Vikings or rugged Highlanders, awaken the romance of the past.

MEDICAL

Set your pulse racing with dedicated, delectable doctors in the high-pressure world of medicine, where emotions run high and passion, comfort and love are the best medicine.

True Love

Celebrate true love with tender stories of heartfelt romance, from the rush of falling in love to the joy a new baby can bring, and a focus on the emotional heart of a relationship.

Desire

Indulge in secrets and scandal, intense drama and plenty of sizzling hot action with powerful and passionate heroes who have it all: wealth, status, good looks…everything but the right woman.

HEROES

Experience all the excitement of a gripping thriller, with an intense romance at its heart. Resourceful, true-to-life women and strong, fearless men face danger and desire - a killer combination!

To see which titles are coming soon, please visit

millsandboon.co.uk/nextmonth

JOIN US ON SOCIAL MEDIA!

Stay up to date with our latest releases, author news and
gossip, special offers and discounts, and all the
behind-the-scenes action from Mills & Boon...

 @millsandboon

 @millsandboonuk

 facebook.com/millsandboon

 @millsandboonuk

It might just be true love...

GET YOUR ROMANCE FIX!

Get the latest romance news, exclusive author interviews, story extracts and much more!

MILLS & BOON

Desire

Indulge in secrets and scandal, intense drama and plenty of sizzling hot action with powerful and passionate heroes who have it all: wealth, status, good looks…everything but the right woman.

MILLS & BOON

MODERN

Power and Passion

Prepare to be swept off your feet by sophisticated, sexy and seductive heroes, in some of the world's most glamourous and romantic locations, where power and passion collide.

Julia James

Heiress's

PREGNANCY
SCANDAL

MILLS & BOON
MODERN

Jennie Lucas

Choosing the

SHEIKH'S ROYAL
BRIDE

MILLS & BOON

Kim Lawrence

A WEDDING
at the
ITALIAN'S DEMAND

MILLS

Sharon Kendrick

The

SHEIKH'S
SECRET BABY

MILLS & BOON
MODERN

Eight Modern stories published every month, find them all at:

millsandboon.co.uk/Modern

MILLS & BOON
MEDICAL
Pulse-Racing Passion

Set your pulse racing with dedicated, delectable doctors in the high-pressure world of medicine, where emotions run high and passion, comfort and love are the best medicine.